LOST SAINTS

Book Two of the Lazare Family Saga

ELIZABETH BELL

Claire-Voie Books

 Created with Vellum

For everyone who supported NECESSARY SINS

CONTENTS

PROLOGUE

CHEYENNE NATION
SUMMER 1840

The name given by the Cheyenne to the Sun Dance is the New-Life-lodge. ... The performance of the ceremony is supposed to re-create, to re-form, to re-animate the earth...

　　Then all returned to the lodge except the Chief Priest and the Lodge-Maker's wife.

　　— George A. Dorsey, *The Cheyenne, Volume II: The Sun Dance* (1905)

"To the bright star, I give my beloved," Zeyá's husband prayed. "To the mountains, I give my beloved..." Okóm was offering her body as a sacrifice in order to give new life to the world.

　　But Zeyá knew the truth: she was not her husband's beloved. Okóm loved her older sister Héshek. He'd taken Zeyá as his second wife only because no one else wanted her. The white scabs sickness had stolen Zeyá's beauty before it could bloom; it had left her entire body pitted with scars.

"To the animals, I give my beloved," her husband continued. "To the waters, I give my beloved…"

When Okóm had pledged to lead the New Life Lodge, he'd expected Héshek to serve as the Sacred Woman. Zeyá's sister had preened like a magpie in anticipation of the honor, which began with her husband's pledge. No one could pass in front of the Sacred Woman, or they would be cursed. Then, as the ten bands of the People gathered, Héshek realized her blood would start before the ceremonies concluded. Zeyá must replace her as the Sacred Woman.

"All the better," their husband chuckled as he drew Héshek against him for the first time since his pledge. The Sacred Woman was not allowed to lie with her husband till she'd made her sacrifice. But Héshek was no longer the Sacred Woman. "Now, I don't have to share you with *anyone*—even a priest."

"But I must share *you!*" Héshek pointed her lips accusingly at Zeyá, who was tucking her sister's children beneath their robe for the night.

Okóm motioned toward Zeyá's pitted skin, which looked particularly ugly by firelight. "You think I enjoy touching *that?*" he asked Héshek as if Zeyá could not hear him. "Lying with your sister is like mating with a lump of granite!"

"Then why do you do it?" Héshek pouted.

"Because she keeps begging me for a child!"

"Aren't *our* children enough?" Héshek tugged playfully at his breechcloth. "I think the sickness made her barren. I think there is no need for you to lie with my stone sister ever again."

Okóm murmured agreement into her neck.

Zeyá held back her tears till she was hidden under her buffalo robe. She reminded herself that she enjoyed lying with Okóm even less than he did.

Now, she must surrender herself to another man, a man nearly her father's age: the Chief Priest of the New Life Lodge.

"How can it be right?" Zeyá wept to her mother the next day. "To lie with a man who is not my husband?"

"While you make the sacrifice, you will not be another man's wife, and he will not be another woman's husband," Zeyá's mother explained. She was a medicine woman who understood these things. "You will be the Sacred Woman, and he will be Maheo."

But surely the Creator wanted a beautiful woman like Héshek.

"You will be the honored mother of us all!" Zeyá's own mother continued. "Through your sacrifice, you will give new life to all our People, to the animals, the plants, the Earth itself."

Zeyá's mother took her to meet the wife of the Chief Priest, the woman who would sacrifice her husband to Zeyá. She herself had been the Sacred Woman a few summers before.

"Were you frightened?" Zeyá whispered.

"The sacrifice must be great, or Maheo and the Sacred Powers will not pity us," answered the Chief Priest's wife. "What sacrifice could be greater than our own bodies?"

ZEYÁ DID EVERYTHING REQUIRED OF HER during each day of the ceremonies. She prepared the ground for the Lone Tipi. She carried the buffalo skull. She let her ugly body be exposed inside the New Life Lodge, her doeskin dress bound up around her waist. Her helpers painted her scarred skin red like the Earth, then painted her with the symbols of the Four Directions, the Sun, and the Moon. They tied sage in her hair, at her wrists, and at her ankles. Through it all, Zeyá stared at the grey-haired Chief Priest and dreaded what was to come.

Finally her husband took up the fire spoon, brought a coal to her feet, and placed sage upon it. In the shelter of a buffalo robe, Zeyá stood over the smoke, purifying her body. Then the Chief Priest purified his body.

Her heart racing in fear, she led him and the other priests from the Lodge into the darkness, toward the East and the promise of the life-giving Sun. The men of the warrior societies stood on either side of their path. One of the other priests prayed to Maheo, the Four Directions, and the other spirits, asking them to accept the coming sacrifice. He prayed that the animals and birds and people and grass would continue to grow, that the Sun would rise in the morning and the clouds would give rain. Then everyone but Zeyá and the Chief Priest returned to the Lodge.

Now they stood together under one buffalo robe, incensing their bodies with sweet grass. Zeyá's voice trembled as she sang, as she and the Chief Priest raised the sacred pipe to the Sky four times. Finally, he laid the robe over the Sun design outlined on the Earth and drew her down next to him.

Zeyá felt the moonlight bright as day on her pitted skin. Even the sacred paint could not conceal her scars, and the Priest had seen her naked before and between each painting. She bent her head in shame and unbound her dress from her waist. She wanted to pull it up again, to cover her chest and back and arms at least. "I can— It's all right if I— Isn't it?"

"Are you cold?" asked the Priest, though the night was warm.

"No; but you don't need to— You don't have to—" Zeyá stopped with only one arm through its sleeve. "I know I am ugly."

"Who told you you were ugly?"

"You saw." She stared down at her scarred skin in the moonlight. "My husband says I look like weathered stone, that lying with me is like…"

"Stone is strong. It endures everything." The Priest touched her bare shoulder—not to push her down against the robe, as her husband would have, but in reassurance. His thumb stroked her skin, and he did not recoil. "Stone is powerful. In the mountains, it reaches to the Sky, yet it is still part of the Earth—the World Below meeting the World Above. Nothing is more holy." The Priest traced his fingers up her neck to her cheek, her lips. "But you do not feel like stone to me. You are soft." He raised his other hand to her sleeve. "I want to see more of you, not less. Will you let me?"

Slowly, Zeyá nodded. The Priest tugged down her dress again, till her shoulders and back and breasts were bare. "Maheo was wise, to give us such a Sacred Woman. You are proof that no matter what we suffer, he can heal us. He can give us new life." The Priest kept tugging, easing the doeskin over her buttocks and down her legs past her feet. All the while, he murmured lies about her beauty. They *must* be lies…

Zeyá was trembling again. She wondered how he would take her, how she should lie down.

The Priest saw her hesitating. "I think *I* should be the Earth, and you should be the Sky." He lay down himself, with his back against the buffalo robe.

Zeyá blinked at him, confused.

"Climb on me when you are ready," the Priest smiled.

Still she stared at him. She always turned away when her sister and their husband were coupling. Sometimes she'd seen them together from the corner of her eye, but her sister had never been *above*… Was Zeyá to *kneel* over the Priest? "Where… Where do my hands go?" she asked aloud.

"One on my chest, one on yourself, perhaps?"

"On…myself?"

"Here." The Priest reached between her thighs and brushed her flesh there—not the place where his *véto'ots* would go but just in front of it. She started at his touch. He stilled his hand but did not withdraw it.

Nor did she pull away. What had her mother called this spot? Her husband always ignored it, and Zeyá had forgotten its name.

"Or I can keep *my* hand here, if you like," suggested the Priest. "We will do only what you like." His fingers began to move again.

Zeyá found herself rising on her knees, pressing closer, her breath catching not in fear now but in anticipation.

When she returned to her husband and the dancers inside the New Life Lodge, Zeyá shouted the words every Sacred Woman shouted every summer. But surely no woman had ever meant them as she did: "Maheo has answered my prayers! I have brought power to you! There is happiness in this power!"

Never before had she understood the power or the happiness

that could flow between a man and a woman. Zeyá knew she would never feel it again. But it was enough—to remake the world, and to remake her.

That night, she and the Priest made something else, too: he gave her a son.

PART I
SO DELIGHTFUL AN
INTERCOURSE

1843-1844

CHARLESTON, SOUTH CAROLINA

Our inexperience of such delights made us all the more ardent in our pursuit of them, so that our thirst for one another was still unquenched.

— Pierre Abélard, *The Story of My Misfortunes* (1132)

CHAPTER 1

And I who looked for only God, found *thee*!
— Elizabeth Barrett Browning, *Sonnets from the Portuguese,*
   XXVII (1850)

J oseph had never wanted to praise God more than he did that
Easter morning. Not only had He died for Joseph's sins and
opened the gates of Heaven, He had made Tessa and sent her
across the ocean to Charleston.

As he performed the rituals of the Mass, Joseph could scarcely
breathe, knowing how near she was, this parishioner unlike any
other parishioner, that if he only turned—

Not here, Joseph chanted in his head. *Not now. But soon.*

Joseph was grateful that Tessa's husband remained absent. He
was also grateful that she knelt before Father Baker to receive the
Eucharist. Tessa understood what would happen when their eyes
met again—what *did* happen when Joseph saw her at his parents'
house for Easter dinner. He could not help but remember his last
sight of Tessa—nearly nude—and it was all he could do to turn
pink instead of scarlet. Tessa blushed too, which only made her
more beautiful.

Impossible desires flooded through him: to deepen that blush by enfolding her in his arms and engulfing her in kisses, heedless of everyone else in the room. Joseph's father and Tessa's brother would not have been surprised by such a shameless display. They might even have cheered, after watching Joseph and Tessa fighting their love for eight excruciating years. But the secret must go no farther.

Joseph tried to focus on his nephew. When prodded, David would talk about school or the medical texts he was memorizing on his own, but little else. Beyond the tasks he had set for himself, his barricade of books, Joseph's nephew seemed to have no other interests or pleasures. David hadn't even reached his twelfth birthday, and already he resembled an old recluse scholar. The boy had inherited nothing but his coloring from his late mother; if Joseph were honest, he would have to describe his sister Catherine as both garrulous and frivolous.

Tessa's brother Liam was even more taciturn, this passionate, gentle Irishman who had been Joseph's brother-in-law all too briefly. *"The last thing I want is for you to spend the rest of your life mourning me!"* Joseph's sister Hélène had told her husband. Perhaps in time, Liam would find the strength to obey. For now, the Irishman resorted to the comfort of a bottle. Agathe had prepared an exemplary Easter feast, but Liam only picked at his food, then excused himself before dessert.

After dinner, Joseph asked to hold Clare—Tessa's miracle, the child she had conceived after her husband had given up hope and agreed to take David as their ward. Joseph cradled Clare's slight weight and gazed down at her in awe, this tiny, perfect piece of the woman he loved.

Joseph's father was not fooled by the way Joseph doted on the daughter and only glanced at the mother, or by the way Tessa maintained a polite distance as well. When Joseph went out to the stable, his father followed him.

While Joseph saddled Prince, his father leaned over the stall and watched him for a minute before he asked: "You've started visiting Tessa in private, haven't you?"

Joseph did not raise his eyes from Prince's billet straps, and he tried not to react. "Possibly."

His father chuckled. "I am pleased to hear it, son."

It was good to hear his father laugh again, after losing Hélène; but Joseph did not like the implication in his father's tone. "I'm not — We haven't—" He snatched Prince's bridle from its hook. "I am still a virgin, and I will remain one."

"All right," his father said doubtfully, his elation—his pride— deflating considerably. Then he added: "I *did* tell you Tessa cannot conceive again?"

"It isn't about that: whether we might be caught!" With the bridle just before Prince's nose, Joseph paused to glare at his father. "Carnal intercourse isn't necessary. I don't need it. I want only to *be* with her."

His father let out a great sigh and turned to go; but before he did, he left Joseph with this: "Have you thought about whether *she* needs it, Joseph?"

Joseph scowled in his wake. Less than two months ago, hadn't his father argued that for a woman, penetration was "tolerable at best"? Tessa did not wish Joseph to repeat the pain her husband had inflicted. She needed Joseph to hold her, perhaps kiss her, in time maybe even caress her—but no more.

Joseph was glad of it, this clear limit amidst such uncertainty. *"I trust you,"* Liam had told him. *"You'll find a line and you won't cross it."* While Joseph had yet to locate that line, he knew this: his nights with Tessa would never include coition. He would never cause her discomfort by even suggesting such a thing. If stopping short of union meant denying his own pleasure, all the better. Joseph could maintain the spirit of Priestly purity, if not its letter. He could make Tessa "unspeakably happy" and still face God and his parishioners the next morning.

This *was*, of course, about whether they might be caught. Joseph's night-time visits must remain rare. The more often he used Tessa's hidden garden gate, the greater the chance would be that someone would learn of it—that her husband would learn of it. As much as possible, Joseph must content himself with visits no one could question: crossing paths with Tessa at his parents' home, or when Joseph went to see his nephew at hers.

WHEN JOSEPH RETURNED to the Bishop's residence, he found his confessor waiting for him in the library. Joseph had known he could not avoid the man forever. He tried not to blanch. "Good evening, Father."

"I haven't seen you for weeks, Joseph," his confessor glowered. "Didn't I tell you that *regular* Confessions are more important now than ever? Have you been avoiding your proximate occasion of sin?"

Joseph couldn't lie. "No, Father." He bowed his head. "Give me your blessing, for I have sinned." Joseph said the words because that was how you always began a Confession; but now they felt empty. He was not certain that he *had* sinned —or at least, that he had sinned mortally. Still, he went through the motions of Penance. He admitted he'd stopped using his discipline and that he'd visited his "proximate occasion of sin" at night, when he knew her husband would be away.

His confessor was aghast, and then furious.

Joseph argued: "We barely touched, Father."

"You have opened the door! You have let in the Devil! You must repent and mortify yourself *at once*! You must tell your superior that you are not strong enough to remain in the proximity of this temptress!"

Joseph's jaw clenched. His confessor had no right to speak about Tessa like that. He didn't know her; he didn't understand how perfect and blameless—

"Would to God *I* could tell Father Baker for you!" But the unbreakable Seal of Confession protected Joseph. "Do you understand what you are risking, if you persist in this sin? Not only eternal consequences but also immediate ones! You cannot administer Sacraments or blessings unless the Holy Spirit assists you. If you continue to offend Him, He may refuse to come when you call on

Him. The power of the Priesthood comes at a price, Joseph. That price is our purity."

"But Saint Thomas Aquinas wrote: 'Christ may act even through a minister who is spiritually dead.'"

His confessor glared at him. "'May act'—not 'will act'! Do you really wish to put Him to the test? To try the patience of Almighty God? Stop looking for loopholes, Joseph! This is the time to fall on your knees and beg His forgiveness. Since you were ordained, how many times have you prayed the Miserére?"

In whole or in parts, Joseph had recited and sung the Fiftieth Psalm every day of his Priesthood. "Thousands."

"Do you remember who composed it, and when?"

"King David—after his sin with Bathsheba."

"Another man's *wife*. As part of your Penance, pray the Miserére again, slowly—and this time, think how every word applies to *you*."

"Yes, Father."

When his confessor had departed, Joseph knelt in the empty cathedral to obey: "Miserére mei, Deus…"

"Have mercy on me, O God… For I acknowledge my transgressions, and my sin is always before me. … Purge me with hyssop, Lord, and I shall be clean: wash me, and I shall be whiter than snow. Let me hear joy and gladness; that the bones which Thou hast crushed may rejoice. … Drive me not from Thy presence; and take not Thy Holy Spirit from me. … My sacrifice, O God, is an afflicted spirit: a contrite and humbled heart…"

But Joseph was *not* contrite. He could not regret what he and Tessa had done or anything they might do. He felt impure when he awoke sticky with a nocturnal pollution, but not when he'd tasted the perspiration on Tessa's skin. His wickedness—if it *was* wickedness—twisted the words of this Penitential Psalm. When Joseph prayed *"Let me hear joy and gladness…"* it only reminded him of Tessa: SHE is my joy! Perhaps God had brought joy to his *youth*; but Tessa…

Joseph brought joy to her too; he knew he did. He could hear her laughter even now. God had "crushed Tessa's bones" so many times: He'd forced her to flee from Ireland; He'd allowed her to marry Edward Stratford; He'd ripped six children from her womb and her adopted daughter from her arms; barely a month ago, He'd taken Tessa's best friend; even her beloved brother had become distant in his grief... Surely the Holy Spirit would not scorn Joseph for restoring joy to such a woman.

King David had cried out this Penance; and yet (having disposed of her husband) he'd kept Bathsheba as his wife. Through their son Solomon descended Joseph's patron saint, and through their son Nathan descended the Blessed Virgin. God had used their sin to His greater glory. God must have sent Bathsheba to bathe on that rooftop, knowing King David would see her, knowing their sin was necessary.

Bereft of Joseph's comfort, might not Tessa sink into despair again? But with a strong mother and a devoted uncle to support them, what might Clare and *their* David accomplish? Tessa's husband wanted nothing to do with the children: Clare was not a son, and David was not *his* son. Tessa's joy, Clare and David's futures—surely these were the greater good.

As she'd promised, Tessa set their blue Argand lamp in her bedchamber window during the day as well, whenever her husband was absent. Joseph tried not to pass the corner of Church Street and Longitude Lane often enough to attract suspicion; but when he noticed the lamp one May morning, he decided to answer.

First, Joseph looked in on Clare (napping like a cherub), then his nephew. He found David in his usual posture: hunched over a book. The boy had made one friend in Charleston, at least, even if his friend wasn't human. After his sister's death, David had adopted her black-and-white cat, Mignon—or perhaps vice versa. Even while David read, his hand scratched absently between the ears of the contented animal.

Joseph and Tessa dared not risk any intimacies with her slaves going about their duties. She asked him into her garden only to see a new rose. "It's come up out of *nothing*!" Tessa explained. "I thought perhaps you could identify it, and tell me how I might encourage it. The scent is magnificent—it reminds me of champagne!"

The fragrance greeted them even before the blossoms: delicate yet powerful, sweet and a little spicy. The canes spurted from the earth like the jets of a fountain, the blue-grey-green foliage reaching nearly to Tessa's waist. The flesh-pink blossoms blushed a darker pink at their centers.

"This is *all* new!" Tessa assured him. "Do you recognize it?"

He did indeed. Yet Joseph hesitated. This rose had been christened half a dozen times over the centuries: Regalis, La Virginale, Incarnata... He might have given Tessa any one of those names. He knew only the name he would *not* be giving her: in France, this rose was called "Cuisse de Nymphe Émue," Thigh of an Aroused Nymph.

Joseph decided on the English name: "It's called Maiden's Blush."

"How lovely! Will she be all right here, in the shade?"

Joseph nodded. "She's an Alba. They're remarkably resilient, wherever they're planted. Years after you think they've perished, Albas will spring up again, as vigorous as before."

"Will she blossom over and over, like the Noisettes?"

Joseph shook his head. "Only once." But in her brief bloom, she would be generous and unforgettable.

He stared at Tessa's chaste tree, which had burst into flower as well: stalks of vivid blue-violet standing out from the lush foliage. Medieval monks had chewed these blossoms to maintain their chastity. Joseph wondered if he shouldn't take a few.

He looked to where Tessa's gardener was pushing a cast iron mowing machine across the grass. Zion wasn't close, but he was too close for Joseph's liking. Joseph lowered his voice. "Tessa... What we did on Holy Saturday, have you confessed it?"

She kept her eyes on the Maiden's Blush but shook her head. She whispered back: "Have you?"

"I *tried*."

Tessa caressed one of her roses. "All those years when I thought I was alone, that you loved me only as a sister, I was certain what I felt for you made me despicable in God's sight. I knew without a doubt that I was damned. But now that I know *you* feel the same... I cannot help but believe that He wants this for us—that He has given us to each other. My turning to you is like a flower turning toward the sun. It would die without that warmth." Tessa also glanced toward the gardener, whose back was to them now. For only as long as she spoke, she squeezed Joseph's hand. "I cannot believe this is sin."

CHAPTER 2

ROMEO: Thus from my lips, by yours, my sin is purged.
JULIET: Then have my lips the sin that they have took.
ROMEO: Sin from my lips? O trespass sweetly urged! Give
me my sin again.
— William Shakespeare, *The Most Excellent and Lamentable*
Tragedie of Romeo and Juliet (1599)

Word reached them from Baltimore: the Fifth Provincial Council had submitted a *terna* to Rome, a list of three candidates from whom they hoped the Holy See would choose the next Bishop of Charleston. Once again, Father Baker was slighted.

Joseph knew their widowed diocese needed a new Bishop; but he also knew this would mean change. Even if the next Bishop did not send Joseph on permanent mission outside Charleston, Joseph would likely share a residence with His Lordship. Such proximity would make night visits to Tessa more difficult. How many times could Joseph claim to be returning from an emergency sick call before the Bishop became suspicious?

Joseph began to watch more assiduously for Tessa's blue lamp. But as he'd suspected, she and her husband soon removed to Sullivan's Island. Edward spent several days in town every month, so he could attend to business, but Tessa and the children remained at the cottage. This was safest, Joseph knew; the sea breezes spared them from the worst of the summer heat and diseases.

Joseph visited when he could, ostensibly to visit his nephew or to say Mass. Even on the island, Tessa was surrounded by her husband's slaves, and often Edward was present too. Joseph and Tessa walked along the sand a few times, one of them carrying Clare, but this was as close as they came to being alone. The most they dared were hand-clasps—except for one reckless morning when Edward was away and they'd wandered farther from the other strollers than usual. Clare lay between them on her mother's paisley shawl, experimenting with the taste of her toes. Pretending to lean over her and coo as they did so often, Tessa kissed Joseph's hand instead, and he kissed hers. It felt like a promise.

IN OCTOBER, Tessa finally returned to Church Street. A few days before her twenty-seventh birthday, Joseph saw the blue lamp shining for him once more. He made sure no one had followed him down Longitude Lane and that no one was approaching. His heart racing nonetheless, he pulled the chain from around his neck and inserted the key. Tessa's garden gate opened easily for him, and he slipped inside, locking it behind him.

The garden was even darker than the lane, and he'd not risked carrying any kind of lantern. But he knew Tessa's paths by heart. Silently he strode past the roses, over the oyster shell walks, and up the steps of the piazza. With as little sound as possible, he opened the unlocked front door and crept up the spiral staircase to the second floor. He'd meant to follow the glow of the blue lamp into Tessa's bedchamber, where the door was ajar; but from the nursery, he heard the murmur of Tessa's voice and her maid Hannah's.

That door was closed. Joseph hesitated. Should he knock? Should he call Tessa's name? However softly he did either of these things, if his nephew were lying awake upstairs, mightn't the boy hear?

Finally, Joseph reached for the handle and turned it with excruciating slowness. When the door had opened a crack, he heard a
gasp from inside the nursery, and the women's voices ceased. He
froze in place. This had been a terrible idea. Tessa and Hannah
were alone in a dark house, with their virtue and two children to
defend. One of them was likely to take him for an intruder and
scream.

Then, he heard the women giggling, followed by Tessa's whisper: "Is that 'my ghostly father'?"

Joseph recognized the appellation from *Romeo and Juliet*. He'd
been particularly interested in the character of Friar Laurence—a
fellow gardener and man of God. In Shakespeare's day, "ghostly"
meant "spiritual." Joseph had to chuckle at the absurdity of this
situation. Very like something from the stage. "It is."

"'Stay but a little, I will come.'" It sounded like Tessa was
quoting again. Had she attended the play recently, to sample from it
so freely? Had she gone with her husband? Joseph felt a ridiculous
stab of jealousy. Inside the nursery, he heard rustlings and more
murmurs.

Joseph felt too exposed in the hall, so he waited in Tessa's
bedchamber. As he pulled off his gloves and unbuttoned his coat
in the warm night air, he eyed the left-most window warily. In
order for Joseph to see the blue lamp from the street, Tessa had to
leave the inner jalousie shutters open, which also meant anyone on
the street could now see *him* if he ventured too close to that
window. Probably he would appear as only a shadow behind the
lamp; but he couldn't risk it. He was nearly a head taller than
Edward.

Their voices were hardly alike either. But Tessa's bedchamber
was in a good position, Joseph decided, even if they had to leave a
window ajar for the breeze. The nearest neighbors were across the
side garden and Longitude Lane or across the front garden and
Church Street—not very near at all. As trysting places went, it was
relatively safe. As long as neither of them became too excited.

And then Tessa joined him. When Joseph saw she was wearing
only her chemise—and presumably drawers, but no stockings—he

sat down quickly on her méridienne, as if it were some kind of statement: *I shall not be moved.*

His own body was belying his resolution. Horrified, Joseph flung one leg over the other and clasped his hands around his knee to hold it in place. "Tessa..."

"Yes, my love?" She closed the door and came to stand before him, the swells of her breasts nearly level with his eyes.

Joseph struggled to look elsewhere. "I—I know it is still warm, but do you think you could find a wrapper, to cover..."

She stared down at herself, and her cheeks went a shade of scarlet that had nothing to do with pleasure. She touched the milk stain on her chemise, and her beautiful face crumpled. "I'm sorry..." She fled through the door to her adjoining dressing chamber.

"Tessa, I didn't—" He called it too loudly and swallowed the rest of the words. With several deep breaths, he fought to dampen his lust. He must explain that it wasn't disgust he felt when he looked at her—without disgusting *her.* Finally he stood and paced to the door of the dressing chamber.

But a single glance inside revealed more of Tessa's bare skin than he'd ever seen before: all of her back and arms and lower legs —everything her drawers did not cover. She'd shed the stained chemise entirely and was opening her wardrobe for another. She glanced at him over her shoulder; she knew he was there, and she did not cry out.

Joseph tried to retreat, but his legs wouldn't move. He tried to look away, but his eyes kept returning. "Tessa, I didn't mean that you or your—motherhood are in any way displeasing to me. I meant the *opposite.*"

She hesitated, her arms in the wardrobe. "The opposite?"

He didn't want to admit this. But she must understand. Her trust in him was humbling—and misplaced. "I meant: I am neither as pure nor as strong as you think me."

She peered at him over her naked shoulder. Her long tresses were done up only loosely: a few bronze tendrils cascaded down the breathtaking contours of her back, between her exquisite shoulder blades. "So if I were to turn to you now, exactly as I am...?"

"I fear I would do more than gaze at you, Tessa." She couldn't *want* him to touch her—at least not yet, when her breasts must be reserved for her child.

Indeed, Tessa was scowling at the very thought. She yanked a new chemise from the wardrobe and dropped it over her head. She covered herself further with a muslin wrapper, patterned white on white; but the garment was so sheer, he could see her arms through it. Head held high, Tessa stomped past him to close the jalousies— as much as a sylph could stomp. Clearly, she was angry with him, or at least disappointed. Apparently she *had* thought he was made of stone, that a Priest should be able to share a bedchamber with a beautiful, nearly nude woman and feel nothing. Saints had done it, hadn't they? Why couldn't he?

"Would you be more comfortable on the méridienne, or on the bed?" she demanded.

"Uh... The méridienne..."

Before he could help her, she snatched up one end of the little sofa, rotated it till its back faced the bed, and dropped it onto the floor again. "'Tis all yours, sir." Tessa herself climbed onto the bed and lay down perfunctorily, flat on her back, staring up at the canopy. She clasped her hands over her abdomen as if she were a figure on a tomb.

Confused but obedient, Joseph perched on the méridienne. In its current position, he was facing the corner like a naughty child. He could not even see her without turning sharply on the seat and craning his neck. Had he mistaken the source of her anger? Perhaps she'd expected him to bring her a birthday present? How could he, when her husband might see it? Women were so irrational.

Tessa proved her volatility by springing up almost as soon as she'd lain down. "Perhaps you would allow me to *read* to you?" She crossed to the bookshelf near the blue lamp. "Something from Scripture?"

"Anything but the Canticles," Joseph said to the wall.

Tessa huffed out a breath. "Would the writings of an ascetic saint and fellow Priest meet with your approval?" She selected a volume and sat on her bed before she read aloud:

"Into the darkness of the night,
With yearning love inflamed—
Oh blessed chance!—
I went forth unobserved,
My house being now at rest."

Joseph recognized the poem at once. The author was Saint John of the Cross. The verses were about the Soul's love for God, and His for her; but to secular ears, they sounded like a shameless young woman sneaking out to meet her *human* lover.

Tessa glanced toward their lamp and continued with more and more fervor:

"This light guided me
More surely than the noonday sun
To the place where He was waiting for me…
On my flowery breast,
Kept wholly for Him,
He fell asleep, and I caressed Him…
I lay quite still, all memory lost.
My head was resting on my Love.
I fainted away in sweet abandonment."

Joseph clenched his jaw at the impiety of her choice in such a context. "Have you read Saint John of the Cross's 'Ascent of Mount Carmel' wherein he explains that each line is allegorical?"

"I think the poem speaks for itself."

"As you said, Saint John of the Cross was a Priest—a man who dedicated himself to God. Everything he did and thought and wrote sprang from his desire to strengthen *that* relationship."

"Do you really think he could write such a poem unless he'd known *human* love as well?"

"With Saint Teresa, I suppose?" This was too much. Next Tessa would be suggesting that Saint Joseph and the Blessed Virgin had lain together as husband and wife.

"Yes: let us see what my patroness has to say," Tessa agreed, though it didn't sound like a concession. She returned to her bookshelf and plucked up another volume. As soon as she began reading, Joseph recognized it as Saint Teresa's *Life*.

"Our Lord was pleased that I should have repeatedly the following vision: I saw an angel close by me, on my left side, in bodily form. ... He was most beautiful... I saw in his hand a long spear of gold... I thought he thrust it several times into my heart, and penetrated my very entrails; when he drew it out, he seemed to leave me all on fire... The pain was so great, that it made me moan; and yet its sweetness was so excessive, that I could not desire it to go. The soul is satisfied now with nothing less... The pain is not bodily, but spiritual; though the body in some measure, yea, in great measure, participates in it. It is so delightful an intercourse..."

Joseph hadn't read Teresa's autobiography since he was a boy. When Tessa excised the references to God, the remaining descriptions sent color to his cheeks. The beautiful angel's "long spear" might almost be taken for—

Why was Tessa reading this to him? She couldn't be telling him she would *welcome* the pain of carnal intercourse.

"I'm not saying Saint John of the Cross and Saint Teresa knew one another physically. I am saying that even while their souls yearned for intimacy with God, their bodies yearned for another kind of intimacy—even if they couldn't admit it to themselves."

But Joseph *had* admitted his yearning, aloud, only a few minutes ago.

"If you'll do no more at night than you will during the day, why are you here, Joseph?"

Before he could answer, her daughter started complaining in the nursery.

"Please don't leave," Tessa begged before she went to Clare.

For a while, Joseph stared at the tiny golden birds perched on the urn of their blue Argand lamp. Each seemed to be waiting for the other to drink. But neither ever would.

He looked to the empty bed. He was afraid to begin because he didn't know if he could stop—and if Tessa did not *want* him to stop, or *thought* she did not want him to stop... That was even more frightening. He *must* stop, regardless of what either of them wanted. He must maintain some semblance of his Priesthood, even here.

He shrugged off his coat, untied his choker, and unbuttoned his boots. He padded to the bed and lay down atop the counterpane, staring up at the rosette in the center of the canopy. He clasped his hands over his chest and tried to pray. *God, grant me chastity and continency—and Tessa. Grant me the strength to give her everything she desires without surrendering to MY desires. Most of all, help me to understand what she desires.*

He wasn't sure how many minutes passed before Tessa returned to the bedchamber. She lit a small glass lamp and blew out the Argand lamp, so that the room was more shadow than light. To allay the suspicions of her neighbors, Joseph guessed.

Still in her wrapper, Tessa climbed onto the bed and lay down next to him on her side. After a moment, she reached out to touch him just above the V of his waistcoat, where the buttons of his shirt were. Joseph started as if she had burned him.

Tessa did not move her hand; she only traced her fingertips over his buttons. He could feel her warmth. As she caressed his chest, she whispered:

"If I profane with my unworthiest hand
This holy shrine, the gentle fine is this:
My lips, two blushing pilgrims, ready stand
To smooth that rough touch with a tender kiss."

She was quoting *Romeo and Juliet* again. Did she have a copy in the nursery, which she had consulted before returning to him? It had been eight years since Joseph had seen the play with his sister, but he could hardly forget such a charged metaphor. He remembered as well that Shakespeare had given that verse to Romeo, not Juliet.

When Joseph turned his head to her, Tessa continued with the male lines: "'Have not saints lips?'"

Juliet had replied with something about saints' lips being reserved for prayer; but Joseph was not about to quote an adolescent girl. He turned carefully on his side. He slid his left hand into the silk of Tessa's hair and let his right hand caress her face. He'd done this so many times in his dreams...

Even in the near-darkness, he found her mouth easily: the warmth of her breath guided him. Her lips were even softer than her throat. He began hesitantly, with a mere brush. Even this was electric, and he felt her smiling, encouraging him. A kiss was a sign of reconciliation, wasn't it? Tessa twined her arms around his back, and the globes of her breasts stroked his chest, their shapes distinct even through four layers of fabric. He raised one knee like a shield, so she wouldn't realize what she did to him.

How many ancients, mystics and saints even, had called a kiss more intimate than coition, because in it you poured your breath—your spirit—into another, and drank hers in return? Saint John Chrysostom spoke of mouths as the entrance to the temple of the body. As their kiss deepened, Joseph finally understood.

When the tip of Tessa's tongue flickered against his lips, all thoughts of saints vanished from his mind. He knew it was an invitation. Very slowly, he began to explore inside her entrance. The caresses of his tongue were not skilled, not at first; and for all her determination, she proceeded cautiously too. Once, they knocked teeth. But they only laughed and plunged back into the sweet fray with even greater ardor.

Joseph did not know how long they lapped at each other's souls like this. It might have been an hour. It might have been two.

When at last he stopped to regain his breath, Joseph whispered: "'Honey and milk are under thy tongue.'" He was fairly certain it had been Solomon who said that, not his bride. Tessa tasted more like wine—or perhaps pomegranate, at once bitter and sweet.

She seemed to read his thoughts; Tessa answered: "'Let my beloved come into his garden, and eat the fruit...'"

If she meant more than kissing, he could not wait to obey, to consume even more of her. But he *must* wait. He must find a pause without Clare's intervention. So he rested his forehead against Tessa's, caressed her hair, and willed himself to be content. They had time. They must save something for the next night, and the night after that... Wherever the new Bishop might send him, Joseph would find a way to return to her.

CHAPTER 3

Oh! Lord! Give me the strength and the courage
To gaze upon my heart and my body without disgust.
— Charles Baudelaire, "Un Voyage à Cythère" (1857)

When Edward removed to Stratford-on-Ashley that fall, he took Tessa with him. For the entire winter. "He wants me to learn how to be a plantation mistress," she explained to Joseph. He knew she loathed the role. "But if I can make those people's lives even a little more bearable... I do not know how many changes Edward or his father will allow me; but I must try."

There was no way for Joseph to spend the night with Tessa at the plantation without someone seeing him. Even while they strolled in the extensive gardens, they had to look over their shoulders. Joseph could not risk more than a brief visit every few weeks, under the guise of spiritual counsel. Edward returned to town periodically, but he allowed Tessa to do so only on Sundays for Mass, and she did not spend the night.

"Do you think he knows?" Joseph whispered in a guarded moment behind a camellia hedge.

"That I care for you? Yes. That we have acted on it? No.

Edward's anger toward you is at a slow simmer. If he does discover the truth, I will know it."

And Joseph could do nothing to protect her. *Edward isn't a violent man,* Joseph kept reminding himself. *He will rail at her; he will find ways to punish her; but he will not harm Tessa physically.*

Except by using her the way all husbands used their wives—with her submission, but against her will.

In MARCH, when the blue lamp shone for the first time since October, Joseph slipped into her bedchamber to find Tessa curled up on the counterpane in her blue wrapper. Her eyes were bloodshot from weeping, and she still clutched a handkerchief.

Quickly Joseph shed his gloves and boots, then remembered about the window. He managed to lean toward it in such a way that he closed the jalousie shutters without exposing anything but his arm to the street. The slats admitted even less than the grille of a confessional: air but no sight. At last, he lay down face to face with Tessa on the bed.

"Edward insisted I wean Clare," she told Joseph in a broken voice. "I would have nursed her for months yet, not only because it makes me feel closer to her, but because it has kept *him* away from me. My milk disconcerted him, so he's let me— He's been satisfied if I only… I thanked God for that reprieve, every time. But now that I have stopped nursing…" Tessa buried her face deeper in the pillow, as if she were ashamed. "Edward…reclaimed me last night —and this morning, before he left."

She should remind Edward that she could no longer conceive, so coition was a sin, even if they were husband and wife. But Joseph knew how ridiculous such advice would sound, coming from the lips of her lover.

"He's even removed the locks on my rooms!" Tessa wept. "He knows I have never refused him!"

Was lying with Edward Tessa's Penance for lying with Joseph? Except she hadn't lain with Joseph. And now that her husband had reminded her how painful coition could be, she would never wish to.

What could Joseph do to assure her that with him, she was safe? Gingerly, he reached out to the loose hair that had fallen across her eyes. As tenderly as he would have touched her daughter, he smoothed the strands behind Tessa's ear again.

She looked up at him. "Would— Would you just hold me, Joseph?"

"Of course."

Tessa tucked herself against him, her head beneath his chin. But he heard her sound of frustration, and he understood; his neck was still bound up in his choker. As quickly as he could, he undid the neckerchief and tossed it on the other side of her. He loosened his collar too. Tessa sighed her gratitude and nestled her face tight against the skin of his throat, her arms curled against his chest.

Joseph enfolded her and sang her a slow lullaby in French until she was sleeping peacefully against him. He was weary himself from his work, but he watched the mantel clock carefully. He couldn't call Hannah to ask her to wake him in a few hours; his voice would disturb Tessa and probably David too. Clare was finally sleeping through the night. Joseph must keep vigil himself. It was a sweet duty.

He suspected he did slumber briefly. When the mantel clock read six, Joseph tried to extract himself from Tessa without waking her; but he did not succeed.

As he slid from the bed, she gave a murmur of disapproval and opened her eyes. "Don't go."

"I must. It's nearly dawn." He located his boots. "I have to prepare for Mass."

When he retrieved his choker from the counterpane, Tessa grasped his waistcoat and pulled him to her for a kiss. "Come back tonight?" she pleaded against his lips. "Edward will still be away."

Joseph had promised himself never to visit two nights in succession. But if the years ahead continued like the last one, with only narrow windows between Tessa's months on the island and on the plantation, she would be alone twice a year at most: once in the spring and once in the fall.

Joseph made a new promise: he promised to return. He also

asked her, as he rebuttoned his boots: "Tessa, the nights Edward spends away from you, do you think *he…*"

She shook her head, staring down at the blue skirt of her wrapper. "I wish he would! I know that is a terrible thing to say: that I *want* my husband to be unfaithful to me. But Edward does it more for himself than for me. The thought of lying with another woman, the risk of disease—I think it disgusts him. Then he uses his faithfulness as a weapon: one way or another, I must always submit, because I am his only 'relief.'"

Joseph came to stand by the bed again. He touched her face. "If I *ever* make you uncomfortable, Tessa—if I do anything to remind you of him—you must tell me."

She smiled and nodded, placing her own hand over his. "But you and Edward are as different as night from day. I could never mistake you, even with my eyes closed." She lowered her lids and her smile widened. "Even your smells are different. *He* is cloying and oppressive; *you* are spicy and mysterious."

"'Mysterious'?" Joseph chuckled. At the moment, he probably smelled more like stale sweat than anything else.

"Absolutely beguiling," Tessa added, bringing her face closer and inhaling deeply.

She was all three of those adjectives and far more. But if he lingered here any longer, he'd never make it to Mass. So he only kissed her again—chastely—and said: "Well, you may sniff me again tonight. Right now, I really must go."

THAT NIGHT BEGAN MUCH LIKE THE LAST, with the two of them lying on their sides on the counterpane, facing one another, him mostly dressed and her mostly undressed. But now, Tessa's eyes glistened only with delight. Her teeth flashed too, her mouth a broad smile. "If *you* were my husband, if this were our wedding night, do you know what I would do?"

Joseph swallowed. "No."

Tessa caught her lower lip between her teeth. "First, I would ask you to lie on your back. Then, I would make you promise not to move, no matter what, unless I gave you leave to do so. Then, very carefully, I would remove each of your garments. I would need you to move a little for that: to lift your arms while I pulled off your shirt, for example. When you were absolutely naked, I would start at the crown of your head and work my way down to your toes, brushing every single part of you with my fingertips. I would still forbid you to move. But I would watch—and listen—for your reactions as I touched each part of you. I would remember the places you liked my touch best. One area, I think I can guess"—her eyes flitted downward wickedly—"but I would want to find all of them. The insides of your elbows? The soles of your feet? Maybe one of those would make you groan too. Then, I would return to the places you liked best—but this time, with my mouth. And this time, I would linger."

Joseph clenched his eyes shut, as if this would banish the images. It was all he could do not to groan *now*, at the mere thought of Tessa's mouth—

"If I were your wife, what would you do to me, on our wedding night?"

He couldn't breathe enough to speak. "I would…"

"Yes?"

"…caress you…"

"Where?"

"…everywhere." He knew it wasn't original.

Tessa didn't seem to mind. "Where would you start?"

He struggled to keep his eyes on her face.

"Nothing you say will make me love you any less, Joseph."

Still he did not speak; but he let his gaze slide down her throat to where the small mound of her left breast was visible even through her wrapper and chemise. Then his eyes returned apologetically to her face.

Tessa only smiled. Her fingers went to the buttons of her wrapper. He watched her unfasten it and did nothing to stop her. Then she unbuttoned her chemise and pulled it off her shoulder, so that her left breast was nearly exposed to him. The upper swell of it *was*. Finally Tessa took his right hand and guided it into her chemise.

Now he did groan, as his fingertips grazed over flesh softer than anything he'd ever felt in his life. The silk of his vestments was jagged glass compared to the softness of Tessa's breast. Yet her flesh was changing under his touch, becoming even more exquisite: puckering, rising to meet his palm. Her breath hitched again and again as his thumb stroked her pebbled areole, her erect nipple; but he wanted more.

He forced himself to be gentle as his hand closed around that magnificent swell of her. He dared the lightest of pinches, and Tessa moaned her encouragement. His mouth rushed to hers, in gratitude, in completion. As his tongue dove inside her, his fingers continued to caress, to squeeze, to play.

He must have done it for five minutes straight before Tessa broke their kiss to whimper: "Joseph...?" It was halfway between a whine and an apology.

Instantly his hand stilled on her breast. "Am I hurting you?"

"No, but...I do have *two* breasts."

Joseph laughed, though he kept his nose against hers. Even in his embarrassment, he could not bear to lose contact with her. "I love you."

"For criticizing you? Or for having two breasts?"

He gave her another quick buss. "For keeping me humble—and for having two breasts." He soon found the second one.

"That's the first time you've said it."

Joseph was slightly distracted. "Said what?"

"That you love me. You have implied it; I have assumed it; but..."

His eyes returned to her face. "I love you, Tessa. Whatever else I say or do, never doubt that."

Tessa grinned. But when he opened her chemise wider to expose her breasts to the lamplight, she hid her face in the pillow. "Please don't examine them *too* closely."

Joseph frowned. "Why not?"

"They have...*declined*."

What she meant by that, Joseph couldn't fathom. "They're perfect,

Tessa. And…unexpected." He pulled away from her a little, so he wasn't blocking the light. No: he hadn't imagined it. He'd seen her breasts before, when she was nursing Clare, but he'd been so careful not to stare—and she'd been in shadow. Tessa's nipples were like the rosebuds of a Maiden's Blush; but beneath that deep pink, the softest, most beautiful shade of brown suffused her areoles, like the coat of a fawn.

Joseph remembered that day on the beach, nearly two decades ago, when his cousin Frederic had stripped to his skin. Joseph had seen the pink of Frederic's genitals and been ashamed of his own, because he was colored, because his father had been born a slave. But Tessa was as white as his cousin—and the hue of her intimate skin wasn't so different from Joseph's after all. "You're *colored* here," he whispered.

"I am?" Tessa peered down at herself and smiled. Then, she squinted at Joseph's chest. "What color are yours?"

He blushed at once, as if she could see anything through his black waistcoat and white shirt. "Darker."

"How much darker?"

"They're *brown*."

"But what shade? Are they like nutmeg, or coffee?"

He sat up, hoping to end this ridiculous conversation.

Tessa sat up too. "Might I see for myself?"

"Of course not!"

Tessa pouted. "You've seen *mine*." When Joseph only glared at her, she gave a deep sigh and clasped her chemise over her breasts. "If you're not willing to reciprocate…"

She couldn't be serious. Did she really mean she would never again allow him—

He couldn't risk it. Joseph's fingers tore through his waistcoat buttons. Then he wrested open his shirt buttons, which ran down a bit farther than the chain holding his key, to the base of the dark swath of hair. Finally, he yanked the fabric sideways, past his right nipple. "See?" He thrust his shirt back in place and reached to refasten the buttons.

Tessa protested immediately. "I didn't get a good look!"

Joseph groaned his frustration and repeated the motion, but left the nipple exposed slightly longer.

Tessa grinned. "Cocoa," she decided.

Why were all her suggestions edible? Again he started redoing his buttons.

"Not *yet*! I haven't seen the other one!"

"They are quite the same!"

"Are you certain?"

"Yes!"

"You don't have a very good angle. I think you'd better let *me* judge."

"Fine!" In exasperation, he pulled open both sides of his shirt at once.

Tessa leaned closer, peering at him as if he were a painting in a gallery. "Mm… This left one, I don't know; I'd think I'd better…" She tilted her head. And then, her mouth darted to his chest. Before he knew what was happening, she'd *kissed* his *nipple*.

Fortunately, it was a single peck. If she'd lingered, Joseph was fairly certain his heart would have burst. As it was, he felt her lips all the way to his groin. He scrambled to rebutton his shirt and waist-coat as if his life depended on it, while Tessa grinned at him.

Before he was quite presentable, she launched herself at him once more, flinging her arms around him and knocking him back to the bed. She bussed his Adam's apple, inhaled his throat, and finally simply clung to him. So closely that, even through the layers of cotton and broadcloth between them, she could not fail to notice his rampancy.

"I'm sorry," he muttered miserably, trying to shift his erection away from her.

She wouldn't release him. She only tilted her face up to his, though he was too ashamed to meet her gaze. "You needn't apolo-gize, Joseph. My body reacts just as fiercely to your proximity—to the very *thought* of you." She was pressing her hips against him, a soft and delicate cradle—such a contrast to his own rude jutting.

"Your body is more discreet about it."

"It doesn't feel 'discreet' in the slightest." Above the back of his trousers, her thumb had slipped inside his waistcoat, and she caressed his skin through his shirt. Her other hand slid up to the hair at the nape of his neck. "Can you understand, Joseph, how precious every inch of you is to me?"

He was beginning to.

They kissed and he stroked her breasts till the threat of dawn forced Joseph back to the Bishop's residence. There, he had only a small mirror for shaving. But that afternoon, he returned to his parents' house. With his mother working in the garden and his father ensconced in his office, Joseph climbed the stairs to his old bedroom. He jammed the door shut with a chair and closed the curtains. He lit a lamp and stood before his old pier-glass.

He was still fully clothed, and already his heart was racing. He was nearly thirty-two years old, and he hadn't done this since he was thirteen. Only furtively even then. To stare at oneself was vanity. It invited impure imaginings about someone staring back at you, touching you... All his life, his baths had been quick and cold.

Slowly, he removed each article of his clothing and laid it on the bed. He kept his eyes averted. Finally, there was nothing between him and the mirror but light, and he raised his eyes.

Was it possible, that someone as beautiful as Tessa should desire *this*? This colored body that he had hated and punished and denied for so long? This body swelling anew at the very thought of her? When Tessa had said "every inch of you," did she mean...? In her imaginary wedding night, she'd reminded him that they could do many things besides penetration, things that would bring her no pain and bring him a great deal of pleasure.

Then Joseph's eyes focused on the other body reflected in this mirror: the small, broken body of Christ on the crucifix hanging next to the door.

Joseph closed his eyes. *Remember what you are—and what you are not. You are NOT Tessa's husband. You ARE—and always will be—a Priest, a "living sacrifice" like Christ. Colored, white, ugly, beautiful, desiring, desired— IT DOESN'T MATTER. The body in that mirror is no longer yours; it was conse- crated to Him, and you will not—will never—inflict it on or permit it to Tessa.*

CHAPTER 4

As each thing to more perfection grows,
It feels more sensibly both good and pain.
— Dante Alighieri, *The Divine Comedy: Inferno* (circa 1308)

Before Joseph was able to visit Tessa at night again, they learned their new Bishop had been consecrated and was proceeding to Charleston: Ignatius Aloysius Reynolds, a native of Kentucky. Joseph hoped their late Bishop was too occupied with the joys of Heaven to take note of developments in his former diocese. Bishop England would not approve of his successor: Reynolds was the protégé of the late Ambrose Maréchal, the Archbishop with whom England had clashed many times.

When Bishop Reynolds arrived, unannounced, Joseph wasn't wearing his choker or even a coat. He had a screwdriver sticking out of his pocket, and he was hanging repainted shutters on the Bishop's residence, where Joseph still lived himself. He'd hoped to complete the project before His Lordship's appearance.

His back to the Biblical garden, Joseph heard a voice call behind him: "Is this the episcopal residence, boy?"

"It is." As he set down the shutter, Joseph frowned. He was taller than most men, and he'd just begun his thirty-third year: he hardly qualified as a "boy" anymore. Then, as he turned, Joseph realized his visitor had seen only the back of his curly black head and that he was engaged in manual labor—so the man had assumed he was colored. Rightly, of course; but he'd probably also assumed Joseph was a slave.

In fact, there were two visitors. The one who'd spoken was a portly white man of perhaps forty-five, whose features reminded Joseph of portraits he'd seen of Napoleon. The second visitor, a tall, solemn black man several years his senior, remained silent.

Now that they stood face to face, Joseph watched the white man assessing him—still trying to judge his color and class. After a lifetime of such stares, Joseph felt only a twinge of apprehension. Whatever suspicions white men might have on first meeting him, they soon dismissed the possibility that he was different from themselves: he was a Priest; he was cultured; he *couldn't* be colored.

This white man asked: "Is Father Lazare at home?"

"I am."

At this revelation, the man's scowl only deepened.

Joseph assessed him, too. The visitor wore a nondescript brown cloak but also a choker. "Dr. Reynolds?"

"The same."

"Welcome to Charleston, my lord."

Even as Joseph knelt to kiss his episcopal ring, the new Bishop motioned to the shutter Joseph had been carrying. "Don't we have servants—or at least parishioners—for such work?"

"There's a father and son who usually do our repairs"—free, pious colored men—"but before the last coat of paint could dry, they were offered a job in Summerville." A job that actually paid. Joseph could not blame them. "They talked me through the final steps." In truth, Joseph had been eager to help. The Biblical garden did not need his attention at the moment, and such manual labor tended to ease the fervor of his dreams about Tessa.

Bishop Reynolds turned to the black man who'd accompanied him. "You ever hung shutters, Thornton?"

"Yes, sir."

"This is my man," His Lordship explained to Joseph. "Do you have one?"

"We have a housekeeper and cook, Mrs. O'Brien, and the Sisters of Mercy help with the cleaning, but I don't— No."

"Well, since we'll be living under the same roof, I suppose you may borrow him from time to time—but ask me first."

Joseph managed not to clench his teeth at this "liberality." "Of course, my lord."

Father Baker appeared, introduced himself, and offered to show Bishop Reynolds the seminary. His Lordship pointed toward the shutter and told Thornton to "Finish up here."

The black man stepped forward to obey; but as soon as their Bishop was out of sight, Joseph assisted. Thornton nodded his thanks, and together they slid the hinges onto the pintles. This really was a job for two men—especially the shutters on the upper windows.

Joseph asked: "You came with Dr. Reynolds from Kentucky?"

"Yes, sir."

Joseph led Thornton to the sawhorses where the next shutter waited. "Did you have to leave family behind?"

The man hesitated. "Yes, sir."

"Do you have a way to contact them?"

"I can't write, Father."

"I'd be happy to take down whatever you wish to say. Do you have somewhere to send such a letter—someone in Kentucky able to read it?"

For the first time, Thornton met his eyes, if only for a moment. "Yes, sir." His smile lasted longer.

Joseph told Thornton about the room in the garret where Bishop England's valet had slept. "I'm afraid you'll have to watch the roof for leaks—as you can see, our buildings here need more than fresh paint."

When they'd finished with the first floor, they brought over the ladder, and Joseph climbed it. Slowly the black man grew bolder with him. Joseph knew that Thornton had realized the truth his master had dismissed. Colored men and women often reacted this way to Joseph. They remained respectful—he was, after all, a Priest—and they said not a word about their shared origins, but they let down their guards.

"I ain't a Catholic," Thornton admitted. "I guess I ought to say that right off. But that don't mean I don't love God. I'm a preacher myself, in fact." He passed Joseph another shutter. "If you wouldn't mind, Father, it would please me to listen to your sermons. They're a help to me, see—since I ain't able to read the Good Book or any of the learned men you can. I like to hear Dr. Reynolds preach, think about what he said, pray about it, and then use bits of it in my preaching."

Joseph smiled. How many times had he himself studied books of sermons, searching for inspiration? "I would be honored, Thornton. Is there anything in particular you would like to preach about?"

"There is," Thornton mused aloud. "All the way from Kentucky, I been thinking about a Bible story I heard a long time ago: a man named Joseph whose own brothers sold him into slavery. But his sufferings were part of God's plan—they came to good in the end. Do you know it?"

"I do. Joseph is my Christian name." His patron saint was New Testament Joseph, but he still felt a kinship with Old Testament Joseph. "And it's time I read those chapters of Genesis again. Perhaps I might read them aloud?"

DESPITE THE DISCOMFORT of sharing a roof with his Bishop—where only a narrow hall separated them at night, and Reynolds just might hear him groaning Tessa's name in his sleep—Joseph had reasons to be thankful. His Lordship decided Joseph should remain in Charleston. Moreover, the climate had weakened his confessor's health, as it did so many Irishmen's. He requested permission to convalesce in his homeland, and Bishop Reynolds granted it. Joseph must find another confessor; but this one would not know of Joseph's history with Tessa, and he would know no more of their present intimacies than Joseph chose to share with him.

Once again, she spent the summer on Sullivan's Island with the children. The first time Joseph visited, he found the three of them seated on the back porch facing the beach, Clare in her mother's lap. Fortunately, Edward was nowhere in sight. David was reading them something from a newspaper. Clare wasn't even eighteen months old—Joseph suspected she understood little; but she watched her foster-brother's face with rapt attention nonetheless.

Then the girl saw Joseph, and a smile lit up her entire countenance. "Fa-Fa Jo!" Clare hadn't managed "Father Joseph" yet. Tessa helped her daughter slide from her lap, and the girl toddled toward him as fast as she could.

"Good morning, *ma petite*!" He caught Clare up in his arms.

She squealed in glee as he spun her around. Then she patted his cheeks with both of her small hands and declared: "Mine!"

"Can you guess what Clare's favorite new word is?" Tessa laughed. "She's already claimed David and me."

Oh, to belong to this precious little tyrant: to be able to guide and protect her every moment; to have been there when Clare spoke her first word and took her first step; to read her to sleep every night and kiss her awake every morning; to share a bed with her mother…

Joseph sat in the chair next to Tessa and grieved, while Clare nestled her soft bronze head against his shoulder and peered up at him with her mother's myrrh-brown eyes. Clare looked nothing like Edward. *"A living miracle,"* Hélène had called the girl. Joseph could almost believe Tessa's husband had had no part in Clare's conception, that Tessa had conjured her daughter through sheer will or that God had implanted the child without any need of a man.

Joseph remembered his nephew. He asked: "What were you reading, David?"

"It's a story called 'The Gold-Bug,' by Edgar A. Poe. It's about buried treasure. It takes place right here on Sullivan's Island."

"Mr. Poe's description isn't very flattering!" Tessa laughed. "He calls our cottages 'miserable frame buildings'!"

They were simple structures, but hardly "miserable." Joseph

could live here quite contentedly. Although that had much to do with the company.

"He's right about us being 'fugitives from Charleston dust and fever,'" David pointed out.

"And about the sweet myrtle growing all over the island," Tessa acknowledged. "Would you read that part again?"

David decided to start over. "The Gold-Bug" included a negro character named Jupiter, a grinning, dim-witted caricature. The man had actually been freed, yet he refused to leave his "Massa." When David noticed Clare's giggling reactions to Jupiter's nearly incomprehensible dialect, he read the lines with particular relish, as if the negro were no relation to him.

Joseph grimaced, and he saw Tessa frowning too. His nephew had always been polite to Hannah and the Stratfords' other slaves, but the boy's mocking portrayal of Jupiter worried Joseph. Finally he interrupted: "David…"

"What?" His nephew stopped reading and glanced up. The look of disapproval on both their faces seemed to be enough. David's eyes returned to the story. "That's what it says. I was only trying to make Clare laugh."

Sensing the tension between them, the girl pouted now. Joseph stroked her back to assure Clare they weren't angry at her. "*Clare* is too young to understand that there is nothing comical about slavery," he admonished his nephew. "You are not."

"But Jupiter isn't a slave," David countered.

"He might as well be," Tessa answered. "Mr. Poe is implying that negroes are fit for nothing *but* slavery, that they crave it, that they're all simple-minded…"

"It's only a story." Joseph's nephew tossed the newspaper onto the table beside him.

"Stories have power, David." Joseph almost reminded the boy about his Yoruba great-grandmother, Ìfé, who'd been part of the Haitian Revolution and still lived on the island. But that story had power too—power to destroy their family. Little Clare remained nestled in Joseph's lap, and a few strides away from this porch was a beach anyone could walk. They couldn't risk it.

If David didn't see negroes as his kin, Joseph knew he was partially to blame. Joseph himself had relegated his Grandmother Ìfé to a mere corner of his thoughts, though his father still wrote to her every few weeks. Joseph's French great-grandfather had forced himself on Ìfé; she'd borne Joseph's father at the age of fourteen, and she had yet to reach seventy.

Joseph always accepted news of Ìfé and their other Haitian relatives like something in amber, a part of their past that didn't affect their lives in Charleston. But David was growing up in a society that enslaved and belittled people of African blood. Joseph's nephew needed to understand Charleston's injustice and hypocrisy—and Joseph couldn't help him understand it unless he cracked open that amber.

THE NEXT DAY, Joseph found his father in his office. "Have you received any more letters from my grandmother?"

"Last week, in fact." His father pulled open one of his desk drawers.

"Might I see it?"

"Of course." Joseph's father offered him the letter.

Joseph struggled with the Creole. Something about rain… This was why he'd always relied on his father to summarize. But holding it in his hands, this tangible connection to Haiti, to Africa—for the first time, it felt not only right but necessary. "Have you replied yet?"

"I haven't sealed it. I'm still adding things."

"Would you— Would you help me understand her, and could I include a reply as well?"

His father smiled. "I would be happy to translate, son."

PART II
A MOVEABLE FEAST

1844-1847

Charleston

If any thing is sacred, the human body is sacred

— Walt Whitman, "Enfans d'Adam" (1860)

CHAPTER 5

Well, if that's divine love, I know all about it.
— Charles de Brosses, on seeing Bernini's *Saint Teresa in Ecstasy* (1739)

I n October, Joseph had Tessa to himself again.

"I was so afraid the rain would keep you away," she said.

"A *hurricane* couldn't keep me away," he grinned as he stashed his umbrella and followed her up the stairs. Indeed, the rain splattering the windows was a blessing. Surely it would conceal any sounds they made, so that Hannah and the children would not even know he was visiting.

Still, little Clare was insatiably curious. Just in case the girl came running before Hannah could catch her, Tessa wedged a chair beneath the handle of her dressing chamber door. In her bedchamber, she tied the door closed by anchoring its handle to one of the bedposts. She used spare corset laces. She had plenty of corsets.

It was at once thrilling and dangerous, this knowledge that no one would see them, no one would hear them; and even if someone did, they could not be disturbed. Joseph had not forgotten how to undress her. He could almost believe Tessa wore all these layers just for him, just to tease and delight him as more and more of her was revealed.

When she was free of her boots, cuffs, collar, gown, petticoats, corset cover, and corset, she sat on the edge of the bed and unbuttoned her chemise. Joseph threw off his coat while Tessa tugged the linen down past her shoulders, then her breasts. They seemed as right as the evening's first stars.

Already her bare flesh was blushing with pleasure, nipples proud, areoles taut. Areole—so close to aureole, the great golden halo that surrounded the Blessed Virgin and the holiest saints in sacred art: a cloud of glory. *Two* clouds of glory, right here in his hands. Two breasts, two hands. Joseph offered a silent prayer of thanksgiving for this divine foresight.

To touch her breasts, he had to stand between her legs. And as marvelous as her breasts were, he couldn't be this close to Tessa and not kiss her. He thought she was pulling him even closer, till he realized she was undoing his waistcoat buttons. He permitted this; but when she reached to drop his braces, he pushed her hands away. In doing so, he lost contact with her breasts. At first, his hands couldn't find them again: she was drawing her legs up on the bed and retreating towards the pillows.

He had no choice but to follow or he would lose her mouth, too. Her legs were still open, so he ended up kneeling between them, crawling on his knees, pursuing her. He caught the skirt of her chemise by accident, pulling it up her right leg till her garter was exposed—and above it, startling and magnificent against her blue stocking: a glimpse of white thigh. He saw it only at the corner of his vision, and he clamped his eyes shut so he wouldn't be tempted to reveal even more. Instead, he fondled the soft under-sides of her breasts, and he chanted Job in his head: *"Hitherto thou shalt come, but no further."*

Yet Tessa kept shifting beneath him, lying back against a pillow, forcing him to lie over her. He settled himself low between her legs, not *quite* making contact—only his abdomen pressing against the juncture of her thighs. Eventually he had to stop kissing her, simply to catch his breath, but he didn't stop caressing her breasts.

As her delicate, soothing fingers played in his hair, Tessa whispered against his lips: "'A bundle of myrrh is my beloved to me; he shall lie all night between my breasts.'" She was quoting the Canticles.

Joseph answered in kind: "'Your breasts are better than wine.'"

Impishness quirked her lips. "How can you be sure? You know 'tis a sin to lie, Father. I mean, you've tasted *wine*, but…"

Joseph smiled back. He remembered his own reaction when she'd touched her lips to his nipple for only an instant. He settled even lower on the bed; slid his hands beneath her back; and slowly, he kissed one rosé peak, then the other. He heard Tessa gasp each time. The rain still pattering on the windows emboldened him; surely the children would hear nothing. He promised: "'Until the day break, and the shadows flee away, I will go to the mountain of myrrh, and to the hill of frankincense.'" To ensure she had no objections, Joseph looked up to her face.

Peering down at her breasts, Tessa wondered aloud: "Which is which?"

He frowned in consideration. *"Vadam ad montem myrrhæ, et ad collem thuris"*: mountain and hill, two distinct words in the Latin. Finally, Joseph chuckled. *"Solomon's"* beloved must have been lopsided."

How he loved Tessa's laugh. So warm and so sincere. It also jiggled her breasts.

He let her guide him. They discovered she liked licking, didn't mind nibbling, and *loved* sucking. But even his lightest touch thrilled her—the mere caress of his breath. Since he had only one mouth, he teased the other nipple with his fingers. He paused to taste her mouth again, and he thought she might devour him in gratitude, so he kissed down to her other breast. With his free hand, he stroked her back just inside her fallen chemise.

Her pants and whimpers became moans. He was more grateful than ever for the noise of the rain. Her fingers tightened on his shoulders till it was actually painful, but he welcomed it. Her head was turned away from him, so he couldn't see her face, but that grip told him he was doing particularly well. Then her hips pressed hard against his stomach, and her legs shuddered. She cried out as if she were scrambling for something *just* out of reach. When she found it, she collapsed.

Joseph's eyes had sprung open in alarm. Tessa lay gasping beneath him, gaping up at the bed canopy, as if she were a newborn seeing the world for the first time. Sweat glistened on her skin where there had been none minutes before.

Could that have been… His father had mentioned it, in his carnal catechism so many years ago: if a woman was particularly sensitive and excited, she might achieve release through her breasts alone.

"Tessa, was that— Did you just…come?"

Even as her breaths calmed, she gazed down at him in wonder. "I don't know—it's never happened before!" She grinned. "I think you'd better do it again, so we can be sure."

Joseph chuckled and kissed her mouth for a very long time. He gave her only one stipulation: "This time, could you try not to turn your face away? I want to watch you."

Tessa blushed even deeper but nodded.

Now he knew better what to do. As her second climax approached, he recognized the signs. But Tessa had forgotten her promise and turned her face to the pillow again. "Let me *see* you," he pleaded between licks. When she obeyed, the sight of her absolutely stunned him. Her nipple slipped from his mouth, and he simply stared.

"Don't *stop!*" she begged, clasping his head in her hands. "I did what you asked!"

Joseph chuckled. "I *understand* now."

"I don't!" she cried. "Why did you stop? Why are you laughing at me?"

"I'm not! I'm laughing at myself." His father had told him that being a virgin made him an idiot. He'd been right. "At Santa Maria della Vittoria in Rome, there's a statue of Saint Teresa by Bernini."

"You told me that years ago," Tessa whimpered.

"But I didn't *describe* it. The position of Teresa's body—her head thrown back, her eyes half-closed, her mouth half-open—she looks *exactly* like you did just now. To illustrate spiritual ecstasy, Bernini used physical ecstasy. Other pilgrims sniggered at that statue or glared at me for lingering there. I knelt before that Teresa for *hours*. I'd never seen anything so sublime in my life, but I didn't understand *why*. I do now."

"It isn't *all* physical ecstasy."

Half of Joseph was still in Rome. He was remembering the marble skeletons watching Teresa—who had nothing below their waists—and envying them all over again. "Pardon?"

"What you did to me. What you *do* to me." Tessa caressed his face. "The physical pleasure is only part of it, Joseph. With you, for the first time in my life, I feel safe and strong and free and *at peace*."

Joseph smiled and resumed his ministrations.

TESSA IMPLORED HIM TO STAY till the end of the night as he had twice before. Joseph claimed the risk was too great: long before sunrise, Charleston began to stir. The longer he stayed, the more likely it would be that someone would see him leaving.

The truth was, he had to return to his own bed long enough to snatch a bit of sleep before Mass. Most of all, he had to sleep long enough to dream, or he would be in pain throughout the following day. His body was incredibly stubborn. Just when he thought it had given up hope, some unguarded thought would inflate it all over again.

One of his fellow seminarians had argued that praying for a nocturnal pollution wasn't a sin. Even if the young man had been wrong, Joseph knew it was less of a sin than unclenching his fists and literally taking matters into his own hands.

CHAPTER 6

God Almighty first planted a garden. And indeed, it is the purest
of human pleasures. It is the greatest refreshment to the spirits
of man.

— Francis Bacon, "Of Gardens" (1625)

The next year was nearly intolerable. Throughout that endless
winter and interminable spring, Joseph haunted the corner of
Church Street and Longitude Lane, but Tessa did not light the blue
lamp even once. When no one was watching, he caressed and
inhaled the Noisette roses draped over her garden wall. They were a
poor substitute, but they were hers. He liked the sweet, sharp,
lemony scent of the Larmarques with their dense white petals remi-
niscent of petticoats. He loved the ever-changing Jaune Desprez:
fragrance as delicious and exotic as pineapple, buds the color of
Tessa's blushes, blossoms the color of her flesh.

Joseph still saw her during the daytime, when they conferred
about their gardens or when he visited the children. So at least
Joseph knew that her desire had not waned—that Tessa was
suffering as much as he was. Her husband simply spent every night
under the same roof with her, like a dragon guarding his treasure.

Joseph crafted mad plans in his head. They could meet during the afternoon in his old bedroom. *With Tessa's brother still grieving your sister? You know Liam doesn't keep regular hours, that he could come home at any time. And what if my mother walks in on us?* Charleston had a dozen hotels to choose from; they could plan a tryst. *How would we pay for it? Edward monitors Tessa's expenditures. Are you going to steal money from the collection plate?* At her father-in-law's plantation, they could duck behind a hedge or escape to the stable loft— *Someone would see us. Someone would HEAR us, or at least her.* Nothing was safe.

As long as you continue to do this, you must do it wisely, Joseph reminded himself again and again. *Think of the consequences if you are caught—the consequences in THIS world.* The scandal would jeopardize Joseph's Priesthood. He would be sent far away from his "proximate occasion of sin." He would never see Tessa again. Yet in some distant parish where no one knew of his fall, he could still be a Priest, albeit a broken one.

Tessa could not start over. If Edward rejected her, perhaps she could take refuge with Joseph's father and her brother. But everyone Tessa ever met would see her—and treat her—as a fallen woman.

Most of all, Joseph must think of Clare. Tessa's daughter would bear the weight of her mother's sin for the rest of her life. She might even *lose* her mother—legally, Clare belonged only to Edward. Little as he cared for the girl, she was his heir, and by the terms of his father's will, losing Clare meant losing his plantation to his nephew. With his precious Stratford-on-Ashley at stake, Edward would never relinquish Clare to the woman who had shamed him.

For all these same reasons, Joseph should cease his intimacies with Tessa altogether. But he couldn't. When she called for him again, Joseph knew he would answer.

He told himself: *The blue lamp, the garden gate—they are working. They are safe. Everyone knows you are David's uncle and Tessa's friend; if you are caught visiting their house at night, you will find an excuse. So you must wait. Even if Edward leaves Tessa alone for only one night a year, that is far better than a lifetime without her.*

That summer, Tessa removed to Sullivan's Island as usual. There, she and Joseph managed a single stolen kiss that left both of them more miserable than before. Joseph promptly threw himself into the sea and swam till he was exhausted. Finally he dragged himself onto the beach and collapsed. But even as the warm water lapped at his waist, calling him back, he imagined it was Tessa's arms encircling him, her lips soothing him.

TWELVE AGONIZING MONTHS, six wretched days, and one unbearable hour passed before Tessa set out the blue lamp again. She left it behind and met him in the garden. Joseph had barely locked the gate before she threw her arms around him from behind. "I was certain I would go *mad!*" Her hair was down, and she'd already shed her corset. She wore only a thin wrapper, a chemise, and possibly drawers.

He cherished the press of her erect nipples against his back, discernible even through broadcloth. "Good evening."

"'Tis *now.*"

Joseph turned into the blissful assault of her lips. In her hunger for him, Tessa shoved him back against the garden wall. It was only by luck that he landed *between* the rose canes and not amidst them. He might have ended up with a crown of thorns, or with his coat torn to shreds. Small prices to pay for such a kiss.

Then Tessa groaned at her haste and yanked him away from the wall, turning her own back to it. She explained breathlessly: "You'll have brick dust on your clothes."

"You're the one wearing white."

"'Tis *my* wall."

Before she could stop his mouth with hers again, a terrifying thought occurred to him: "Tessa, wait." He stared at the house in dread. "Did you meet me out here because Edward is *still* home?"

She shook her head fiercely. "He's gone. But I couldn't bear to lose a minute with you."

Joseph exhaled with relief. He inhaled the richness of loam, the fruity sweetness of the roses, the heady fragrance of Tessa's perfume —and beneath them, his favorite scent of all: the unmistakable tang of her desire for him.

Even as they kissed, she tore off his gloves. He tore open the buttons of her wrapper and chemise till his hands found her breasts. In answer to her pleas, his mouth trailed lower and lower and finally closed over one of her nipples. He sank to his knees, heedless of stains now, as Tessa gasped and writhed against him. Church Street stood only a few yards away; but darkness and evergreen leaves sheltered them from curious eyes.

When her moans threatened to draw curious ears, Tessa clapped a hand over her own mouth and muffled the last triumphant cry. Then her legs gave out, and she collapsed on top of him. She'd already undone the buttons of his coat. Now Joseph yanked its front aside so she could sprawl across the softer fabric of his waistcoat.

He lay back on the grass, feeling her bare breasts press against his chest with each pant, and willed himself to ignore the demands of his own body. But Tessa's right elbow was dangerously close to the truth.

He stared up at the half-moon, reflected in the pale glow of the Lamarque roses above them. In vestments, white was the color of joy—and purity. He realized some of the petals had fallen into Tessa's loose hair, and he thought them the perfect adornment. Like the Blessed Virgin, ever sinless, this woman could never be impure —even flushed with pleasure, even with her breasts bare to the stars. Especially not now. This wasn't Tessa defiled but Tessa fulfilled—like a flower turning toward the sun or a butterfly opening its wings.

When his arousal had subsided and he thought she had regained enough breath to answer, Joseph asked: "In the Language of Flowers, do white roses mean 'purity'?"

Tessa nodded against his shoulder. "They can also mean 'secrecy and silence,' 'eternal love'—or even 'I am worthy of you.'" Tessa raised her head, and he knew she was grinning at him.

He looked to the Jaune Desprez. "And yellow roses?"

Tessa sat up suddenly, as if he'd said something wrong. "Those *aren't* yellow, remember? They're far more pink, and pink roses mean—"

"Tessa?" Joseph sat up too. "What do yellow roses mean?"

She was rebuttoning her chemise. "It doesn't matter. Those dictionaries are absurd."

The Jaune Desprez roses draped over the garden gate; Joseph passed beneath them every night he visited her. "What do yellow—"

Finally she looked back at him, though her face was a blank in the darkness. "'Infidelity.' But pink roses mean 'perfect happiness.'" Tessa stood and offered him her hand.

After a moment, Joseph sighed and accepted it.

In her bedchamber, Tessa gave him a quick kiss and asked him to wait just a minute while she ran to her dressing chamber. Joseph closed the jalousies, then doffed his coat and inspected it for brick dust. Indeed, the black broadcloth now carried a film of powdery red. He frowned.

Tessa reentered the bedchamber, sans wrapper and slippers now. She smelled more strongly of gardenia; she must have reapplied her perfume. Joseph was disappointed, though he supposed it was for the best. All the time he'd had her pressed against the garden wall, he'd been wondering what she would taste like *there*. If he pulled up her chemise, perhaps she would even permit it. But the moment he uncovered her, he would want to do more than taste. He would want to bury himself inside her.

Joseph showed her his coat. "Do you have a clothes-brush?" Her husband must—but they could hardly use that one.

Tessa covered her mouth with her hand and giggled. "Your trousers are even worse!"

He looked down. She was right. He'd slapped away most of the grass clippings outside, but his knees were smeared with soil. "I dirty my clothes all the time," he reasoned.

Tessa raised an eyebrow. "Ministering to other lonely female parishioners?"

In spite of himself, Joseph flushed. "No! In my own garden, or helping Henry in my mother's garden."

"Well, you are not lounging on my clean bed looking like *that*." She rounded him and assessed his buttocks. "The back is nearly as bad!" She laughed and tugged at the hip of his trousers. "We shall simply have to remove these."

Instantly, his arousal returned. Joseph stepped away from her, and his trousers slipped from her grasp. "I-I can't, Tessa." He couldn't return to the Bishop's residence and change, either; he couldn't risk waking His Lordship.

"Why not?" Tessa pursued him.

Joseph retreated till the back of his legs bumped the seat of her méridienne and he could go no farther.

Tessa reached for his trousers again, but this time she was facing him. Her fingers slipped under the hem of his waistcoat and pinched the top of his fall. Such an appropriate term; and the flap that made urination easier also made other things easier. Even closed, his fall left room for the bulge just below Tessa's hand, and she understood perfectly well what it meant. "Are you afraid that once you liberate this gentleman, you won't be able to stop him?"

She had no idea. He—it—was anything but a gentleman. "Yes," Joseph choked out.

Tessa smiled, caressing the center button with her thumb. "I should have told you this last time. You've been so patient with me, and I haven't been fair to you. But everything was so new, and I wanted to savor it. I'm ready, Joseph. You don't *have* to stop. You have my consent."

Still trapped against the edge of the méridienne, Joseph only gulped.

Tessa frowned. "You do *want* to…" She dropped her eyes to the rug. "Does the thought of touching me there disgust you?"

"Quite the opposite."

"Then why are you hesitating?"

For a moment, Joseph simply stared down at his own erection (still clothed, but increasingly ravenous). "How can *you* want that, after…" He looked vaguely in the direction of Edward's bedchamber. Joseph couldn't bring himself to say her husband's name.

Tessa's right hand remained poised at Joseph's fall. Her left hand stroked his cheek. Shining with trust in the lamplight, her eyes answered even before her lips: "I know it would be different with you."

Would it? Joseph had no experience whatsoever—only raw

hunger. Surely in his lust and his ignorance, he would hurt her as much as her husband did. If they used olive oil, the scent would remind her of Edward; and if they didn't, Joseph's intrusion would hurt her even more.

By now, Tessa had an uncanny way of reading his mind. She assured him: "I don't even think we'll need any… I told you how my body reacts to you."

Joseph closed his eyes, more grateful than ever for her gardenia perfume.

"You know there's no risk I'll…" Tessa's voice was barely a whisper, and shame crept into it. "You know I am truly barren now?"

Such a harsh word: it conjured an image of parched earth breaking a plow. Tessa was neither dry nor resisting; she'd just told him so.

"At least it won't ever be the wrong time of the month." He thought she must be smiling, however timidly.

It didn't matter. It didn't matter if their union would be tolerable or even pleasurable for her—because he knew without a doubt that it would be pleasurable for him. "I'm sorry, Tessa." He opened his eyes to see her frowning at him. "I can't."

Her face tightened in worry. "You can't what?"

He stroked his fingers through her hair, which still contained petals from the Lamarques. "What we've done thus far, your *beautiful* pleasure—I cannot regret it. But it's different for me. You know that. At my ordination, I promised God a *lifetime* of sacrifice. If I sacrifice nothing, how can I ask Him for anything in return?"

Her expression became incredulous. "But—you must be in pain."

That was the point. Had she forgotten her catechism? Suffering was part of God's plan. It taught you humility. It purified you. It was an invitation to holiness. "Pain is the price of my Priesthood, Tessa."

She dropped her hand, relinquishing his fall; but her expression clouded into something even darker: jealousy. "You sacrifice every *other* night to God. You have sacrificed thirty-three years to Him. You will never hold your own child in your arms. We will never be able to live as husband and wife or even walk out in the street holding hands. Isn't all of that sacrifice enough?"

Her mention of his age only reminded Joseph of Christ, and how *He* had sacrificed everything.

"You want to please me and still be a good Priest?"

"Yes."

Before the word was even out of his mouth, Tessa assaulted him. She shoved him down onto the méridienne.

The back of his head hit the wall above the sofa—not hard, but enough to stun him while she climbed on top of him. Naturally his penis had no use for his head. Elated, it strained frantically against every one of his trouser buttons.

When Joseph flung up his hands to dislodge her, Tessa took control of the motion, pinning his wrists against the wall. Straddling his legs, she sank the inverted cup of her hips over his erection. "Then I have a bargain that should meet everyone's needs: yours, mine, and God's," she nearly growled against his lips. "To administer His Sacraments, to preach His Word, God needs only your hands and your mouth." She withdrew her lips and squeezed his immobile wrists. "Reserve those for Him—and let me have the rest of you."

That left nearly everything—including... He struggled to push her aside, except his hips were the only thing moving. "It doesn't work that way, Tessa."

"We've already decided the rules don't apply anymore!"

"Of course they do! I just have to find them!" At last he managed to shove her sideways and stand.

Tessa pulled her legs up onto the seat of the méridienne and tucked them beneath her chin, breathing raggedly like someone mourning.

He turned away, then turned back, muttering: "I thought you liked what I did with my hands and my mouth."

"Of course I did!" Tears overflowed from her eyes. "I don't *want* you to accept! I am trying to make you see how ridiculous you're being!"

Helpless to do anything else, he fished his handkerchief out of his pocket and offered it to her.

Tessa snatched it. "We have an expression in Ireland, Joseph: 'One might as well be hanged for a sheep as a lamb.'" She blew her nose. "It was inspired by the brutality of English law, which imposed death for small thefts and large ones alike."

Joseph thought he understood. "'In for a penny, in for a pound'?"

"*Yes.*"

"That is profligacy and hedonism, Tessa. There are venial sins and there are mortal ones—and the difference between the two is salvation and *damnation.*"

She stared up at him miserably. "What about your shirt? Are you ever going to let me remove *that?*"

"It would be unwise."

She could hardly speak through her sobs. "Are you saying I must wait for you, day after day, month after month, year after year—and one glimpse of your chest is all I'll ever have of you, because you are too *holy* to come?"

Joseph clenched his teeth. "I am saying I think I should leave now, before one of us says something we'll regret." He turned to go.

But Tessa caught his hand. She stood and tightened her arms around him, but she did not stop weeping. Amidst her own grief, she caressed his skull where he'd hit the wall. "Is your head all right?"

"More or less." Joseph stroked her hair and felt her trembling against him. Fifteen minutes before, at the garden wall, she'd been shuddering in pleasure, not pain. He hadn't anticipated this: that Tessa would desire union as much as he did. He took her head in his hands and kissed the tears on her cheeks, on her throat. *I still love you, Tessa,* he told her without words.

Fresh tears kept cascading down her face. They soaked into the fabric of her chemise. He undid the buttons and kept kissing her. He drew her back to the méridienne. He'd intended to take one of her nipples in his mouth, to make her "perfectly happy" again; but she only curled against him, locking her arms around his waist and tucking her head beneath his.

While his hand caressed her back and her tears penetrated his shirt, Joseph contemplated a practice he'd read about years ago, a way for a husband to please his wife while minimizing his own sin: *coitus reservatus*. He entered her and moved within her for as long as it took to bring her to climax. Then he withdrew; he did not allow himself to come. At all.

But Joseph knew he was incapable of such restraint. Two seconds after he sank into Tessa's fragrant wet heat, he would explode—a duration that would please her very little. So she would argue that they should try again, and again: better to be damned for a dozen adulterous climaxes than only one. Better still to try for a thousand!

But that wasn't the way God's law worked. If you sinned and repented, you could be forgiven. If you sinned, repented, and then repeated the same sin, clearly you were not repentant. And there was no sinner more despicable than a Priest who pursued his own pleasure. That was why he must never open this door. Why he must never open the fall of his trousers.

CHAPTER 7

But those pleasures of love, which we enjoyed together, were so
sweet to me, that they can neither displease me, nor glide from my
memory. Wherever I go, they present themselves to my eyes, with
all their allurements. Neither are their illusions wanting to me in
my dreams.

— Second Letter of Héloïse to Abélard (circa 1133)

Again, Tessa spent the fall and winter at the Stratfords'
plantation. After they returned to Charleston for Race Week,
Tessa did not set out the blue lamp. This time, Joseph was not
entirely certain whether this meant that Edward remained at
Church Street—or that Tessa no longer wished Joseph to visit her at
night. When they saw one another during the day, she remained
civil; but she was also more distant than she'd been in three years—
since she'd confessed her love for him.

In May, Joseph began to lose hope. Surely Tessa would summer
on Sullivan's Island again. David's school term had nearly
concluded. Soon there would be no reason for her to remain in
Charleston.

Joseph's own desire did not ebb. He toiled in his Biblical garden to distract himself. While pruning the Damask rose, he contemplated the statue of Saint Rose with her crown of spikes. He knew that was only the beginning of her mortifications. All these nights without Tessa—even nights *with* Tessa—Joseph might have felt as if he lay on a bed of thorns and broken glass, but Rose had done it literally. Joseph also meditated upon Saint Francis and Saint Benedict, who had thrown themselves naked into thorn bushes to mortify their flesh. His pain was nothing next to theirs. Purposefully, Joseph pressed the pad of his thumb into one of the rose thorns, till a drop of ruby red blood beaded on his finger.

Suddenly he felt the warmth of Tessa's lips at the nape of his neck. He jumped, and the thorn sank even deeper into his flesh. As blood welled from his fingertip, he glanced nervously toward the cathedral and the Bishop's residence. What did she think she was doing? They were far too exposed here.

Tessa only grasped his wounded hand, slipped his thumb inside her mouth, and closed her lips around it. While Joseph gaped at her, she smiled and sucked on his flesh till he couldn't breathe. When she finally let his thumb slide from her tongue, she whispered: "Now I have African blood inside of me, too."

All at once, Joseph didn't care if he was a Priest, if she was another man's wife. He needed to be truly inside her, or he would die. He would repent later. He gripped her hand in his. "Will you take more of me?"

Tessa smiled and touched his face. "Joseph. The answer has always been '*Yes*.'"

He pulled her after him, past Saint Rose suffering in silence, toward the little garden house where he stored his tools and cuttings. Joseph slammed the door behind them and slammed Tessa against the wall, kissing her brutishly. She clung to him just as fiercely, from tongue to toes. Even through her petticoats, he could feel her legs parting. One of her boots hooked around his ankle.

He tried fumbling at her back, but he accomplished nothing. "Turn around," he gasped. "I can't reach your buttons."

"My drawers are open in the middle, remember? *Yours* are the only buttons we need to reach." Already her hands were at his fall.

"But you're wearing a corset," he argued. "Won't you faint, when…"

"Will you catch me?"

"Of course!"

"Then stop talking and *help* me, Joseph!"

Between them, they dispatched the twelve buttons of his fall and his drawers in a matter of seconds. After thirty-four years, he was finally free. But he knew he couldn't let her hand close around him, or this would be over before it began.

Amidst a duet of groans—some of pleasure, some of frustration—they bunched up her mass of skirts and petticoats, and she wrapped one of her bared legs around his. *So close* now; but out of the corner of his eye, Joseph saw his rake—two feet away, caked with manure. "This isn't what I wanted for you, Tessa. You deserve a feather bed, not the wall of a garden house."

She gripped the back of his neck, holding him to her. "As long as you're in front of me, Joseph, I don't care what's behind me."

That was enough. He found her entrance and plunged inside her. He wasn't sure which of them moaned louder. Dear God, why hadn't he done this a decade ago, the moment he first laid eyes on her in this garden?

SOMETIMES, HE DID. Joseph had had this dream about Tessa in the garden house dozens of times. It was hardly surprising that it had returned to torment and relieve him now.

Sometimes in the dream, he and Tessa left little Thomas slumbering on the bench and disappeared into the garden house before they'd spoken a single word to each other, because they'd said everything they needed to say with their eyes. He was twenty-three and she was barely nineteen. He wasn't yet a Priest, and she wasn't yet anyone's wife.

Because it was a dream, even as a virgin, he knew exactly how to pleasure her; and even as a virgin, she felt no pain when he thrust into her, only wave after wave of ecstasy. They came with the force of an earthquake, simultaneously, and they collapsed onto the feather mattress that was suddenly inside the garden house.

Her first coherent words to him were: "You'll marry me, won't you?"

Joseph laughed and tortured her for a minute with pretended indecision before he answered. He didn't say: *"I am a Deacon—it's already too late; I already belong to God."* Instead, he dipped his fingers between her slickened folds and said: "As long as you allow me *this* for the rest of our lives, I will marry you tomorrow."

Because in a dream, there were no such things as celibacy or miscarriages. In a dream, you could have whatever you wanted.

CHAPTER 8

I have been here before...
I know the path beyond the door...
You have been mine before...
Then, now,—perchance again!
O round mine eyes your tresses shake!
Shall we not lie as we have lain
Thus for Love's sake,
And sleep, and wake, yet never break the chain?
— Dante Gabriel Rossetti, "Sudden Light" (1870)

Joseph was hunting amongst the books in the library for sermon ideas when someone rapped on the door of the Bishop's residence. He knew neither His Lordship nor Thornton were home, so Joseph answered the door himself.

It was Hannah standing on the porch. Nervously, she glanced behind him. "You alone, Father?"

"Apart from you and God, I am."

Hannah withdrew a small box from her skirt pocket. "Miss Tessa wanted me to give you this message." She bobbed a curtsey and left him.

Joseph hurried upstairs and closed the door of his bedchamber before he opened the box. It contained candied pink rose petals and a note:

I will light the blue lamp tonight.

Joseph kissed the note, burned it, and then savored each rose petal.

TESSA WAS WAITING FOR HIM on the other side of her garden gate. This time, she sat serenely on one of the green wrought iron benches, fully dressed in a gown that looked grey, though it was difficult to tell by moonlight. Normally, the garden would have been uncomfortable in May, but God had blessed them with cooler weather and fewer mosquitoes these past few days.

Tessa did not turn as Joseph approached, holding herself aloof. So different from the brazen woman in his dream. If it had been daytime, he might have believed they were courting chastely, superintended by a chaperone on the piazza.

Without looking at him, she asked: "Did you enjoy the petals?"

"They were better than pineapple." He sat down beside her. "Which rose did you use?"

"The Maiden's Blush." She nodded in its direction. Even from here, Joseph could smell its spicy champagne fragrance. "Because your father told me its French name."

At once, Joseph blushed himself. He'd just savored a dozen nibbles of Aroused Nymph's Thigh. When he thought how he'd allowed each petal to dissolve on his tongue—how he'd moaned at the first taste...

Tessa kept her eyes on the roses. "When you were in Paris, did you visit the tomb of Héloïse and Abélard?"

Joseph shook his head.

"But you're familiar with their story?"

"Yes." Six centuries ago, Pierre Abélard had been a renowned philosopher, theologian, and canon at the cathedral in Paris.

Though he was not ordained, he was expected to remain celibate. Then he met Héloïse, the most remarkable woman of her day, as brilliant as himself. In her uncle's home, Abélard tutored her—and became her lover. She bore him a child, and they married in secret. But even that was not enough to quell the wrath of Héloïse's uncle. He had Abélard attacked and castrated. In his shame, Abélard became a monk and urged his wife to become a nun, while his family raised their child. She became an abbess and he an abbot. In their seclusion, Héloïse and Abélard wrote one another beautiful, heartbreaking letters. She remained devoted to him and longed to renew their intimacy, at least on paper. He preferred to thank God for his chastisement, call Héloïse his sister in Christ, and call their love foul lust.

"Have you ever read Alexander Pope's poem about them?"

"No."

"For a man, Pope describes female desire remarkably well—a woman's hopeless yearning for a man she cannot have. Héloïse says to Abélard: 'Give all thou canst—and let me dream the rest.'" Slowly, Tessa took one of Joseph's gloved hands in hers. Her eyes remained lowered, her voice almost shy. "Do *you* dream of *me*, Joseph?"

"Nightly."

"In your dreams, do we…"

"Yes."

"Will you tell me one of them?"

Hesitantly, then more confidently, he told her his dream about the garden house. As he spoke, Tessa removed his gloves, so she could hold both his hands with nothing between them. She pleaded for more detail, until it became *their* dream. He could almost feel her fingers at his fall; her breath hot in his ear; her wet, welcoming body arching against his.

In reality, Tessa only stroked his hands. "Even in your dreams, you are solicitous." Her voice broke. "I understand that you will never succumb like that in waking life. But whatever you *will* permit yourself, my answer will always be 'Yes.' Whenever you come to me at night, my body is yours, Joseph."

If she truly meant that... Now that she understood the rules, surely it would be safe. "Then...might I see you, Tessa? All of you?"

He heard her breath catch, and her hands tightened on his. "You wait till I am nearly thirty to ask me this?"

He caressed her face, so familiar to him that the darkness didn't matter. "You have never been lovelier."

She gave a soft laugh. "You had better mention that fib to your confessor."

Despite himself, Joseph chuckled back.

"I don't suppose you'll be satisfied with moonlight?"

"No—but two Argand burners should be just right." Joseph sprang to his feet, pulling her with him.

In a dance of kisses, he led her across the garden, up the piazza steps, through the hall, and up the spiral staircase. The second-floor hall smelled strangely of her gardenia perfume. In her well-lit bedchamber, safe behind the door and the jalousies, they undressed her together, peeling away each layer as if for the first time. They paused frequently for more kisses. Why should anyone need to copulate, when they had *this*?

Her corset wasn't white. He hadn't expected that. It was a deep, rich bronze, the same color as her hair. In the lamplight, the silk shimmered like metal—like the armor of a goddess. Above it, within the flimsy shield of her embroidered chemise, her breasts rose with each hurried breath.

The night was cool, and Tessa wore her usual number of petticoats. He dropped a white one to the floor, then a grey one, a blue one—and there were even more beneath. Joseph remembered a story he'd read to Clare several days ago, by a Dane named Hans Christian Andersen. Joseph smiled at the memory and plucked at Tessa's fourth petticoat. "Is there a pea under here?"

"You *could* call it a pea—or a pearl..." The way Tessa was peering at him over her shoulder, the way she was biting her lower lip...

Suddenly, Joseph understood that she was alluding to a certain sensitive part of her anatomy. He colored, and then he chuckled. *Dear God, I love this woman. Dear God, thank You for every word that comes out of her mouth, every inch of her skin, and every moment I spend in her presence.*

But when Joseph dropped her last petticoat and she stepped out of them, Tessa tried to flee from him—even before she was free of her corset.

He caught her wrist. "Where are you going?"

She was blushing furiously now, and he knew it wasn't with pleasure. "Clare spilled the last of my perfume; but I have rosewater in my dressing chamber…"

So that explained the scent of gardenia in the hall. Tessa's daughter was three years old now, and Joseph had seen the girl tearing through the house, shrieking with delight, while Tessa and Hannah chased after her to keep her out of mischief. But what did spilled perfume have to do with Tessa's sudden desire for flight?

"I bathed not two hours ago, I swear it…" Tessa pleaded, still trying to pull away from him.

Then he realized how strong it was, now that her skirts were gone, now that her motions had excited it: the unadulterated fragrance of Tessa's arousal. "You don't like your own scent?"

She stilled then, peering back at him doubtfully. "You…do?"

"Tessa, you are intoxicating."

She only wrinkled her brow, as if she still didn't believe him.

"Will you let me prove it to you?"

Slowly, Tessa nodded.

She let him near enough to unlace her corset. He stepped closer still to press his lips to the nape of her neck. Then he peeled her chemise over her head, exposing her sinuous back; her hair was still pinned up. He draped the chemise like a blanket over her méridienne: they would need it soon. She shivered as he kissed each shoulder and each shoulder blade.

Finally he loosened the tie at the back of her frilly drawers. They slipped to the floor, and she wore only her stockings. Tessa's legs were the eighth wonder of the world. But he must not rush this. He let his fingertips glide down the curves of her back to the curves of her buttocks. He cupped her there with both hands, caressing each hip with his thumbs in languid circles.

Tessa's breaths grew quicker and quicker. She turned at her waist and leaned back to kiss him, but he denied her.

"Sit on the méridienne," he instructed, "on the edge." He motioned to the side where he'd draped her chemise, to protect her bare flesh from any dirt he'd left in the upholstery during his last visit.

When Tessa obeyed, he saw her *mons veneris* for the first time. The delicate thatch there shimmered bronze in the lamplight. He had suspected it would match the tufts beneath her arms, but he hadn't been certain.

On the edge of the méridienne, Tessa kept her magnificent thighs together, till he knelt before her and parted them—only a little, enough to untie her left garter. It was lovely: floral embroidery on a pink ribbon. But he was far more interested in the skin underneath. He let the garter drop to the floor and peeled her white stocking away from her knee, so he could press his lips against her exposed flesh.

As he pulled her stocking down her calf and over her foot, the muscles of Tessa's slender leg tensed with apprehension, as if she might kick him away from her at any moment. On the green upholstery of the méridienne, she'd tightened her hands into uncertain fists.

Joseph forced himself to look upward, not inward, to meet her eyes. "You may slap me at any time, Tessa." He returned his gaze to her thigh and kissed her again, a little farther from her knee, a little closer to her center. "I will stop." He tilted her leg wider so his mouth could reach the middle of her thigh. "But only if you *want* me to."

When his lips neared the edge of her bronze thatch, she looked especially anxious. So he turned his attention to her other garter, and she seemed to relax, even when he kissed inside her other knee. He freed her right leg of its sheath. She wore nothing but hairpins now, and surely her legs quivered only with pleasure. He tucked a hand beneath each of her knees, his thumbs soothing her into contentment.

Still forcing himself not to look, only to breathe her in, he assured her: "You are sweeter than any gardenia, Tessa." Her own scent was just as heady, but more like... "More like the Maiden's Blush," he decided.

He was lulling her into some sort of daze. Tessa's hands were limp now, her head sagging back, eyes closed, lips slack. "Don't you mean 'Cuisse de Nymphe Émue'?" she sighed.

Thigh of an Aroused Nymph, indeed. Joseph grinned and agreed: "Champagne and spices." Phrases from the Canticles welled in his mouth, and he rained them onto her inner thigh with each kiss: "'Spikenard and saffron; calamus and cinnamon; frankincense, myrrh...'" Yes: myrrh, which bloomed when it burned.

At last, he allowed his eyes to feast. Dear God, she was beautiful. *Dear God, how can You deny your Priests such a sight—"last and best of all Your works"?*

But it wasn't God who had denied Priests wives—it was the Church.

Joseph had seen the diagrams in medical texts, yet the reality was something else entirely. The crescent of bronze hair protecting but not concealing what lay within. The impossibly simple, impossibly complex slit of flesh, trembling with each of her breaths. Its petals seemed to blush even as he watched: rose becoming claret, plump and slick with something far more precious than wine. Where should he begin?

With her "pea," of course. Better to call it her pearl. Joseph kissed her exactly there.

In an instant, Tessa awoke from her daze. She cried out and tried to clamp her legs shut, but he was in the way.

"*Shhhh,*" Joseph warned, purposefully drawing out the syllable, blowing warmth against Tessa's pearl and making her shriek again. "You'll wake the children."

Tessa's entire body was blushing now. She'd clapped both hands over her mouth. "I didn't think you'd—" She loosened her fingers slightly, but her voice was still muffled. "I thought you'd *stop!*"

"You haven't slapped me yet."

Her brow furrowed endearingly. She stared down at him in horror and yearning for a very long time. She dropped her hands and caught her lower lip between her teeth. Her myrrh-brown eyes settled not on him but on the tasselled pillow propped against the arm of the méridienne. She seemed to be giving it great considera- tion. Finally Tessa snatched up the pillow, stuffed it behind her, and flopped backward—which opened her thighs even wider. "I can't," she sighed at the ceiling. "'Tis a mortal sin to strike a Priest."

Joseph laughed till tears leaked from his eyes. He kissed her again and again—not only her pearl but all along her petals. "I love you," he told Tessa's vulva.

The woman attached to it hadn't surrendered quite yet. Her hands were still clenching and unclenching, her face crinkled up in disgust. "Joseph, you really don't have to— It must taste *terrible*."

"No." It wasn't dessert wine, but neither was it unpleasant.

Curiosity crept into her expression. "Is it...like my saliva?"

"A little." He licked experimentally, in order to taste her better. "Closer to...lemonade." Joseph smiled. "Not only do you look and smell like a rose, you taste like one too—or at least, you taste like the Lamarque roses smell."

Tessa covered her mouth with her hand again, but she failed to contain her giggling.

He returned his attention to her other lips. "You know what Solomon called this?"

Tessa frowned and shook her head.

"A 'goblet never wanting liquor.'"

"I remember that verse!" Tessa objected. "'Tis about his beloved's *navel!*"

"Is it? Remember, you're reading a translation of a translation." Joseph raised his head a little and peered into Tessa's lovely—but very empty—navel. "I don't see any liquor *there*." He grinned and lowered his gaze. "*Here*, however..."

Tessa's laughter made her goblet run over. "I love you!"

Best of all, when she came, her liquor grew sweeter.

CHAPTER 9

Give me a thousand kisses, then another hundred,
then another thousand, then a second hundred,
then yet another thousand more, then another hundred...
— Catullus, Poem 5 (circa 60 BC)

Before dawn, Joseph slipped back into the Bishop's residence as quietly as he could. Today His Lordship would be ordaining two men from the seminary and then leaving on another tour of his diocese; he needed his rest.

After Mass, in the Biblical garden, little Clare ran ahead of her mother and tugged on Joseph's chasuble. She made scissors motions with her first two fingers and asked: "Why?"

"Why did Bishop Reynolds cut off a bit of the men's hair?" Joseph guessed.

Clare nodded.

"It's called a tonsure—or at least, it's symbolic of a tonsure." He hesitated. This was hardly something he could explain in the language of a three-year-old. "It...shows that Mr. O'Connell and Mr. Kennedy are special, that they are going to be Priests."

"Why?"

Clare might have meant *"Why are they going to be Priests?"* But Joseph decided on the simplest interpretation: "Because sometimes we change our hair when there's a change in our lives." He smiled at the approach of his lanky nephew, who would turn fifteen next month. "The way David is growing a mustache to show he's becoming a man."

Clare thought for a moment. "The men are sad?"

Joseph glanced to Tessa, who seemed just as puzzled by her daughter's conclusion. Surely Clare couldn't know that seven years ago, her mother had cut off her hair out of grief for the children she'd lost.

"Why do you think they are sad?" Tessa asked.

"Because!" The little girl looked to David for help.

Joseph's nephew ceased stroking his sparse mustache. "Clare is always asking me questions about what I saw out in the territories. Last week, I told her that Indians cut their hair when they are in mourning." He crouched down to his foster-sister. "Is that why you think the men are sad?"

Clare nodded.

"Mr. O'Connell and Mr. Kennedy aren't sad at all," Joseph assured the girl. "Today was a celebration—like a birthday. They were born again in the Church, just like I was. *I'm* not sad."

But Tessa's own smile was heartbreaking. She led her daughter a few steps away to look for fritillary caterpillars on the Passion-vine.

Joseph's nephew remained with him. David's inquisitiveness warred with his shyness, as it always did, though the boy seemed especially uneasy today. "In Europe, don't Priests and monks *shave* their heads?"

"It varies between orders," Joseph explained. "Secular Priests shave only a small spot about the size of the Host." He pointed to the crown of his head, though his hair had grown back long ago. "I did that my last years of seminary, while I was in Rome. But in a missionary country like the United States, we don't maintain the tonsure—for the same reason we don't wear our soutanes outside church grounds. It would invite persecution."

Still David would only glance at Joseph out of the corner of his eyes. "Where does it come from? The tonsure?"

"It goes back to ancient times. The Greeks and Romans shaved the heads of their slaves, to facilitate identification in case of escape."

"We do that to prisoners today," his nephew interjected thoughtfully. The Charleston Jail stood only one street behind his grandparents' house.

Joseph nodded. "Early Christians then began shaving their heads as a sign of humility, to show their total devotion to God. It proved they cared nothing for the fashions or esteem of the world." Other churchgoers were enjoying the Biblical garden as well, and two bewhiskered gentlemen passed their little group. "For the same reason, *I* can't ever grow a beard or mustache," Joseph told his nephew. "The Bishop wouldn't permit it. Priests must remain clean-shaven, as a way of setting us apart and as a sign of respect for the Blessed Sacrament we consume."

Tessa must have heard this last bit. As soon as Clare drew David's attention away, Tessa glanced meaningfully at the visitors' bushy facial hair. Then she leaned close to Joseph and whispered: "For once, I am grateful for the Church's rules. If *you* had such whiskers, you would give me a terrible rash!"

Joseph fled to the sacristy, where he could blush and snigger in relative privacy—though his young altar server did look at him strangely. Then Joseph returned to the Bishop's residence for breakfast. Fortunately, His Lordship was absorbed in the latest issue of the *Miscellany*.

This gave Joseph the freedom to relive last night's feast in his mind. Last night's libation? The word was certainly grander, but a libation was an offering to a god, and *Joseph* had been the worshipper, Tessa the goddess. Or at least a saint: last night, she'd resembled her patroness more than ever before. In her ecstasies, Saint Teresa had levitated. Tessa had come very close; the force and totality of her climaxes had surpassed anything he'd achieved with her breasts. She was always surprising him, always delighting him. The range of sounds he could produce with only his—

Suddenly Bishop Reynolds interrupted his thoughts: "Did you visit one of our parishioners in the middle of the night, Joseph?"

He very nearly choked on his mouthful of egg.

His Lordship only glanced at him; his attention remained on the newspaper and his toast. "Are you all right, Joseph?"

"I'm fine." Joseph realized the first question hadn't been an accusation, only mild interest. But if Bishop Reynolds had heard him come home in the small hours of the morning, Joseph knew he must offer *some* explanation. "It was a sick call, my lord." That was only a white lie, Joseph told himself. One *might* refer to it as a sick call: Tessa was lovesick, and he'd eased her suffering. Repeatedly.

"I didn't hear the knock," Bishop Reynolds observed. "Was it Mrs. Taylor?"

So much for a white lie. Joseph shook his head, guzzling his coffee to buy himself a moment to think. He tried desperately to appear grave, rather than panic-stricken. "Mr. O'Reilly."

His Lordship sighed. "I suppose you and Father Baker will have said his funeral Mass before I return to Charleston."

That was precisely why Joseph had chosen Mr. O'Reilly. Bishop Reynolds was departing to tour his diocese immediately after breakfast; and a dead man would be unable to expose Joseph's lie.

Whose name would Joseph give next time?

ON MONDAY, A LEGITIMATE SICK CALL made Joseph several minutes late to his final class of the day. He taught mostly at the seminary, but he also assisted Father Magrath by teaching courses at the school for younger boys. All spring, David had been one of his pupils. He was a model student: not only uncommonly bright but also uncommonly sedate. This was the last week of the term, so the other fourteen-year-olds were particularly restless. Even from the hall, Joseph could hear them arguing inside the classroom.

When he crossed the threshold, his pupils hushed and took their seats. But as Joseph strode to the lectern, young Mr. Lange spoke up: "Is kissing a mortal sin, Father?"

"Saint Alphonsus calls it an 'imperfect act,'" chimed in another boy.

Perhaps hoping Joseph wouldn't recognize his voice in the rising chorus, a third student called: "Have *you* ever kissed a girl, Father?"

Joseph knew at once it was Mr. Kelley. At first, Joseph answered only with raised eyebrows and a pointed, wordless stare in his direction.

Young Mr. Kelley dropped his gaze at once. Amidst the sniggers of the other boys, he qualified: "I meant *before* he was a Priest..."

Joseph might have answered: *"No"*; technically, he'd never kissed a *girl*, only a woman. He might also have answered: *"Throughout Friday night, into Saturday morning—and more intimately than some of you have ever dreamt possible."* Instead, Joseph rounded the lectern, leaned back against it, and crossed his arms over his chest. He did not glance toward David. "This may come as a shock to you, gentlemen, but the answer to Mr. Kelley's question is: 'Yes.'"

Gasps and excited murmurs followed.

Joseph cleared his throat loudly. "Nor have I forgotten Mr. Lange's question: 'Is kissing a mortal sin?' The answer to *that* depends entirely on the kiss."

More sniggers.

"I *don't* mean: 'Is one's tongue involved?'" Joseph clarified. "I mean: '*Whom* are you kissing, and *why*?' The briefest kiss can be sinful if it is done for the wrong reasons. Are you kissing this young lady merely for your own pleasure—so you can say you have done it, so you can brag about it? Or: do you wish to know more of this particular lady, to communicate something to her alone, to give *her* pleasure? If *those* are your reasons—and if you remember that it was God Who brought her to you, God Who made her so soft—then no, I don't believe *that* kiss is a mortal sin. I don't believe it's even a venial sin. It is far from 'imperfect': it is the most perfect act imaginable."

For a moment, his students only gaped at him. Then one of them ventured: "And...if you intend to marry the lady, right, Father?"

"Of course." Joseph attempted to smile. "That goes without saying, doesn't it?"

AFTER HIS LECTURE, Joseph's students filed out of the classroom— all but one. His nephew remained at his desk, utterly silent, frowning at the cover of his Latin text. Joseph had sensed that David wanted to speak with him since Saturday, but they'd not had a chance. The boy was so unreadable; his somber expression might have meant a hundred things. Cautiously, Joseph crossed to the door and closed it.

Without looking up, David whispered: "I know you visit Tessa at night sometimes, when Mr. Stratford is away. I heard you arguing last October, and...*not* arguing on Friday night."

Joseph closed his eyes and steeled himself. "You have every right to be angry, David, to despise me..."

"I'm not. I don't." The boy's voice broke, but Joseph did not think it had anything to do with his changing vocal cords. "Forgive me, Father, for I have sinned."

Joseph stared at him. "*You* have sinned?"

David nodded, his eyes still averted. "You're bound by the Seal of Confession, right? You won't tell anyone else?"

"No one," Joseph promised.

"What I feel is envy, Father. I know Tessa loves *you*; I know she is supposed to be my *mother*; but...after I returned to my bed on Friday, I dreamt she was with *me*."

"Ah." Joseph sat down beside his nephew. "You are nearly fifteen years old, David. All boys your age have such dreams, such desires —else why would your classmates have been so interested in kissing?"

David's voice trembled with the effort of restraining his tears. "But we were doing more than kissing; and Tessa is—"

"Tessa is *not* your mother or even your aunt. She *is* a beautiful woman whom you see every day."

His nephew still wouldn't meet Joseph's eyes. "That wasn't the first time I've dreamt about her. Sometimes, I'm not even asleep."

His cheeks turned an even deeper shade of scarlet. "I know it is sinful and ridiculous…"

"It is *normal*, son. Understand that first."

Finally the boy glanced up. "I…don't disgust you?"

"No, David. I know this is hard to believe, but you won't feel this way about Tessa forever. Your mind is simply experimenting. Before you know it, you will have focused your attention on someone else— someone your own age who returns your affections. One day, all of this—the lust *and* the guilt—will be only a memory."

David frowned. "You think I should marry?"

"Not immediately," Joseph chuckled. "*Eventually.*"

"Even with our blood the way it is?"

"You will need to choose your bride carefully; you will need to find someone you can trust—but every man must do that." Joseph sighed. "I know what it is like to live without a wife, David—and I know what it is like to find happiness. When the right woman enters your life, I pray you will recognize her and never let her go."

"Grandma said it's all up to me, now: I'm the last Lazare."

"She's right." As part of the agreement between Edward Stratford and Joseph's family, David had adopted his mother's name.

"So I *have* to get married?"

"Of course not. You must make your own choices. But I hope that you will learn from our mistakes. Mine especially."

"*I'm* so afraid of making a mistake—so afraid that Tessa will realize how I feel about her." A tear finally escaped, but David wiped it away at once. "And I want to punch Mr. Stratford: for making her miserable, for *existing*. I've been thinking about where I should attend school. I'd planned on the College of Charleston. But staying under the same roof as Tessa is a proximate occasion of sin."

"Have you considered Georgetown?"

The boy nodded. "I know how smart the Jesuits are; but they expect you to remain there even between terms. I'll be going so far away for medical school, and I'm not…" His cheeks colored again. "Grandma wants me nearby, and I learn so much from Grandpa."

Joseph struggled not to smile. He remembered his own loneliness in Rome, and he understood what his nephew was *not* saying: He wasn't ready yet to leave everything he knew. Charleston to Missouri to California back to Charleston, the deaths of his parents and siblings—already the boy had endured so many changes in his short life.

"I thought— Mr. Stratford wants me to go to South Carolina College. Columbia isn't *so* far, and I could return over the summer. It's easier when we're on the island—I can get away and swim."

"Swimming helps," Joseph agreed. "You'll come back for Christmas too, won't you?"

The boy nodded haltingly. "I-I think I can bear it that long."

"I'm sorry, David. I've made you uncomfortable in your own home, haven't I?"

"It's not your fault. She's just so *perfect*, so kind and beautiful, with hair like honey…"

Joseph could only smile.

"I'll need your help, Father, before they'll accept me in Columbia. I think my Latin is good enough, but my Greek isn't."

"Of course I will help you, son."

CHAPTER 10

The people are in great distress for want of food, yet there is
plenty and to spare of food in the country—that food however…is
being sent out of the country and the people are looking to receive
food five thousand miles away…

— Editor John B. Knox in his *Clare Journal* (October 5, 1846)

That September, Joseph's father took David to Columbia to
begin his Freshman year at South Carolina College. The day
after Tessa's thirtieth birthday, when Joseph answered the blue lamp,
he was glad to know his nephew would not be listening.

Joseph slipped upstairs to find Tessa seated at her dressing table,
fully clothed. She was gazing at herself in the mirror, so absorbed
she did not even notice his entrance. As beautiful as she was, to his
knowledge, Tessa had never committed the sin of vanity before.
Now, her countenance radiated loss and despair.

Happily, he'd brought her a birthday gift she would never forget
—and one her husband would never spy: carnal knowledge. Experi-
mentation could be delightful; but in their ignorance, he and Tessa
had been neglecting half the experiments. Joseph had finally worked
up the courage to ask his father's advice. There were more ways to

make a woman come than Joseph had ever dreamed. He didn't even need his penis.

First, he caressed Tessa's shoulder and kissed the top of her head. "It's only a number, darling. It doesn't make me love you any less."

"What?" Tessa seemed genuinely confused, as if he were pulling her out of another world.

"Weren't you searching for wrinkles? Lamenting your thirtieth birthday?"

"No." Yet her voice wavered with unshed tears. She looked back to the mirror. "I was staring at my jewels"—emeralds dangled from her ears and her throat—"and my gown and thinking about all the things I have and do not need, while my countrymen..." She grasped his hand, still on her shoulder, and gazed up at him through the mirror. "You know half the potato crop failed last year in Ireland."

"Yes."

"But there have been losses before; we thought the farmers could recover this year." She turned to him. "Except the crop is failing again, Joseph. I've had a letter from my father. The blight is even worse now."

"This goes beyond County Clare?"

Tessa nodded, and tears spilled from her eyes. "'Tis all over Ireland! Already the newspapers are reporting deaths from starvation."

"And your family?"

"They are suffering, but not nearly as much as the *very* poor..."

Joseph grabbed a chair so he could sit next to her. He grasped both her hands in his. "I'll talk to Bishop Reynolds tomorrow. I'll speak about Ireland in the cathedral on Sunday. We'll solicit donations and find somewhere to send them."

"Thank you," she wept.

"If it's food the Irish need, surely we can convince some of the planters to provide rice and corn as well as funds—men like Mr. Lynch who come from Ireland themselves."

Tessa nodded, brightening just a little. "I'll ask Edward and his father. If they refuse, I'll sell my jewelry."

Joseph stroked the backs of her hands with his thumbs. "Your family and your countrymen will be in my prayers every day till this crisis has passed."

Tessa sighed with relief and leaned over to embrace him. She pulled back only to caress his face and stare desperately into his eyes. She whispered: "Make love to me, Joseph? Make me forget?"

Gladly. He had only to find the right words. He would borrow someone else's. Fortunately, Joseph had attended *Antony and Cleopatra* last month with his father and David. Joseph had thought Shakespeare's description of the Egyptian queen so appropriate for Tessa, he'd looked it up afterward and memorized it for her birthday:

"Age cannot wither her, nor custom stale
Her infinite variety."

Tessa smiled, so he continued:

"Other women cloy
The appetites they feed, but she makes hungry
Where most she satisfies…"

Realizing he'd just said "hungry," Joseph grimaced. Tessa wanted to *forget* the Irish famine, at least until tomorrow. "I'm sorry. That was a poor choice."

"I liked the first bit," Tessa told him with a weak shrug. "And if you were any better at wooing, I might be worried."

A year ago, she'd suggested much the same thing: that he might visit other women as he did her. Perhaps it had not been in jest. He took her face in his hands and gazed sincerely into her myrrh-brown eyes. "There is only you, Tessa."

"Truly?"

"How can you doubt that?"

"You are such a beautiful man, Joseph. I've seen the way other women stare at you, choker or no choker." She fingered its folds. "They must have done it all your life—and the years are only improving you."

She was going to make *him* commit the sin of vanity. He resisted a glance at his reflection. Beauty was in the eye of the beholder. If Tessa found him pleasant to look at, that was all that mattered. "I may have *lusted* after other women," he admitted, "especially when I was younger." He saw the pained look in her eyes and added quickly: "But I did nothing about it—and you are the only woman I have ever *loved*, Tessa. The only woman I can ever imagine loving."

Shyly—or perhaps coyly—her smile returned. "That's *better...*"

"And every word is true. Couldn't you tell the first time I kissed you that I'd never done it before?"

"Neither had I. I mean, not like *that*."

So her husband was inept even at kissing. While they were making confessions: "And...in all your years together, you've never come with Edward?"

She dropped her eyes and shook her head. "When your father wrote me that long letter, just after my marriage, I was so grateful to him for the care he put into those words. But I read them and I wept all the more. I knew I would use almost none of his advice. I could have shown that letter to Edward; I could have made things easier between us if I'd only tried harder. But the truth is, Edward may be talentless and rough and selfish—but at least he is quick. The things your father wrote about... I didn't *want* to experience them with Edward. It would have felt like my own body was betraying me. I was waiting for you."

Joseph wanted to say: *And I was waiting for YOU.* But he hadn't waited; he'd married Holy Mother Church instead.

"You won't make me wait *too* much longer, will you?"

Joseph smiled, undressed her, and carried her to the bed. There, he proved how talented, gentle, selfless, and indefatigable *he* was.

～

THE NEWS FROM IRELAND grew more and more terrible. All across America, the compassionate responded. Not only those with connections to Ireland but also Jewish congregations, free colored communities, and even Cherokee and Choctaw Indians sent funds, food, and clothing.

It was not enough. Hunger, disease, and exhaustion extinguished thousands upon thousands of lives. The British government offered public works, but they turned many away; and with the rising price of food, they did not pay the workers enough to survive. If the Irish families straggled back to their cottages to die, many found their homes destroyed by pitiless landlords who'd seized the chance to evict them. So an exodus began. Those who still had the strength— and who could pay for the passage—made the only choice they had left: they abandoned their beloved island for an uncertain future on a distant shore.

Month after month, Tessa waited in an agony for tidings from her family. She'd sent them everything she could—everything Edward would permit her. Late that spring of 1847, she finally received word that three of her brothers, their wives, and their children had arrived in New York. There they would stay; Tessa had written her family long ago about Charleston's heat and its fatal fevers. Tessa's mother accompanied her brothers across the Atlantic. Typhus had taken her father.

JOSEPH ANSWERED THE BLUE LAMP the night after Tessa learned of his death. Joseph kissed the lids of her bloodshot eyes and soothed her: "You'll see your father again. Not in this life, but you *will* see him again."

She seemed to sigh with relief. Joseph intended to make her forget as he had last October, to make her happy for a few scant hours before reality assaulted her anew. When he pulled off her chemise, Tessa did not resist.

But when he began caressing her in earnest, Joseph realized she wasn't making the right sounds—that she was too numb with grief to respond to him. So in the end, he only took her in his arms and whispered empty promises: "I'm here, darling. I won't leave you."

He *would* leave her, well before dawn; and this time next week, Bishop Reynolds might send him to another parish. Joseph would have to obey.

Throughout those precious hours, as Tessa clutched him against her beautiful body, Joseph tried not to be disappointed. He had no right to be. These nights were supposed to be about what *she* needed, about *her* pleasure. Not about his need to vanquish her pain. Not about his pleasure at watching her come.

LIAM AND TESSA had not seen their mother, brothers, or sisters-in-law for twelve long years. There were new nephews and nieces to meet, and Tessa was eager to introduce them to Clare. Edward had no interest in attending the reunion, but there *would* be a fourth person travelling to New York.

Tessa told Joseph her plans on the beach at Sullivan's Island. Clare and Hannah sat on a blanket a little apart from them, playing with the girl's dolls. They were enacting some great drama, and the forty-year-old negress seemed to be enjoying herself nearly as much as her four-year-old charge. Joseph could tell by Hannah's smiles, though the sounds of wind and surf snatched most of their dialogue.

Certainly none of the other strollers or swimmers were close enough to hear Joseph and Tessa, but she spoke in a low voice nonetheless. "I've been thinking about Bishop England's valet Castalio, how he accompanied His Lordship to Philadelphia and never returned... Did you know Hannah's son Caleb escaped north two years ago?"

Joseph nodded.

"He was able to get a letter to her last month. Caleb is married now, and he's about to give her a grandchild. But of course Hannah worries about him—and I worry about her. I'm afraid that if Edward ever realizes you... Won't he also realize that Hannah knows about us? His father *sells* slaves who displease him. I tried to talk to Edward about manumission, indirectly. I didn't realize how difficult 'tis to free a slave—'tis nearly impossible. And even if it were easy, Edward would never do it." Tessa drew in a deep breath. "So, I've made a decision. When I visit my family in New York, I will take Hannah with me. Edward won't give it a second thought: a lady never travels without her maid. Once we are safely there, Hannah will send word to Caleb. She's certain he can have free papers forged for her. I wish I could make it legal, but at least I can give her a chance, a start. I know it will be painful for Clare, to lose Hannah—and *I* will miss her terribly. I owe Hannah so much, for keeping our secret. But that is why I must let her go. I can do so little for Edward's slaves, but I can do this, for her."

Joseph could not help but anticipate Edward's response. "You are very brave, Tessa."

She looked back to her maid. "Not as brave as Hannah."

"EDWARD IS FURIOUS, ISN'T HE?" Joseph asked after Tessa returned from New York without Hannah.

Tessa nodded. "I had to pretend that *I* was furious too—that I felt betrayed." Tessa rolled her eyes. "He's bringing out another maid from the plantation for me, but now I have an excuse not to let her sleep in the house when he's away, because 'I'll never trust a negress again.' All the while, I pray for Hannah's safety. Trying to make Clare understand has been difficult, too. She feels as if Hannah abandoned her. 'Slaves have families too,' I told her. 'They have whole lives apart from us.' Many adults can't even understand that."

Finally, Joseph asked a question that had been haunting him: "Tessa, when you saw your family, did you tell them about me?"

"Of course. I've always mentioned you in my letters. They even asked about you."

"But…they know me as simply your Priest."

"I've called you a friend. My brothers and their wives still don't know you're anything more. In letters, I could deceive even my parents. But it was different face to face. My mother saw through my words."

"How did she respond?"

Tessa looked away. "She said: 'I am so happy for you, Tessa— and so frightened for you.'"

PART III
PASSION PLAY

1847-1850

CHARLESTON

There are no Romish priests…who cling more to the spirit, and less to the letter of the law, than the Roman Catholic priests of the United States.

— Alexis de Tocqueville, *Democracy in America* (1840)

CHAPTER 11

Do not suppose me well, lest you should deprive me of the pleasure of a remedy. … Do not suppose me strong, lest I should fall
ere you can sustain me.
   — Second Letter of Héloïse to Abélard (circa 1133)

At the end of August, a hurricane roared past Charleston.
Joseph was visiting the mission at Summerville, and the
inclement weather persuaded him to remain another night with one
of the Catholic families. He ensured that Prince was as comfortable
as a horse could be in a storm. Then he prayed for everyone in the
path of the hurricane.

Finally, Joseph said an extra prayer for Tessa and the children.
Surely the rising winds had warned them to abandon Sullivan's
Island in time. The ferry had been operating and steady. Now, they
were safely ensconced in the Charleston house with all the windows
shuttered tight. If waves surged over the sea wall, the flooding would
not reach Longitude Lane. *Please, God, let that be true.*

Late the next morning, after he'd aided and comforted the resi-
dents of Summerville, Joseph and Prince picked their way back
toward Charleston. They were navigating a swollen stream when

Joseph looked up to see Tessa's husband approaching. Edward's valet trailed close behind his master on another horse.

Joseph attempted a smile. "Good morning, Mr. Stratford! I see you survived the storm."

"As did you," Edward observed. He'd already averted his eyes.

Prince emerged from the stream. Tessa's husband and his valet plunged in without stopping; Joseph had to twist in his saddle and call over his shoulder to continue the conversation. "And my nephew? And...the rest of your household?"

"They are well enough." Edward did not bother to turn. "They certainly have no need of a Priest."

Joseph watched Tessa's husband and his valet disappear behind a stand of pines. Edward must be riding out to assess the state of his plantation after the storm. His tone had hardly been friendly. But it had been a grumble of annoyance, not hatred, Joseph told himself: the way one might react to finding a burr stuck to one's backside. Tessa's husband did not *know*.

EVIDENCE OF THE STORM lay littered all about the streets and yards: fallen tree limbs, fences, and roof slates. But at least in the upper wards, only a few isolated, predictable places had flooded. By Charleston standards, the impact had been minor. Joseph knew he should report to Bishop Reynolds, but first he directed Prince down Church Street. Joseph wanted to see for himself that David, Clare, and Tessa remained unharmed.

Fortunately, Zion was tidying the front garden just inside the Church Street gate, so Joseph didn't have to wait long for admittance. "We been counting our blessings, Father," the gardener told Joseph. "We come through all right—except for Miss Teresa's accident this morning."

Fear clutched at Joseph's heart. "She is hurt?"

"Only her ankle. Your father said she'll be mended in a month or so."

Joseph raced up the staircase to find Tessa lying supine on her bed, her left foot elevated on pillows, her bare toes peeking from a bandage. The mosquito netting hanging from the canopy had never looked so much like a shroud.

When he gasped at the sight, Tessa opened her eyes and propped herself on her elbows. "Joseph! I was so worried! Are you all right?"

"*I* am fine!" He hurried to her side—as close as he could come with the netting between them. "What happened?" He nearly added an endearment; but at the last moment, he swallowed it. Tessa should have called him "Father"; but Joseph was fairly certain no one was close enough to hear.

"'Tis only a mild sprain," Tessa explained, though she had grimaced and lain back again. "My pride hurts as much as my ankle. I simply wasn't watching where I was going! First thing this morning, Clare was eager to see how her garden plot had fared in the storm."

Together, Joseph and Tessa had planned a bed just for Clare, filled with plants sure to fascinate a four-year-old: lambs' ears, Chinese lanterns, and the like.

"She dashed down the steps before the slaves could clean up the garden paths. I chased after her—and I *tripped* on a fallen branch! But God was watching over me: David was only a few steps behind. He carried me back into the house, and he knew exactly what to do. He will be an excellent doctor. I'm so grateful this happened before he returned to Columbia."

David had probably enjoyed carrying Tessa in his arms and tending to her naked ankle. Joseph banished the thought. *I am NOT jealous of my sixteen-year-old nephew!* For all Joseph knew, David had overcome his infatuation with Tessa. Joseph hadn't asked about it again, and his nephew hadn't volunteered.

"He fetched your father himself, and now he's entertaining Clare for me."

At that very moment, Joseph heard the girl's voice from the third floor: "*Hurry*, David!"

The boy's footsteps hastened down the stairs. Joseph crossed to the hall in time to see his nephew dashing back up with an umbrella. He smiled at Joseph and glanced toward the play-room.

"Apparently the Flood is coming—according to Clare, last night was only the beginning."

"David?" Tessa called from the bed.

He came to the threshold, the closed umbrella propped against one shoulder. "Do you need something?"

"No; I just wanted to say 'Thank you.'"

The boy shrugged. "I'd rather play Noah's Ark than review algebra." He ran back upstairs.

Tessa asked: "Would you check on Clare for me, Joseph? She was so distraught earlier, when she realized I was hurt. She didn't want to leave my side, but your father insisted she let me rest."

Joseph nodded and followed his nephew. He knew the moment Clare saw him, she would rush to him, her game forgotten; so Joseph remained out of sight in the hall.

"You got back just in time!" Clare told David. "It's *really* raining now, and Mignon was getting wet! You *know* how he feels about water!"

Quickly David opened the umbrella to protect Clare and the black-and-white cat from the imaginary downpour. In actuality, Mignon did not seem distressed in the slightest. He lay curled on the rug, and Joseph thought he detected a purr.

"We have to find *all* the animals before it's too late!" the little girl declared.

David chuckled. "You hid them while I was gone, didn't you?"

"No! They were scared of the thunder, and they hid themselves!"

"Well, I see the giraffes…" He leaned down to rescue them.

"You have to make the sounds!"

"I don't think giraffes make a sound."

"Oh." Clare pouted.

"But here are the cattle! *Moooo!* Like that?"

She grinned and nodded. Clare tucked two zebras into the Ark, neighing them into place. Then she instructed David: "Don't forget the lions!"

He smiled, then did a decent approximation of a roar, which made Mignon raise his head in confusion.

Clare clapped her hands. "Do the wolves next!"

David threw back his head and cried: "Ah-oooh!"

Joseph left them howling with laughter and returned to Tessa. "Clare is in good spirits—and in good hands," he assured her. Then Joseph glanced toward the hall again. As far as he knew, all the slaves were outside dealing with the storm mess. Still, he pushed the bedroom door almost but not quite closed—a closed door would only arouse more suspicion. Then he whispered: "I passed Edward on the road outside Charleston."

She exhaled a nervous breath. "Did you?"

"I imagine he'll be spending the night at the plantation?"

"Most likely."

Joseph hesitated. Earlier that summer, after the Ursulines had left Charleston, Bishop Reynolds had moved into their former convent, which was larger and better cared for than the old Bishop's residence. For the moment, Joseph lived alone again, though another Priest might join him at any time. While he still had the freedom to come and go unobserved, Joseph longed to seize the day —or at least the night. But he looked back at Tessa's bound ankle. "I suppose you'll want me to stay away too."

"Of course not." Her voice dropped even lower. "I *always* want your company—although we *may* need to limit our...activities tonight."

"I'll sit on the méridienne," Joseph resolved. "I won't even touch you." Yet even to have this mosquito netting between them was maddening.

"You may touch me *a little...*" Then Tessa's grin became a frown. "Speaking of where you will spend the night, have you been back to the Bishop's residence yet? I mean, *your* residence?"

"No."

"I think something happened to it in the storm. When your father came to look at my ankle, he said: 'Tell Joseph he can sleep at my house.' But I'm afraid he'd given me laudanum, and I was falling asleep—that's all I remember. I'm sorry!"

"That's quite all right. You *should* rest." Another gale of laughter from the play-room prompted him to add: "And you needn't worry about Clare."

"She's good for him too, isn't she?" Tessa smiled. "I can't even remember the last time I heard David laugh."

THERE WAS A TREE lying on Joseph's bed. Or at least, half an oak had crashed through the old Bishop's residence into Joseph's bedchamber. He was wondering if it was safe to venture up the stairs when His Lordship emerged from the seminary. "Joseph! I'm glad you're still with us. 'Many hands…' as they say."

"Is Thornton all right?"

"Oh, yes. He's securing us an ax. This house did not fare as well as our persons, as you can see. I've decided not to rebuild. You know I've been planning a larger cathedral."

Numbly, Joseph nodded.

"Well, it will take up this space. So it doesn't make sense to repair something we'll be demolishing anyway. Father Baker says we can convert one of the rooms in the seminary for you."

"My father offered to let me stay with him tonight."

"Good, good!" Bishop Reynolds nodded toward the crushed house. "See what you can salvage from the library in there, will you?"

JOSEPH HAD FEW BELONGINGS to begin with, and even fewer thanks to the storm damage. He gathered them into his portmanteau and saddlebags and dined with his parents that evening. "You are welcome to stay here permanently, son," Joseph's father offered. "Now that Liam has left us and David is in Columbia most of the year, your mother would be delighted to see more of you. So would I."

Liam had decided to settle in New York, to be close to his mother and brothers. *"Tessa has you now,"* Liam had reasoned to Joseph. *"And Charleston only reminds me of Hélène."*

"We're only two streets away from the cathedral," Joseph's father continued, "and your horse lives here already."

Since the arrangement would save the diocese money, Bishop Reynolds embraced it at once. Joseph was relieved that he could now come and go at any hour of the night without attracting the suspicions of another Priest. His mother was deaf, so he could hardly disturb her. His father already knew Joseph's nighttime destination—and approved. That tree had been a figurative windfall as well as a literal one. Surely it was a sign: God was giving Joseph and Tessa His blessing.

But the night after the hurricane, when Joseph slipped through the garden into her bedchamber, he found Tessa's daughter curled up beside her. *Of course.* Hannah was no longer in the nursery to keep Clare company or to quell her fears.

Inside the transparent mosquito netting, the myrrh-brown heads of mother and daughter turned toward one another in sleep. Neither sheet nor counterpane covered them; the sultry air was blanket enough. Damp with perspiration, Tessa's short, thin chemise clung close to her breasts and her hips. She was not wearing drawers, so most of her slender limbs were entirely bare. Even with a swollen ankle, her legs were spectacular. Joseph could feast his eyes for a few minutes before retreating...

Then a mosquito attacked him. He slapped at it instinctively, before he could reflect on the consequences of the sound.

Tessa opened her eyes and smiled in greeting. Gently, she roused her daughter. "Father Joseph is here, *a chuisle*. Remember I told you he was coming?"

Clare whined and nodded.

"You also remember that Mama wants to be *alone* with Father Joseph?"

"Yes," the girl pouted.

"You have me the whole year round," Tessa reminded her daughter. "So Father Joseph is going to carry you to your own bed, and you must try your very best to stay there, *a chuisle*."

"What if there's another storm and I get scared?"

"Then you must *knock* and wait for one of us to open the door. If you hear any strange sounds *inside* this bedchamber, what did I tell you about those?"

"That I shouldn't worry, because the sounds mean you are happy."

Through the netting, Tessa glanced slyly at Joseph, who was closing the jalousies. "Exactly."

"Don't *I* make you happy, Mama?"

Tessa caressed the damp curls clinging to her daughter's forehead and kissed her left cheek with the two small brown moles. Mother's marks, Joseph had heard them called. "You have made me happy since the moment you opened your eyes, *a chuisle*. But this is a special kind of happiness, one only grown-ups share. I shall tell you all about it when you are older."

Clare didn't seem entirely satisfied by this answer, though she allowed Joseph to carry her back to the nursery and tuck her into bed. In the light of her little night-lamp, Tessa's daughter must have seen his troubled expression. "I know you're a secret, Father," the girl grinned up at him. "I'm not going to tell. That wouldn't be any fun."

Joseph smiled and kissed Clare's forehead in thanksgiving. Still, he was glad that he and Tessa had decided not to tell her daughter that he was really a colored man—not yet.

Joseph secured the mosquito netting around Clare's bed and asked her about her day. At first, the girl chatted excitedly; but soon, she was yawning. Finally, he blessed Clare's dreams and returned to her mother.

Her mother had vanished.

Joseph frowned and peered at the door to her dressing chamber, which was closed. "Tessa?"

"I-I'll be only a minute," she called back, sounding strange—sounding worried. What could have compelled her to climb from her cocoon of netting and limp into the next room on a sprained ankle?

"Can I be of any assistance?"

"Stay where you are!" Now Tessa sounded panicked.

Naturally this ejaculation only made Joseph more concerned. In spite of her injunction, he stepped closer to the dressing chamber door.

She must have heard his footfalls. "If you love me, *stay where you are!*"

In the next instant, Joseph's nose informed him *why* she wanted him to keep his distance. He couldn't help it. He burst out laughing.

He also retreated to the far corner of the bedchamber, near the open windows (open to the breeze but not to the eyes of neighbors, thanks to the jalousies). While he waited for Tessa to reappear, Joseph divested himself of as many layers as he dared: hat, coat, boots, socks, choker, and waistcoat.

In the dressing chamber, he heard the little grunts that told him she was closing up the commode—so that it might be mistaken for a small chest of drawers again—and maneuvering herself to the bidet and the washstand. She was deliciously clean, his Tessa: after trips to her dressing chamber, it wasn't only her hands that smelled like lily of the valley soap.

When the scent of her gardenia perfume reached him as well, he knew she was ready to return. Joseph crossed to the dressing chamber again. "Will you let me carry you back, at least?"

"No!" Yet by the time she achieved the door, Tessa was panting. When she emerged, she wouldn't meet his eyes. Her head was bowed in shame, as if she'd committed a sin. Probably in an effort to contain the lingering unpleasantness, Tessa tried to slip through the door quickly, but her sprained ankle impeded her: she had to brace one hand against the wall to take some of her weight.

Joseph took *all* of her weight before she could protest, catching her up in his arms and shutting the door by leaning his own buttocks against it. Some of the unpleasantness escaped nonetheless. He resumed chuckling; but he also strode quickly toward the bed.

Tessa buried her face in his neck and whimpered: "You'll never want to kiss me again…"

"Impossible." He laid her down on the mattress and let his lips hover just above hers, promising to prove her wrong. But for now, it was only a promise; he preferred to tease her a little longer. "Did you really think I didn't know what you were doing, when you disappeared into your dressing chamber on other nights?"

Tessa turned her face away, determined to maintain her dignity. "I was refreshing my perfume!"

Joseph laughed and turned his attention to her swollen ankle, installing it carefully on its mound of pillows. "What did you think *I* was doing when *I* disappeared?"

"Praying!"

Now Joseph guffawed.

Tessa hid her face in her hand, but she was laughing too.

"You *should* be ashamed of yourself," he told her as he restored the mosquito netting on her side of the bed. "A proper hostess would have *shown* her guest the commode. I had to find it myself."

"I left a little lamp on top!"

Joseph crossed around to the other side of the bed, then stopped smiling. A mosquito was buzzing at his ear; he wanted to join Tessa on the bed for more reasons than one. But he must think of her sprain. "My weight on the mattress will disturb you, won't it?"

Tessa lowered her hand and assessed him in the lamplight. The way she caught her lower lip between her teeth revealed the bent of her thoughts even before she spoke. "You would weigh less if you were naked."

The idea was very, very tempting. He'd donned fresh clothing before coming here, and already every inch of it was soaked with sweat. Surely he could discard his shirt, perhaps even his trousers... Tessa was injured; she wouldn't risk—

The look in her eyes told him she would.

So Joseph shed only his braces before he slipped inside the netting. He felt as if he were shedding far more: as if in this room, on this bed, he became another man. As he closed the netting around them, he felt as if he were shutting out the world.

Tessa understood. "'Tis almost like a cocoon, isn't it?"

Joseph nodded, settling down next to her as gently as he could: he on his side, she on her back so she could keep her ankle elevated. Her beautiful face was turned toward him, her myrrh-brown eyes liquid with longing. Joseph brought his face so close that their noses nearly touched. "Or like our own little island."

Tessa tilted her lips even nearer. "A raft in the eye of a storm."

He kissed her, almost chastely and without hurry. "An oasis in the midst of the desert."

"A republic of two," she breathed against his mouth. "A tiny country where we can write our own rules."

If only that were true. But Joseph had only to glance at Tessa's leg to remember: the world reached even here. Every single moment, they must watch where they stepped, or there would be consequences far more terrible than a wrenched ankle.

Then Joseph realized that Tessa was unbuttoning his shirt. Any sudden move of protest might hurt her, he told himself. And after all, the buttons reached only to the base of his breastbone. It hardly seemed worthwhile to grab her wrist. Still, he could *voice* his disapproval. "Tessa..."

"I'm being a good hostess," she reasoned. "I'm making you more comfortable."

She was right: it made all the difference, that tiny bit of openness between his throat and his nipples. The way the shirt fell, the left one was nearly exposed to her... But Tessa was bunching up the fabric at his navel instead, pulling the tail of his shirt from his trousers. That felt wonderful too: the kiss of the breeze against his bare skin. Slick with sweat, the cotton between them had never seemed so insubstantial, so inconsequential...

She is injured... he told himself again and again. Did that mean they should do less, or that they could do more?

Tessa certainly wasn't behaving like an invalid. When he felt her hand exploring *beneath* his shirt, he slipped his fingers between hers and drew it out. Her hand tightened on his, pleading wordlessly, while objections bubbled from her throat. He swallowed them, though he still had a decision to make and a kiss was hardly conducive to thinking.

Especially when she responded like *this*, when she made these little moans of pleasure and encouragement. They reminded him of the longer, deeper moans she made when his mouth was on her nipple or her clitoris—how her whole body would rise to meet him and press against him—how when she came, her limbs would tense and thrash…

Which was precisely why they could do no more than kiss tonight.

He kept his hand clasped in hers to prevent it from wandering. It was difficult for Tessa to use her other hand without turning, which she couldn't do without disturbing her ankle. She seemed content enough with his mouth.

After perhaps a quarter of an hour, Joseph disengaged their lips enough to grin: "And you thought I'd never want to kiss you again."

Tessa was smiling too, but her voice sounded mischievous. "When I said 'kiss me,' I *meant*…" She glanced downward.

His own gaze lingered there, on the triangle of bronze hair visible through her thin chemise. Much as he longed to… "If we do *that* tonight, you will be lamed for life."

She pouted.

"Besides, it is far too hot—and David is upstairs."

"He knows, doesn't he?" For a moment, Tessa squeezed her eyes shut. "Is he terribly disappointed in me?"

"Not at all. Still, I would prefer he were not within earshot."

"Am I so very loud?"

"Yes, you are," Joseph chuckled. She looked almost repentant, so he assured her at once: "And I adore every syllable." He pressed his lips to the source of those wild, beautiful sounds—to the delicate Adam's apple hidden inside the slender column of her throat. Tessa rewarded him with a resonant sigh. Very slowly, he kissed his way back to her mouth.

It was almost as if they were starting over. They had so much to look forward to.

CHAPTER 12

How might any pain be more than to see him that is all my life, all
my bliss, and all my joy, suffer?
— Juliana of Norwich, *Sixteen Revelations of Divine Love* (circa
1400)

They were not alone again till the following spring—on Joseph's
thirty-sixth birthday, as it happened. He unwrapped Tessa
faster than ever before; and as soon as he had her naked, he
intended to devour her. But she braced her hands on his shoulders
and kept him at a distance. "Tonight, 'tis *your* turn, my love. Or *my*
turn, depending on how you look at it."

Joseph averted his eyes, because his penis had leapt for joy at the
mere suggestion. "Tessa, I told you—"

"I know; I know." She rolled her eyes. "I shan't profane anything
covered by your trousers or your shirt. But surely you will allow me
the other bits?"

Since that left very little, Joseph nodded haltingly.

"Then first, you will sit. You will do nothing else till I return."
Tessa motioned to her méridienne. Joseph obeyed, and she disap-

peared into her dressing chamber. She said her left ankle had healed, but she still seemed to favor it a little.

Tessa returned with a blue-and-white basin half-filled with water and a chunk of soap. She set the bowl beside his feet and sank to her knees. The sight was incongruous and exciting all at once: to be fully clothed and have a beautiful, naked woman kneeling before you like a penitent.

He wasn't fully clothed for long. Tessa unbuttoned his boots and pulled them off. Then she reached for the hems of his trouser legs. Joseph flinched.

Tessa scowled up at him. "I'm not anywhere near your precious, inviolable manhood. I'm simply keeping your cuffs dry." When she'd rolled his trouser legs partway up his calves, she peeled off his socks. Joseph grimaced. He knew his feet smelled; he'd been on them most of the day. But this must be why she'd brought the basin.

Even with his dirty feet, she was remarkably tender. She placed them into the cool water and washed them without hurry: working a lather from his ankles to his toes, then rinsing them clean with a pitcher. Washing someone's feet was supposed to be a sign of humility, but it was Joseph who felt humbled.

When she'd finished, Tessa unpinned her long hair, smirked up at him, and used the silken tresses to dry his feet. The sensation was surprisingly arousing. Joseph thought of Mary Magdalene; but he was not Christ.

Neither did Tessa seem the least bit repentant. She leaned closer and kissed the top of Joseph's left foot at the ankle, trailing downward till her lips reached the base of his large toe. Then, her tongue slipped *between* his toes. Joseph started and yanked his foot back, beneath the méridienne.

Tessa narrowed her eyes at him. "You *said* I could have the bits that weren't covered by your shirt or your trousers."

Slowly, he relaxed his feet. Tessa caressed every inch of them with her fingers and kissed just about everything. Finally, Joseph watched with wide eyes as she lifted his right foot, drew it to her breast, and pressed the sole against her erect nipple. He fell back against the méridienne and panted at this ridiculous pleasure. As long as he didn't come, surely it was all right...

Next she led him to the bed, where she ripped off his choker. Then she sucked on his Adam's apple as if she intended to pull it through his skin. She stroked his neck, toyed with his hair, and kneaded his scalp. She'd touched him tenderly so many times during their nights together, and those caresses had thrilled him; but they had been nothing like these. Now her movements were concentrated, purposeful—skillful. Had *she* consulted with his father too? With the inhabitants of a brothel? Joseph knew he shouldn't be allowing this; his body was consecrated; but Tessa was doing *incredible* things to his ears...

She saved the best for last. She kissed each of his palms as she had after his ordination, as though granting him a new chrism. And then, she took each of his fingers into the warm, wet hollow of her mouth and sucked on them, just as she'd done in his dream. As long as he didn't come...

He was very, very close; and Tessa had not relinquished the possibility. Perhaps imagining she'd lulled him into consent, she slid one of her hands downwards. She'd undone one of his trouser buttons before Joseph mustered the strength to stop her.

Pouting, she let his thumb slip from her mouth, though it hovered hopefully at her lips.

"Tessa," he gasped, still holding her hand away from his erection, "it is hard enough—"

"'Tis, indeed." She glanced downward and grinned wickedly.

"It is *difficult* enough to fight myself," he amended. "Please don't make me fight you, too."

"You could stop fighting."

Fortunately, he was very good at distracting her. There were so many things they still hadn't tried (besides *that*). One in particular, he had been saving. It was his birthday, but maybe, just maybe, she'd enjoy it as much as he did. There was a way he could enter that beautiful, secret gateway without his penis. It was the closest approximation he could allow her.

He'd stroked her clitoris and fondled her labia with his fingertips; but he'd dipped inside only with his tongue. That was softer and a good deal shorter than his fingers. He'd waited because he was afraid he might press too forcefully or at the wrong angle. He wanted it to be perfect, and this time, he knew he was prepared. He always kept his nails short; but tonight, he also knew for certain they were smooth and clean.

He still had to make sure she was ready. Her mouth already swollen from his kisses, he closed his lips around one of her nipples now, letting his hand explore even lower as they lay side by side. His fingers quested past the adorable dip of her navel and through the curled hair between her thighs.

His thumb lingered at her clitoris—the part of it at the surface —while his other fingers teased the parts hidden beneath her labia. *"If you look closely, you'll see the 'pearl,'"* Joseph's father had told him, *"but don't let that deceive you: there is a whole 'shell' underneath, as large as an erect penis—and with twice as much nerve fiber!"*

Finally, Joseph's fingertips discovered what he truly longed for: that indescribable liquor, fragrant as myrrh and slick as holy oil. But before he did any more, he wanted her consent. He raised his eyes to hers.

Tessa understood. She encouraged him with the Canticles: "'My beloved put his hand through the keyhole...'"

Solomon's beloved had *probably* meant that verse literally; but couched in such poetic language, who could say?

"Or at least, a finger?" Tessa suggested.

Joseph smiled, and very slowly, he started to obey. He was certain her sigh was one of gratitude; but he whispered: "Tell me if I hurt you."

She nodded. Her eyes said: *"You won't."*

He remembered to distribute her liquor—to anoint her clitoris —and then his forefinger sank blissfully all the way to the last knuckle. Already he could feel her tightening and trembling. Her eyes closed but her lips parted wider. He thought she was inviting what he wanted too. He slid a second finger beside the first and pressed upwards.

Tessa moaned, and tears spilled from beneath her eyelids.

Joseph stopped at once and tried to withdraw his fingers; but she clamped onto his wrist with her own hand. "I'm hurting you, darling!" he argued.

Tessa shook her head, though her breaths were so shallow, she managed only one word: "Opposite." Now her fingertips slid inside his shirt cuff. Though the tight passage would barely admit her, she stroked his skin till he understood: these were not tears of pain. Or at least, not the kind of pain you fled.

Joseph recalled the most famous ecstasy of her patroness: *"The pain was so great, that it made me moan; and yet its sweetness was so excessive, that I could not desire it to go... The pain is not bodily, but spiritual; though the body in some measure, yea, in great measure, participates in it. It is so delightful an intercourse..."*

It *was* an intercourse, a communion as profound and miraculous as transubstantiation: liquid becoming solid, solid becoming liquid...blood rushing to pearl, myrrh dripping from keyhole... Her innermost parts swelled and molded around his searching fingers, seeking him as fervently as he sought her. Tessa clasped her arms around his woolen back and hooked a leg over his woolen hips, till every bare inch of her clung to every clothed inch of him.

She gave him a hurricane of his own, almost terrifying in its violence. Yet this storm was not destructive but curative, and the calm in its wake was most astonishing of all. Tessa seemed at once comatose and blooming.

Only when Joseph withdrew his hand was her moan truly one of pain. One of loss. He might have remained there forever. Instead, he tugged a handkerchief from his pocket, trailed its linen between his fingers to collect her myrrh, and folded it with infinite care, as if around a relic. Across the world, Catholic churches enshrined the blood, tears, and even breast milk of saints—why couldn't he preserve this?

Tears still glistening on her cheeks, Tessa slid one hand to his face. "How I wish I could give you this: this *peace*."

"You have, darling."

Thanksgiving, even yearning, drained from Tessa's expression.

They left only anger and despair. She pulled away from him and turned her face to the far wall. "In your *dreams?*"

Joseph shook his head. "Right now." Gently, he turned her face back to his. "The sight of *you* is all I need."

It was only a white lie.

CHAPTER 13

If you have a garden and a library, you have everything you need.
— Marcus Tullius Cicero (circa 45 BC)

During his second year at South Carolina College, Joseph's shy nephew surprised all of them by joining the Shakespearian Club. "It's not *me* up there," David explained at his grandfather's table that May. "They only let me have small roles, anyway. But I love the *rhythm* of Shakespeare's language. It's mesmerizing, almost literally. It's like I'm dreaming, and I never want to wake up."

They begged David to perform something. He gave them Hamlet's "To be, or not to be" soliloquy and made them believe every word. Joseph would have preferred something less melancholy. He *hoped* his nephew was acting. At their applause, David blushed and smiled. The boy seemed to be enjoying himself, and that was what truly mattered.

Joseph's nephew was also learning to fence at college. One Sunday afternoon, when both Edward and his slaves were out, Joseph visited Tessa's house to find David and Clare crossing "swords" in the garden. From their color and suppleness, Joseph guessed the swords were parkinsonia branches divested of their thorns. Joseph and Tessa lingered in the shadow of the sweet olive hedge to observe. After she confirmed that no one was watching *them*, Tessa tucked her arm in Joseph's.

David made a weak parry (Joseph suspected it was intentional) that allowed five-year-old Clare to stab him in the heart. The boy practiced his acting by dying dramatically. He clutched at his chest, gasped, and rolled in agony on the grass, much to Clare's amusement. At last he gave up the ghost, closing his eyes and letting his tongue hang out.

Still giggling, the girl knelt down beside him and poked his cheek. Whereupon David sprang back to life, but only long enough to die a second time. Clare shrieked with surprise and then delight. Finally David tucked his hands under his head, sighed with contentment, and stared up at the evergreen branches of the Arbor Vitae as if he wished never to move again.

Mignon appeared from the underbrush and rubbed against her, but Clare's gaze remained on her foster-brother. She sat down Indian-style beside him and stroked the cat distractedly, her voice apprehensive now. "David?"

"Yes, *souris?*"

"Am I *almost* as good as a brother?"

He glanced over at her and smiled. "You are *better* than a brother."

The girl grinned. "I am?"

He nodded, though his eyes returned to contemplating the tree. "Boys can be very stupid and mean. My classmates, for example, think it is entertaining to get drunk, shoot out windows, and set a dog's tail on fire." When Clare whimpered, he turned his head toward her and added quickly: "I'm sorry, *souris*; I shouldn't have mentioned that. The dog survived—I tended her wounds myself." David seemed about to sit up, but Mignon climbed on his chest and perched there like a victorious warrior, making both children laugh.

Clare scratched beneath the cat's chin. "You'd teach those nasty boys to behave, wouldn't you, Mignon?"

Tessa squeezed Joseph's arm then to draw his attention. She

asked in a low voice: "How much has David told you about his time at the college?"

"Not as much as I'd like," Joseph admitted.

She nodded in sympathy. "I have more chances to ask, and still I must construct the picture from bits and pieces. David won't say it outright, but I know he's unhappy there."

Joseph sighed. "I wish he'd gone to Georgetown."

"I think David felt obligated to attend Edward's *alma mater*— since Edward is paying for his education."

Joseph did not comment on his nephew's other motivations.

"I wish Edward had thought about what *his* precious college would be like for David. Or perhaps Edward *intended* that David should understand his 'place': he is only a planter's *ward*. The other students are the *sons* of planters. They have been pampered all their lives, and they think the world belongs to them. I suppose South Carolina *does*. These boys think nothing of beating the college's slaves or challenging someone to a duel for the smallest of reasons. Our David is there to *learn*. I praise him for his diligence, his restraint. His future wife will praise him for it. But the other boys must see him as a kill-joy and mock him."

"He is also a Catholic," Joseph added. "David did admit to me that one of his *professors* thinks 'Catholicism is the work of Satan.' He's published a pamphlet on it!"

Meanwhile, Mignon leapt from David's chest, drawn to some scurrying creature in the flower bed. The boy had imparted his interest in natural science to Clare, so both children followed.

"With that tail, it must be a skink," David declared.

"Can *you* catch it?" the girl begged.

"I'll try." They disappeared behind the camellias, while Tessa and Joseph strode closer. After a minute, David cried: "Got him!"

Clare shrieked. "I didn't want you to *hurt* him!"

"I didn't!"

"But his pretty tail broke off!"

"The skink did that on purpose, *souris*. He was trying to distract me so he could escape."

They waded back out to the grass where Joseph and Tessa stood.

David held the struggling skink, a slender black lizard with pale stripes.

Clare held its brilliant blue tail. Still her voice wavered. "Can you fix it?"

"I don't have to; the tail will grow back."

"Really?"

"Really."

"He's *so* cute!" Clare reached out to touch one of the creature's tiny feet with its long toes. For a moment, the skink remained still and permitted this; then, he began wriggling in David's hand again. The girl frowned. "He isn't happy, is he?"

David shook his head. "Can I let him go now?"

Clare sighed and nodded. They made sure Mignon had stalked off after other prey. When the skink had darted back into the camellias, the girl asked: "Can I keep his old tail?"

David glanced to Tessa. "I think you'll have to ask your mother about that, *souris*."

The girl hurried over with her prize. "Look, Mama! It's the same color as David's and Father Joseph's eyes!"

"Beautiful," Tessa agreed.

Joseph knew how difficult it was for her to deny anything to her one surviving child. Even he had to admit that, for a detached lizard tail, it was lovely: such a brilliant blue it was nearly purple.

"May I keep it, Mama?"

"It isn't like a feather, *a chuisle*," Tessa reasoned. "I don't think it *will* keep."

"Not even for a few days?"

"You know your father gets upset when you bring creatures into the house."

"But it's only a tail! It can't crawl under his door like the walking-stick!"

"Even so, I don't think he'd—"

The girl scowled. "Father wants to get rid of Mignon too. He's mean and I don't care what he thinks!"

"But you *should*, Clare. We must—"

"He doesn't even like me!"

Tessa looked away. "I know your father doesn't *show* that he loves you, Clare; but he—"

The girl hugged Joseph's legs, since she wasn't tall enough yet to embrace him properly. "I wish you were my father."

I wish that too, Clare, Joseph tried to tell her with only his hand on her head.

She pouted up at him. "*You* like me, don't you?"

"Of course I do, *ma petite.*" He glanced to David. "Or should I call you 'ma souris'?"

"That's what David calls me." She brightened a little. "He was reading, and I snuck up on him and made him jump. He said: 'You're as quiet as a mouse!'"

"When she *wants* to be," David chuckled. "I've been teaching her French, and she's so fond of small creatures—it seemed appropriate."

"Tell Father Joseph what *else* 'souris' means!" Clare urged.

"Father Joseph's French is even better than mine—I'm sure he knows already."

"*Souris* also means 'smile,'" Joseph supplied with one of his own. "David is right: *souris* is perfect for you."

"I like Mama's name for me even better. She's been teaching me Irish."

"And you are a very good student, *a chuisle mo chroí.*" Tessa glanced up to Joseph. "Have I ever told *you* what that means?"

"No; I only know it's an endearment."

"'Pulse of my heart,'" Clare translated with a grin.

Tessa nodded, stroking the girl's cheek. "It means: 'You are as precious to me as my own heartbeat.'"

Clare still held the skink's blue tail, and she remembered her disappointment. "But I can't keep it?"

"We should leave it here," David answered so Tessa wouldn't have to. "The skink will come back for it."

"You said he'll grow a new tail."

"He will—but first, he'll eat the old one."

The girl's eyes went wide. "He eats his own tail?"

David nodded. "Like a real-life ouroboros."

Clare frowned. "Our...?"

"Ouroboros. That's an image of a snake or a dragon devouring its own tail. It's an ancient symbol of eternity and rebirth. I'll show you a picture later."

The girl nodded eagerly. "First, we have to give the skink his tail back! We should put it where you caught him!" She led him back to the camellias.

"So many times, I have wondered if I did the right thing, bringing David to live with us," Tessa told Joseph. "But when I watch him with Clare, I know he belongs here. He's such a fine tutor for her. And Clare is giving him another childhood. You remember, after his parents died, how somber and withdrawn he was?"

Joseph nodded.

"It was as if he wouldn't give himself permission to play. With Clare, he has a second chance. I am so grateful they have each other, even if 'tis only a few months a year. I cannot give Clare *everything* she needs, and it isn't any easier for her to make friends than 'tis for David. Edward doesn't want her associating with most of the girls who attend the cathedral, because their families are poor. But Clare's cousins in Edward's family and his friends' daughters look down on her, because *I* was poor. I've carried Edward's name for more than a decade; Clare was born in Charleston; yet we will never be one of them. I don't *want* to be, but..."

For all those same reasons, Tessa was isolated too. Against the odds, she'd found Hélène, then Hannah—and lost them both. She'd even lost Liam to distance.

Joseph made sure neither the slaves nor her husband had returned before he clasped Tessa's hand and whispered: "You have me."

She smiled weakly. "I have *some* of you."

CHAPTER 14

I have wanted to place locks on their sacred thighs. I have attempted to place the restraints of continence upon the genitals of the priesthood, upon those who have the high honor of touching the body and blood of Christ...

— Cardinal Saint Peter Damian, *De Caelibatu Sacerdotum* (circa 1060)

The next night he and Tessa met, she tried again, even though it wasn't his birthday. This time, when she slid her hand downward, she didn't bother with his buttons at all: she only cupped him there through his trousers. Before he could argue, she pleaded: "Won't you at least let me hold you? Just for a minute?"

Was this what it felt like for her, when he cupped his hand over her vulva? It was uncanny, this concentrated embrace—almost chaste in its restraint. Why did he feel as connected to her now as he did when their tongues slid against each other, or when he sucked on her clitoris—*more* connected? Why did he feel as though she held his heart in her hand?

But it wasn't enough for her, any more than it was for him. She couldn't keep her hand still. She managed to undo *two* of his trouser buttons before he wrested her hands away. Tessa groaned out her frustration—as if it could be anything next to his—and flopped back against the pillow. She flung the back of her wrist against her forehead and declared: "*Dum spero, spiro!*"

Joseph recognized the Latin. Taken from Cicero, it was the state motto of South Carolina, on her Great Seal since the Revolution: *As long as I breathe, I hope.*

But Tessa suspected her mistake and glanced back at him. "Did I say that right?"

"You switched the verbs, actually." Joseph restored the last of his buttons. "You said: 'As long as I hope, I breathe.'"

"*That* is also true," she sighed.

JOSEPH WAS CAREFUL to visit Stratford-on-Ashley only rarely, since it was difficult to predict Edward's absence. But between Christmas and New Year's Eve, Tessa, Clare, and David would be spending a few days at the plantation; and Joseph's nephew had alerted him that Edward would stay one more night in Charleston before joining them.

Unlike the winter of Clare's birth six years before, the weather was blissfully mild. Joseph found Tessa and her daughter on the double staircase at the back of the mansion. A portico projected from the veranda, and twin stairs curved down from either side of it. The final steps faced each other, forming a broken circle. In honor of the season, pine garlands twined through the balustrades and banisters.

Clare was using the double staircase as a race-track, squealing with delight as her mother chased her up one set of steps and down the other. As Joseph emerged from the lower veranda and the portico, the girl whirled about and began pursuing Tessa instead, while her mother laughed and pretended to flee.

When Clare saw Joseph, she gripped the banister to stop herself and cried: "Father!" She darted down and embraced him on the brick pavement between the ends of the steps. "Look, Father." The girl motioned to the double stairway. "I didn't see it till we put up the garlands, but it's a circle! Like an ouroboros: it never ends!"

"And what is this?" Joseph asked, pointing to the flash of blue-green at her wrist.

"It's my Christmas present from David!" Clare exulted, thrusting the bracelet toward Joseph for inspection.

No doubt drawn by their voices, the seventeen-year-old appeared on the portico. "It was my *idea*," David corrected. "Aunt Tessa found it."

"Clare has been drawing ouroboroses for months now, so we thought she might like it," Tessa explained, then quirked her mouth. "Ourobori? What's the plural of ouroboros?"

Joseph chuckled. "I think it's ouroboroi—it's Greek." He bent to admire Clare's new bracelet. True to the symbol, it was a snake nibbling its own tail, with a black onyx eye and an articulated body of turquoise scales. It was exquisite—and very pagan.

Trying to decide whether to admonish Tessa for her choice, Joseph looked up to her. Tessa sat on the stairs now, reaching under her mass of petticoats to rub her left ankle.

"It's still bothering you?" Joseph asked.

"It only feels a little weak, now and again." Tessa smiled bravely. "'Tis nothing, really."

"Should *I* take over the chase?" David offered. He scrunched up his nose and curled his fingers as if they were cat claws. "I'm coming to get you, *souris*!"

Clare shrieked with joy and took off running again, this time into the gardens.

Joseph sat down beside Tessa on the staircase. "You're all right?"

She nodded and smiled at him with her eyes as much as her mouth, in the way that meant: *More than all right—you're here.*

Joseph and Tessa spoke of everything and nothing. From their perch halfway up the stairs, they watched his nephew chase her daughter around the hedges of the garden, and vice versa, till David came back to them carrying the girl over his shoulder like a barbarian with a war prize. But his prize was giggling.

TESSA DID NOT RELINQUISH her own slow conquest. The third time, she'd undone the three center buttons of Joseph's fall before he even realized her hand was there. That was all she unfastened; she ignored the nine remaining buttons and simply slipped her hand inside. She still wasn't touching *him*—his drawers and the tail of his shirt were in the way—but it was a very convincing approximation.

He couldn't object, because his tongue was tangled with hers. Each time he tried to break the contact, her mouth would pursue him relentlessly. Even her left hand at the nape of his neck served to trap him as much as caress him. Her siege was carefully planned. At first, she only cupped him as she had before. She waited for him to accept the onslaught of pleasure before she attempted her next attack. She lulled him into the delusion that this was somehow right —that this was somehow *his* right.

Gradually, her hand moved: tiny fingertip strokes that soon became more insistent. He knew this had gone far enough; he knew he should pull her hand out of his fall; but his own hands were in such delicious places: one teasing her breast, the other clasping her buttock. He could permit this a *little* while longer, couldn't he?

Even if he never withdrew her hand, the sin was in consent, and he hadn't actually consented; he hadn't *asked* her to stroke him like this, to press, to squeeze... *Now*—he must move her hand *now*...

But his own hands refused to obey him. The problem was not the weakness of his flesh; the problem was its strength. He felt each and every sensation blaze through him, but his body had become disconnected from his mind. He'd even lost control of his voice: he was grunting like some kind of animal. He could no longer delude himself that he hadn't consented, that he didn't want this, because his body was pressing toward hers: straining, shoving, rutting, leaping, twitching, jetting—all of him pouring into her hand, groaning into her neck, gripping her flesh, leaving and dying...

Sometimes he slept through his nocturnal pollutions, and sometimes they woke him. Never before had he been fully awake from beginning to end; never had he experienced in its full undiluted fury this blinding, deafening possession—like something demonic overtaking his body, his very will. He understood now: the lack of control had had nothing to do with fighting his way up from sleep. The punch of exhaustion had nothing to do with sleep either; it was simply the searing wake of this cataclysm. Other men *sought* this helplessness?

Having accomplished its vile work, the hand in his trousers had stilled, but Tessa continued caressing his hair. His face was buried in her neck now, and she turned her head to kiss his temple. As if she were praising him. When she'd just humiliated him.

He shoved her away from him and sat up, though his head swam with dizziness. The proof of what she'd done to him rearranged itself wetly inside his drawers. He tried to swallow his revulsion and spoke through clenched teeth. "Don't *ever* do that again."

"Was I pressing too hard? Should I have—"

His hands were fists, though Joseph didn't know who—or what —he intended to punish. "That's *not* why I'm here, Tessa!"

"I know that."

He forced his hands open, still trying to steady his breath. "If I can make *you* happy, that is enough."

"How can I be happy, when *you* are miserable?" Gingerly, she touched his face.

Joseph slapped her hand away. "I'm not miserable! I'm— I am *filthy*." He half-fell from the bed and staggered to her dressing chamber like a drunkard—which allowed the foul substance to dribble down his thigh. He slammed the door behind him, caught himself on the wall, and yanked out his handkerchief.

Tessa came to the door, but she didn't open it. "You said once that my pleasure was beautiful."

"It is!" The words came out sharper than he'd intended. He raised his eyes from the mess only to see himself framed in her dressing glass.

"Then how can *your* pleasure be filthy? How can it be wrong?"

How could she even ask such a question? Anyone else who saw him in this moment would be horrified: Father Lazare, "another Christ," standing here half-erect, sticky with sin, exposing himself in the dressing chamber of another man's wife. What Tessa had done—what he had allowed her to do—was nothing less than sacrilege: the profanation of his consecrated body.

He dropped his eyes from the mirror and attacked his testicles with the handkerchief. "Because *I* am a Priest, Tessa! After I leave you, I have to face not only God but also our Bishop, other Priests, seminarians, altar servers, communicants, penitents: hundreds of people who rely on me to remain holy—*incorrupt!* Hundreds of people who have far more of a claim on me than *you* do!" Couldn't she understand how selfish she was being?

Tessa said no more. In the silence, he cleaned himself up as best he could. Even after he'd scrubbed himself with soap, he still felt filthy.

He knelt and tried to pray. But in a room where he'd seen Tessa naked, he couldn't truly repent. He must return to the cathedral and make a proper Penance to the Real Presence on the altar. He also needed to change these fouled clothes.

As he crossed back into the bedchamber, he kept his eyes cast down. He had to find his socks. Only when he noticed how ragged her breathing was did he glance at Tessa. At least she wasn't naked anymore; she'd covered herself with her blue wrapper. Tears shining on her cheeks, she sat limply on the edge of the bed, watching him. She was only a few feet away, yet she seemed so distant now—so divorced from him.

When he sat on the méridienne to pull on his socks, she murmured: "'You must give yourself permission to experience this pleasure.'" It didn't sound like a command or even advice; it was simply an echo. Joseph recognized the words as his father's, written to her long ago.

Joseph didn't reply; he only tugged on his left boot.

"You'll come again, won't you?" Tessa realized her poor choice of verb, grimaced, and amended: "I mean: you won't stay away, because of this?"

He pulled on the other boot. "I don't know."

Tessa hurried to kneel at his feet. "I only wanted to give you what you have given me." She grasped one of his knees.

His fingers did not pause in fastening his boot buttons. He still couldn't look at her.

She was weeping again. "Do you think it has been easy for *me*: to offer up every inch of my body to your gaze, to your hands, to your mouth? Do you think I haven't been terrified? But *I trust you*, Joseph. Why won't you trust me?"

This wasn't *about* trust, let alone being terrified! It was about him being a Priest and nothing more.

"Tell me what to do, Joseph." Tessa clutched both of his legs now, as he struggled to retie his choker. "Tell me what to do to make it easier."

He stared past her to the bed they'd shared for so many nights now—the bed they would never share. Some wicked part of him answered: *You could tie me to the bedposts.* Aloud, he said only: "Promise me you won't ever try that again."

As fresh tears descended her cheeks, Tessa bowed her head and nodded.

He stood and pulled his coat back on. Since the bedchamber door was still tied shut, he left through the dressing chamber door. Dislodging the chair was easier. When he entered the hall, he saw Clare standing in her doorway, glaring at him. Joseph hesitated only a moment. What could he possibly say to her?

"You're supposed to make Mama *happy!*" the girl flung at him.

He hurried past her down the stairs.

Behind him, Tessa spoke to her daughter in a voice still thick with tears: "Please don't yell, *a chuisle*."

"You and Father were yelling!"

Joseph did not stop until he'd changed into clean clothes and prostrated himself in the cathedral for the Act of Contrition: "'Oh my God, I am heartily sorry for having offended Thee and I detest all my sins because of Thy just punishments, because I dread the loss of Heaven and the pains of Hell...'" He rose to his knees and struck his breast thrice, as if he were saying Mass: "'Lord, I am not worthy that Thou shouldst enter under my roof; but only say the word, and my soul shall be healed'—and my body shall be cleansed. Please, Father, have mercy on me. Do not withdraw Your grace because of this. Do not take away my Priesthood. I am nothing without it—nothing without You..."

CHAPTER 15

But none ever trembled and panted with bliss
In the garden, the field, or the wilderness,
Like a doe in the noontide with love's sweet want
As the companionless Sensitive Plant.
— Percy Bysshe Shelley, "The Sensitive Plant" (1820)

God must have accepted his contrition. A few hours later, when Joseph took the Body of Christ into his mouth, He made no sign of His displeasure.

Joseph dreaded facing Tessa almost as much as facing God, but he knew he couldn't stay away permanently. At night perhaps, but not during the day. He had to think of the children. They needed a father, and Edward wasn't interested in the role. "Everything they do irritates him," Tessa had told Joseph. "That plantation is the only 'child' he cares about." This week, her husband was supervising the sowing of his rice fields.

Yesterday, hours before Tessa had ruined everything, Joseph had suggested that he and Clare plant something too, a species that had fascinated him as a child. He'd promised to bring her the seeds today. His return would show Clare that a quarrel didn't mean he'd stopped loving her mother—or her. Having been given this time to reflect, perhaps Tessa would even apologize.

She'd left the blue lamp in her bedchamber window, but she'd extinguished it for the daytime. That *should* mean Edward was still absent. Even if the man appeared, Joseph told himself, he had a legitimate excuse to be visiting.

Tessa and her daughter sat on the piazza, their heads bent over a small book that they read aloud together: Tessa the questions, and Clare the answers. Joseph recognized it as Bishop England's catechism. The girl was preparing for her First Confession.

"'Can anyone come out of Hell?'" her mother read.

Clare answered solemnly: "'No; out of Hell there is no redemption.'"

And Tessa wondered that Joseph should fear offending God. The stakes could not be higher: they were gambling with their immortal souls. He must make Tessa understand. He was the Priest; he was the one who knew just how much they could dare to wager.

Mother and daughter saw him then. They both frowned, but Joseph forced himself to smile as if last night had never happened. "Good afternoon, ladies! I brought those seeds I promised Clare."

The girl brightened, albeit cautiously. "The sensitive plant that closes up when you try and touch it?" He knew she was eager to see it for herself: how at a single touch, the fern-like leaves would fold in on themselves, as if the plant were some shrinking maiden.

Joseph nodded. He pulled the botany book from his coat pocket and opened it to the color plate with the sensitive plant. He showed Clare the bipinnate leaves and the puffy pink flowers, but he concealed the text with his forefinger. "Do you remember the plant's Latin name? The genus and species Linnaeus assigned to it?"

Clare twisted up her lips, trying to remember. "*Mimosa...*"

Tessa set aside her catechism. "*Prudica,*" she finished before Joseph could.

He frowned and corrected: "*Pudica.* That's Latin for 'shy,' 'bashful,' or 'shrinking.' Besides 'sensitive plant,' another of its common names is the 'shy plant.' I've also seen it called the 'humble plant'— even the 'shameplant.'"

"Or: *Noli Me Tangere*," Tessa muttered, standing and pacing to the balustrade.

Joseph hadn't heard the Latin equivalent used, but he nodded. He continued to address her daughter. "It's called 'Touch-Me-Not' too—although that name is a bit misleading. Now, when it's mature, *Mimosa pudica* has prickly stems, and you wouldn't want to touch those. But the leaves won't hurt you at all—and your touching them won't hurt the plant. You shouldn't stroke it *too* often, I suppose— that would probably exhaust it." He withdrew the folded paper from his pocket. "I think Our Lord made it the way He did on purpose. He must have known how such motion would fascinate humans." Joseph opened the paper and showed Clare the small brown seeds. "But for all their sensitivity when they sprout leaves, the seeds are quite tough. Before they'll germinate, we'll need to scarify these and soak them."

Clare frowned. "We have to *scar* them?"

"It's a strange word, I know. It simply means we have to break through this hard coat"—he tapped a seed with his fingertip—"and expose the core. We can scarify them with a knife, a file—or a grater. I thought we might go to your kitchen, because we'll need to drop the seeds into boiling water after we've scarified them."

"It doesn't hurt them?"

"Not at all. It helps them. They need it to grow."

The girl nodded and stood. She stepped toward Joseph, then returned to take her mother's hand. Tessa had been doing her best to ignore Joseph. Clearly, she wasn't going to apologize any time soon. But Tessa would never neglect her daughter. When Clare asked: "You'll come too, won't you, Mama?" Tessa followed, however reluctantly.

The Stratfords' cook was shelling peas in the yard. Joseph saw smoke already drifting from the kitchen chimney, so he inquired: "May we borrow one of your burners, Tilly?"

"And the nutmeg grater?" Clare added.

"You gonna make a pudding?" the cook smiled, though she kept at the peas.

"I'm afraid not," Joseph answered.

"Well, suit yourself, chile."

While Clare selected a pot, Tessa found the grater and Joseph located a ceramic bowl. Mother and daughter filled the pot halfway from the water barrel. Tessa set the pot on the iron stove and then retreated. Apparently she loathed Joseph's presence so much, she would rather shell peas. But the kitchen windows were open, so he knew Tessa could still hear him.

Joseph spread the *Mimosa pudica* seeds on a cutting board and showed Clare how to scarify them with the grater. As she worked, the girl scowled in thought. Finally, she asked: "Father?"

"Yes, *souris?*"

"Why couldn't you—" She glanced toward the open windows and broke off. Tessa had schooled her well. "I mean: Why can't Priests get married?"

Joseph himself was more aware of Tessa's ears than those of any eavesdropping slave. "Well, Clare, we *are* married; and a man cannot have more than one wife."

"He can if he's an Indian."

Joseph smiled. "You are correct. But do you really think that is what God intended for us? Don't you think the wives might be jealous of one another? How could the husband love them equally? He'd have to split his heart in two."

"Who— Whom are you married to?"

"Have you heard the phrase 'Holy Mother Church'?"

"You marry your mother?"

"Not quite!" Joseph chuckled. "We say that a Priest enters a mystical marriage with the Church. The Church is the Mother, and the Priest is a Father to all believers. That's why you, and everyone else, call me 'Father.' A Priest tries to be like Christ. *He* never married, yet He is the Father of everyone. A Priest cannot marry because he must love everyone the same—he must treat everyone as his family."

Clare was frowning.

"Celibacy—that means 'remaining unmarried'—simply makes sense for Priests." Joseph strode to the stove, where the pot of water was beginning to boil. "You have to understand, *souris*: what *I've* been able to do—remain in the same parish for more than a decade, the parish where my family is—that is *very* rare. A Priest must be ready to go wherever he is needed. That might be on the other side of the world. It might be someplace dangerous, like China or India. The Priest might be killed for what he believes. But if that happens, he doesn't have to worry about leaving a widow or orphans. You see?"

"I guess." Clare was finished scarifying the seeds, so she only stood staring down at them.

"Here's another example: a few years ago, a man came to the Bishop's residence late at night and begged for my help. His daughter was sick with measles, and he needed a Priest. This man was an Episcopalian; but when he'd asked his own priest to come, he'd refused! The Episcopal priest had children too, and he didn't want to bring the measles back to them. So the father of the sick girl turned to a Catholic Priest—a *true* Priest with no other commitment but the care of souls." The pot was ready, so Joseph found a rag to protect his hand. "Not only did that girl recover from the measles, Clare, she and her family now attend Mass at our cathedral!"

Outside, Tessa muttered something unintelligible.

Joseph plucked the boiling pot from the stove. "*That* is why a Priest cannot have his own family." He poured the hot water into the ceramic bowl, then motioned for Clare to drop the seeds in the water. "Next time you see Bishop Reynolds, look at his left hand, and you'll see his ring. That symbolizes his marriage to the Church."

Clare paused, still holding the seeds, to stare at Joseph's left hand. "But *you* don't wear a ring."

Tessa entered the kitchen and threw down her peas, which leapt and shuddered in the bowl. "There is a band around his *heart*, Clare. Think of it like that."

CHAPTER 16

I speak to you, o charmers of the clergy, appetizing flesh of the devil...you bitches, sows, screech-owls, night-owls, she-wolves, blood-suckers...through your lovers you mutilate Christ... You snatch the unhappy men from their ministry of the sacred altar, in which they were engaged, that you may strangle them in the slimy glue of your passion. ... You suck the blood of miserable, unwary men... They should kill you...
— Cardinal Saint Peter Damian, *De Caelibatu Sacerdotum* (circa 1060)

It made no sense whatsoever. Any other woman would have sold her soul for a lover like him. He was practically Tessa's servant! She'd come how many times now, without his *ever* asking for anything in return? And *she* wasn't satisfied? Had she forgotten how much he risked simply to be with her?

No wonder Priests didn't take wives. God was easy to please by comparison. Women were impossible.

When they saw each other during the day, Tessa continued to ignore Joseph, snap at him, or stare at him with a haunted expression he might almost have mistaken for pity. With Clare and David, she was as tender and attentive as ever.

This was all for the best, Joseph told himself. Even if Tessa lit the blue lamp again, he wouldn't answer. He took the key to her garden gate from around his neck and deposited it at the back of his bureau drawer. Their nights together had gone far enough—too far. He and Tessa would return to being brother and sister. He would concentrate on being a proper Priest, and she would concentrate on being a mother.

Except he couldn't concentrate on anything but visions of her. He snatched the key back from his drawer. Tears stung his eyes at the feel of the iron between his fingers, as if by holding the key he were somehow holding Tessa again.

Day after day, year after year, Mass after Confession after sick call after Office for the Dead—his Priesthood allowed him to do so much good, but sometimes it all seemed like a relentless mill wheel grinding him down, drying him out. Tessa was his oasis, his "well of living waters." He could not bear to lose her.

But he was *not* going to apologize. *He* had done nothing wrong— or at least, not without her assistance.

ONE EVENING THAT JUNE, Joseph was trying to compose a eulogy at the desk in his bedchamber when his father leaned against his door-jamb. Without any other greeting, he crossed his arms over his chest and demanded: "What have you done?"

Since this question was rather vague, Joseph scowled and opened his mouth to make some clever rejoinder.

His father did not wait. "To Tessa," he clarified. "The pair of you have been moping about since March."

"What makes you assume the trespass is *mine*? In point of fact, Tessa—"

"Because that woman *loves* you, Joseph. If *she* were the one to blame, she would have apologized weeks ago." His father turned on his heel before Joseph could reply.

Joseph almost ran after him. What exactly was his father implying? That Joseph did *not* love Tessa? Did his father really think Joseph
would have risked his Priesthood, her reputation, and their immortal
souls for the sake of *lust*? If his father only knew what had caused
this impasse—how much Joseph had suffered for her—how little he
thought of himself. Everything he'd done had been for Tessa!

Summer passed into fall, and then the day came: the blue lamp
appeared in Tessa's window once more. Joseph knew if he returned
that evening, the burners would be lit. David had begun his final
year at South Carolina College. Joseph and Tessa could be alone
tonight.

He would go to her. He couldn't leave things as they were.

After Joseph made his way through the darkness of the garden
and the empty house, he found her pacing beside their lamp. Was
she still debating whether to extinguish it?

Tessa saw him and stopped. She came to him without a word.
She slid her arms around him and pressed her cheek to his shoulder.
He suspected this was her apology—or the nearest thing he
would get.

He closed his eyes and embraced her in return. But he knew
they were not yet reconciled. He let the silence drag out, to offer her
one last chance to repent, but still Tessa said nothing. Finally he
reminded her: "The night we saw *Lucia di Lammermoor*, you said:
'Whatever you can give me, Joseph, I will accept it gladly.'"

"I thought surely, once we were alone together, *you* would be the
one begging *me* for more." Her breaths grew unsteady. "I was
prepared for *that*." She pulled back just enough to gaze up at him
with those eyes of liquid myrrh. "There is nothing I wouldn't give
you, Joseph—nothing I wouldn't do for you."

He touched her face, letting his thumb caress her cheek. "Then
will you stop asking me for something that is impossible?"

Tessa closed her eyes. Her lashes were damp with tears. She
turned her face away. "Thy will be done."

Joseph frowned at this near-blasphemy. But tears were escaping her closed eyelids now. He pressed his lips to her cheeks and tasted the salt. "It will simply go back to the way it was before," he assured her.

But this proved impossible too. He did all the things he knew she liked best, yet Tessa's responses were nearly as weak as they'd been the night after she learned of her father's death. Her sole climax was a struggle for them both. Even then, it felt more like a capitulation than a celebration. Somehow the joy of it had vanished, leaving only a scrabbling desperation.

HE WOULDN'T FAIL HER a second time. He would find a way to delight her again. In the spring, he came to her full of plans.

"I have an idea. We'll pull the curtains closed around your bed. We won't be able to *see* anything, but losing one sense will make the others more acute. You'll have to trust me, but you said..." He trailed off. She'd smiled when he'd entered, but with every passing moment, dread overtook more of her features. "Tessa? What is it?"

"Do you think perhaps we might simply hold each other tonight, my love? I am so tired, and..."

"Are you ill?"

"No; but..." Tessa averted her eyes.

"It's Edward, isn't it?" Joseph squeezed her arm just above the elbow, willing her to look back at him. Tessa winced. He dropped his hand at once. "What has he done to you?"

"Sometimes, when I have made him angry and he has drunk too much, he is...especially rough."

Joseph kept staring at Tessa's left arm. Slowly, he reached for the buttons of her chemise. Tessa did not fight him; she submitted without a word, just as she always submitted to her husband. As tenderly as he could, Joseph peeled her wrapper from her left shoulder and eased the wide neck of her chemise down to her elbow. A purple bruise the size of Edward's hand stained her pale skin. Joseph let out a shaking breath. "You told me he never struck you."

"He hasn't," she said quickly.

This was hardly better. Were there other bruises? Did her husband think he was asserting his ownership by branding her flesh in this way? He was lower than a dog pissing on a lamppost. "Tessa, is this because of me?"

She shook her head. "Edward doesn't need a reason to do what he does."

Joseph still felt responsible. If *he* were Tessa's husband... Joseph wished he could challenge Edward to a duel—or at least throttle him. Instead, he only bent his head and brushed his lips over her bruise, as if he had the power to heal it with a kiss.

Tessa stared down at him, her eyes pleading. "Could we simply..."

"Whatever you need, darling."

~

HE AND TESSA WOULD FIND EACH OTHER AGAIN, in spite of her husband, in spite of Joseph's Priesthood. It was a new year, halfway to a new century. They had every reason to be hopeful. If the slave states and the free states could reach a compromise, then so could he and Tessa.

But the Compromise of 1850 came at a terrible price: a new fugitive slave law. The free states were no longer truly free. On pain of imprisonment and crippling fines, not only federal officials but also ordinary citizens were now required to assist slave catchers in hunting down runaways. "Just when Hannah and her family have become settled, they must flee all over again," Tessa muttered.

1850 brought other changes too. The Holy See divided their vast diocese into two, allowing Bishop Reynolds to concentrate on their new cathedral. He began by permitting another fair—with stipulations. Last year, the *tableaux vivants*, the fortuneteller, and the young ladies selling confectionary in the shape of kisses might have been the most profitable booths; but these were not appropriate ways to fund a house of God.

At least this year's raffle proved a success. The grand prize was a complete set of parlor furniture donated by one of their colored parishioners, whose skill with wood was extraordinary. The building fund passed $20,000 that summer, which emboldened His Lordship to engage an architect and lay the cornerstone at last.

Their new cathedral would be Gothic in style and almost four times the size of Bishop England's wooden structure, with a spire reaching over two hundred feet into the sky—higher than any other building in Charleston, including the Protestant churches. Joseph only regretted that the larger cathedral would obliterate most of his Biblical garden. The ground where he'd met Tessa would be consecrated as a chapel.

That May, Joseph's nephew (almost nineteen now) graduated from South Carolina College. David would finish his medical studies in Paris; but for the next two years, he would remain in Charleston. He intended to go into practice here, and the Low Country had its own unique disease climate. So David would begin by apprenticing with his grandfather and attending lectures at the Medical College of the State of South Carolina. Most men would do no more than this—or even less—before hanging out a sign and attaching "Doctor" to their names.

David agreed with his grandfather: such behavior was irresponsible. "Medicine might be an imperfect science," Joseph's nephew admitted, "but every year brings new discoveries. My aunt had to endure surgery in a state of terror, fully conscious and sensible to each slice and probe. Now, ether and chloroform are changing that. Perhaps someday, we'll understand the inflammations that follow surgery. We might even be able to prevent puerperal fever."

Joseph knew David was thinking of his mother and baby brother.

"Why do *some* transfusions of blood succeed and others fail?" the boy continued passionately.

Joseph smiled his encouragement. "Perhaps *you* will be the one to tell us, David."

. . .

CLARE WAS DELIGHTED to have her foster-brother back under the same roof. David warned her that his studies would occupy him most of the day, even into the night. But after his return to Charleston, he permitted himself a week's furlough before he began training with his grandfather. Clare immediately re-enlisted David as her play-fellow. "Mama isn't any good at playing a boy!" the girl complained. "Her voice just sounds silly!" And of course Edward would never dream of indulging his daughter.

At the end of that week, Joseph climbed the stairs to the playroom to find Clare using one of her mother's petticoats as a tipi. She sat cross-legged inside it, her hair in two braids with a turkey feather tucked behind one ear. She still wore her ouroboros bracelet.

Joseph chuckled and looked to his nephew. "I see Clare is an Indian princess again."

David nodded. He was on his knees before the tipi with a pile of toys beside him. "An Indian princess who is *impossible* to please. I am a brave who's trying to woo her. But none of my gifts have impressed her. I went all the way to Africa and brought her back zebras, and still she won't have me."

"I'm not 'impossible to please'!" the girl objected. "I want only one thing."

"Will you tell me what it is then, Princess?" David pleaded.

"All the other braves have two, three, six wives! I want you to promise that you won't ever take another wife—that you'll love only me."

"That's all?"

"Do you *promise?*"

David placed a hand against his heart and bowed his head in mock solemnity. "I promise, Princess."

"Then you may kiss me." Clare climbed out of the tipi, leaned into him, and tapped her cheek. David smiled and obliged. She threw her arms around his neck. "Do you mean it?"

"Mean what?"

"That you won't have any wife but me?"

He pulled back. "Um, Clare— Princess— Which one of you is asking?"

Neither seemed to have heard the question. The girl only kissed *him* on the cheek with great enthusiasm. "I love you, David!"

"I love you too, *souris*; but you understand that I was only *preten*—"

She didn't let him finish. She stood up abruptly, curtseyed a greeting to Joseph, and sauntered into the hall, humming to herself.

David frowned after her. "She doesn't understand what being a wife really means." He looked to Joseph. "Do you think I should talk to her?"

Joseph couldn't resist. "About what being a wife really means?"

The boy colored at once. "O-Of course not; her mother will do that. I mean about Clare being *my* wife; I mean—"

He was only growing more uncomfortable, so Joseph suggested: "Do you have another young lady in mind?"

"No; not at all."

"Well, by the time you do, I'm sure Clare will be old enough to understand that there's a difference between romantic and brotherly affection."

David nodded. "I have to concentrate on medical school and then…" He stood. He was as tall as Joseph now. "I know I'm the last of the Lazares. I know it will disappoint Grandma, and I think Grandpa wants me to marry too. But I'd rather be like you, Father. I mean, without— I would rather be celibate and devote myself to my work."

"By celibate, I hope you also mean chaste?"

The boy blushed anew. "Of course, Father."

"If that will make you happy, then I applaud your dedication to your vocation, David." Joseph put his hand on his nephew's shoulder. "Fortunately, *you* will be able to change your mind at any time."

CLARE'S HAPPINESS DID NOT LAST LONG. The next evening, Tessa's husband evicted David over dinner. "Since you'll be apprenticing with your grandfather, it makes sense for you to live with him,"

Edward had observed. "Besides, Archdale Street is closer to the Medical College."

By now, Tessa and David knew how the man worked. Edward wasn't making a suggestion. He was giving a command.

Clare had understood too. She'd burst into tears.

The move was logical. "But I hate the thought of leaving Tessa and Clare alone with that brute," the boy seethed to Joseph. "We've had rows about it: me defending Tessa or Clare, telling Edward he has no right to speak to them like that, and him yelling that I've no right to say anything at all. He knows I'm not afraid of him anymore. I think *he* is afraid of *me* now. Edward is a coward at heart. *That's* why he wants me gone—so he can abuse his wife and daughter unchallenged."

With a great deal of effort, Joseph swallowed his fury and his impotence. "What does he do to them?"

"He grabbed Clare and shook her once. I don't want to think about what he does to Tessa when the door is closed. Mostly he just flings words—but they cut as deep as daggers. The smallest thing will infuriate Edward—anything he can construe as defiance." David rubbed a hand over his mouth. "I don't know; maybe *I* made it worse. Maybe he'll calm down now that I'm gone."

Silently, Joseph prayed that would be true. "And do you think Edward will keep his promise to pay for your medical training?"

"I think so. If he doesn't, Grandfather and I could sue him for breach of contract, couldn't we? *That* would bring dishonor to the illustrious name of Stratford." David rolled his eyes. "Edward would never risk that. Terrorizing his wife and daughter, on the other hand, is perfectly acceptable."

PART IV
THE PEARL OF GREAT PRICE

1850-1851

CHARLESTON

Yet each man kills the thing he loves…

— Oscar Wilde,
The Ballad of Reading Gaol (1898)

CHAPTER 17

I saw a dream that affrighted me: and my thoughts in my bed, and
the visions of my head troubled me.
— Daniel 4:5

David's absence from Tessa's house meant Joseph could not
visit her as often—at least not openly. To make matters
worse, her husband slept at home every night in October. Then
Tessa and Clare spent November at the plantation with him. It was
well into Advent before they returned to Church Street, and nearly
Christmas before Edward left his wife and daughter alone. At last,
Tessa set the blue lamp in her window once more.

The Jaune Desprez roses had surrendered for the winter, but the
Lamarques persevered in spite of the chill. Tessa was waiting for
Joseph near their ghostly white blooms. As soon as she saw him, she
unclasped her hands from her shawl to embrace him.

He thought of the bruises Edward had left on her skin—and
how the time before that, no matter how Joseph had tried, he'd
brought her so little pleasure. "I am still worth the risk?" he
whispered.

"I need you now more than ever, Joseph."

Upstairs, they performed their rituals of enclosure: they shut the jalousies, wedged the chair beneath the door handle in her dressing chamber, and anchored the bedchamber door to the bedpost. Joseph added logs to the fire in her hearth, and Tessa extinguished their lamp.

He undressed her first, layer by magnificent, blasted layer. To his relief, Joseph saw no evidence of her husband's abuse tonight. At last, Tessa stood naked before him, her tresses cascading nearly to the floor, the firelight gilding her perfection. His fingers ached to caress her shoulders, her breasts, the thatch of hair at her center. But already he saw the sorrow in her eyes, as she gazed at him with equal yearning.

She began reverently, with the garments he always allowed her to remove: his coat, choker, shoes, socks, and waistcoat. She knew not to try for his fall. But when she reached for his braces, he did not stop her. His trousers weren't going to fall down between here and the bed.

He heard her breaths quicken with excitement as she raised her hands to his shirt buttons next. Her motions tickled the sparse mat of dark hair at the top of his chest. He did his very best to stand as still as a statue and not to respond. He let her pull his shirt free of his trousers. She'd done as much the night after the hurricane, and he had withstood it.

As Tessa slipped her hands *beneath* his shirt, her grin spread to her eyes—even to the tendons of her neck and the pitch of her shoulders. How he'd missed that expression, that whole-hearted joy. He felt it too, the thrill of this difference. However thin the barrier of a well-worn cotton shirt, skin to skin was something else entirely.

Her fingers kept climbing. By clasping his hands over hers through the fabric, he arrested her just beneath his nipples. "Not so far."

So Tessa skimmed her hands around his sides to his back, learning every contour of his skin, lingering at each vertebra as if it were made of gold. Inside his shirt, she teased the edges of his shoulder-blades as if they contained invisible keys. He felt the music resounding inside him.

She kissed his Adam's apple as she had so many times before. Then she pulled one hand from beneath his shirt. When her fingers brushed the hair on his chest, Joseph flinched. But Tessa only grasped the key to her garden and draped it between his shoulder-blades like a scapular.

Her hands returned to exploring his back, sinking lower, while her lips glided down his throat with torturous slowness. She pressed her mouth to every inch of exposed skin, even the hairy parts. She kissed him deeper and yet deeper, till her teeth were grazing his flesh. At his back, her fingers slipped inside his drawers, clutching the upper curves of his buttocks.

He couldn't take much more of this. He suspected she couldn't either. He brought her mouth up to his and stopped all her objections.

Together, they stumbled to the bed. There, he regained control, and she surrendered willingly. She also seized every opportunity to slide her hands beneath his shirt again. Her sighs and moans were very encouraging. He hadn't lost his skills after all. Her clitoris didn't lie.

And then, without warning, she was shoving his head away. Like a child determined to keep a sweet, his hands clung instinctively to her buttocks. But her heels scrabbled against his shoulders, and she managed to sit up in spite of him. When Joseph started to protest, to ask what he'd done wrong, Tessa clapped her hand over his mouth.

Her eyes were wide with horror, but she wasn't looking at him. He followed her gaze to the bedchamber door. The handle was still tied to the bedpost; but it was *rattling*.

In that moment that lasted a lifetime, as he lay there propped on his elbows between Tessa's bare legs, a dozen thoughts plummeted through Joseph's brain: *It's Edward! He's returned early! How much did he hear? Can I climb down from the piazza before he decides to try the windows there? I don't have time to find all my clothes! I can't leave Tessa alone with him! He'll see us together, like this! He'll THROW me from the piazza and strangle Tessa...*

Then, on the other side of the door, a feeble voice called: "Mama?"

Joseph and Tessa both exhaled.

"I told you to *knock*!" Tessa groaned. But she was the first to leap from the bed.

"I f-forgot." Clare sounded as if she was speaking through sobs.

Tessa was already dashing to her dressing chamber. She paused on the threshold. "What's wrong, *a chuisle?*"

"I had— It *must* have been a dream; but…"

"I will be there in only a moment." Tessa retrieved her gold silk dressing gown and fastened it quickly.

Safely away from the incriminating bed, Joseph tidied his face with his handkerchief, then assessed his own attire. He was barefoot, but his trousers were intact. A shirt was an undergarment, yes; but would Clare even see him? He buttoned frantically nonetheless.

"Let me *in*," the girl begged while Tessa struggled to untie the door handle. As soon as it was open, Clare flung herself at her mother. When Tessa urged her into the hall, the girl cried out: "Please don't make me go back there!"

"'Twas only a dream, *a chuisle*. 'Tis over now. You can tell me all about it in your own bed."

"No!" Clare shrieked. She tore away from her mother and ran to the méridienne, where Joseph was donning his socks. Clare pounced on the seat, threw her arms around his waist, and buried her face in his shoulder. "Don't make me go back!"

Tessa sighed and came to stroke her daughter's hair. "All right. You may stay—for a little while."

The girl scowled down at the boot in Joseph's hand. "You'll stay too, won't you?"

He hesitated. "Do you *want* me to stay?"

She nodded fiercely. Her nose dripped. Normally, Joseph would offer a weeping female his handkerchief… Fortunately, Tessa pulled a fresh one from the little table at her bedside. Clare released her grip on Joseph so she could blow her nose. After Tessa sat down next to her daughter, he took the opportunity to add more wood to the fire.

Her eyes on her snotty handkerchief, the girl asked: "Father, do you know what dreams mean, like Joseph in the Old Testament?"

He adjusted the last log, then returned to the méridienne. "If you tell me your dream, I can *try* to interpret it."

"We were visiting Aunt Amelia in Greenville. Father wanted—" Clare looked back to Joseph. "Not you, Father. *My* father wanted to buy some land there for himself. I went with him to see it. I don't know why you weren't there, Mama. It was just me and Father. We got up to the highest mountain, higher than I've ever been. I wanted to see everything below, so I got closer and closer to the edge. But then the rocks slipped out from under me, and I started falling. I caught myself on this little tree, but I didn't know how long I could hold on. I looked below me, and everything was twice as far as before!" Clare glanced between her mother and Joseph, as if afraid they wouldn't believe her. "I called and called for help. Finally, I saw Father. I know he saw me—he was looking right at me! But he didn't move. He didn't say a word. He just stared at me, like he *wanted* me to fall. My arms hurt so much. I tried to keep holding on, but I couldn't." She was sobbing again. "I fell and fell… Even when I woke up and saw my own bed, I could *still* feel myself falling, like there was no mattress, no floor—nothing underneath me. I thought I'd *never* stop falling…"

"But you *did* stop, *a chuisle*—you were never falling at all," her mother assured her, squeezing her hand. "You are perfectly safe."

Clare gazed up at him pleadingly. "What does it mean, Father?"

It means you don't trust your own father—and you shouldn't. But one glance at Tessa reminded Joseph that she would not permit him to disparage Edward. "Well, *souris*, I think…you are feeling alone because David doesn't live here anymore, and you know he will be going away for school in a couple of years. You're afraid that if you're ever in trouble, no one will come to help you." Joseph looked back to Tessa. "But your mother loves you more than her own heartbeat, Clare, and *she* will never leave you." He took the girl's small hand and brushed his thumb across its back. "If you ever need *my* help, I will come running too. We will never let you fall."

Slowly, grasping both their hands, the girl nodded, though her face was still tight with fear.

"I know dreams can be very convincing—so convincing that

your body believes they're real. But they're not. They never happened, and they never will happen."

Clare's chin quivered. "But what if I go back to sleep and I have the same dream?"

"You won't," Tessa told her.

"But how can you—"

"Because I am going to bless you, Clare," Joseph said. "I will ask Our Lord and your guardian angel to protect you. Together, we are better than any pagan charm." He gave a little tug on the ouroboros bracelet she apparently wore even to bed.

The girl sniffled and managed a smile now. "And then, will you sing me that lullaby about the hens?"

Joseph chuckled. "I promise."

"And you'll say the towns, Mama?"

"I will."

"The towns?" Joseph asked.

"Sometimes I send her to sleep with the names of towns in County Clare," Tessa explained. "We both find them soothing."

Her daughter slid down from the méridienne—only to bound across the room and up onto her mother's bed.

"Clare!" Tessa chided, standing up. "I didn't mean— I want you back in your *own* bed."

"No!" Clare planted her head against the pillows and flung the sheet up over her. "I'm staying *here*!" At least there was more obstinacy than terror in her protests now.

Tessa let out a great sigh and looked to Joseph. "I'm sorry," she whispered.

He felt the lost chance just as keenly; but he answered in a low voice: "You don't have to apologize. You are hers first." *And mine, not at all.*

Tessa yanked down the sheet to reveal Clare's giggling face, then joined her on the bed. Tucked close to each other, the bodies of mother and daughter formed a sort of loop. Very like the girl's bracelet. The only empty space remaining lay at Clare's back. When Tessa noticed this too, she asked her daughter to "move over, just a bit" so that Tessa herself could shift to the middle of the bed.

Standing beside them on the rug, Joseph hesitated, knowing he did not belong. But Clare reminded him: "You promised to bless me and sing to me!"

"I can do that well enough from here."

"I want *all* the verses!" the girl insisted.

"Stay with us," Tessa implored.

Joseph decided on a compromise: he blessed Clare *before* he climbed into bed with her mother. Narrow as the space was allotted to him, curled as she was, Tessa's silk-clad buttocks were impossible to avoid. Clearly, Joseph needed to spend more time on this side of her. She did not seem to mind his proximity. In fact, she settled her warm curves more snugly against him, though her eyes remained on her child.

Miraculously, Joseph remembered all seven verses of "Une petite poule grise." The words were silly: about hens laying eggs everywhere from a church to the moon. But in French, it all rhymed, and his voice seemed to please Clare. It pleased her mother too. She managed to twine one of her slender legs between his, as if anchoring him to her bed.

Finally, Tessa kissed her daughter's forehead and added her own lullaby. "In County Clare, there is Ballygareen, Ballymaconna, Carrowlagan, Cloonteen, Derrycarran, Doonsallagh, Glascloon, Killernan, Knockalisheen…"

Joseph's blessing, the French rhymes, or the Irish invocation lulled Clare back to sleep. Lying there with his head propped on one elbow, watching the girl's untroubled breaths, Joseph could almost believe that nothing and no one would ever dare distress her again.

"When your father told me I had a daughter," Tessa whispered, "I knew Edward would be disappointed—but *I* was relieved. My husband would dote on a son, but he would also mold him in his own image. I thought a daughter could be *mine*." Her voice darkened with bitterness. "But Edward is beginning to realize that girls grow into women. More and more, he voices his displeasure at my 'little Irish hoyden.' He wants to control Clare now, to remake her. I am so frightened for her, Joseph—for her future. What will her life be like ten years from now?" Tessa had turned partway toward him, though she could not tear her eyes away from Clare for long—as if her daughter might be snatched away if she did not keep watch. "The men Edward will push her toward, the men he'll want as a son-in-law, the heirs of the great plantations—most of them are worse than he is. He is cruel only when he is drunk. But the other men of his class… They behave like English aristocrats. They expect the world to bow at their feet. If anyone does not grovel sufficiently, they resort immediately to violence. By the time these men court Clare, they'll already have forced themselves on their slaves. The 'best' ones are simply frivolous. I wish I could take her away from here, start again somewhere Clare could make her own choices, somewhere she could marry for love and not money." Tessa's eyes were swimming with tears now. She clasped the hand Joseph had laid on her waist. "I want Clare to know what I have known with you: what 'tis like to be loved by a good man for *herself*—not for her dowry or her exterior."

Joseph had been listening—truly he had—but he was also relishing Tessa's warmth, how every soft curve and crevice of her fit against his own body. She was quivering with the passion of her words, and the vibrato was thrilling. He was wondering if they might slip into her dressing chamber and finish what they'd started without disturbing Clare. He kissed Tessa's hair at her temple, where the strands shone like honey in the firelight. "I happen to be very fond of your exterior."

The way Tessa glowered at him, Joseph knew at once he'd made a mistake. "If Clare were *your* daughter, you would not be so flippant."

He sighed and looked back to the girl sleeping beside them. "I'm sorry. I pray for her every day, Tessa—and for you."

She turned away from him again. "I've been reading about the history of this country, so that I can teach it to Clare. During the Revolution, Thomas Paine wrote: 'If there must be trouble, let it be in my day, that my child may have peace.' If I could believe that everything I've endured has a purpose… That is why I married Edward: to give my children a better life than my own. But I didn't understand then…"

"We live in a fallen world, Tessa. No mother can guarantee her child's happiness—not on this side of the grave. But she *can* direct her child toward God's peace."

As Clare's spiritual Father, Joseph should be doing the same. Instead, he was here: in her mother's bed with his penis pressed between Tessa's buttocks. This was not the path to peace, not for any of them.

He knew Tessa was right to worry about her daughter. He couldn't stop thinking about the girl's dream. Had it been a premonition, like those in the Bible? If Edward learned of Tessa's "fall," would he punish Clare for it too? Neither South Carolina nor the Church would allow him to divorce Tessa, but Edward could prevent her from seeing her child.

Tessa would not survive such a separation. She might even... Joseph would never forget her despair when she'd lost Clare's brothers and sisters: Tessa had wanted to destroy herself. If Clare survived the loss of her mother, and if she married a man of Edward's choosing, she would be a very different woman from the thoughtful, vivacious girl she was now.

God had been merciful. He had given Joseph the chance to repent of his selfishness and choose the right path before it was too late. Clare's dream had been a sign of things "Yet to Come," like the Third Spirit in that Christmas story by Dickens. Joseph must never visit this house at night again.

But when Clare had interrupted them, Tessa had been *so close...* One more time. One more time, and he would find a way to end this. For all their sakes.

CHAPTER 18

Why has our author selected such a theme? ... Is it, in short, because a running underside of filth has become as requisite to a romance, as death in the fifth act to a tragedy? Is the French era actually begun in our literature? ... The whole tendency of the conversation is to suggest a sympathy for their sin, and an anxiety that they may be able to accomplish a successful escape...

— Reverend Arthur Cleveland Coxe, "The Writings of Hawthorne" in *The Church Review* (1851)

When infirmity prevented his parishioners from attending the cathedral, Joseph brought the Sacraments to them. In April, a few days before Easter, he visited Lucy Carmody, a young crippled woman. He had just removed his violet stole when Lucy's mother returned with the washing. Their home consisted of a single room, and she did not bother to knock.

"Did you confess your wicked book?" Mrs. Carmody pressed her daughter. "You won't believe what I caught her reading, Father —this very morning, when she *should* have been preparing her soul for you! I could tell it was a wicked book from the title." She plucked a brown cloth volume from the refuse bin, yanked open the cover, and shoved it in Joseph's face. It smelled like onions. The title page read:

THE SCARLET LETTER,
A ROMANCE.
BY NATHANIEL HAWTHORNE

"Tell her, Father. Tell her she's committed a mortal sin by reading such filth."

"I..." Joseph stammered. Romantic novels tended to be frivolous—venial sins—but filthy? "I'm not familiar with—"

"Then take it, Father. By all means, take it out of this house. Open it to any page and you'll see how depraved it is."

Reluctantly, Joseph accepted the book.

Lucy gazed at it with longing. "But everybody's reading it, Mama!"

"Then 'everybody' is going to Hell in a hand-basket! The 'heroine' is a scarlet woman, Father! This Hawthorne compares her to the Blessed Virgin! Makes a living martyr out of her and expects you to feel sorry for her! Not only is she an adulteress—the partner in her sin is her own priest!" Mrs. Carmody planted her hands on her hips and narrowed her eyes at him. "I see you going pale, Father. I looked just like that when *I* read it. At least this Hawthorne fellow has the decency not to make his fornicator a *Catholic* priest. Nobody would believe that! That's why I am proud to call myself a Catholic." Mrs. Carmody thumped her chest. "*I* can hold my head high, with a man like you as my curate. I can say to myself: *My Priest is a proper Priest!* He wouldn't even *dream* of touching a woman! Pure as the driven snow, he is!"

Joseph dropped his gaze to the floor. Only last night, he'd dreamed wetly of Tessa. Usually this calmed his restlessness at least a little; instead, he'd been in a foul mood all day. He was convinced now: their spring chance had passed, and he and Tessa would have to wait until fall to be alone again. It was the middle of Holy Week, and all he could think about was the body of another man's wife.

If you only knew... The thought echoed again and again, not only as Joseph fled the Carmodys, but as every other parishioner greeted him that day. *Why do you trust me?* he wanted to shout at them. *Why do you think me so far above you? Can't you see what I am? I have corrupted an innocent wife and mother! If you knew what I've done, what I long to do...*

By the time he finished his parish calls, Joseph had nearly forgotten what had prompted all this shame and contrition: the novel at the bottom of his portmanteau. He supposed he had been trying willfully to put it out of his mind. The romance of a priest and an adulteress? Joseph certainly couldn't let the Bishop see him with this.

But if "everybody" was devouring *The Scarlet Letter*, other penitents were sure to ask their Priest if reading it was a mortal sin or only a venial one. Joseph had a duty to advise them. He could ask Bishop Reynolds or Father Lynch if the Church had already condemned the book...or he could read it for himself.

In the privacy of his bedchamber, with a lamp glowing on the bedside table, Joseph began to read. Set in Puritan Massachusetts two centuries before, *The Scarlet Letter* told the story of Hester Prynne and the consequences of her adultery with her pastor, Arthur Dimmesdale.

Sometimes, Hester reminded Joseph of Tessa. She was stubborn —and braver than the priest she had loved in secret. Standing at the pillory, staring into his eyes, she still refused to condemn him. "Would that I might endure his agony, as well as mine!" she cried.

Joseph admired her along with Dimmesdale: "Wondrous strength and generosity of a woman's heart!"

But of course it was the priest himself who transfixed Joseph. Hawthorne disparaged the true Church—he called it "the old, corrupted faith of Rome." Yet as this fictional Puritan clergyman wrestled with his conscience, Joseph felt as if the author had stolen his own thoughts:

> It is inconceivable, the agony with which this public veneration tortured him! ... He longed to speak out, from his own pulpit, at the full height of his voice, and tell the people what he was. "I, who have laid the hand of baptism on your children,—I, who

have breathed the parting prayer over your dying friends...I, your pastor, whom you so reverence and trust, am utterly a pollution and a lie!"

In the end, the priest's guilt destroyed him. But when Joseph closed the novel, it was another declaration that resounded in his head, rebuttal, justification, and lodestar: "What we did had a consecration of its own." Marriage was a Sacrament, a pouring out of God's grace; but what Joseph and Tessa shared was a union far holier than her contract with Edward.

WHEN TESSA AND CLARE removed to Sullivan's Island for the summer, Edward permitted Joseph and David to visit. Or at least, he did not expressly forbid it.

In July, Joseph's nephew helped Tessa's daughter build a great sand castle. Joseph and Tessa brought out two folding wooden chairs to watch their progress. But in truth, they only glanced toward the children for the sake of appearances. He and Tessa left enough space between them that anyone passing would not raise an eyebrow; and when anyone did pass, their conversation shifted.

Tessa wore a sheer white dress, more transparent than her finest wrapper. Her petticoats covered her from her feet to her waist, and the bodice was lined to conceal her corset. But her slender arms tantalized him behind the thinnest veil of muslin, as did her nearly-bare shoulders and throat. A day dress that revealed just as much skin as an evening gown—it would have been scandalous if it weren't the latest fashion. For a Charleston summer, it certainly made sense. *It must be cool,* Joseph thought, as he perspired in his own ecclesiastical black. He'd left his coat and gloves at the cottage, but he dared not remove any more in company.

With her left hand, Tessa kept hold of her parasol. With her right, she leaned down to undo her boot laces. "May I tell you a secret?" she asked over the crash and murmur of the waves.

"Of course."

"I'm not wearing garters." Tessa grinned and peeled off her stocking.

Joseph chuckled, staring enviously as she wiggled her toes in the wet sand.

"Surely you could do the same?" she suggested as she started on her other boot.

His socks didn't require garters. Joseph glanced about for spies but didn't see any. Then he freed himself of his boots.

Tessa sank both feet into the sand and gave a little moan of contentment. "May I tell you another secret?"

"Please."

"I'm not wearing drawers, either."

This time, Joseph laughed loud enough to attract Clare's attention. She left David at the sand castle and hurried over. Before the girl reached them, Joseph glared at her mother and muttered affectionately: "Temptress."

"What?" Clare inquired upon her arrival, glancing between Joseph and Tessa. "Did Mama tell you a joke? I want to hear it too!"

"It was a grown-up joke," her mother assured her.

"Tell it to me," the girl begged.

"I will tell you when you are…fifteen."

"But I'm barely halfway there!" Clare groaned.

"As Father Joseph will tell you: 'Patience is the greatest virtue,'" Tessa admonished, though she tossed him a smile.

Joseph tried to *stop* smiling and nod with Priestly gravity. "*Tout vient à celui qui sait attendre.*"

"Do you know what Father Joseph just said?" Tessa prompted.

"'All things come to those who wait.'" Clare rolled her eyes and stalked back to David.

Yet waiting to have Tessa again was driving Joseph mad. He must find a way to distract himself from her bare skin and lack of drawers. He stared down at his feet submerged in the sand. "How have you been faring with Edward?"

"For the moment, he is ignoring us again." Tessa sighed. "He is busy training his protégé."

"Edward has a protégé?"

"Technically, Mr. Cromwell is his secretary; but Edward treats him more like the son I never gave him—or at least a favorite nephew. The man is David's age, and according to Edward, twice as brilliant. I told you Edward's father left the estate in debt when he died? Even more than most?"

"You did." Year after year, the elder Mr. Stratford had continued to spend beyond his means, throwing too many lavish balls and investing in too many unreliable racehorses.

"Well, Mr. Cromwell is helping Edward balance his account books. Today they're out inspecting a parcel of Sea Island property. It will mean more debt initially, but you know how successful long-staple cotton has been." Tessa squinted at him. "Or perhaps you don't. *I* know far more about Carolina plantations than I would care to. But not, apparently, as much as a twenty-year-old Englishman."

"Not only is his name Cromwell, he is actually English?" Joseph chuckled. "No wonder you dislike him!"

"Am I so transparent?" Tessa laughed too, at least a little. "He is not the 'butcher of Drogheda'; I know that. And still, I do not trust him. He is *too* polite. Compliments roll off his tongue like…tobacco spittle. Not that Mr. Cromwell chews tobacco—he is far too fastidious! 'Tis only…he has made himself indispensable so quickly." She shook her head. "Perhaps 'tis nothing; perhaps 'tis only my Irish prejudice, and Mr. Cromwell is the Godsend Edward thinks him. After all, if *I* had the ability to discern a man's heart from so brief an acquaintance, I would not be Edward's wife." Before Joseph could offer any words of comfort, Tessa went on: "And you, my love?"

Joseph glanced about them again. Even the children weren't near enough to hear, but he wished she would refrain from such endearments outside of her bedchamber.

"Until I mentioned my garters, you seemed so somber. Is it something you can tell me?"

Slowly, Joseph nodded. "Bishop Reynolds has made his decision. He will not be reopening the seminary in the fall. Much like a plantation, a diocese must be mindful of its account books—and what will drive it further into debt."

He saw her hand twitch instinctively—he knew she wanted to reach for him; but the distance was just too far. "Oh Joseph, I'm so sorry. You'll miss teaching, won't you?"

He looked past the children and their sand castle to the sea. "I'll still be a catechist; but that is nearly all rote. It is different, being a professor. Sixteen years ago, when Bishop England first asked me to teach at the seminary, I was terrified. I thought I would loathe every minute. But now… The chance to affect so many lives—the lives of Priests, men who will affect so many others—the excuse never to cease learning myself…" Joseph looked back to Tessa. "I will miss it very much. And I also think…this may mean other changes." He dropped his eyes to his feet again. "Bishop England kept me in Charleston largely to *be* a professor, because my education in Rome qualified me so well. Now that the seminary is closed…"

Joseph was not ambitious; he didn't expect or even want a bishopric; but to be trapped in the limbo of curacy for the rest of his life… While Father Baker was pastor at the cathedral, he'd given Joseph a great deal of freedom in the exercise of his office. If a parishioner wished Joseph to administer a Sacrament, Father Baker had always allowed it. His concern was for souls, not which of them received donations for services. But four years before, Bishop Reynolds had moved Father Baker to St. Mary's and advanced Father Lynch to the cathedral. Joseph was five years his new pastor's senior, yet he had to seek Father Lynch's permission for every Baptism, Viaticum, Extreme Unction, and wedding Mass. Often, Father Lynch refused Joseph's requests and performed the Sacrament himself—unless, Joseph had noticed, the parishioners were colored. "I am nearly forty years old, yet I am still a curate, while parishes go to younger and less experienced men," Joseph muttered.

He heard Tessa's breath catch as she realized that the three parishes in Charleston already had capable pastors, that a promotion would mean his leaving. "Are you saying that I am about to lose you?"

"I know nothing for certain," he admitted, meeting her eyes again. "With so few seminarians to teach these past few years, I have wondered that Bishop Reynolds has not assigned me elsewhere already. I have wondered if he knows my secret." At Tessa's fearful expression, Joseph smiled wryly. "My *other* secret—the one about my Haitian grandmother. Perhaps my perpetual curacy is due to my color, to the fact that our Bishop does not trust me to manage my own parish."

"Surely by now you have proven yourself."

"Apparently not."

"I am sorry, my love. I had not thought about how remaining a curate might grate on you." Tessa shook her head. "I am selfish: whatever our Bishop's reasons for preferring other men, I want only what keeps you beside me."

"We've always known this would not last forever, Tessa. We should be grateful for the years God *has* given us, even if they end tomorrow." There—he had done it: prepared himself for the worst, and prepared Tessa too. If Bishop Reynolds did give him his own parish, Joseph would embrace the opportunity. Through His Lordship, God would effect what Joseph could not seem to accomplish on his own: to end this adultery before her husband realized its depth. The next night Joseph and Tessa met—if there was a next time—they would find a way to say good-bye.

She only closed her eyes and murmured: "*Dum spiro, spero.*" *As long as I breathe, I hope.*

CHAPTER 19

Take me to you, imprison me, for I,
Except you enthrall me, never shall be free,
Nor ever chaste, except you ravish me.
— John Donne, Holy Sonnet 14 (circa 1609)

God was merciful. In October, Joseph remained in Charleston, and Edward visited his Sea Island plantation again. He would miss his wife's thirty-fifth birthday, but he considered his first cotton harvest more important.

That evening, Tessa waited for Joseph at the garden wall, leaning back between the Jaune Desprez and the Lamarques, gazing up at the waning moon. Over her chemise, she wore only her blue wrapper, the one bordered in pomegranate blossoms and gold. As Joseph locked her gate, Tessa turned her head, and he was sure he could discern a smile even in the pale light. But she did not move from the wall, as if she were one of the roses. So he came to her.

Tessa tugged on their key where it hung around his neck. When she'd confirmed his solidity, she grinned up at him. "'Tis my birthday today."

"I know," he whispered back, letting his own hands find her hips through her wrapper and chemise. But he was wearing gloves, so the sensation was muted.

On his chest, just above their key, her thumb began making affectionate circles. "I liked very much what you gave me the last time we met."

He chuckled. "Don't you mean: what I *tried* to give you?"

She unbuttoned his coat. "Clare didn't interrupt the important part."

"Yes, she did!"

Tessa shook her head. "What I liked best of all, you gave me before we ever touched the bed." Now she reached for the first button of his waistcoat.

Instinctively, Joseph glanced to either side of them, but he saw only the cascades of roses and the shelter of evergreen leaves.

"Tonight, I want only one thing from you, Joseph." She slid a hand between his braces and the cotton of his shirt, distressingly near his left nipple. "That is why I came to meet you out here. If you refuse to grant it…you might as well leave me now."

He pulled her hand from his chest and laced his gloved fingers through her bare ones, staring down at their hands instead of her face. "How many times must I tell you this, Tessa? Birthday or no birthday, I remain a Priest."

With her other hand, she touched his face, returning his attention to hers. "The gift I want isn't the thing you think. Well—'tis the thing you think, but…" She caressed his cheek. "Five years ago, when I met you in this garden and we talked about our dreams, you asked to *see* me. For five long years, every time you've dreamt about me, you've been able to conjure every inch of me in your mind, because you know exactly what I look like. But *I* still have to imagine *you*. Just once, Joseph: let me see you?" She withdrew her hands and clenched them into fists. "I promise I won't touch you. You can bind my hands if you don't trust me. But please: let me look at you?"

This would be their last night together: he'd promised himself that over and over. For a long moment, he stared down at the fallen roses between their feet. "All right."

Tessa drew in a sharp breath, as if she hadn't believed he'd agree. "Truly?"

He raised his eyes again. "Truly."

"I don't mean by moonlight."

"*I* don't intend to disrobe in the middle of your garden!"

Tessa grinned. "No?"

"No." She herself was gorgeous by moonlight. He started to sink his fingers into her hair (bound up only loosely) but groaned in frustration when he remembered his gloves.

Before he could remove them, Tessa grabbed the lapels of his coat and pulled him even closer. "But you'll kiss me here, won't you?"

He obeyed at once, if only in teasing pecks, pressing his lips against hers between each phrase. "When you say—'Kiss me'—do you mean…?" His forehead still brushing hers, he canted his head away just enough to glance downward.

Even in the moonlight, Tessa understood perfectly well, because she giggled. "I think we'd better save *that* for inside, too—we wouldn't want to dirty your knees. But there *is* something we can do standing up…" She reached for his right hand, popped open the two buttons at his wrist, and drew off his glove. Then she brought his hand to her mouth and kissed his palm.

She tried to take control of his wrist, but he eluded her grasp. When she whimpered, Joseph reminded her with a chuckle: "Patience is a virtue, darling." He wanted to fill both his hands with her softness. So he yanked off his other glove, undid the sash of her dressing gown, and unbuttoned the embroidered neck of her chemise to expose the curves of her breasts. "Are you wearing drawers tonight?" he asked in her ear as he gathered up her skirt.

Tessa looped her arms around his neck. "I am…but you are always so busy *untying* my drawers, I don't suppose you've ever noticed the slit at their center?"

He resented the silk of her stockings and the linen of those drawers, shielding her glorious long legs from his touch. But the slit was a marvelous convenience, not only allowing her to relieve herself without disrobing but also allowing him to reach up just like this and...

"I could be fully dressed—corset, petticoats, and all—and you wouldn't have to remove a single article of my clothing to..." Her words shattered as he found the slit and slipped his hand inside.

He had only to graze the back of his fingers against one of her inner thighs, and Tessa gasped, her white neck arching in pleasure. Joseph kissed the delicate hollow at its base, then dipped his mouth lower, tasting the perspiration between her breasts. He feinted toward one nipple, then nibbled his way to the other. All the while, beneath her skirt, his right hand brushed across her hair, her petals, closer and closer to her center.

"You won't change your mind?" Tessa panted.

"About what?" he asked against her nipple.

"You'll let me see you? *All* of you?"

She was already wet; but he knew she had more to give him, and he wanted all of it. Very gently, he tugged at her labia, as if he were urging a blossom open. "I promise."

Tessa sighed out her last reservations and bloomed in his hand, plump and succulent, more like a fruit than a flower now. He sank in his forefinger and inspired a moan.

"*Shhh*," he reminded her with a chuckle. He didn't have a hand free to muffle her cries. How he wished he could hear her scream to the stars; but they must not forget the nearness of Church Street, her gate onto Longitude Lane, or the slave quarters. There were only so many secrets her garden could keep.

When he brought her nectar to her clitoris, Tessa began attacking his choker. He didn't understand why until she tore it from his neck and clamped the silk between her teeth. It softened her moans; and everyone around them *should* be asleep...

As his fingers teased and caressed, he pressed his mouth to her throat again, to the source of that mellifluous, muffled voice. Above and below, he followed each vibration to the secrets hidden inside her, to each trembling well of joy. In spite of his braces, she worked her hands beneath his shirt to his skin. Every bite of her nails was its own song of praise. But the honor he cherished most was like applause and embrace at once: the sudden, strong shudder of her intimate muscles clasping his fingers, holding him ferociously inside her.

Even that possession did not dispel Tessa's desire. Her heart still racing beneath his hand, she pulled the improvised gag from her mouth and tilted her face down to his. "You still haven't kissed me— not properly," she pleaded.

He stuffed his choker into his coat pocket beside his gloves. Then, he kissed her—quite *improperly*, by anyone else's standards. This time, he felt each of her cries reverberate inside his own throat. All around them, her roses seemed to tremble in sympathy; but surely it was only a breeze. He slipped both his hands into her drawers now, till the tremors and pulses coursed through her again. They might just set a new record tonight. But before he inspired any more climaxes, he needed to get her safely inside.

Her legs were so weak now, he had to carry her most of the way. She wobbled like a newborn foal, murmuring adoration in his ear with every step. If he didn't know better, he would have thought she was drunk. Only on him. Pride was a mortal sin, but he couldn't stop grinning. As they passed Clare's bedchamber, he prayed silently that God would give the girl only sweet dreams tonight. Joseph had plans for her mother.

He laid Tessa on her bed to recover while he secured the jalousies and the doors. When he shrugged off his coat, she cried out an objection and stumbled to the floor. "*I* want to do that!" He assisted her to the méridienne. There, she sat grinning up at him as she helped him shed his waistcoat and braces.

At the prospect of unbuttoning his shirt, she managed to stand on her own. She pulled the tail from his trousers, and he raised his arms so she could draw the shirt over his head. Above his waist, he wore only their key now.

Vanity (another mortal sin) got the better of him. He let Tessa admire his body as long as she wanted—though she was breathing so rapidly, he feared she might faint. Swimming, gardening, and fasting kept him trim; but finally, he could not believe his bare chest was so endlessly fascinating. He made the mistake of glancing down at himself.

Whether she'd been waiting for such an opportunity, he couldn't say; but in his moment of distraction, Tessa flung her arms around him. She tucked her head beneath his and pressed herself against him all the way to the tips of her toes. Her unbuttoned chemise covered *most* of her breasts; only part of one smooth swell peeked from the opening to unite with his own flesh.

He should be pushing her away; he should be reminding her that this wasn't part of their bargain. But once she'd embraced him, she did not attempt any other caress. She only stood there holding him against her, Tessa's warm, wordless pants against his shoulder expressing thanksgiving and exultation without demanding anything more.

So Joseph closed his eyes and inhaled the scents of roses, gardenias, and satisfaction wafting up from her body. He'd hoped *not* to be in a state of arousal when she saw him, but there was no chance of that now. He closed his arms around her too, wishing away her wrapper and chemise, his trousers, and both their drawers—wishing they might join skin to skin *just once...* Perhaps he was strong enough to—

Fortunately, Tessa broke his reverie. She pulled back just enough to bring one of her hands to his face and gaze into his eyes. "I love you so much," she breathed against his lips. She slid her fingers down his bare chest, just past the chain of their key. Since she stopped short of his nipple—barely—he left her hand where she placed it, on his heart. "I will always remember this: not only every magnificent inch of you, but that you trusted me, that you let me see what no one else has seen."

"No *woman* at least."

"What?"

"Nothing—I was a boy." He saw Tessa was still scowling. "Before they let me attend seminary, a doctor had to examine me," Joseph explained. "He had to confirm that I was 'whole'—that nothing was missing." He glanced down at his bulging fall. "Nothing is missing," he assured her in an exaggerated whisper.

He was trying to make her smile, but Tessa was frowning instead. Her eyes had followed his; and they hadn't left his trousers. "They had to confirm you were a man before forbidding you to be one? They had to confirm you were capable of fathering children before taking them away from you?"

"I— It's called a sacrifice for a reason, Tessa."

Despair began overtaking her face. "You would have had such *beautiful* children, Joseph—beautiful and brilliant and kind..."

Only if they were yours.

She reached for the buttons of his fall then, but only numbly, as if she were completing a task. All joy had drained from her countenance.

Gently, he lifted her hands away. "My boots first."

She nodded solemnly and knelt before the méridienne.

He sat so she could pull off his boots and his socks. When he stood, he stepped away from her. "I think I had better do the rest myself."

Tessa remained subdued; she did not protest. She only lifted herself to the seat of the méridienne and watched him disrobe without another word. It was eerie, this silence; it reminded him of her grief. At last, he unbuttoned his drawers and let them slide to the floor. Her gaze travelled slowly up his legs, lingering at the white birthmark on the outside of his thigh. The discipline hadn't left any scars. Finally, her attention came to rest on his alert genitals. On the parts of him she'd been pursuing for so long.

Still Tessa said nothing. He tried in vain to read her expression. Surely longing radiated from her eyes, from the slight parting of her lips; but there was something else too. What surprised Joseph most were his own feelings: how little shame or fear remained in him. After all these years, revealing himself to her seemed as natural and inevitable as genuflection. But he wished Tessa would *say* something. Perhaps she wished him to *turn* as well? She *had* asked to see "all of him."

So Joseph obeyed her unspoken command, showing her his back and buttocks, peering over his shoulder as best he could. "I think you might have left a few nail marks earlier—do you see any?"

She did not answer. When Joseph looked back to her, he saw tears spilling from her eyes. "Tessa?" he asked in alarm.

"This was a mistake," she whispered in such a trembling voice he barely caught the words.

But he'd given her exactly what she wanted! Was the sight of him really so horrible? Joseph snatched up his drawers, and his erection finally began to subside. What else could it do, in the face of such rejection?

She couldn't even look at him now. "I thought..." Using the arm of the méridienne, Tessa forced herself to her feet. Tears dripped onto the floor as she shook her head. "I can't do this anymore."

But she'd seen his nipples before; she must have known the skin of his penis and scrotum would be the same shade. Was it the brown skin in combination with the woolly black hair? She'd claimed his color didn't matter to her, but the reality of his body—dark and ugly with lust—must be very different from her fantasies.

Without another word to him, she moved like a sleepwalker toward her dressing chamber and pulled the door closed behind her.

Hurriedly Joseph buttoned his drawers and went to the door. "Tessa?"

He heard only sobs. He waited, but no reprieve came.

"Do"—he choked on the words—"do you want me to go?"

She kept wailing as if she'd lost something precious.

Of course she couldn't bear to look at him. He could hardly bear to look at it himself. It was a miracle anyone of any race managed to copulate with such an obscene appendage. Tessa had desired him only in the abstract—only the idea of him. Forbidden fruit was more delicious in the mind than in the mouth.

Still Joseph dressed himself as slowly as he could, hoping—even praying—that Tessa would return to him before he finished. It wasn't supposed to end like this. Their last night together, he'd meant to leave her in a stupor of happiness like the one he'd achieved only minutes before. Instead, *Tessa* had left *him*, and now she was trapped in an agony he couldn't comprehend. Did she mean their entire affair had been a mistake? That she never wanted to see him again, even clothed in daylight?

Finally Joseph stood fully dressed before Tessa's wall mirror, lacking only his choker. She'd torn holes in it with her teeth, back at the garden wall, when he'd made her whimper with desire and not disgust.

Inside her dressing chamber, Tessa continued weeping. She still wanted him gone.

Joseph put the choker on anyway. He wrapped it around his neck so many times, no one would notice the tears.

CHAPTER 20

For we did not meet in the holy night,
But in the shameful day.
— Oscar Wilde, *The Ballad of Reading Gaol* (1898)

At least it was easy to lose himself in his work. There were always Sacraments to administer, parishioners to counsel, and prayers to recite. If he could fill a morning with such duties, he could fill a day—a year—a lifetime. It would not be a life of joy, but it would be a life of purpose.

Twelve hours after he'd left Tessa sobbing, Joseph was trying to read his breviary on his parents' second-floor piazza when he heard the gate creak. He looked up to see Tessa entering the garden, Clare trailing behind her like a duckling. They wore matching dresses of changeable silk, midnight blue shot with violet. Joseph's breath caught, and he stood up at once. Tessa came to visit his mother and David often; but why was she carrying a valise?

Tessa saw him above her. The sunlight seized the violet in her dress as she stopped on the garden path to stare up at him. Her eyes were terribly bloodshot. Her jaw tensed, but she said nothing.

Joseph's gaze darted to Archdale Street, where anyone walking past might see them. He wasn't wearing his coat, but it wouldn't have saved him from the chill sinking into his spine. Why would Tessa risk such a meeting? Had Edward returned from his Sea Island plantation? Had they quarrelled? Had he hurt her? Anger kindled in place of fear.

Joseph was grateful that his parents and nephew weren't home yet. He hurried down the stairs, and Tessa met him in the entry hall. With that valise, she looked like a refugee. Joseph longed to embrace her, but he didn't think she would welcome it anymore. He tried to read her face, but *nervous* was the only emotion he could name.

Joseph turned to Clare. Whatever Tessa's reasons for coming here, this would not be a conversation for eight-year-old ears. He stooped down to the girl. "Has David told you that Persephone had her kittens?"

Clare's eyes widened with interest, and she shook her head.

"They're behind the stable. Henry will show you where. Why don't you go play with them for a few minutes so your mother and I can talk?"

The girl hesitated and glanced to her mother, who nodded her assent.

Joseph directed Tessa into his father's office, since he could hardly take her up to his bedchamber. While he closed the curtains, she settled uneasily onto the chair in the center of the room. In the sudden dimness, her dress looked almost black. Tessa set her valise on the floor beside her. Her breaths remained hurried. She clenched and unclenched her hands like a defendant awaiting trial.

Joseph asked in a low voice: "What has Edward done?"

"Nothing. He's not back yet."

Joseph sighed with relief and sat on the edge of his father's desk. He still didn't understand why Tessa carried a valise. Was she donating some of her old clothing? "Do you want me to speak with Bishop Reynolds? To *request* a re-assignment, whatever the position, so long as it isn't Charleston?"

She'd been undoing the buttons at the wrists of her gloves. She stopped. "*No*, Joseph!"

"But won't that make it easier for you, if you don't have to see me even at—"

She gaped at him. "I don't want you to leave!"

Joseph frowned. "Then...why are you here?"

Tessa stood and crossed the space between them. Her dress shimmered from blue to violet and back again. In spite of her reddened eyes, she radiated desire: her breaths coming in little pants through her parted lips. She grasped Joseph's hand in hers. "Come away with me, my love."

Joseph opened his mouth, but his first question died on his tongue. She couldn't mean— What else *could* she possibly mean? "But...y-you said we were a mistake."

Tessa frowned. "No I didn't."

"Last night, when I— As soon as you saw me, you said: 'This was a mistake.' You said: 'I can't do this anymore.' You ended it. Now, you want to—?"

She gripped his head in her gloved hands. "I meant: I cannot abide by your rules anymore! I cannot bear to see you and never touch you, Joseph!" She clasped her arms around his shoulders and seemed to waver. He caught her instinctively. Tessa held on like a drowning woman, each ragged breath hot against his ear. "I want— I *need* to be part of you, for *you* to be part of *me*."

You are—I am, he wanted to answer. *We have been part of one another for sixteen years.* But he knew that was not what she meant.

She had no right to do this to him, to tempt him in this way— not when he'd finally made his peace with the truth. *This must end now,* before he ruined her life, before Edward discovered them.

Joseph was not sure how long he stood there gathering his strength, letting the scent of her wash over his tongue and the warmth of her seep into his bones, knowing once he let her go, he would never hold her again. He stared over her shoulder at the *Noli Me Tangere* behind her till tears began to blur his vision: Mary Magdalene always reaching toward Christ, He always denying her. Joseph dropped his eyes to the valise. "Where would we go, Tessa?"

"Anywhere!" He heard the hitch of excitement in her voice.

She'd taken his words as encouragement instead of reason. She pulled back. "New York, Paris… Clare already speaks French."

He could *see* them, Tessa, Clare, and himself: strolling through the Jardin des Plantes, laying flowers on the tomb of Héloïse and Abélard… Joseph and Tessa were no longer young, but neither were they old; they might spend thirty, even forty years together before death parted them. Half a lifetime, with the purgatory of her marriage to Edward left far behind them, blotted out by their rapture…their delicious sin… "How would we live? I have one horse and no money."

Tessa tugged a reticule from the pocket of her skirts and tumbled two pearl earrings into her gloved palm. "We could live for months on *one* of these!"

"And after that?"

"You could teach! I could teach! We could open a school!"

On Joseph's left, Saint Denis and his fellow martyrs sacrificed everything for their faith and earned their eternal reward. On his right, from his father's painting of the Holy Family, the green eyes of the Christ Child stared at Joseph in accusation. "Who in God's name would entrust their children to a debauched Priest and his whore?"

Tessa sucked in a breath and stepped back from him. Her blue-violet skirts knocked over her valise. She brought a hand to her mouth and turned her face from him.

"I'm sorry." He reached out, but he didn't know where to touch her, and he was afraid she'd slap his hand away. "I didn't mean that, Tessa. You know that's not how I see you. But you must understand: that is how everyone else would see you."

She still gripped her pearl earrings, as if relinquishing them meant relinquishing her plan. "Not if they don't know who we are!"

"So you would have us change our names? Masquerade as husband and wife?"

"Yes!"

"Is that really how you want to live, Tessa?" Gingerly, Joseph placed his hands on her arms. "We would be looking over our shoulders for the rest of our lives, in perpetual fear that someone might discover us. We must think of Clare."

"I *am* thinking of her! She needs a father. And you know she adores you."

"In the eyes of the law, Clare belongs to Edward. Surely your brother has explained that to you. No court on Earth would allow a child to remain with an adulteress, especially when her wronged husband is one of the wealthiest—"

"Edward doesn't even *like* Clare!"

"She is his only heir. Do you honestly think he will just let her go?"

Tessa evaded his hands and dropped the earrings back into her reticule. "He would have to find us first."

"You told me he paid some English 'detective' only to learn about Mr. Cromwell's past. You are his *wife*. We would make Edward a laughingstock. He would pursue us to the ends of the Earth out of spite."

Tessa raised her chin. "Wherever we go, however long it lasts, together you and I can give Clare a better life than she would *ever* have here."

"In the beginning, she might think it a great adventure," Joseph acknowledged. "But she would grow to despise us, Tessa. Clare might betray us by accident; she is a child who loves stories. If any of our neighbors learned that you were married to another man, or that I was colored, let alone a fallen Priest… We would make Clare an outcast too."

"Better an outcast and the daughter of a whore than married to a man who thinks her his property."

Joseph averted his eyes again. He wished he could take back that word.

Tessa's voice grew suddenly quiet. "You would tire of me, day in and day out."

He met her gaze at once. "Of course not." The opposite was true. Even *he* wasn't strong enough to spend every day—every night—in her company and not succumb to her. But that was exactly what she wanted, part and parcel of this elopement: to be husband and wife in body if not in name.

Joseph had to believe that God would forgive what he and Tessa had done thus far. For all the nights Joseph had spent in her bed, he'd always knelt at the altar the next morning, and she'd endured Edward as her own Penance. But if Joseph deserted his Priesthood, if he and Tessa lived together for forty years of ceaseless, unrepentant mortal sin, as if his ordination and her marriage had never happened, when nothing in Heaven or on Earth could unmake them...

"I cannot go back there, Joseph."

What she suffered with Edward, it was *finite*—just as her pleasure with Joseph would be. Hell was infinite. What use would it be to save Tessa in this life only to damn her in the next?

"I am sorry, Tessa—more sorry than I can say." The pain in her eyes nearly stopped his heart. He had to look away again. "If there is anything else I can do for you or for Clare, I will do it; but I cannot run away with you. You know it's impossible—that I can never stop being a Priest. Hundreds of people—hundreds of *immortal souls* yet to be born—are relying on me. I cannot abandon them."

"So you choose to abandon me instead?" Fresh tears trickled from her beautiful, bloodshot eyes. "Your parishioners need a Priest —that is all! I need *you*."

"Think what the scandal would do to our Church, Tessa." Joseph could scarcely speak through the tightness in his own throat. "Every Priest would be doubted. You are one of the holiest women I know. You have simply forgotten—"

Tessa clenched her hands into fists. "I am so tired of being holy! I want to be *whole*!" She clung to his waistcoat now, on either side of his hips, pulling their bodies together till her skirts all but swallowed his legs.

Joseph braced his arms on her shoulders and pushed her away from him. "This body does not belong to me."

Tessa let him go and caught herself on the back of the chair. Not only her face but her entire frame crumpled—as much as a corseted woman could crumple. Her breaths were as labored as his. "As my body belongs to Edward. We are both of us slaves."

"Tessa!" She knew it wasn't the same.

She glared at him, refusing to apologize. "The negroes have one consolation, at least: they know their sufferings are unjust. They can hope for deliverance. You and I chose our own masters. We have no one to blame for this misery but ourselves."

Before Joseph could formulate a reply, they heard a timid knock on the door to the hall. "Mama?" Clare ventured.

Tessa wiped angrily at her tears before she answered: "I'm here, *a chuisle*. I'm still here."

The door opened, and the girl peered cautiously inside. Her eyes settled on Joseph. Sorrow tightened every line of her young face, but there was no surprise in the expression. "We're not going anywhere, are we?"

Joseph couldn't speak. He turned away from her, toward the front windows. Through the thin curtains, he could just make out the silhouette of St. John's Lutheran Church.

"Not today," Tessa managed in a quavering voice as she gathered her valise from the floor.

"Not ever," Joseph whispered. He meant it more for himself than for Tessa, but she muffled a moan as if he'd struck her. He forced himself not to turn, not to embrace her. What would that accomplish now? He longed for her forgiveness, but he'd committed no sin. Quite the opposite. He was finally standing his ground.

Then why did he feel so ashamed?

After he heard the front door close, Joseph trudged into the hall, mounted the stairs, and returned to his breviary on the upper piazza. But he did not open it. Below him, across the garden and the sidewalk, the sunlight jumped off the changeable silk of Tessa's dress.

She was crossing Archdale Street as if she'd gone blind. Clare had to yank on her mother's sleeve to keep her from colliding with a passing carriage. As it was, Tessa dropped her valise. It sprang open, spilling her fine undergarments into the muck of the street in front of the church.

Joseph gripped the balustrade as if he might vault all the way to the ground. He wanted to run to her. He wanted to help her. But he remained where he was. He only watched while Clare and a Good Samaritan helped gather up the soiled linens.

Tessa sank to her knees in the street, but she only held the gaping valise. She must have sensed him standing above her; she looked up. Joseph knew he should retreat, but her eyes riveted him in place. Across the distance, she gave him one last message, signs she'd learned from his mother long ago. Her dress shimmering violet, her eyes shimmering with tears, Tessa placed both hands against her heart. Then she lifted her right hand from her breast. She extended only her index finger to make a circle in the air, as if she were tracing the infinite loop of the ouroboros. *I will love you always*, she told him without words.

Joseph clutched the railing till his knuckles went white, forcing himself not to reply, because other people were starting to stare at him too.

Tessa lowered her eyes and closed her valise. She stood, clasped her daughter's hand, and returned to her husband. Joseph watched till she turned the corner and was lost to him.

CHAPTER 21

Lay thee down and roar…
— William Shakespeare, *The Tragedy of Othello* (1603)

The end of October meant one last trip to the mission at
Summerville. Fever season had passed, and the planters were
returning to their country homes. Edward, Tessa, and Clare had
already settled in at Stratford-on-Ashley, according to David. He still
visited his foster-sister when he could. He'd borrowed Prince for a
day. Edward had been out hunting and Tessa had kept herself shut
up in her bedchamber, so David had been unable to give Joseph a
full report.

Joseph and Prince passed the Stratfords' plantation on their way
to Summerville. Tessa remained in his thoughts through every
Sacrament he performed. It had been scarcely a week since she'd
begged him to elope with her, but it felt like a year.

On his return to Charleston the next afternoon, Joseph decided
to risk a visit. He was the Stratfords' curate; it would look suspicious
if he *didn't* pay them a call from time to time.

If God was with them, no one who knew her had seen Tessa
with that valise. If Joseph could speak to her in private just once

more, he would have a chance to end things less bitterly. He could explain himself better and see her smile one last time, even if it was a wistful smile.

Joseph directed Prince down the alley of live oaks with their shrouds of Spanish moss. As soon as he'd dismounted, Joseph heard Tessa's daughter screaming inside the mansion. He froze.

The words were so hoarse, he could hardly understand them. Clare was shrieking the word "No," then "She's *my* Mama! You can't make me—"

An unmistakable sound interrupted her: the sound of a hand striking flesh.

Joseph did not bother to tie up Prince or even knock. He raced up the steps of the piazza and flung open the door as if Clare were his to defend.

But someone else was hurrying up the stairs in the front hall. When the man reached the landing, he saw Joseph and hesitated. Barely across the threshold, Joseph did too. He recognized Mr. Cromwell, Edward's young, blond, English-born secretary whom Tessa disliked. Joseph had met the man only once and hadn't made up his mind about him quite yet. At least Mr. Cromwell looked as distressed as Joseph was by the sounds from upstairs.

Yet it wasn't Edward's voice hissing at Clare, as Joseph had expected. It was a woman's voice: "You'll wake your father!" Her accent sounded very much like Edward's.

"Clare's aunt—Edward's sister Hortense," Mr. Cromwell supplied, glancing up the stairs again. "She came over from her son's plantation, after…" Mr. Cromwell's voice trailed off. He looked back to Joseph and seemed to frown at his empty hands. "Did you bring your things, Father? Your case?"

"I…" Upstairs, Joseph heard Clare sobbing, a final admonishment from her aunt, and a door closing firmly. "It's still on my horse."

"Don't you need it?"

To comfort Clare? Joseph moved to the first stair, eager to go to her, though surely Tessa would be there already. "For…?"

"For the Last Rites—Sacraments, whatever you call them."

If Joseph hadn't grasped the banister, he would have fallen to his knees. "Last…?" he echoed again stupidly, all strength bleeding out of his voice. Above them, around them, the house had gone terrifyingly quiet.

Mr. Cromwell's shoulders sagged in realization. "Of course: it's too soon. You're here on your own. Our messenger hadn't reached you yet."

"What messenger?" Joseph choked out.

"I'm sorry, Father. She was gone before we found her. But Clare insisted we send for you anyway."

"*Who* was…" But Joseph already knew.

A slave appeared in the doorway behind him like an angel of death, bearing Joseph's portmanteau. Joseph opened his hand to accept it; his fingers closed around the handle; but he felt too weak to carry it. Somehow, he pulled himself upwards till he reached the second floor, forwards till he reached the bedchamber on the right. He stopped on the threshold as if he could stop time, when he needed to turn it backward.

Tessa lay clothed and motionless on her four-poster bed. From this angle, Joseph couldn't see her face; she was only a mound of petticoats and skirts, a day dress of cream-colored cotton printed with a delicate pattern of flowers. But the blood staining her pillow told him the truth.

"It must have been an accident," Mr. Cromwell explained, lingering in the hall beside Joseph. "She must have slipped coming down the back stairs, the ones off the veranda. We found her at the base of the steps, Edward and I."

"How long…?"

Before he answered, Mr. Cromwell consulted his pocket watch. "Not quite two hours ago."

Two hours… If Joseph had stopped here yesterday on his way *to* Summerville, Tessa would have been alive. She'd been alive when he'd celebrated Mass this morning… How could he not have *known*, not have *felt* it when such a light went out…

"Edward is inconsolable," Mr. Cromwell continued. "He wouldn't leave her. His sister and I had to put laudanum in his brandy. Hortense may have done the same with Clare. In any case, I'll make certain you're not disturbed, Father."

Mr. Cromwell left him. Left them. Though there wasn't any *them* anymore.

Joseph staggered into the room, shoved the door closed, and caught himself on one of the bedposts like seaweed snagging against a pier. His vision was blurring. He nearly lost hold of his portmanteau, then snatched it up again. Inside, the candlesticks jangled. Only two hours gone. No one knew how long a soul might linger inside a body after the breath stopped; there was still a chance the holy oil might cleanse her, might save her…

Someone had crossed Tessa's hands over her breast, so like the sign for *I love you*—the last thing she'd ever said to him, as if she were assuring him even now. Or reproaching him, even in death. Why hadn't he returned the sign? No one but Tessa would have understood it. The last thing he'd said to her was *"Not ever."* He'd actually called her a whore…

Dear God, it can't end like this. Dear God, bring her back, just for one hour —one minute! You have done it before, to allow time for the Last Sacraments! One tiny miracle is all I ask! You must allow me to cleanse her, to purify her, to tell her I am sorry… You must give her a chance to repent…

Joseph fumbled with the straps of his portmanteau. He mustn't waste even a moment. *Dear God, don't let it be too late…* He retrieved his violet stole and the small brass container of holy oil. He screwed open the lid and pressed his thumb into the oil-soaked cotton. He tried to ignore Tessa's ravaged flesh. Someone had attempted to clean her wounds, but only hastily. The right side of her face was scraped raw.

He was trembling so much, those long, myrrh-brown lashes grazed his fingertip before he made the Sign of the Cross on the eyelids that would never open again. They were still warm. *"Through this holy anointing and through His tender mercy,"* Joseph prayed in Latin, *"may the Lord forgive thee whatever sins thou hast committed by the sense of sight…"*

His tears dripped onto Tessa's forehead as he anointed her earlobes and her nostrils—the senses of hearing and smell. Then he pressed his thumb across her lips. They still gave beneath his touch, those lips as soft as the petals of a Maiden's Blush; but no warm breath emerged to caress his skin. *"May the Lord forgive whatever sins thou hast committed by the sense of taste and the power of speech..."* These lips had opened and swelled so often to his kisses, had set free that witty, wicked tongue and the angelic voice he would never hear again...

Her knuckles were bruised and bloody. To anoint her palms, he lifted each hand with infinite tenderness, as if he could hurt her any more. *"May the Lord forgive whatever sins thou hast committed by the sense of touch..."* These clever fingers, that could play him as skillfully as she played the piano, were already growing cold.

He dragged himself to the end of the bed and undid the buttons of her boots as he had so many times before. Not so many: sixteen years they'd had together, and only seventeen nights. Not nearly enough. They might have had forty more years, if he'd fled with her.

He fumbled under her petticoats and tore away Tessa's garters, her stockings. At last her feet were bare, and he made a cross with his thumb on each sole. *"Through this holy anointing and through His tender mercy, may the Lord forgive whatever sins thou hast committed by the power of walking. Amen."*

He sank to his knees at the end of the bed, clutching her still-warm feet against his forehead. What if it hadn't been an accident? What if she'd purposefully leapt from the veranda? Had she *tried* to step into the path of that carriage on Archdale Street?

Nothing in Heaven or on Earth could cleanse her of *that* sin, of willfully destroying the life God had given her... She'd spoken of suicide before, after she lost her sixth child. Tessa had warned Joseph, so many times:

"I need you."

"My turning to you is like a flower turning toward the sun. It would die without that warmth."

"I can't do this anymore."

"I cannot go back there."

"As long as I hope, I breathe."

Joseph had abandoned Tessa when she needed him most. He'd ripped her last hope from her hands, so she'd stopped breathing. As surely as if he'd pushed her from that veranda, he'd killed her. He'd killed the only woman he had ever loved and damned her for all eternity. He'd left her only child an orphan—worse than an orphan, with a father like Edward.

Even if it *had* been an accident—if that weak ankle and the distraction of her misery had made Tessa lose her footing at the wrong moment—she'd gone to her grave cursing holiness and wanting to elope with a Priest. She'd died in a state of mortal sin, unrepentant. Holy oil and a thousand Masses could not save her soul now.

"Lord, have mercy on us," Joseph pleaded through his tears. *"Christ, have mercy on us. Lord, have mercy on us…"*

Why hadn't Joseph gone with her? Better to be hanged for a sheep than a lamb.

Joseph crawled up the bed, along Tessa's body, till his face was buried in her neck and she was clasped in his arms. The holy oil must be leaking onto the sheets; his tears and snot were soaking into Tessa's dress and her skin; he was probably wailing loud enough for the whole household to hear; but he didn't care. He would come away with her blood smeared across his clothes and his skin; but it was exactly what he deserved.

He'd had her in his arms, beautiful and breathing, this woman more precious than rubies, this pearl of unimaginable price, and he'd thrown her away.

I am the Priest! he screamed to God in his head. *My sin is greater! Punish ME!*

But what punishment could be greater than to damn Tessa and leave him alive? Joseph wanted to race to the back of the veranda and throw *himself* from the balcony. He didn't want to live in a world without Tessa. He didn't want to achieve Heaven if she wouldn't be there to greet him. What was that horrible Irish proverb? *"Three who will never see the light of Heaven: the Angel of Pride, an unbaptized child, and a Priest's concubine."*

At a knock on the bedchamber door, Joseph started and raised his head. The door was still closed. "Father Lazare?" Mr. Cromwell's voice called from the other side. "We need to prepare the body."

Joseph did not move. "I-I need a few more minutes."

Mr. Cromwell did not answer, but neither did he enter.

"*The body.*" Slowly, Joseph raised himself to his elbows. He knew this wasn't Tessa any longer. Still he kissed her cool fingers. He released her, dug in his portmanteau, and located the little scissors he used for snipping candle wicks. He found a lock of her long myrrh-brown hair unstained by blood and cut it. He curled the lock into his Ritual, then shut everything back into his portmanteau.

He stood over her one more moment, tears falling ceaselessly. He stared at her face one last time. With his hands, he told her: *I will love you always.* With his voice, he begged her: "Forgive me."

When he emerged into the hall, Mr. Cromwell had gone, because of course it wouldn't be *him* preparing Tessa's body for burial. Instead, two solemn slave women followed Joseph into the bedchamber.

He knew he must go to Clare. Joseph opened her door as quietly as he could. He hoped the dimness of the room would obscure Tessa's blood on him. The girl was curled around Mignon on her bed. Joseph set down his portmanteau and approached.

The cat's tail thumped impatiently, and he strained to leave his mistress, but Clare clutched him tighter. Her honey-brown hair was a dishevelled tangle, and she'd lost a slipper. The girl's face was nearly as changed as her mother's: reddened and bloated with grief. Clare kept her eyes squeezed shut, but she must have sensed Joseph's presence. She whispered: "Is Mama in Hell?"

Never in his life had Joseph wanted so much to lie. Finally he answered: "Only God knows that."

The bloodshot brown eyes opened, demanding more. "But you were too late. She was supposed to confess her sins, and she didn't."

"A-At the last moment, when she was dying, she could have repented on her own. There is a *chance*, Clare."

Tessa's daughter shook her head. "Something was wrong with her. She was *broken*."

"What do you mean?"

"Mama wouldn't look at me. She *yelled* at me! She stopped loving me!" Alarmed by the stridency of the girl's voice, the black-and-white cat managed to squirm away. Clare whimpered anew at the loss.

Joseph knelt by the bed so his face would be closer to the girl's. He kept his own voice calm. "Of course your mother still loved you."

Clare sat upright—suddenly, Joseph was looking up at her. "Then why did she leave?"

The girl had just described the behavior of a suicide, if Joseph had had any doubts. Still he insisted: "It was an *accident*, Clare." He reached out to touch her face in reassurance.

Tessa's daughter slapped it away. Her voice continued to grow louder: "Two weeks ago at Mass, you said: 'There are no accidents with God'! 'All things work together for good'! But *this* is bad! It won't ever be good!" Clare was shrieking now, her hands fists at her sides. "You're wrong! And so is God, if He doesn't fix Mama and give her back! Tell Him to give her back!"

From a room down the hall, Joseph heard a groan. Edward's voice. In Joseph's moment of distraction, Clare slid from the bed and padded over to the window. She still wore a single slipper. Seeking some way to be useful, Joseph peered under the bed, looking for the second shoe.

Down the hall, Edward's sister Hortense chattered in an effort to soothe her brother. Clare was struggling with the lock of the triple-hung window. Joseph went to help her. As they raised the lower sash, Edward's sister appeared in the doorway behind them, hands on hips.

"You've upset him again." Hortense glanced to Clare, who was peeling off her remaining slipper and fighting new sobs. "You've upset both of them, *Father*! You've chanted your Mumbo Jumbo—it is high time you left us in peace."

Tessa's daughter escaped through the floor-length window onto the veranda. Joseph called out and ducked after her. Behind him, he heard Hortense muttering. Joseph glanced back to see his portmanteau being defenestrated, but he did not stop—he must catch Clare, who was racing away from him. He must keep the promise he'd made to Tessa the night she'd borne her daughter: that he would be the girl's "soul-friend."

Then Joseph reached the back of the mansion. Heedless of her stocking feet, Clare ran ahead of him, down one of the half-circles of stairs that curved from the portico. The sight of those steps, of this balcony, stopped Joseph like a block of ice to the chest. He caught himself on the balustrade. This was where Tessa had...

What had he been thinking, trying to comfort Clare? *He* was the one who had broken her mother. The girl had every right to despise him. He would never be able to keep his promise.

At the base of the steps, Joseph heard splashing, then a strange, repeated scraping sound. He peered over the balustrade to see a slave woman on her knees, scrubbing Tessa's blood out of the bricks.

Joseph stumbled backwards and fled. He barely remembered to snatch up his portmanteau. Somehow he mounted his horse. He let the reins hang slack. Prince knew the way.

WHEN THEY REACHED HIS FATHER'S, Joseph all but fell from the saddle, and he offered Henry no explanation as he staggered into the house. There, another set of stairs met him. They were more than he could bear. Joseph collapsed to his knees and began climbing that way, dragging himself upwards by the banister, as if these were the Scala Sancta and every step he achieved meant nine years' indulgence. But he was already in Hell.

His father found him there, less than halfway to the top. "Joseph?" He noticed the red stains on Joseph's hands and cuffs. "You're wounded!"

"It's not my blood."

"Whose blood is it?"

"She's *gone!*" Joseph cried, each word like a blow to his back. "Tessa is dead!"

"Oh, Joseph..." His father looped an arm beneath his shoulders and helped him up the rest of the stairs. "How did it happen?"

"She *fell*—they say she fell..."

His father deposited Joseph on his bed and closed the window curtains. "I'll tell Father Lynch you are ill."

Before grief overtook him completely, Joseph heard his father explaining to David that Tessa was dead. "I'm going to Clare," his nephew announced. "I don't care what Edward or his secretary say. She shouldn't be alone."

JOSEPH CURLED UP in the darkness and tried to die.

His father and mother were having none of it. His mother felt his forehead and begged both of them to tell her what was wrong. Joseph refused to answer, and his father feigned ignorance. They stripped off his clothes, sponged off Tessa's blood, and cleaned him when he didn't make it to the chamber pot. They enlisted May too, till all of them were forcing broth and bread into him.

Joseph had no idea how long this went on, how many Masses he missed. The sun seemed to rise and set several times, but he did not count. Even the thickness of his beard wasn't a gauge, since he'd never let it grow before.

Joseph understood now why Liam had sought refuge in alcohol after Hélène died. Joseph decided to start drinking. Better yet, his father must have laudanum in his office. He would swallow the entire bottle. But Joseph didn't even have the strength to crawl from this bed.

Somewhere in the haze, David reported: "They're keeping her above ground till her tomb is ready. Edward bought this metal case, this iron coffin with a window over her face, to preserve her like some kind of saint..."

EVENTUALLY, HIS FATHER THREW OPEN the window curtains. Joseph groaned and covered his face with his hands.

"I know you are in pain, Joseph. But I do not intend to clean up your shit for the rest of my life, and I won't let May or your mother do it either. You are nearly forty years old. It's been two weeks; did you know that? You cannot remain shut up in this room forever. I cannot continue fending off your fellow Priests. I had to invent an illness that was highly contagious but never fatal."

His father's warped sense of humor had never been less welcome. Joseph tried to shout at him, but it came out as a croak. "You don't understand!"

"Then tell me, son."

"It's *my* fault." Joseph slammed his fist into his chest. "Tessa came here, begging me to elope with her and Clare. She told me she couldn't go back to Edward—and I abandoned her! I left her in despair. I think she *purposefully...*"

"I cannot believe that," his father concluded at once, as if he'd already discussed this with someone. Did David suspect suicide too? "That ankle kept giving her trouble; I think—"

"Even if she slipped, she died in a state of mortal sin. She had no chance to repent!"

"I refuse to inhabit any heaven that would shut its gates to Tessa." His father strode to his bedside. "She was far 'more sinned against than sinning.'"

"Shakespeare was not a saint! And I sinned against Tessa more grievously than Edward ever did! She is dead because of *me*. I could have saved her."

"You think I haven't blamed myself over and *over* for Hélène's death?" His father pressed his own fist to his chest. "I have asked myself a thousand times: Should we never have operated? Should we have operated earlier? Should I have found another surgeon, or treated her fever differently? But I did what I did, Joseph. I can't change it now. Nor can I curl up in bed and will away the world, because I am a doctor. People depend on me. You are a Priest. For better or worse, you chose your Priesthood. Abandoning it now won't bring Tessa back."

When his father turned to go, Joseph realized his nephew had been standing in the doorway. He heard David ask: "Is he any better?"

Joseph pulled his pillow over his head.

THE NEXT DAY, David came to Joseph on his own. His nephew closed the door and crossed to the window. He waited till Joseph rolled toward him before he spoke. "I know what it is like, to face the most important decision of your life and make the wrong choice. I know what it is like to bear the weight of an innocent's death—someone who was relying on you to protect them."

Joseph swallowed. "You made a mistake with a patient?"

"No. I think I could forgive myself for that." He turned enough to glance at Joseph over his shoulder. David looked so much like a man, standing there. He *was* a man: twenty years old now. "You are still a Priest, Father, bound by the Seal of Confession? What I say to you will not leave this room?"

Joseph's violet stole was out of reach, but at the very least, a Physician of the Soul shouldn't hear a Confession while lying on his side like an invalid. He managed to sit up. "It will not."

"You will never tell my grandparents what I tell you?"

Joseph propped a pillow against the headboard. "Of course not."

David drew in a deep breath and let it out. "Ten years ago, I told you and everyone else that my baby brother, your nephew Ian, died of puerperal fever with our mother at Independence Rock."

Joseph settled back against the pillow and frowned. "Yes."

"I lied, Father. I killed my brother."

PART V
POSSIBILITIES

1841, 1851

The Unorganized Territory and Missouri,
Charleston

Many of my friends tried to dissuade me from going, telling me of
the many dangers and difficulties I should have to go through,
exposed to hostile Indians and the wild beasts… Mr. Greene said
there was a *possibility* of my returning, but not a probability.

— Reverend Joseph Williams, *Narrative of a Tour from the State of
Indiana to the Oregon Territory in the Years 1841-2*

CHAPTER 22

Ten Years Earlier
Summer 1841
The Unorganized Territory

Accidents will happen; but God permits them for his own wise purposes... It became necessary for us to cross the Platte River. It was about a mile wide, full of islands, and had a strong current. John Grey went in search of a ford... We were nearing the other bank when suddenly I beheld the wagon upset...
— *The Rocky Mountains, Memoirs of Father Gregory Mengarini* (1888)

The first person to die shot himself by accident. When Pa came to tell them, David laughed. He thought it was a joke, because the man's name was Mr. Shotwell.

"There is nothing funny about the death of a Protestant," Mama scolded him.

The old Methodist minister spoke over Mr. Shotwell's grave. "'For ye know neither the day nor the hour!'" Reverend Williams boomed in a voice like thunder. "'Take heed...and pray always, that ye may be accounted worthy to escape all the things that shall come to pass!'" He glared at the Frenchmen standing nearby, the ones who drove the Jesuits' mule carts. Whenever the drivers cursed at their animals, Reverend Williams muttered about the men's wickedness under his breath; David had heard him.

Reverend Williams made David glad he was a Catholic. The Jesuits did not thunder that everybody except David's family was going to Hell, because they were Protestants or just plain godless. The Jesuits were kind. They had horses and mules; they could have travelled much faster on their own; but they matched the slow pace of the oxen and wagons instead. That was how missionaries should be, Pa said: "A spoonful of honey will catch more flies than a gallon of vinegar."

Since Mama had forbidden David to visit the trappers, he visited the Jesuits instead. Father De Smet overflowed with stories: he'd been through this country last year on his first journey to the savages. It was easy to tell the Priests apart, unlike all the Williamses (who were no kin to the Reverend) and Kelseys (four brothers with three wives and six children).

The Italian Jesuit, Father Mengarini, was a nobleman—or he would have been, if he hadn't become a Priest. He was from Rome and almost the same age as Uncle Joseph. Father Mengarini even remembered talking with him at a concert once. In the evenings, Father Mengarini often played his violin. Sometimes Father De Smet joined in on his clarinet. Pa would set up Mama's piano so she could play too, but mostly she was busy cooking.

Father De Smet was from Belgium, a bit fat, and usually laughing. "If you *really* want to hear music," he joked, "listen outside our tent tonight! Brother Specht snores like a steam-engine! He runs through all the notes of the chromatic scale and closes each movement with a deep sigh which harmonizes with the prelude."

The third Priest, Father Point, was from France, and he liked to draw. Sophie found out by peering over his shoulder one nooning. Father Point was drawing Father Mengarini napping beside a mule cart. He'd also made a sketch of Mr. Grey, who was half Indian but dressed like a white man. "Do me! Draw me!" David's sister begged. Father Point promised he would the very next day.

For David's tenth birthday, Father Point gave him a sketch of the forty Cheyenne braves who'd frightened Mr. Dawson while he was hunting and followed him back to camp. (Their guide, Mr. Fitzpatrick, knew how to talk to the Indians in signs like Grandma's. He convinced the braves to smoke a peace pipe instead of scalping everybody.) David thought it was the best present ever.

But later, David wished Father Point had drawn Pa instead, while he still could. Because Pa was the second person to die.

It happened while they were crossing the North Fork of the Platte. The water was high and the current was swift. Mr. Fitzpatrick said it was melted snow that had come all the way from the mountains. Underneath the river, there were rocks in some places and quicksand in others. Everyone was being careful, but as Pa and Brother Claessens tried to float it across, their family's wagon started tipping.

Pa went under, and something must have hit him. When he surfaced, he didn't kick or cry out. The water just dragged him like a fallen tree. Mama wouldn't let David go after Pa, no matter how much David pleaded.

When Brother Claessens and Mr. Bidwell finally pulled Pa out of the river, he didn't cough up the water. He didn't seem to be breathing at all. Father De Smet anointed him anyway. When they were sure Pa was dead, they used boards from the broken wagon to make him a coffin.

Sophie clung to Mama as if something might happen to her too. "Can we go home now?" she whimpered. Mama only stared down at her big belly.

David wondered if he was going deaf like his grandmother. When the Priests spoke to him, he could barely hear them. He felt as if *he* were underwater. He tried to find the surface. Reverend Williams came too and patted his shoulder. "You're the man of the family now, David. You must take care of your mother and sister. You must lead them in the paths of righteousness."

Father Point burned Pa's name into a board for a marker, and they piled rocks over him so wolves couldn't dig down. David wanted to do more, but all he could think of was to scratch the shape of a Saint Andrew's cross into a rock at Pa's feet.

Mama's piano was ruined; they had to leave it on the bank. David lost his microscope and all but one of his books. The things that had survived the river they added to their cart or distributed among the other wagons. The other families took the wheels and spare parts, and they said it was good to have extra oxen. Asa Williams, who was fourteen, helped David look after them. Asa's father had been teaching him. He still had a father.

Three days later was Independence Day, but they didn't feel like celebrating. The next morning, Mama's baby started coming. They camped at Independence Rock on the Sweetwater River, and the women gathered around Mama in the tent. They wouldn't let David in. When his sister started bawling like a baby herself, the women let her visit Mama for a little. Then Winnie and the older girls tried to keep Sophie occupied.

David had been looking forward to climbing Independence Rock ever since they left Missouri. It was a rock the size of a mountain in the middle of a plain, shaped like a whale breaching the surface of the ocean. But he couldn't go exploring or carve his name till he knew Mama was all right. He'd seen baby animals born on their farm. He knew lots of things could go wrong.

David tried to read his book, but Mama's moans filled his head. He didn't get any farther than the first page. "Let us submit to God's will," it said.

David had packed a whole crate of books, and *The Swiss Family Robinson* was the only one God had spared from the river. God must be angry that David had given away all the books about saints that Uncle Joseph had sent him. David had brought only the books that Grandpa had sent: the ones about natural sciences and faraway places, the journals of Mr. Darwin and Captain Cook. David's wicked books couldn't be the reason their wagon had capsized, the reason Pa was dead—could they?

Sniffling, Sophie sat down beside him and rested her head against his shoulder. "Tell me a story, David?" His sister was always begging stories from him. She had even in Missouri, since Pa and Mama were usually too busy or too tired to read to her. David picked the bits of his books he thought she'd like best, or he told the stories in his own way. But he'd only just started *The Swiss Family Robinson*, and right now, he didn't think she'd want to hear about a shipwreck.

Instead David asked: "Do you know how Independence Rock got its name?"

"Winnie says it's because it's 'independent' of the other mountains."

"Maybe that's part of the reason they picked it. But mostly, it's because years ago, Mr. Fitzpatrick and some other trappers camped here on Independence Day."

His sister waited a moment, then leaned away so she could scowl at him. "*That's* not a story!"

David smiled a little. Sophie never let him get away with a lazy story. "Then do you know why Devil's Gate looks the way it does?" He nodded toward the gorge in the distance. David knew his sister wouldn't want to hear the truth: that the Sweetwater River had simply carved through the granite over years and years.

So he told Sophie the Indian legend about a great beast with tusks, a beast that loved to trample tipis. She giggled and gasped exactly where he intended. Finally a party of braves managed to corner the monster against the side of a mountain. To escape their arrows, the beast used its tusks to rip straight through the rock and then disappeared.

His sister frowned. "You mean, the beast didn't die?"

"He disappeared," David repeated.

"But he could come back?"

"He didn't."

"But he *could*?" Sophie insisted. "It's *possible*?"

By then, they had to run under one of the Kelsey wagons for shelter. He and his sister compared their loose teeth till the rain stopped. A thunderstorm came every afternoon now, but it didn't last long, and a rainbow usually followed it.

This rainbow was the best one David had ever seen: it was

tripled, with the middle bow connecting the other two. Did this mean Mama was having triplets? Or only that God really, truly wouldn't send them any more disasters?

David and Sophie were admiring the triple rainbow when Mama stopped moaning and a baby started crying. Finally Mrs. Williams and her daughter Martha came out of the tent.

"Your Mama is just fine," Mrs. Williams told them. "And you have a healthy new brother."

"He was born with a caul!" Martha put in. She was twelve.

"A *what?*" David asked.

"He had this sort of veil over his head, till Ma peeled it off."

Sophie stuck out her lower lip at Mrs. Williams. She looked like she was about to cry. "You said nothing was wrong with him!"

"There isn't! A caul isn't bad! It's *good!*" Martha babbled before her mother could answer. "It's like a four-leaf clover! It means your brother will be lucky and that he'll do something great one day. He might see the future, or heal people like Jesus! He can share his luck too: if you dry the caul and keep it, it's a love charm, and it protects you from drowning."

David had to sit down again.

"That's enough now, Martha." David could tell by the way Mrs. Williams went pale that at least *she* hadn't forgotten about his Pa already.

Martha kept chattering over her shoulder as her mother led her away: "But your Ma thinks a caul being lucky is only an old wives' tale—so *we* get to keep it!"

Even if he wasn't lucky, David liked the idea of having a brother. But he'd be useless for years yet. And right now, he was rather ugly: his skin was purple, his face was swollen, and his head looked kind of pointy. Mama said all that was normal because he'd been through a lot.

"Can I hold him?" Sophie pleaded.

"If you're very, *very* careful," Mama told her. "He's a hundred times more fragile than Lisette." That was Sophie's china doll, whom she'd lost in the river. David thought it helped that his sister was sitting Indian-style, so it was basically impossible for her to drop the baby.

Still Mama kept a close eye on them. "I thought about naming him Peregrine after your father. But I'm afraid that would condemn him to a life of wandering too." Mama looked to David. "When you were born, your father suggested Ian. It's Scottish for John, so it *is* a saint's name—it still means 'gift of God.'"

This news made David feel strange, like he might have been a different person. "Why didn't you name me Ian?"

"I liked David. I thought Ian sounded too foreign. But I think your father deserves..." Mama looked away. "Your father deserved more than I gave him."

David frowned, wondering what she meant.

Then Mama asked: "David, do you remember Charleston at all?"

"I...remember the museum with the animal specimens."

Mama smiled for the first time in days. "I thought you would. Your great-great-granduncle Thierry's butterflies are part of that collection. He also left books to the Library Society—I know you'd like to read *them*."

Now David was truly confused. Why was Mama getting so excited about a place they were never going to see again?

"You were born in Charleston too, Sophie; but you were so small when we left. You probably don't remember your Grandma and Grandpa, or your Aunt Hélène and Uncle Joseph."

Sophie thought about it. "Uncle Joseph is the one who sends us seeds and flat flowers?"

"*Pressed* flowers," Mama corrected, smiling again. "And your Aunt Hélène's letters usually make us laugh."

"Grandpa sends good presents," Sophie added. He'd sent her doll and David's microscope.

"How would you both like to live with them in Charleston?"

"You mean, we'd turn back?" David asked.

Mama nodded. "We're not even halfway, and the most difficult part of the journey is still ahead. We would have to cross not only mountains but a desert. No one has ever done that with wagons before. Even the trappers don't want to risk it. Before Fort Hall, Mr. Fitzpatrick and the others are going to leave on their own or with the Jesuits. After that, all the settlers have is a map. Even if we made it... Do you *want* to live in California?"

David stared down at the moccasins he'd gotten at Fort Laramie. What was that expression? *"I've seen the elephant."* He'd seen the Indians. He didn't need to stay and be scalped. It was one thing to read about adventures. It was another to have to survive them. He thought of Pa. "I wanted to go at first. I don't anymore."

Mama touched his book. "There are good schools in Charleston, David. You could even go to college."

"And there's a beach?" Sophie cut in. "With shells and pelicans?"

"And dolphins!" Mama smiled again. "And more kinds of flowers than you can imagine. But going back will be hard, too. I'll need you both to be very brave and very strong for me. Do you think you can do that?"

David and his sister nodded.

MR. PIGUE, A RED-HAIRED FRENCH TRAPPER who'd been helping the Jesuits, agreed to stay with David's family. Mama seemed relieved it would be him, and David was surprised. Weeks ago, she'd said to Pa: *"I can't put my finger on it, but that Mr. Pigue is odd even for a trapper."* Some of the others whispered about him, though David hadn't been able to catch enough of it to understand why. All he knew was, one of the trappers had told David to stay away from Mr. Pigue. The Frenchman had a scar under one eye, so he looked kind of mean, but he wasn't. In fact, he had better manners than the other trappers. That must be why Mama trusted him.

He would take them back at least as far as the two forts where the Laramie River met the Platte. (There had been a trading post at the fork for six years now; and that spring, rival traders had built a second post a mile away.) From there, Mr. Pigue thought they could return to Missouri alongside empty supply wagons or some other company. Mama still had the money Grandpa had sent them for starting in California—that would help. Maybe Mr. Simpson or Mr. Mast would still be at Fort Laramie. They'd come along for the adventure and the hunting but had decided to turn back too.

The other women tried to convince Mama to keep going. Mrs. Gray (no kin to the half-breed Mr. Grey) had been a widow when she'd started. One of the Mrs. Kelseys also had a baby, and David overheard her arguing with Mama in a low voice: "But you'll need me to nurse Ian, until your milk comes in."

"I *told* you, Nancy: I am a doctor's daughter—and Ian is not my first child. What I have now is called colostrum, and it's *good* for him."

Even Martha came back to give Mama advice. "I know you're sad about Mr. McAllister. But my Papa says there will be scores of husbands to choose from once we cross the mountains. He says *I'll* probably get proposals, because California has so few white women."

When Martha left, Mama was especially quiet. David figured she was thinking about Pa, but it turned out she was thinking about something else, too. Sophie had gone outside with Martha, so David was alone with Mama and baby Ian, who was sleeping.

Mama said: "There's something you need to understand, David, before we return to Charleston. I think you're old enough now." She played with the pale wisps of hair on the baby's head. "Ian and Sophie take after your father, thank God. But you'll have to be more careful, because you take after me. And I'm *not* white—we're not white."

"*What?*"

For once, Mama didn't scold him for being impolite. "My father, your grandfather René, he was born a slave on Saint-Domingue— it's called Haiti now. His mother was a *mulâtresse*." Mama told David about his great-great-grandmother Marguerite bringing his baby grandfather René to Charleston, a story he thought he knew. "We're colored, David, and if you have children, they will be colored too. They might even be darker than you; they might look like— I've heard that can happen." She looked back at baby Ian. "You can't imagine how terrified I've been, every time."

Even though David was sitting, he still felt dizzy.

"I agreed to come to the frontier with your father because color matters less here. But *this* isn't the life I want for you." Mama looked up at the tent roof, then tugged on the leg of David's coarse trousers. "You're so bright, David—like your Uncle Joseph. You could make something of yourself: live in a fine house, wear the clothes of a gentleman. If we're found out…well, *then* you can move to California. But you should hold onto Charleston as long as you can."

THE OTHER TRAVELLERS needed to get over the mountains before the snows started, so they couldn't wait with David's family any longer. Before they separated, they all tried to guess who would need what most, and they traded supplies. The families who still had wagons kept Pa's oxen, but Mama got an extra mule. David renamed it Sacagawea, to go with their cart mules, Lewis and Clark.

The three Mrs. Kelseys washed their family's dishes and clothes so Mama could keep resting. Mrs. Williams gave them fresh bread and strawberry preserves. Mr. Grey brought back pieces of a new-killed buffalo, and Mr. Pigue set to cooking and drying them. Martha gave them a book. It was fairy stories, but David thanked her anyway.

Father De Smet baptized baby Ian, just in case, and he heard the Confessions of David's family (even Sophie, who was seven and old enough to sin now). All the Priests blessed them. Father Mengarini gave Mama a rosary he'd gotten from the Holy Father himself.

Now David had time to explore. His family and Mr. Pigue would stay at Independence Rock a couple more days till Mama and baby Ian were stronger. David climbed all the way to the top of the Rock and watched the missionary carts and the wagons trail away into the distance, past Devil's Gate and around the bend till they disappeared from sight.

Mr. Fitzpatrick and Mr. Pigue agreed that the Indians who roamed between Independence Rock and the two forts were mostly friendly. Perhaps baby Ian *was* lucky. He'd chosen a good place to be born, like an oasis. The Sweetwater River wove along beside their camp, which meant good water and grass for the animals. There were even trees for shade and wood. From atop the Rock, David could see buffaloes and antelope too. They would have fresh game whenever they wanted.

Yesterday, they'd also seen wolves.

CHAPTER 23

We arrived at Rock Independence, and felt ourselves in a new region... I was startled by its surprising likeness to the scenery of Eastern Africa.

— Richard F. Burton, *The City of the Saints* (1861)

L ate that morning, David and Mr. Pigue had a contest to see who could shoot better. Mr. Pigue could hit a rattlesnake right through the head at forty yards, so he won. But he helped David improve his aim and told him he only needed more practice. "You have to account for the wind out here," he explained.

Even though they'd gone to the far side of the Rock, Mama heard the bangs, and she scowled when they got back. "You startled Ian and made him cry."

Standing just outside the tent, Mr. Pigue took off his hat and said he was sorry.

"Won't you attract Indians that way?"

"It's possible, Madame," the trapper admitted. "But they'll be too curious to hurt us. Indians in these parts haven't seen a white woman or children before."

"I will not have savages poking their dirty noses in this tent!" Now *she* startled baby Ian. "I don't want them touching my children!"

"I'll make sure they don't, Madame," Mr. Pigue promised.

When Sophie came out to pee, David shook the dead snake's rattles and made her shriek.

Mr. Pigue was a good cook, at least of meat. Mama was not surprised. "He's French, isn't he?" Still, she treated him like a servant. David didn't think she liked having to rely on a trapper, even though he hardly ever cursed near her.

That afternoon, Mr. Pigue showed David where he'd carved his name on Independence Rock before David was even born, on a place where the wind had rubbed the surface smooth. Father Mengarini had left his hammer and chisel, and Mr. Pigue demonstrated how to use them. Some of the others in the wagon train had only painted on their names with axle grease, but Mr. Pigue said that would come off.

David wanted *his* name to still be here a hundred years in the future. This was the farthest West a McAllister had ever come. It was probably the farthest West a colored boy had ever come, too.

Mr. Pigue could see that his horse was wandering off, so he had to climb down. David stayed on the Rock for a while. He was glad for the chance to be alone. David kept thinking about what Mama had said, that he was a half-breed—or something like it. He tried to do the figures. Maybe a sixteenth-breed? Was that even a word? Mama had said his children might be darker, so he had to be more than one-sixteenth, didn't he? Like the darkness was hiding inside him, just waiting?

This was why Mama always got fretful when he didn't wear his hat. She was afraid his color would come to the surface and everyone would realize what he was. Mama didn't know that he'd become brown all over since leaving Missouri; out of sight of the women, he'd been swimming naked with no trees to shade him.

David tried to stare at his face in the blade of his knife. He pulled out a few strands of his hair, so curly they were springy—and black as sin. After he'd gotten his microscope on his ninth birthday, he'd examined his hair so carefully. Why hadn't he realized what it meant?

David remembered Mama's reaction when Grandpa had sent him Mungo Park's *Travels in the Interior Districts of Africa*. When she'd seen him with it, Mama had demanded: "Why would you want to read such a thing?" Because it was fascinating! "Dr. Park is Scottish like Pa, and a botanist like Uncle Joseph," David had argued. But Mama had taken the book away, and he'd never seen it again.

David also remembered their first summer in Missouri, just before school started, when he'd gone fishing and brought back a negro boy along with the bass.

Mama had been on the porch, peeling sweet potatoes. She looked up at him and the negro, and her eyes went wide. "What is this?"

Didn't she mean *who*? "This is Noah. I met him down on the river."

Mama gripped her knife as if she might use it on something besides potatoes. "Well, he isn't welcome here."

David answered quickly: "I know he isn't Catholic, Mama, but he isn't a slave, either. He's free."

"So he's a beggar."

"No! I wouldn't have caught anything if it weren't for Noah—he shared his bait. I told him about the sweet potato pie you're making for dinner, and—"

"He is *not* staying for dinner!"

David hesitated. "What if I share my piece with him?"

"Absolutely not!" She stood up and glared at Noah. "Get away from my son this instant! And don't you *ever* come near him again!"

David tried to offer Noah half the fish they'd caught, but the boy fled. David wheeled back to Mama. "You told me I should make friends!"

"Not with *his* kind! Do you hear me?" She gripped David's shoulders. "Do you?"

"Why not?"

"You associate with negroes, and you'll become lazy and coarse, just like them!" She shook David by the shoulders till his head ached. "Negroes don't know right from wrong! They lie and steal and kill you in your sleep the moment you let down your guard! Is that who you want to be?"

"No, Mama."

"Every time you see them, you remember, David: 'I will not be *that*.'"

"Yes, Mama."

ONCE THEY RETURNED TO CHARLESTON, they would be surrounded by negroes. And Grandpa was one of them. Grandpa had been a slave, at least when he was a baby. How could a baby be a slave? How could a slave own slaves? None of it made any sense.

David almost wished they were still going to California. But he didn't want Mama or Sophie or his baby brother to die like Pa.

Now that no one could see, David let the tears come. He stayed on top of Independence Rock till he heard thunder rolling in the distance. He knew he must get back to the tent. He wiped his face on his sleeve.

About halfway down the southeastern slope, David found a kind of cave, and he climbed inside. Here the Rock wasn't smooth at all but a jumble of boulders. The rain started pelting, but it didn't matter, because the rocks above protected him. He still needed to carve his name. Inside this space, the weather couldn't reach it. There was plenty of light, too: the cave was open at both ends.

"I don't want you up there during the storms," Mama frowned when he got back. "It isn't safe. You could slip."

"I *was* safe, Mama." David told her about the cave and the rest of his explorations. "Even *Indians* like to leave their names here, or some kind of markings. They call it Painted Rock. Mr. Pigue showed me..." Maybe Indian signs weren't the best thing to tell Mama. "On the top of the Rock, there are these bowls that collect water and dirt. Some have long grasses growing in them. One of the bowls actually has a tree—a little pine."

Mama did like that. "A bird must have dropped a cone." Then she became serious again. "I suppose our family is like that, aren't we? Dropped somewhere we don't belong, with the shallowest of roots, buffeted by storms, trying to survive against the odds."

Did she mean they didn't belong here, or they didn't belong in Charleston? David didn't ask, and he didn't say that the tree had been tilting, as if it might fall over before very long.

When his sister found out about the cave, she made David take her back there and carve her name beneath his. When he was finished, he let Sophie dot her i's. She stuck the tip of her tongue through her lips at the effort. Then David carved

CHARLESTON, S. C.
JULY 1841

underneath, so everyone who saw their names would know how far they'd come and when they'd been here. He let his sister do the S. C. dots, too.

That evening, Mr. Pigue showed David and Sophie the trade goods he'd brought along to make the Indians like him: glass beads, red paint, and small mirrors. The trapper called it "foofuraw." Sophie started whining till Mr. Pigue gave her a few beads. Mama helped her make them into a necklace.

When they lay down to sleep, Mama was shivering. "It gets so cold here at night," she complained.

David wasn't cold yet; the sun had only just set. He thought it was plenty warm in the tent. But you could never tell with women, especially a lady like Mama. "I'll fix it, Mama." David grabbed one of their extra blankets and hurried outside. He would prove how little negro blood was in him. Negroes were lazy—Mama and everybody else said so. *He* would be industrious.

Mr. Pigue was still outside his own tent, smoking by the fire-pit where he'd cooked supper. David got his permission but refused his help. With their shovel, David rolled a few rocks away from the coals. Then he wrapped them in the blanket, dragged it inside their tent, and tucked it next to Mama's feet. She said he was a good boy and settled in with baby Ian.

But in the night, Mama kept tossing and turning and murmuring. David could even hear her teeth chattering. He whispered: "Should I heat up some more rocks, Mama?" But the ones he'd given her were still warm. "I don't need two blankets, Mama; do you want one of mine? I'm not cold, honest." She accepted and blessed him.

When dawn came, Mama had kicked off all three of her blankets. She was still trying to sleep, so David leaned over her to pull one back on. The moment he brushed her belly, she screamed.

Beside David, Sophie started awake, her hair wild, her eyes wide as plates. Of course baby Ian woke up too and started crying.

"What happened?" Mr. Pigue threw aside their tent flap, letting in the sunlight.

Mama's face was red like she'd been running up a hill. She was breathing fast too, when she hadn't even sat up. She kept trying to touch her belly and clenching her hands instead.

Now Mr. Pigue cursed.

Was this David's fault? Had the rocks he'd brought in made her *too* hot?

"What's wrong, Mama?" Sophie begged.

"It's nothing." Mama tried to smile, even though her hands were still fists. "I'll be all right in a little while."

David ran out to their trunk, to their supply of medicines. He came back with the bottle of laudanum.

At first, Mama only stared at it, even though she kept gritting her teeth in pain. She looked over to the unhappy baby Ian, whom Sophie was trying to calm. "If only my father were here," Mama whispered. "This might stop my milk. Or it might go into Ian and harm him."

Finally Mama agreed to swallow a little of the laudanum mixed in water. When she opened her mouth, David saw that her tongue was coated white.

The laudanum made Mama sleepy and dulled the pain in her

belly, but it didn't lower her fever. Baby Ian slept even more than before. David had to wake Mama so she could wake the baby so he could eat. He still had an appetite, and he kept soiling his diapers.

Sophie had washed them before, but now she was acting more like a two-year-old than a seven-year-old. She even sucked her thumb, something she hadn't done in years. If David insisted, his sister would hold baby Ian and get him to burp. But she refused to do anything that required her to leave Mama's side.

"What's wrong with you, Mama?" Sophie asked a second time.

"Sometimes mamas get sick after they give birth," she murmured.

"But they get better, right?"

Mama didn't answer.

"They get better, right?" Sophie demanded.

Mama had fallen asleep again. His sister reached out to shake her, but David stopped her. "Let her rest, Sophie. She needs to rest."

"She's *been* resting—ever since Ian came! She's just getting worse!" Sophie stuck her thumb in her mouth again and started rocking.

So David had to wash the baby's diapers. Disgusting as this was, at least it gave him something to do besides worry. He knew it was silly, but he wished they'd kept Ian's caul for good luck.

The first time David hurried down to the river with a filthy diaper, he passed Mr. Pigue, who was making Mama some meat broth. "You'll look out for rattlesnakes?" called the trapper.

David nodded. "I remember you said they can swim."

It took David a long time to get the diapers clean. Their contents were blacker and stickier than anything that had ever come out of David. He wondered if his brother was ridding himself of his negro cells.

Even when baby Ian's diaper was fresh, something in the tent smelled rotten. David thought it was coming from Mama. Finally he got brave enough to ask her if he could help. She cried and let him. He cleaned her up the best he could, but the bad smell came back.

Outside their tent, Mr. Pigue mostly paced. Toward evening, he convinced Mama to drink a tea he'd learned about from the Indians. It seemed to help with her fever, but not much.

Mama kept kissing Ian's head and murmuring, "Please let my baby live," while she clutched the rosary blessed by the Holy Father. Sometimes she changed it to: "Please, God, let my babies live," while she gripped Sophie or David's hands so hard it hurt. She was strong enough to do that.

After they ate a little supper, when Mama and the baby were sleeping again, Sophie begged for another story. David was glad to think about something besides Mama's sickness. First, he lit their lantern. "Do you know about Mr. Glass and the grizzly bear?"

His sister shook her head.

"Well, many years ago, there was a trapper named Hugh Glass. He was with a bunch of other trappers at a fort when Indians attacked them. Half of the trappers got killed, and the rest ran for their lives. Mr. Glass went ahead scouting for the others, but he came across a grizzly bear and her cubs. Before he could escape or even grab his rifle, the grizzly tore into him with her claws and her teeth. Finally Mr. Glass killed her with his knife."

"What happened to the cubs?" Sophie wanted to know.

Mr. Fitzpatrick, who'd told David the story, hadn't mentioned their fate. "They're not important."

"But—"

"The cubs got away," David decided. "They were old enough to survive on their own."

"I don't like this story," Sophie pouted.

"You will—I promise. The other trappers found Mr. Glass. They took care of his wounds as best they could and made a *travois* to drag him behind one of their horses. But the Indians were still after them, and dragging Mr. Glass was slowing them down. The leader of the trappers said two men should stay behind with Mr. Glass till he died. They'd get half a year's extra wages. The youngest of the trappers, Mr. Bridger, said he'd stay. He needed the money: he was an orphan, and he had a sister back in Missouri to take care of. A man named Mr. Fitzgerald also agreed to stay, and the other trappers took off."

"*Our* Mr. Fitzgerald?" his sister interrupted.

"Our guide was Mr. *Fitzpatrick*. He met Mr. Bridger later."

"Oh."

"Mr. Fitzgerald and Mr. Bridger dug a grave for Mr. Glass and waited and waited. While he was sleeping, they spotted Indians in the distance, and Mr. Fitzgerald said he wasn't going to wait any longer. Mr. Glass was a goner, but there was no sense in all of them dying. Mr. Bridger didn't want to abandon their friend. But Mr. Bridger wasn't even twenty years old, and it was his first time in the wilderness. He was scared. He knew he couldn't fight off the Indians alone—and his little sister was depending on him. He had to make a choice. Finally he decided to save himself. Mr. Fitzgerald wasn't sorry at all. He even took Mr. Glass's provisions and his rifle. They planned to tell everybody they'd stayed till he died, see, and a dead man doesn't need a gun. Mr. Fitzgerald dragged Mr. Glass into his grave and they left him."

"I *really* don't like this story," Sophie whimpered.

"It isn't over yet. Mr. Glass didn't die. When he woke up and realized his friends had abandoned him, it made him angry, and he wanted revenge. He crawled out of his grave and found some berries to eat. He killed a rattlesnake with a rock and ate it raw. He couldn't walk, but he started crawling to the nearest fort—even though it was three hundred miles away."

When he'd told the story, Mr. Fitzpatrick had explained how Mr. Glass had left the maggots in his torn-up leg: they'd actually helped him, because they ate only the dead parts of his flesh. David had been fascinated, but he didn't want to give Sophie nightmares.

"Remember, Mr. Glass didn't have any food or even a gun. After a while, he found a couple wolves who'd just killed a buffalo. He scared them off and ate the meat himself. Eventually some friendly Indians found him. They treated his wounds and gave him a little boat so he could make it the rest of the way to the fort.

"When Mr. Glass reached it, the trappers there took him for a ghost, because everybody thought he was dead. Mr. Bridger was still there, but when Mr. Glass saw how sorry he was, he decided to forgive him. Mr. Fitzgerald still had his rifle, though. Mr. Glass tracked him down at another fort. Mr. Fitzgerald thought Mr. Glass would kill him for sure. But once he got his rifle back, Mr. Glass decided to forgive him too."

Sophie frowned at him. Her face said: *Is that it?*

"All of that really happened!" David said. "It goes to show: Even when you think it's hopeless, it isn't!"

His sister still wasn't satisfied. So David read her a story from the book Martha had given them, about an orphan girl with a mean stepmother. For a while, the girl had to work as hard as a slave, but then she married a prince. Sophie liked that story better, even though none of it was true. She smiled and sighed and fell asleep as if everything would be better when she woke up.

David checked on Mama, who was still sweating. Then he took the lantern outside and sat with Mr. Pigue by the fire.

"Are they all sleeping?"

David nodded.

"You should rest too, David."

He couldn't. Like Reverend Williams had said, David was the man of the family now. Mr. Pigue wasn't kin, and he wouldn't be with them forever. It was up to David to look after Mama and Sophie and the baby. He couldn't do that if he fell asleep. In a couple hours, he had to wake Mama to feed Ian.

The trapper offered him a pipe. David shook his head. Mr. Pigue didn't say anything else; he only looked at David sadly, like Mama was already—

Even by the fire, it was cold. But David was afraid if he returned to the tent, Mama *would* be…

Men were brave. David crawled back in the tent. Mama was the same. He would stay awake right here and watch over his family like Pa would have done.

In the end, sleep was stronger than he was.

When baby Ian's wails speared through his brain, David jerked awake. Then Sophie started wailing too. This time, Mama didn't wake up, even when David shook her. He only needed to touch her once, and he knew for sure. She wasn't soft or warm anymore.

Mr. Pigue stumbled in like he hadn't slept much either. He knelt beside Mama for a moment, crossed himself, and left the tent. In a few minutes, David heard the horrible sharp sound of their shovel scraping down into the Earth.

Baby Ian's bawling soon drowned even that.

David staggered out to watch Mr. Pigue, who had chosen a spot right next to Independence Rock. "Wh-Why did she die?"

The trapper kept digging. "You'll have to save that question for the Jesuits, son."

"No, I mean: She was fine after the baby came; she was fine the day before yesterday…"

"I'm not a doctor, David. I can't explain it. I'm sorry."

David frowned even more then. "What did you mean, about asking the Jesuits? We aren't going to see them again."

"We have to catch up to the wagons now."

"But we're going back East."

Mr. Pigue glanced over his shoulder. "Even if we cached the cart and most of the supplies, it's at least four days' hard travel back to Fort Laramie. Your brother can't survive that long without milk. We *might* find an Indian woman between here and there who's able and willing to help, but we can't risk it. Even if we did, the wet nurse wouldn't want to leave her family and go all the way back East with you."

David supposed Mr. Pigue was right. They couldn't leave baby Ian with a savage woman to reclaim at some future time—they might lose him forever. And David and Sophie couldn't live with the Indians. Mama wouldn't want that for either of them.

"We know for a fact that one of the Mrs. Kelseys is nursing," Mr. Pigue reasoned. "She is your brother's best hope."

"But they left two days ago."

"We've got mules. We can travel twice as fast as the oxen. The wagons will have to take the pass—I know the way. We should catch up to them early tomorrow. If we can get him to drink some sugar water, I think your brother can survive until then."

"We'll have to stay with the wagon train? We'll have to go to California?"

"You don't have any other choice."

Baby Ian was ruining everything. The Kelseys and Williamses and the widow were nice enough, but David didn't want any of them to be his new parents. He and Sophie still had a family, only they were in Charleston. How would he and his sister ever get back there now?

Mr. Pigue interrupted his thoughts: "Could you collect some rocks for me, son?"

David got a blanket from the tent. Sophie wouldn't leave Mama, and at least she was holding baby Ian. All he did was cry. David was glad to keep away from him. He went to where there had been a rock slide and piled several on the blanket, then dragged the rocks back to the grave. David did this again and again till the trapper told him he could stop.

Mr. Pigue wrapped Mama in a quilt. When he picked her up, her rosary fell to the ground. Sophie grabbed it without dropping baby Ian. "She'll want this!"

"We should throw it in the river," David muttered.

"Don't say that!" his sister gasped. "You'll make God angry!"

"What difference could that possibly make?" David shot back. "He can't do anything else to us!"

Sophie ran after Mr. Pigue. She put the rosary and some flowers with Mama.

The trapper asked: "Did you learn any Latin in school, David?"

He nodded.

"Did you understand any of the prayers the Priests said over your father? Do you remember any of them?"

David knew he should say something, even if he didn't believe it. "I remember the parts they said more than once." He repeated the words in English: "'Eternal rest grant unto her, O Lord. And let perpetual light shine upon her. ... Lord, have mercy on us.'"

But He wasn't merciful at all. That rainbow had been a lie.

Even when David had helped Mr. Pigue pile the rocks on top of Mama's grave, there was no time to rest. They collapsed the tent and gathered the dried strips of buffalo. None of them felt like breakfast, except baby Ian. Mr. Pigue mixed sugar into water, soaked a handkerchief in it, then showed Sophie how to pretend her fingertip was Mama's nipple. Baby Ian sucked for a little while, then seemed even angrier than before. Sophie tried to keep him from fussing, but it was useless. His cries wound up and up till he was red-faced and bawling like some sort of windstorm.

David could barely hear Mr. Pigue asking him: "You think you can drive the mules?"

David nodded and shouted back: "Pa taught me!"

"We'll have to ford the Sweetwater nine times before we reach the pass," the trapper warned him. David was sure he'd heard wrong, but Mr. Pigue repeated it: *nine times*. "The Sweetwater keeps winding back on itself," he explained. "But it isn't deep, and you can see how narrow it is—almost a creek."

It looked like a river to David. Why hadn't they kept the baby's caul?

"I'll be right beside you," the trapper promised.

Pa had also taught David how to harness and hitch Lewis and Clark, but he needed Mr. Pigue's help. Together they loaded trunk after barrel after box after parcel onto the cart, or strapped it to Sacagawea and Mr. Pigue's pack mule, Molly. Before they were through, every muscle in David's body felt like jelly.

Finally everything was ready, only Sacagawea had gone down to the Sweetwater for a drink. Mr. Pigue mounted his horse and went after her. He'd almost reached the mule when his horse shrieked and reared up. He called out, but he couldn't control her, and he couldn't hold on. He fell to the ground with a great splash. When David ran to the bank, he saw a rattlesnake sliding away across the surface of the river, as if it were walking on water.

David ignored the fleeing horse and mule and hurried down to the trapper. "Mr. Pigue?"

Sophie was close behind him with the wailing baby.

"Mr. Pigue, are you all right?" He lay half in the river and perfectly still. David shook him. Then he saw the blood discoloring the water and the submerged rock under Mr. Pigue's head.

"Is he dead too?" his sister whimpered.

David sank to his knees in the mud and nodded.

"You said God couldn't do anything else to us!" Sophie screamed over the baby's cries. "I told you you'd make Him angry! This is your fault!"

CHAPTER 24

Sickness and death in the states is hard but it is nothing to be compared with it on the plains…
— Lydia Allen Rudd, "Notes by the Wayside En Route to Oregon, 1852"

"We're not *leaving* him, are we?"

David was marching to their mule-cart. He turned back sharply to his sister. She didn't have to make this harder. David had already apologized in his head. "It would take hours to bury him, Sophie! *If* we could even drag Mr. Pigue up the bank!"

"But we can't—"

"There's no time. We have to reach the wagon train as soon as possible."

"But I don't want to go to California! I want to live with Grandpa!"

"So do I!" David yelled back. He glared at the complaining baby. David hadn't eaten since supper yesterday—even longer than the baby—and he wasn't crying about it. "But he needs milk. He'll die if he doesn't get it. We have to find Mrs. Kelsey. We don't have a choice."

David gave up on catching Mr. Pigue's horse or the pack mule who'd seen the snake; they were nowhere in sight. Mr. Pigue had already tied Molly to the back of the cart, and Lewis and Clark were hitched. While his sister climbed onto the seat, David held the crying baby at arm's length.

Then he climbed up beside Sophie, took the reins, and yelled at the mules to move. Mr. Pigue had said they'd catch up to the others tomorrow morning. That wasn't so long. He could do this. Even if they did have to ford it nine times, the Sweetwater was nothing like the Platte. All they had to do was follow the wagon tracks to the safe spots.

But when they rounded Independence Rock, Lewis and Clark turned back their ears and stopped. David let the reins go slack and simply gaped. Between them and Devil's Gate, the plain had become a black ocean of buffalo. He'd thought the herds they'd seen these past weeks were large, but those had been nothing compared to this. The trappers had told him there were millions of buffalo on the prairie. Until now, David hadn't believed them.

He stood up on the seat and tried to find where the herd was coming from. Maybe the cart could get around behind them. But the buffalo continued in one single moving mass all the way to both horizons. There was no end to them. No way through, either. The mules had already refused to go any farther. And if even one buffalo decided to charge them...

David's legs wobbled and he sat down again. His head ached, and the baby's howls were making it worse. David closed his eyes for a moment. He'd hardly slept last night. His brain felt fuzzy. He wanted to curl up under a tree, but he couldn't. Everything was up to him now. His sister was depending on him. He had to decide what to do.

He remembered Mr. Pigue telling him that a few years back, he and a fellow trapper had watched a herd pass for two full days before the last animals straggled out of sight. Even when the buffalo were gone, how could he possibly follow the wagons now? Beyond Devil's Gate, David had no idea which way to go; and any tracks not wiped out by the thunderstorms would be tramped out by the buffalo.

What had he been thinking? They *had* to go back to Fort Laramie. At least they'd been that way already. He knew where the sloughs were and which water was alkali. They could follow the Platte most of the way. The buffalo were an omen. He turned the mules.

"What are you doing?" his sister demanded.

"We can't go that way." David rubbed his eyes. "We have to go back."

"But you said Ian would die if he doesn't get milk!"

As if it understood, the baby started wailing at a new pitch.

David clenched his jaw. "Yes."

"We can't let him die too!"

"We can't go forward, Sophie. If we try, we will *all* die. Even if there weren't any buffalo, I don't know the way. Do you understand?"

"Yes, but—"

"The baby is going to die no matter what we do."

As they rounded Independence Rock, that baby kept howling and howling. David couldn't think with this noise rattling his skull. He couldn't save his sister.

At the southeastern slope, David stopped Lewis and Clark. "Hold these." He gave Sophie the reins. She took them all in one hand, still protesting. David jumped down from the cart and held out his hands. "Give it to me."

She clutched the baby to her. "He's not an 'it'! His name is Ian!"

"It's not a doll, Sophie!" David shouted through the baby's cries. "You can't keep it alive by petting it and singing to it!"

"I know that!"

"Do you? Do you want to stop every few hours and wash its diaper?" David stretched up on his toes and tugged at the baby's skirt, trying to grab it.

Sophie wouldn't let go. "What are you going to do to him?"

"Nothing!" David yelled over the baby's wails. "I'm not going to hurt it! But it's pointless to take it with us! It's going to die anyway!

Do you want to listen to it howling hour after hour, day and night, until that happens? Indians will hear it and come scalp us!"

His sister kept pouting. She wasn't convinced. "*He* is our brother! We won't ever have another one!"

"That's right, Sophie. We're orphans because of *him*. Maybe it's my fault Mr. Pigue died." David glared at the baby. He wasn't lucky. He was cursed. "But it's *his* fault Mama died."

That made his sister hesitate. She lessened her grip just long enough for David to snatch the baby. Sophie tried to grab it back too late, and she only got its frilly bonnet. Carrying his squalling burden out in front of him, David raced up the slope of the Rock. He responded only once to Sophie's cries: "Don't let the mules move!"

He reached the cave and ducked inside. The baby's wails bounced off the rock walls, attacking him again and again. David knelt and stared down at the red little face. The baby was baptized. It would go straight to Heaven. Leaving it here was better than leaving it with a savage.

David had to save Sophie. He couldn't do that with the baby slowing them down and making him crazy. His mind was made up.

Suddenly, the baby quieted. It only hiccupped and gasped. Its tiny lips trembled, its tiny hand reaching out. Uncertain now, David brought it closer. Then the baby blew out snot and rooted against his chest like a piglet, as if trying to find a nipple. Wanting the impossible.

David pushed the baby away from him. He laid it on the floor of the cave and let go. He closed his eyes, pressed his hands over his ears, and turned around.

When he got back to the cart, David didn't hear a word Sophie said. For miles and miles, all he could hear was the pounding of blood in his ears and the cries of the baby behind him.

By the time David halted Lewis and Clark for the midday rest, his sister had stopped talking to him altogether.

He dug through the provisions under the cart's little canvas and told her what food they had: jerked buffalo, dried apples, and hard-tack. "What do you want?"

When Sophie did not respond, David looked up to see her scowling at him. She was still clutching the baby's bonnet.

"We're *not* going back!" he yelled loud enough for the baby to hear.

If they were going to survive, they had to keep moving forward. They couldn't go back, no matter how much David wanted to.

When they'd travelled with the wagon train, they'd always unhitched and unpacked the animals during nooning. But David was afraid he wouldn't be able to put everything back together, at least not quickly. It was all so heavy and complicated, and he was already so tired.

David told Sophie to wake him the moment she started feeling sleepy. He thought she enjoyed shaking him extra hard. The mules' rest hadn't been much of a rest either, so they were reluctant to start again. When David finally got them going, he thought about grabbing the baby's bonnet from Sophie and throwing it out of sight.

Toward evening, David found the copse of red willows where their wagons had camped on Independence Day. There was a good spring here and grass, so he stopped for the night. At their approach, a rabbit darted out of the willows. David grabbed his shotgun, but he was too late.

His sister still wasn't speaking to him. She obeyed only half of his commands, but eventually they unhitched and unharnessed Lewis and Clark; unpacked and unsaddled Mr. Pigue's Molly; got the tent put up; and built a fire of sagebrush. Sophie ate dinner with her back turned to him. It was the same as lunch.

"We can't always get what we want, Sophie," David told her. "When you're older, you'll understand."

His sister crawled into the tent without even looking at him. She was cradling the baby bonnet as if it were a tiny doll. She did not ask for a story.

They'd lost a lot of food when Sacagawea ran off. David wouldn't have known how to cook most of it anyway. They'd also lost their extra clothing and their shovel. David dug through Mr.

Pigue's packs. He found a pistol, powder, and balls. He found a coffee grinder, a skillet, and a pot, but no beans.

He lit the lantern and looked again, just to be sure. He had to stay awake tonight to guard Lewis and Clark and Molly. He couldn't let wolves get them. He couldn't let Indians get them either. His life and Sophie's depended on those mules.

Finally David gave up on the coffee. The cold was making his hands stiff. He bundled himself in Mr. Pigue's buffalo coat and a blanket to keep watch by the fire. The moon was rising fat and yellow in the east. It was waning but more than half full, so it helped some.

David kept picturing the baby, alone in that cave. If Ian was still alive, this cold would kill him. But no matter what they'd done, they couldn't have saved him. He still would have starved, and they didn't even have a shovel to bury him. A wolf would have carried off his little body. In the cave, he should be safe from that. When some trapper or some later wagon train found him, they'd bury him proper. It was better for all of them this way. Not good, but better. Things were different out here on the trail.

Turning back had been the right thing to do. They couldn't get lost on the way to Fort Laramie. When he and Sophie were coming down that big hill, David had already seen the Platte River to the east. All he had to do was follow the north bank till he found a ford, and then follow the south bank all the way to the fort. They'd get across somehow, caul or no caul.

Even if their supplies washed away, he and Sophie wouldn't starve. Even a savage could find food in summer. Maybe David couldn't bring down anything big like a buffalo, but eventually he'd hit a sage-grouse or catch a few fish. They'd find berries.

It was less than two hundred miles back to Fort Laramie—far less than Mr. Glass's journey. John Colter had walked just as far, after savages had stripped him naked and tortured him. Even injured and without mules, those men had survived. David and Sophie would too.

He wasn't the helpless city boy who'd left Charleston. He'd learned from Pa on the farm and from the other men on the trail.

He was ten years old now—almost a man himself. David's patron saint had slain Goliath when *he* was only a boy.

Then, far too close, high-pitched yaps pierced the night like gunshots. Next a single, sad howl filled the darkness till countless others joined it. The cries molded into one, and David felt colder all at once.

The three mules bunched up together in fear, as fast as they could in their hobbles. Inside the tent, his sister whined. It ended like a question.

"I think it's coyotes," David told all of them. He called them coyotes on purpose, instead of "prairie wolves," because it didn't sound as bad. He still got up to put more sagebrush on the fire. He still checked that his shotgun was loaded.

They just had to make it back to Fort Laramie, David told himself over and over. A trader there had been friendly; he'd given all the children lemon drops for free. The trader would help David find someone trustworthy who'd take him and his sister back to Missouri. They'd stay with one of their old neighbors, and they'd write to Grandpa. He'd come and get them, and they'd never be alone again…

David remembered how warm it was in Charleston and how soft the mattresses were. His head kept sagging forward. Surely he could close his eyes for a little while.

HE STARTED AWAKE to the shrieks of the mules. In the dim light of the fire and moon, David picked out one dark shape already thrashing on the ground—a fallen mule. A flurry of dog-like shapes darted toward it. David sprang up, raised his shotgun, and fired. He winced at the recoil against his shoulder, but at least two coyotes yipped in greater pain, and all of them took off.

Quickly David lit the lantern again and reloaded his gun. He heard no snarling, and the coyotes did not reappear. On his way to the mules, he passed his sister, who knelt just inside the tent flap, peering out and shivering.

"Go back to sleep, Sophie. They're gone."

For how long?

The mule on the ground—Clark—was still struggling. His knees were bloody, but they looked like scrapes, not bite marks. Clark must have tried to run and tripped in his hobbles. David unfastened them, and the mule rose shakily. Clark limped, but neither leg seemed to be broken. David had helped Pa treat a calf's scraped knee once. He found one of Mama's petticoats, tore it up, and dipped it in the spring. He used the cloth to clean the wounds and then wrap them.

As he worked, the mules nickered to each other, as if discussing him, as if they were complaining. David knelt for a long time staring at Lewis and Molly's hobbles in the lantern light. If he left them like this and the coyotes returned, worse might happen. The mules might break their legs trying to escape. At the very least, the hobbles would make them easy prey for the coyotes. With their legs free, the mules might run off, but he had to trust that they'd come back.

He couldn't leave the mules helpless. He'd already done enough damage. He wouldn't be responsible for any more deaths.

He tried and tried to stay awake this time; but he couldn't do anything right.

In the morning, the first thing he saw were the skeletons of the sagebrush in the fire pit. David forced himself to his feet. Molly was there, grazing near the willows. Clark lay close by, collapsed on his side. When David rushed over in a panic, the mule raised his head; he was only resting his wounded legs. But David didn't see Lewis anywhere.

"Lewis! Here, boy! Lewis?" David ran to the other side of the little copse. He climbed the nearest hills and peered down. Nothing but sagebrush. Had the coyotes run Lewis off while David was sleeping? Were they feasting on him in some gully? Or had the mule simply abandoned them?

Very slowly, David walked back to camp.

His sister emerged from the tent, rubbing her eyes. She still had the baby bonnet; David saw the edge of it sticking out of her pocket.

He tried to ignore it. "Sophie, have you seen Lewis?"

She shook her head.

David sighed. He stared over at Clark. One of his bandages was coming loose. David should check his wounds again. Maybe they'd be all right without Lewis, but they couldn't lose *two* mules.

David was starting toward Clark when Sophie's stomach rumbled. She whimpered.

He turned back to her. "We have cornmeal and salt. Do you remember how to make mush?"

She shook her head again.

David frowned. "You've watched Mama a hundred times. You've helped her."

Sophie's chin began trembling. She looked like she was going to cry.

She was my Mama too, David thought. But he was older and a boy, so he had to be strong. He snatched up the empty coffee pot and handed it to his sister. "You can fill this, at least, from the spring?"

She sniffled and nodded.

David dragged the sack of cornmeal next to the fire pit. "If I make you breakfast, will you speak to me again?"

She shook her head fiercely.

David boiled the water in the coffee pot and stirred in the cornmeal. The mush burned at the bottom and was lumpy all through. They didn't have any sugar or molasses, let alone butter. Sophie scowled at the mush and then at him.

"If you think you can do better, you try it tomorrow."

His sister made a show of flinging away the burnt parts and the biggest lumps, but she ate the rest. When she was finished, Sophie pulled out the white baby bonnet and stroked it.

David set down his own mush and snatched the bonnet from her.

"Give it back!" his sister cried, speaking to him at last.

David threw the bonnet onto the fire and stopped her from grabbing it back. She hit him a few times, then settled down to sob.

The bonnet caught more easily than he'd thought it would—but it had been a flimsy thing, after all. He added more sagebrush to encourage the flames. When the cotton was only fine ashes, he fetched more water and poured it on the remains.

"David?" his sister whined.

He concentrated on drowning the last of the coals. "We have to forget him, Sophie."

"David!" This time, it was a shriek.

His head snapped up. Her whole arm shaking, Sophie pointed behind him. David twisted around to see what she saw. Coming down one of the hills were Indians on horses.

David sucked in a breath. There were two of them: an old savage and a young one, who both carried bows. Afraid to take his eyes from them, David backed toward his shotgun. "Get inside the tent, Sophie!"

The older savage lifted his right hand and drew his finger across his neck, as if promising to cut their throats.

David tripped over the rocks he'd set around the fire. He crashed backwards into the wet ashes and coals. His chest seemed to clamp shut, but he rolled sideways and grabbed his shotgun. Bracing the stock against his shoulder, he aimed the long barrel at the Indians. "I won't let you hurt my sister!"

The younger savage snatched an arrow from his quiver. Before he could place it in his bow, the older Indian held up his hand and spoke in their language. The young savage frowned at him but lowered his bow. They both stopped their horses.

His backside aching, David staggered beneath the weight of the shotgun as he stood. "Please don't hurt my sister..." If he fired, would the pellets kill *both* of the savages, or only make them angry? Before David could reload, one of the Indians would surely kill him, and then Sophie...

The older savage placed his palms together, extended his arms, and turned his left hand downward. Was that a promise to knock David down again? These were signs, he knew—the way Indians from different tribes communicated with each other and with white men. He'd seen Mr. Fitzpatrick teaching some of the signs to the men in the wagon train, but Mama had called him away before he could learn much of anything. Why hadn't he asked Mr. Pigue?

The Indians were both scowling. They looked around at the tent and the packs and the mules and discussed something in their language. The younger savage seemed angry. They did not advance, and they did not reach for their bows, but David was afraid to lower his shotgun.

In his head, he kept seeing the older Indian drawing his finger across his neck. He kept seeing them cutting Sophie's throat and tearing off her long blonde hair. Maybe she was imagining it too: he could hear her whimpering inside the tent. If they came any closer, he'd have to shoot them. He'd have to try.

Then the Indians turned their horses and galloped away.

David sagged with relief and rested the shotgun on the ground.

His sister ran out to him. "You did it! You scared them away!"

"They might come back. They might bring others." Maybe the Indians intended to torture David and Sophie before they killed them, and they needed an audience? David slapped the black ashes from his trousers as best he could, but the stain clung to him. Then he loaded Mr. Pigue's pistol, which was easier to keep on him than the shotgun. "I need your help, Sophie. We have to pack up and get away from here as quickly as possible."

For once, his sister obeyed without question. While she folded up the tent, David tended to Clark. The wounds looked worse in the sunlight. They'd have to lighten the load in the cart as much as they could. At least Lewis and Clark had been hitched in tandem, so harnessing a single mule would be easier. "You can rest till I get Molly packed," David told Clark.

Unless Molly could help Clark pull. Maybe she was harness broke. There was only one way to find out. David carried Lewis's bridle to Mr. Pigue's mule. The moment the bit got near Molly's mouth, she flicked her head up out of his reach. David tried again and again. Once, he nearly got the bit in, but before he could slip the headstall over those long ears, Molly flung off the bridle.

They didn't have time for this game. David looked back to the hill where the Indians had been. Still empty—for now.

He'd have to pack Molly. She let him attach the lead rope to her halter, but she started wandering off before he could fetch her saddle blanket, so Sophie had to hold her. The top of David's head only came up to Molly's withers, but he managed to throw the pack-saddle up onto her back. He'd helped Mr. Pigue with this yesterday, but it was much more difficult on his own.

David also had to decide in an instant which things to leave behind. Sophie argued with him about keeping Mama's belongings, but they couldn't ask the mules to carry useless weight. David hung everything he could from Molly's saddle, then tossed and looped rope around the packs. Half the time he was standing on his toes and stretching as far as he could reach.

Finally he was ready to hitch Clark, who still lay on the ground. David tugged at his halter. "Come on, boy—get up!"

The mule agreed to a sort of sitting position, with his back legs tucked under him and his bandaged forelegs stretched out. But he refused to stand, no matter how much David yanked and pleaded. "There's hardly anything in the cart now: you'll just be pulling Sophie and me!"

"The coyotes will get you for sure if you stay here!" his sister added, tugging with all of her small might.

"I know you want to rest, but you *can't!*" Was the damage deeper than David could see, or was Clark simply being stubborn? For the hundredth time, David looked up to the hill. Those Indians might return any moment.

Then David heard a horrible clattering noise behind him. He spun around. He saw Molly's tail swishing between two willows. The mule must have squeezed between them on her way to the spring. Half of Molly's packs had fallen off. Blankets, sacks of cornmeal, and tins of trade goods lay strewn all over the ground.

Sophie ran to collect them. David sank onto his knees and closed his eyes. The packs wouldn't have come off if he'd tied them right. This couldn't be happening. It was only their first morning alone.

Four days, he'd been telling himself. Four days, and they'd be back at Fort Laramie. But Mr. Pigue had said it was *at least* four days' *hard* travel *if* they packed light. It had taken the wagon train *twelve* days to get from Fort Laramie to Independence Rock. If David and Sophie had to lead Molly and walk…

They'd be *lucky* to make it in twelve days. Every muscle in David's body was already screaming at him, and he'd never be able to stay awake all those nights. They still had to cross the mile-wide river that had killed Pa, alone.

They had no one to help them. No one else to keep watch or hunt or care for the animals properly. He and Sophie were going to die out here. They were going to drown or be eaten by wolves or get scalped right here beside the willows.

It was like that verse in the Bible: *"For what things a man shall sow, those also shall he reap."* David thought of little Ian crying alone in the cave. What kind of a monster abandoned a baby—abandoned his own *brother*? There were no excuses for something like that. David had proven he was a lazy negro after all. He hadn't wanted to care for Ian. He hadn't wanted to watch him die. Negroes didn't know right from wrong, just like him.

David deserved to die for what he'd done, but Sophie didn't. Maybe if David prayed for *her*, God would listen. *Please don't punish Sophie for my sin*, he begged. *She didn't do anything wrong. She wanted to take Ian with us. She wanted to go back. You can do anything You like to me. Hit me in the head with a hailstone the moment we reach Fort Laramie. But please, please help me get Sophie there.*

Molly let out her strange roaring bray, and his sister gasped. The Indians had returned. This time, there were three of them.

Sophie was still holding one of the tins from Mr. Pigue's packs; it rattled as she ran to David. He yanked the pistol out of his pocket and forced back the hammer.

The newest savage—neither young nor old—repeated that sign where he placed his palms together, extended his arms, and turned the left hand down. But he also called out, words David realized he actually understood. The Indian was speaking French. "We are friends," he was saying. "We are not here to fight. We are here only for those." He seemed to be nodding toward the willows. "We use them for smoking."

David kept the pistol aimed. This could be a trick. Sophie clung to him and whimpered.

All the Indians had halted their horses. The French-speaking savage glanced around. "Where is your father?"

David swallowed. "Our father is dead."

The savage frowned. "You are alone?"

The Indians were more likely to murder him and his sister if they thought no one would seek revenge. "Our grandfather is at Fort Laramie," David lied quickly.

Beside him, his sister scowled. "No he——"

"Shut up, Sophie!" David hissed back in English. He had to think. The first two savages must have left so they could bring back the one who spoke French. Why would they have done that if they only meant to kill him and Sophie? They weren't grabbing their arrows and drawing their bows. The new Indian had a rifle, but it was slung over his back. Slowly, David lowered his pistol. "Do you know it? Fort Laramie?"

"Yes," answered the French-speaking savage. "I go there often to trade. I know your language because my father was French."

The man was a half-breed, like Mr. Grey. Like David himself. This made him feel a little better. "Could... Could you take my sister and me back to the fort?"

The half-breed frowned.

David grabbed the tin from Sophie and opened it to show the beads. "We have things to give you."

The oldest Indian seemed to ask the half-breed a question in their own language. The half-breed answered, and the young one scoffed.

David swallowed. He'd insulted them.

The half-breed glanced to the mules.

"You can have them, too!" David decided. He still had Grandpa's money. He could buy new mules and supplies at the fort. What he and Sophie needed was a guide——someone to get them safely across the Platte River.

The half-breed seemed to be considering. "How long have you and your sister been alone?"

"Since yesterday. Will you help us?"

The half-breed nodded. "I will help you."

David let out the breath he'd been holding.

The old Indian seemed to give the young one a command. He scowled but followed him to the willows.

"What kind of Indians are you?" David asked cautiously.

The half-breed brought his horse to them and dismounted. "Your people call us Sioux." He drew his finger across his throat, just as the oldest Indian had. Was that their tribal sign? "But Sioux is a name our enemies gave us." He peered down at David. "Are you our enemy?"

David's eyes widened and he shook his head.

"Then you must call us Lakota."

David nodded.

"Myself, I am called Yellow Shirt." He glanced toward the other savages. "With me are Standing Bear and Rides Twice."

The young Indian said something that made Yellow Shirt laugh. He translated: "Rides Twice says your name must be Black Rump."

David's face went hot, and he slapped at the ash stain on his backside. "David McAllister! My name is David McAllister!"

Yellow Shirt led Molly back to the things that had fallen. He asked: "Your father, we must put him in the ground?"

David saw Sophie open her mouth, and he glared at her to keep quiet. But Mama had been right when she'd told him once that lies always bred more lies. He must stay as close to the truth as he could. "No. He fell in the river."

Yellow Shirt strapped one of the packs back on Molly. "You are sure he is dead?"

David's throat closed up. What if Mr. Pigue *hadn't* been dead? Yellow Shirt was waiting for him to answer. "He is dead. He hit his head on a rock." David continued quickly, before the Indian could ask any more questions: "How much do you want, to take us to the fort?"

"*I* do not need your things. But others in my village will be happy for more beads. And since you have two guns, maybe you will give us one?"

Yellow Shirt insisted that David and Sophie stay in his village that night, that they should start for Fort Laramie tomorrow morning. David nodded to all of it, because he could do nothing else. Clark was more cooperative when a man was telling him what to do, and Yellow Shirt helped David hitch him to the cart.

As soon as they were on the seat together, David whispered to his sister: "Stay with me every minute. Even when one of us has to pee."

Sophie nodded.

Standing Bear and Rides Twice strapped bundles of willow to their horses and rode ahead of them back to the village. It wasn't far.

As they approached, David saw a crowd of Indians gathering outside the circle of tipis. Mostly they were children, but there were a few men and women. One of the women was nursing a baby.

Sophie saw her too. She gripped David's sleeve. "We can go back and get Ian!" she cried in English. "He'll have milk now!"

David lowered his eyes to Clark's back. "It's too late, Sophie."

"No it isn't! He could live a day without food!"

"Remember how cold it was last night? He couldn't have survived that."

For a moment, she only stared at him. "If we'd kept him with us, we could have kept him warm!"

"You think I don't know that?!"

She started crying. "Even if Ian is dead, we can bury him. We have to tell Yellow Shirt—"

"We can't tell *anyone*, Sophie. Ever!" He squeezed her arm to make sure she understood. "Not now, and not when we get back to Charleston. We have to tell Grandpa and everybody else that Ian died of fever like Mama."

"But that would be lying!"

"You said it, Sophie: If we'd kept him with us, Ian would still be alive. That means I killed him. If anybody finds out, they will hang me." David wasn't sure if they would or not, but it was easier if Sophie believed it. "Do you want them to hang me?"

"No..."

"Then we have to say Ian died of fever."

"But lying is a sin!"

"I'll do the sinning." It hardly mattered, if he was already damned. "I'll say how Ian died. All you have to do is keep quiet. Do you promise to keep quiet?"

At last, Sophie nodded.

CHAPTER 25

Oh what a tangled web we weave,
When first we practice to deceive!
— Sir Walter Scott, *Marmion* (1808)

It took them nearly two months to get back to Missouri, and in all those weeks, Sophie didn't ask David for a story even once. She spoke to him only when she had no other choice. All he had left of his family was a sister who hated him, or at least didn't trust him anymore.

That first night in the Lakota tipi, Sophie even murmured: "If I get sick, will you leave me behind, too?"

"Of course not!" But nothing David said could make her believe him.

In Missouri, after their old neighbors helped them write to Grandpa, David was finally able to confess to a Priest. "Pray, Father, give me your blessing, for I have sinned. I confess to almighty God, to blessed Mary ever Virgin, to Michael the Archangel, to blessed John the Baptist, to the Holy Apostles Peter and Paul, and to all the

Saints that I have sinned exceedingly, in thought, word, and deed, through my fault, through my fault, through my most grievous fault." David struck his breast with his fist till it hurt. "Since my last Confession, which was two months ago, I accuse myself of lying... and of killing my baby brother."

On the other side of the confessional grille, David heard the Priest draw in a sharp breath. He was horrified. "Tell me what you mean by that, my son."

"I lied about killing my brother. I mean: I killed my brother, and ever since, I've been lying to everyone about how he died." David explained how first Pa had died and then Mama and Mr. Pigue. How he had chosen not to go after the other wagons because of the buffalo. How he had abandoned baby Ian and forced his sister to keep quiet about it.

The Priest listened without saying a word. When he finally spoke, it was almost a whisper. "You should not have had to make such choices at your tender age. Circumstances put you in an impossible situation."

David wondered how a situation could be impossible if it had really happened.

"Would a savage wet nurse have kidnapped your brother? Could you have remained with him without you and your sister being killed or becoming pagans? Impossible, as I said. But to *abandon* a child is monstrous. You understand that?"

"Yes." David choked on the word.

"You are contrite—I can hear that—so I can give you Absolution for sinning against your brother. But as you yourself admitted, that was not your only transgression. You have also sinned against your sister, by making her an accessory to your sin. You *must* tell your grandfather and the rest of your family the truth. If you continue to lie—even if you remain silent and simply allow your family to go on believing that your brother died of fever—you continue to sin, mortally. I cannot grant you Absolution for a sin you intend to keep committing. Do you promise to tell the truth?"

"I-I promise," David mumbled.

"As to your Penance...no amount of Our Fathers or Hail Marys can compensate for the death of an innocent. When you chose to abandon your brother, in a single act you committed multiple mortal sins, my son. Anger, because you blamed him for your mother's death. Pride, because you did not wait for Our Lord to spare your brother or take him. Sloth, because you knew caring for a baby would be tiring. But each mortal sin has its conquering virtue. To conquer anger, you must practice patience. To conquer pride, you must practice humility. To conquer sloth, you must practice diligence. Do you know what that word means?"

David nodded. "Working very hard."

"We must all work out our salvation; but you will have to work harder than most, my son. You are young and you have many more choices ahead of you. As you make each of those choices, I urge you to remember your brother. Live your life for him as well as yourself: say prayers and do Works of Mercy for *two* boys. Live your life for your brothers—and sisters—in Christ. Think about them first and yourself second. As our Catechism says: 'The virtuous person… pursues the good and chooses it in concrete actions.' Most of all, pray about your vocation."

"You mean"—David swallowed—"I have to become a Priest?" After seeing—and smelling—what intercourse had done to Mama, the thought of celibacy was not so terrible. But the thought of spending every moment praising God…

"We all have a vocation, my son, whether or not we are called to Holy Orders. Think about how *your* vocation might serve as a Penance for your sin against your brother—how it might teach you patience, humility, and diligence. Perhaps you could run an orphanage or become a physician to the poor. Our Lord promised us: 'Blessed are the merciful: for they shall obtain mercy.' If your life becomes a Work of Mercy, you can please Our Lord as much as you have displeased Him. Even your brother will smile on you from Heaven, because he will see that his death was part of Our Lord's plan—that his sacrifice taught you virtue and allowed you to save thousands of other lives."

.   .   .

DAVID HADN'T MEANT TO LIE to a Priest. But the more he'd thought about it, the more convinced he became: he could never tell his grandfather or anyone else the truth about his brother. If he did, nothing would ever be the same between them. His confessor had called David monstrous. His family would look at him and see a monster too. They would never forget what he'd done, and they would hate him like Sophie did. Maybe, David had told himself, if he did enough Penance—if he became a doctor and saved as many lives as he could—God might still forgive him.

For more than a decade now, David had kept his secret and guarded that hope. But he'd killed his brother to save his sister, and barely a year later, God had taken her, too. Was Sophie's death an omen that David's sins were unforgivable?

Every day since, he'd ached to tell *someone* the truth, to make a full and true Confession at last. Who better to hear it than Uncle Joseph, who knew what it felt like to be a monster?

Joseph listened to David's Confession without a word. When David fell silent, his uncle said many of the things the Missouri Priest had said, with less confidence but more kindness. Joseph disagreed about the lie; he absolved David of that, too. His uncle said nothing could be gained now by telling David's grandparents the truth about Ian's death. The truth wouldn't bring his brother back.

CHAPTER 26

For he who lives more lives than one
More deaths than one must die.
— Oscar Wilde, *The Ballad of Reading Gaol* (1898)

D avid's Confession should have increased Joseph's burdens.
Another secret laid on his shoulders. His tiny nephew not lost
but abandoned. Yet somehow, sharing David's grief began to dispel
Joseph's. Not entirely—that was impossible. David's baby brother
and the woman Joseph loved were still dead, and each of them was
still to blame. But if a ten-year-old boy could become a fine young
man beneath the weight of such a cross, Joseph could carry his too.

When David left his chamber, Joseph slid from his bed and
washed himself for the first time in a fortnight. He pulled on fresh
clothes, lathered his face, and scraped away his beard. Priests were
not allowed whiskers.

When his mother brought him beef tea and a salad, Joseph
consumed them of his own accord. He also apologized, though he
could not explain *why* he'd put her through purgatory these past two
weeks.

He imagined himself making the signs: *I loved Tessa, Mama. I loved her almost as much as Papa loves you. But I didn't love her nearly enough.*

Then he imagined his mother's confusion: *What do you mean, Joseph? Priests don't fall in love. God is everything they need.*

Not everything, Mama.

After his mother had kissed his forehead and left him alone again, Joseph bundled himself in a shawl like the invalid he still was —in mind, if not in body—and passed through the hall onto the piazza. He tried not to think about his last sight of Tessa from this balcony, but he thought of her nonetheless.

Joseph sat down at the back of the piazza, away from the street. Instead of his breviary, he'd brought *The Scarlet Letter*. He returned to its penultimate chapter. As the priest breathed his last, the lovers parted for all eternity:

"Shall we not meet again?" whispered she, bending her face down close to his. "Shall we not spend our immortal life together? Surely, surely we have ransomed one another, with all this woe!"

Dimmesdale doubted it:

"It may be, that, when we forgot our God,—when we violated our reverence each for the other's soul,—it was thenceforth vain to hope that we could meet hereafter, in an everlasting and pure reunion. ... His will be done!"

And with that, the priest expired. Hawthorne concluded:

Among the many morals which press upon us from the poor minister's miserable experience, we put only this into a sentence: —"Be true! Be true! Be true!"

The words rang in Joseph's head like an admonishment, an instruction—as if Hawthorne had written them solely for Joseph and God were speaking to him through this writer who was not even Catholic. But what did "Be true" actually *mean*?

Should Joseph have been true to Tessa? Should he have eloped with her? Should he have been true to his Priesthood? Should he never, ever have answered the blue lamp in the first place? Or had there been some way to "be true" to both Tessa and his Priesthood simultaneously which Joseph had failed to discover?

For so long, Joseph had been certain that he'd found the right path—that not only would God permit him those nights with Tessa, He wished Joseph to have them: to learn, to grow, to drink of her strength, her wisdom, and her joy—but never to be one flesh with her as if they were husband and wife. Surely God understood that Joseph had never forgotten Him, and that everything Joseph had done *was* out of reverence for Tessa's soul, even more than her body.

That precious soul lay in the hands of her Maker now. He was wiser than Joseph; surely He would not let her go.

WHEN JOSEPH'S FATHER FOUND HIM seated on the piazza, he smiled. "I see you've decided to rejoin us."

Joseph closed *The Scarlet Letter*. "More or less."

"Good!" his father declared as if Joseph had been equally enthusiastic. "Because I need your help."

"With?"

His father's mood grew solemn now. He leaned against the balustrade facing Joseph and dropped his voice. "You know Father Wallace died this past January?"

Joseph nodded. In the first years after their meeting, he'd corresponded with Father Wallace and Sarah from time to time. Occasionally, one of their sons would contribute a few lines. Little James must be approaching manhood now: fifteen, perhaps? Joseph's letters had lapsed long before Wallace's death, but he knew his father had been more faithful.

"Wallace was buried with the full honors due a Priest at St. Peter's in Columbia, since anything else would have invited scandal. He left most of his estate to the Church; but that was not enough for our Bishop or his secretary." Joseph's father glanced in the direction of the new cathedral (still under construction). He referred to Dr. Reynolds and Joseph's own pastor, Father Lynch. "They claimed Wallace's *entire* estate—including his wife and sons. Wallace freed Sarah, Andrew, George, and James in his will; but Dr. Reynolds and Father Lynch managed to have his will thrown out."

Despicable as it was, the news did not surprise Joseph. Both Bishop Reynolds and Father Lynch had been reared in the South, and both were already slave-owners. This was hardly the first time rival heirs had refused to treat a man's beloved black family as anything more than valuable property. Although the man in question was rarely a Priest.

"Sarah's own health had been failing for months; flight would have been difficult for her. But she's followed her husband now, so there is nothing holding their sons here any longer. Andrew, George, and James have every right to their freedom. They have secured passes to 'play at a ball,' so at least they won't be missed till tomorrow. Slave catchers *may* already be in pursuit of Andrew's fiancée; she is with them. We need to get them all on a ship tonight. But the captain I've used in the past is dragging his feet now, because of the new fugitive slave act."

"The captain you've…" Joseph echoed, also in a whisper. "You've helped runaways before?"

"When I can. I suppose it's my way of keeping Hélène alive. It was her idea first. She just didn't remain with us long enough to see it through."

Joseph stared down at the brown cover of *The Scarlet Letter* as if it were a catechism. *Is it ever permissible to defy not only state and national law but also your pastor and your Bishop?* the question might read. *To break your solemn vow of obedience?* The wishes of Bishop Reynolds and Father Lynch in this matter were quite clear. Their diocese was poor; naturally they coveted the labor of these three able young negroes for the rest of their lives. The wages of the Wallace boys would help raise the cathedral, heat the Bishop's residence, put new vestments on Joseph's own back.

His father continued: "This captain, he's a very God-fearing man. He attends Mass at the cathedral every time he's in Charleston. He told me he's found *your* homilies particularly edifying. As you know, my pockets aren't deep enough to tempt him with much of a monetary reward. But if *you* can assure him that God approves of this endeavor, I think it will tip the balance in our favor. Will you help me, son?"

Joseph sensed the question didn't apply only to *these* fugitives. Without letting go of *The Scarlet Letter*, he pushed himself from his chair to look down from the back of their piazza. Past their outbuildings, between their neighbors' roofs and trees, he could just see the high wall surrounding the yard of the District Jail. If Joseph and his father were caught, *that* would be their new address.

Three decades ago, Denmark Vesey and his conspirators had been confined in that yard before they were hanged. Even now, the jail yard held slaves awaiting the auction block. Men, women, and children who'd committed no crime whatsoever.

Between Joseph and the jail stood a place of even greater cruelty: Charleston's Work House, remodelled only the year before to resemble some romantic castle, complete with towers and crenellations. Paupers in the British Isles might dread their Work Houses, but Charleston's belonged amongst the Circles of Hell. Its only inmates were slaves who had somehow offended their masters: by attempting to run away or simply by "insolence." If Andrew, George, and James were caught, Bishop Reynolds would send them there.

For a fee, the Work House officials would punish the Wallace boys on their Bishop's behalf, either by flogging them or by forcing them onto the tread-mill. This massive machine ground corn for meal and stones for roads, but mostly it broke spirits and bodies. Weeks into their punishment, if one of the Priest's sons became so exhausted that he simply collapsed, the merciless tread-mill would devour his arm or his leg, maiming him for life.

If the wind was wrong, the screams from the Work House carried all the way to this piazza. Joseph had heard them most of his life. But he'd always stopped his ears.

Sixteen years ago at his ordination, Joseph had chosen to sacrifice himself for the greater good. The men, women, and children in that yard and that Work House had never been given a choice about anything. There was a greater good here, too: greater than the law, greater even than their Bishop.

Joseph could not save everyone held in bondage. He was not Moses. But just because you could not help everyone, that did not mean you should help no one. Aiding the three sons of a Priest seemed a fitting beginning.

As Hélène herself had reminded him: *"To him therefore who knoweth to do good, and doth it not, to him it is sin."* Wherever Tessa was now, Joseph knew she would applaud this work too. He looked down at the spine of *The Scarlet Letter*. What better way to "Be true": to his grandmother Ìfé, his father, his sister, and his beloved all at once. What was that prayer attributed to Saint Teresa? *"Christ has no body now but yours, no hands but yours…"* As long as he had breath in his body, Joseph could be Hélène's and Tessa's hands too. A part of him had died with each of them; but sometimes, to die was gain: only by dying could you be reborn.

"Will you help us?" his father asked again.

Joseph nodded. "I will."

PART VI
THE FOUNDLING

1841-1849

It is difficult to find any Cheyennes without a strain of foreign blood…

— George Bird Grinnell,
The Fighting Cheyennes (1915)

CHAPTER 27

> God moves in a mysterious way,
> His wonders to perform…
> He treasures up his bright designs,
> And works his sovereign will. …
> The bud may have a bitter taste,
> But sweet will be the flow'r.
> — William Cowper, "Light Shining Out of Darkness" (1773)

They were approaching Painted Rock when Zeyá pulled her horse away from the others and stopped, letting her sister and their husband pass her by. But Zeyá did not dismount. She only sat staring at the stone mountain.

Náhgo and his wife Wotoná stopped too, watching their youngest daughter. The wind tugged at the short hair Zeyá had cut in her mourning. Náhgo had undone his own braids, so that the strands tangled about him now, obscuring his sight as grief obscured his thoughts. He knew his daughter was suffering even more; he knew it had been agony for Zeyá to leave the body of her little son behind. Hevávkem was her only child, and he had been with them such a short time. But their scouts had reported the great herd of buffalo passing to the south, so their village had followed.

Zeyá turned back to Náhgo and Wotoná then. Tears stained her face, yet their daughter seemed to be smiling. "Do you hear it?"

"Hear what, my daughter?" Wotoná asked.

"My son! He is calling to me!"

Wotoná frowned and glanced at Náhgo before she replied: "We do not hear anything, daughter—only the wind."

"We left him too soon!" Zeyá insisted. She urged her horse forward again, toward Painted Rock.

Wotoná shouted after her, but Zeyá did not stop. Wotoná cried out in frustration, looking back at the pony drag behind her horse. She could not follow easily through this sagebrush.

"I will bring her back," Náhgo promised.

When his horse reached his daughter's, she did not slow. As they rounded the great turtle shell of Painted Rock, Zeyá only called over her shoulder: "Hevávkem must have become lost trying to find the Hanging Road to the Land of the Departed!"

Náhgo opened his mouth to reply, to tell her as gently as he could that her son was already beyond their reach. But then, he heard it too: the thin, desperate wail of a baby.

Zeyá glanced back at him. "Now do you hear him?"

"Yes," Náhgo answered in disbelief. Did a spirit make the sound, or a living child? Instinctively, he gripped the tip of the bow that hung behind him. This was the edge of Crow territory. The Zizistas were at war with the Crow; and any Crow could see by their hair and clothing that Náhgo and his daughter were Zizistas. They hadn't passed any lodges, but Painted Rock was vast; they had not yet ridden around every side. "My daughter! We must be careful! This baby might belong to an enemy!"

At last, Zeyá halted her horse—only to leap from its back. "A mother knows her own child." She was still smiling. When she was happy, the scars from the white scabs sickness seemed to vanish from her face. She ran to the edge of the mountain and began to climb. She did not let her dress slow her; she tugged its skirt to her knees, revealing her fringed leggings.

Náhgo swung his bow and quiver around his body and followed his daughter. The way was sometimes steep. He braced his hands against the rough, sun-warmed rock when he could. On this side of the mountain, boulders cascaded down the back of the turtle.

Halfway to the sky, Zeyá rested without sitting. When Náhgo came closer, she turned back to him, still breathing hard. "Is it true that medicine men can recapture the souls of the departed and return them to their bodies?"

"Men with more power than I have." Náhgo wished he had such medicine. The loss of Hevávkem had been great not only for their family and their village but for their whole tribe, because of the way the boy had come to them in the New Life Lodge. They had all expected Hevávkem to grow into a great medicine man himself.

His daughter lowered her eyes. "Then I will stay with Hevávkem. I will guide him to the Land of the Departed. My son is too young to go on such a journey alone."

"You will not be able to return, my daughter."

"I know, Father. I am ready."

Náhgo imagined his wife's face if he returned without Zeyá. Could Wotoná survive the loss of her grandson *and* her daughter?

Could he?

Zeyá frowned at the side of the mountain. The child's cries had faded. "Hevávkem? Where are you, little one?"

Náhgo thought he heard a whimper, but in the push of the wind, he could tell nothing for sure. He held his breath to listen. His daughter whispered a prayer. As soon as she opened her eyes, a flicker of orange and black drifted past them.

"He is showing us the way!" Zeyá cried, darting after the butter-fly. Perhaps she was right: she had named her son Hevávkem after this powerful little creature. "Wait for us, my friend!"

The butterfly did not seem to heed her. It flitted between the boulders and disappeared from sight.

Zeyá gasped, and one of her moccasins slipped. Náhgo caught her before she fell. Her eyes did not leave the spot where the butterfly had vanished. "There!" she cried.

Náhgo saw it too: a tall slit of shadow, a crevice between the boulders. Zeyá led the way eagerly. As if they were dancing, they stepped up and then down again, until they reached a space like a cave.

Mountains were sacred, because there the Earth met the Sky. But caves were also sacred. That was why they had laid Hevávkem to rest inside a little cave near their last campsite. Long ago, the Zizistas had lived in a great cave, in a womb beneath the Earth. To glimpse the World Below, here on this path to the World Above... Surely a powerful spirit dwelt here.

Yet this cave did not lead into the depths of the Earth but to the Sky: at the far end of the space, another gap in the boulders let in the sunlight. At the edge of the yellow glow, Zeyá knelt on the floor of the cave, before the child who had cried out to them.

A living child. And no ordinary living child. It wore a long shirt made not of animal skin but of white cloth like the traders wore. Instead of red-brown, the baby's skin was pink. On its head, the wisps of hair were as white as the downy bundles around milkweed seeds. And when Náhgo crouched beside the baby, he saw that its wide eyes were *blue*. Grey-blue like a sky full of storm clouds. This child could not belong to any tribe Náhgo knew.

The baby gasped—the sound was too weak to be a cry or even a whimper—and Zeyá reached toward it.

Náhgo laid a hand on her arm. "It is a *veho* child!"

In the last moon, a messenger had brought word to their village of a band of *veho* moving westward along the Moon Shell River, led by Black Robes and the fur man called Broken Hand. Many of the Zizistas and their allies had begun to doubt that the *veho* even had women of their own. But the warriors who had smoked with Broken Hand and the Black Robes said they'd seen them with their own eyes: a handful of *vehoá* and even pale children.

That band of *veho* must be camped near Painted Rock. But why had they left such a young child alone? Perhaps it was a test of strength. The parents would be angry if they returned to find Náhgo and Zeyá with their child. When *veho* were angry, they reached for their guns and did not stop to talk.

"We must leave this place," Náhgo whispered to his daughter.

"I cannot leave my son! He may *look* like a *veho* now. But you know the *veho* do not have souls. My son has used the body of this boy to come back to me! I *knew* his medicine was strong!" Before Náhgo could stop her, she gathered the baby—they did not even know it *was* a boy—into her arms. "You are filthy, little one!" she scolded it, pulling a damp hand from beneath its loins. "I had heard the *veho* smell terrible! Did you think about that, before you chose this body?" She kissed the top of its head. "I do not care! I do not care, my little one. You found a way to return to me. I will wash you and rub you with mint and you will smell like a Zizistas again." Holding the baby close against her, she hurried past Náhgo and out of the cave.

"My daughter!" he called. He had no choice but to follow her. "Wait!"

Zeyá did not listen. Deftly she carried the baby out of the cave and down the side of the mountain, beyond their grazing horses to the edge of the river. There, she freed him from his *veho* clothing, revealing two things: he was in fact a boy, and he could not be more than a few days old; he had not yet shed the stump of his cord.

Zeyá let the river carry away the dirty *veho* cloth. At the touch of the cool water, the baby started and gave a weak wail. But then Zeyá opened the nursing seam of her dress and offered him her breast, still full of milk. The boy made a tiny sound of pleasure and began suckling at once. His small hand gripped the fringe of her sleeve. Zeyá grinned for the first time since her son's death. "You see, Father? He knows me too."

Náhgo frowned. Could it be? He would have to pray about this. He glanced nervously in all directions. Even if Hevávkem had returned in the body of this *veho*, the other *veho* would not understand that.

"You saw the butterfly," Náhgo's daughter reminded him. "It was a sign." As he nursed, she stroked the baby's wispy hair. "This is like the white hair inside milkweed pods—the plant that feeds the orange-and-black butterflies. But you must have a new name, my son, after this great deed you have done. Let us see... Your eyes are the color of the Sky now, and you returned to us from the Sky." She smiled and glanced up at Náhgo. "So perhaps your grandfather will name you 'Ésh,' after the Sky."

Now that the baby had calmed, his skin had become even paler. But seeing his daughter so happy, Náhgo could only agree. "Ésh is a good name. A holy name. It will make him strong."

CHAPTER 28

My Indian mother was as good and kind to me as any one could be… During this sickness and delirium of grief, she dreamed that her youngest boy came back to her, and he was white. This dream put into her mind the strange notion that she wanted a white papoose.

— Elijah Nicolas Wilson, *The White Indian Boy* (1919)

Ésh fell asleep with his little mouth still open in contentment, and then Zeyá wrapped him in a doeskin from her saddlebags. Náhgo led his daughter and grandson back to his wife. Wotoná fell in love with Ésh almost at once.

A few boys stayed back from the buffalo hunt to explore around Painted Rock. They found evidence that the band of *veho* had camped there, but no living *veho* remained. There was a mound of rocks that might protect a dead *veho*, and a dead fur man lay at the edge of the river. He must be a fur man, since he looked like a *veho* but he wore buckskin clothing. They wrapped him in a buffalo robe and laid him to rest in the branches of a cottonwood.

When Náhgo returned to the cave to offer tobacco in gratitude for Ésh, he saw something he had not noticed before. Someone had carved markings on the wall. Náhgo knew the *veho* could speak to each other through such markings, and that they liked to make their marks on Painted Rock. Did these markings tell about the child? If they did, no one in his village could understand them.

Náhgo and the others thought the mound of rocks might contain the baby's mother, and the fur man must be his father. But why had the fur man placed his baby in the cave? The tracks around Painted Rock were muddled by buffalo and thunderstorms, but there seemed to be hoof-prints and wheel-prints leaving in both directions, west and east. Nearby, two of the village boys captured a mule packed with *veho* food and clothing, but this did not solve the mystery.

At the buffalo camp, another village joined them, a village that was honored by a halfman-halfwoman called Hóxovôho'o. When he heard about the dead fur man, about his red hair and the scar beneath his right eye, Hóxovôho'o began to wail. The fur man had been his friend, Hóxovôho'o explained—another two-spirit person. So the fur man could not have been the baby's father.

Who *was* the baby's father, then? Two moons later, the Zizistas learned that their allies the Inviters had helped two *veho* children reach the village of the fur men on Goose River. But these children had never mentioned a baby, and now they were gone.

None of this mattered to Zeyá. She remained certain Ésh was her son, in spite of his strange new appearance. When his skin turned an angry red and peeled from the sun, she smoothed cactus juice on his burns, made him a cap of rabbit skin, and sang him to sleep. He responded to her voice as if they had never been parted.

The more Náhgo watched them together, the more convinced he became that Zeyá was right: his grandson had returned to them. Children born of the union between the Chief Priest and the Sacred Woman during the New Life Lodge were holy, brimming with *exhastoz*. This resurrection was their first proof of the boy's power.

Maheo had given them Zeyá's child just after the People made peace with three of their long-bitter enemies: the Greasy Wood People, the Rattlesnake People, and the Occupied Camp People.

Náhgo had been certain their Creator was blessing this alliance. Then the breath left his grandson's little body after only three moons, and Náhgo had struggled to understand. Now, the Sacred Powers had returned this holy child, in a way none of them could have imagined.

Most of the People agreed with Náhgo about the signs. His apprentice found further proof in the boy's abandonment. "It is just like Sweet Medicine!" the young man declared in council. "Maybe the baby's *vehoá* mother was also a virgin ashamed of a child she could not explain. Already Ésh has died and been reborn like our prophet!"

"Why did he return in such an ugly body?" Xomoo joked, though some of the men looked more serious.

"Which one of us can say that he does not carry the blood of another tribe beneath his skin?" Maahe pointed out. "That a grandfather did not marry an Inviter or a Cloud Woman, that a grandmother was not captured from the Crow People or the Sósonée? This does not make the Zizistas weaker; it makes us stronger." Náhgo and the other men murmured agreement. "We take the medicine of other tribes and make it our own, just as we take scalps. Why should the tribe of the *veho* be any different?"

"The *veho* do not have our understanding, and they do not know our ways," Heahke worried. "If they see one of us who looks like one of them, they will think he has been stolen. Our people are at peace with the *veho* now, but we do not want to make them angry. We have seen how strong their medicine is." Solemnly he brushed his fingertips over the scars on his arm left by the white scabs sickness. "Sweet Medicine himself warned us about these *veho*."

"Keeping another *veho* child among the People may be dangerous," his brother added. "He may bring bad luck."

"I think Ésh will bring good luck!" Náhgo's apprentice argued. "He will give to us some of the *veho* medicine."

"You mean, he will teach us to make guns from trees?" one of their chiefs smiled.

"Maybe he will not need a gun! Maybe he will spit bullets!"

suggested Xomoo. Then in the firelight, his eyes gleamed with even more mischief. "Or piss firewater!"

In the chief's laughter, he nearly dropped the pipe, which would have been a very bad omen. But in this as in all things, the Sacred Powers blessed them. Ésh remained with Zeyá.

WHILE ZEYÁ DOTED ON THE BOY, Héshek and their husband Okóm would look on and chuckle to each other. Náhgo thought they behaved as if Ésh were Zeyá's pet, not her son—like the girl in the village who had trained a young raven to eat from her hand. As if Zeyá would tire of Ésh someday and leave him behind when they moved camp. Náhgo and his wife knew better.

Zeyá was a good aunt. She cared for Héshek's young son and daughter, Háhkota and Pákehe, as if they were her own, and they loved her in return. But Héshek teased Zeyá about the ugliness of her son. Héshek said they belonged together: Zeyá with her scars and Ésh with his pink-white skin.

Their husband Okóm seemed to agree. When he had Ésh's ears pierced, he gave away only one horse. For each of Héshek's children, he'd given away three.

The older children in the camp began calling Ésh "Little Owl," because his hair was pale like the feathers of that ghost-bird and his eyes were rounder than theirs. As if afraid he might miss something important, Ésh kept his eyes open wide as he peered over his mother's shoulder or out from his cradleboard while she scraped hides, dug for turnips, or stitched beads.

Those eyes did not remain sky-colored; by his first spring, they'd turned the color of young sagebrush. Náhgo thought this was another sign of his grandson's great medicine: green was the color of the morning star, the color of rebirth. The boy's wide green eyes were so trusting, his little hands always reaching out for affection, even when someone was mocking him. He was still too young to understand what they said, and the other children were too young to understand that someone so small and strange-looking could carry great power.

Ésh must be saving his medicine for a day when the People truly needed him. The hunters and warriors who believed in his rebirth and offered him gifts did not find success more often than those who doubted. But the boy blessed Zeyá every day: he filled her with happiness.

Héshek's son Háhkota was a quiet boy only five winters old, but he had a good heart like his aunt. Náhgo was hopeful that as they grew older, Háhkota would help protect his pale-skinned little brother.

Like many Zizistas men, Zeyá's husband Okóm had obtained a small mirror from the traders. He used it when he plucked out his eyebrows, hung his earrings, and applied war paint. Little Ésh noticed the way sunlight bounced off this mirror and tried to reach for it. When Zeyá or Wotoná brought him closer, he was delighted by what he saw inside. He giggled and babbled. But Ésh seemed to think it contained another little boy; he kept trying to look behind the mirror.

When he was old enough to wobble toward it on his own, he played with this little boy, pressing his forehead against the glass like he was sharing a secret. His favorite thing was to dance with his friend, though Ésh was still so new to walking that he often lost his balance and fell onto the buffalo robes. He never cried—Zeyá had taught him not to, the way Wotoná had taught her. He only pulled himself up using one of the willow backrests, and soon he would be dancing away again.

"Are you recounting your brave war deeds to your friend?" Zeyá would ask her son. In his second winter, she set him in her lap facing the mirror. She tapped and then named his nose, his ears, his fingers —all the parts of his body. At last her son understood that the boy in the mirror was *him*.

Soon, she could say: "I love your *mahtsé'oo*—where is your *mahtsé'oo*?" and Ésh would proudly show her his elbow. Zeyá would praise him and kiss his elbow, or his chin, or his ankle. He began to mimic her words in his bubbly little voice till he could name every

part himself. Even as he grew older, Ésh would often pull Zeyá to
the mirror, crawl into her lap, and beg her to play the game again.

During his fourth winter, Ésh, Zeyá, and Náhgo were the only
ones in the tipi when the boy asked: "Mama?"

"Yes, my son?"

Ésh was silent for a moment. Náhgo looked up from grinding
bitterroot to see that his grandson was staring at their images in the
mirror and twirling his pale hair around his fingers. "When will I
start to look like you and Grandfather?"

Zeyá lowered her eyes from the reflection of her scarred face to
her scarred arm. "What do you mean, *nae'ha?*"

"When will my hair turn black and my eyes and skin turn
brown?"

Náhgo heard his daughter's breath catch in pain. "I do not think
that will ever happen, *nae'ha.*"

Ésh frowned. "Why not?"

Zeyá tried to smile. "Because you are special, *nae'ha.*" She
touched his pale cheek. "Maheo made you different from all the
other children."

"You are sacred, *nish,*" Náhgo agreed. "White and yellow are
sacred colors, just as red and black are sacred colors."

"You are rare and precious like the white buffalo," Zeyá
told him.

The boy's green eyes grew even wider. "Is that why the traders
are dangerous? Because they want my hide?"

Mostly the traders let the People come to them; but sometimes,
a *veho* would ride into their village leading mules loaded with beads,
cloth, and metal pots. When Ésh had been a baby strapped to her
back, Zeyá had gone up to see what such a man brought without
even thinking. And then she saw how the *veho* stared at her son. The
trader said nothing with his voice, but his cold blue eyes said: *That
baby does not belong to you.* Zeyá had hurried back to her lodge, and
with Náhgo and Wotoná she had decided that Ésh must never come
within sight of a *veho* again.

"The traders would not kill you," Zeyá explained to her son
now, "but they would take you away with them."

"I do not want to go away with them!" Ésh cried, flinging his arms around her neck. "I am yours, not theirs!"

"I will never let them take you," Zeyá assured him. "I will die first."

"I don't want you to *die!*" the boy wailed.

"No one will die, *nish,*" interrupted Náhgo. "When you are older, I will teach you how to use your medicine—how to protect yourself and your mother."

Slowly, the boy loosened his grip on Zeyá's neck. He peered up at Náhgo, his green eyes still swimming with tears. "Can you make me the same colors as you?"

Náhgo set down his grinding rocks. "No, *nish.* I am sorry."

The powdered root seemed to give Ésh an idea. He stood up. "Then we will make lots of paint, and—"

Náhgo reached out to brush his fingers over his grandson's head and face. "This pale hair, this pale skin, these green eyes—they are gifts from Maheo. They are part of your medicine. He made you this way for a reason."

Still the boy's chin trembled. "What reason?"

"I do not understand that yet, *nish.* I have been praying for a vision, but none of the Sacred Powers have shown me yet. We will understand someday."

CHAPTER 29

Little Old Man, a very brave man, donned his war-dress, mounted his war-horse, and rode through the camp with a lance in his hand, shouting, "If I could see this thing [the cholera], if I knew where it came from, I would go there and fight it!"
— George Bird Grinnell, *The Cheyenne Indians* (1923)

Náhgo stroked a porcupine-tail brush through Wotoná's hair. Sitting with her quillwork in her lap, his wife glanced over her shoulder and smiled in the sunlight. "*É-péva'e, na-momóonéham,*" she murmured in approval. Her voice still rippled into a giggle like a girl's when she called him her "love-captive," as if he were the only husband who dressed his wife's hair, as if it wasn't a pleasure.

The sheer cascade finally reached past her waist again, after she'd cut it to her jaw line in sympathy with their daughter, in mourning for the boy they had not really lost. Many of the strands were grey now. But Náhgo was ahead of Wotoná in that race.

As they grew older, Zeyá teased them, they were starting to look more and more alike. When he was a young man, such a thought might have bothered Náhgo. Now, he knew who he was. When he and Wotoná slipped under their robes at night, it was clear enough who was who and what was what.

It was good to have a day like this, Náhgo thought as he braided his wife's hair. That spring, more *veho* than ever had come flooding across the People's lands. As they lumbered westward, the *veho* camped at all the best watering places and cut down all the firewood —trees that had stood for generations. The *veho* animals ate all the grass, and their presence frightened off the buffalo.

Then Náhgo, Wotoná, and their apprentice had prayed to the Sacred Powers, begging them to pity the People. The Sacred Powers had listened: scouts found a small herd, and yesterday there had been a great hunt. Last night, there had been a feast, and today, everyone's bellies were full. There was still much work to do, drying the meat and tanning the hides. But the People knew that the Sacred Powers had not forgotten them.

Before Náhgo could tie off Wotoná's second braid with a deer-skin string, her hair slipped from his grasp. His wife sat forward suddenly and peered to their right, tilting her head as if she heard something.

Náhgo frowned. "What is it, *na-méo?*"

Soon young Wohtan came running between the lodges. He stopped long enough to brace his hands on his thighs, yet he began before he caught his breath. "There is a messenger." The boy's brows were gathered together in worry. "He will speak with no one but a medicine person."

Náhgo stood. "We will come."

"I will fetch our medicine bundle," Wotoná said. Together they followed Wohtan to the edge of camp.

Well beyond the circle of tipis, a thin young warrior of perhaps twenty-five winters waited on his horse. Even from this distance, Náhgo could see how lathered the animal was. The warrior looked even more exhausted. "Do not come any closer!" he called, though Náhgo and Wotoná were not close at all. "You are medicine people?"

"We are," Náhgo answered.

"Then I pray your medicine is strong enough." The warrior

held his middle, but Náhgo saw no blood. "I am Hewovetas of the Masikota Band," he said in a weak voice. "I was one of a war party returning from a raid on the Wolf People. Along the Moon Shell River, we saw the rolling things the *veho* use to travel. But we did not see any *veho* moving among them. Their animals stood doing nothing, so we thought we could capture them. And then we smelled the *veho*." Hewovetas grimaced. "Their bodies were *blue*."

Behind Náhgo and Wotoná, a crowd was gathering, and people began to murmur in fear.

"A few of the *veho* were still moaning, lying there in puddles of their own waste." Hewovetas glanced behind him as if he were being pursued. "And whatever killed them, it followed us. Many of my band are already dead."

"Ma'eóome?" cried the chief's daughter. Everyone knew Ma'eóome was her sweetheart.

Even before Hewovetas spoke, they saw the answer on his face. "He was one of the first to die."

The chief's daughter collapsed to her knees and began keening like a widow.

"Vóaheso?" shouted Tameesá'e. Her son had married into the Masikota Band.

"When I left, he was still alive, but his daughter… You must run from this spirit before it kills you too."

That had helped before: dispersing across the prairie where the sickness could not find them all. Náhgo thought of Zeyá's scars. "It is not the white scabs?"

"Something different." Hewovetas hunched more deeply over his horse. "It kills so quickly…"

"Rest with us," Náhgo urged. "I will build you a shelter if you are afraid to enter the camp."

"I will make a tea to keep you strong," Wotoná added.

"We will call your spirit helper."

Hewovetas shook his head. "I cannot… I must warn others." He tugged on the rein of his reluctant horse, and they started toward the north.

Náhgo had barely turned back to the crowd when several people gasped at once. He whirled around to watch Hewovetas fall from his horse. As Náhgo and Wotoná ran toward him, the warrior bunched up in pain. He clutched his stomach and moaned.

Wotoná reached him first. Hewovetas lay still on his face and did not respond to her gentle shakes. When she turned him, she revealed the blank stare of death. The young warrior's lips were almost blue, and his fingers were wrinkled like those of an old man.

Náhgo knelt beside them, but his wife held out her hand. "*I* will prepare him, *na-eham.*"

Náhgo hesitated, then nodded. He wished he had reached Hewovetas first; he wished he could spare his wife this task.

"He is dead?" someone called from the crowd.

Náhgo stood. "Yes."

Many of the women cried out and ran for their lodges.

"What should we do?" someone asked.

"We should leave this place—now," Sénáka argued. "We should go farther from the Moon Shell River and the *veho.*"

"We cannot leave!" Sénáka's wife objected. "We have hides to tan! And the meat will not be dry for days! You men kill the buffalo, and then you think the work is over!"

"Before we do anything else, we must pray," Náhgo insisted.

"I will build a sweat lodge," Náhgo's apprentice offered.

"*I pray your medicine is strong enough,*" Hewovetas had said. Perhaps Náhgo's medicine was not strong enough—but a channel of far greater medicine waited within their village. His grandson was not yet nine winters. But Sweet Medicine had performed his first miracle when he was only ten winters.

Náhgo found Zeyá in the crowd. She was staring toward Wotoná, who sang over Hewovetas. Náhgo tried not to worry about his wife. Instead, he asked their daughter: "Is Ésh still in the play camp?"

Slowly, she nodded. "Do you think he can help us?"

"I think today is the day we have been waiting for." What better time for his grandson who looked like a *veho* to use his medicine than against a sickness that had come from the *veho*?

Náhgo hurried through the village. Many families were arguing.

Others were gathering at the chief's lodge. Tameesá'e and her daughter clung to one another and wept.

Náhgo continued beyond the edge of the village to the children's camp. They were still at play; they did not know about Hewovetas. Here the children had built miniature lodges, and good-natured dogs served as their horses. Most of the children were recreating yesterday's buffalo hunt. Boys carrying prickly pear cacti on sticks played the animals, either fleeing or charging their hunters.

Náhgo found Ésh lying on his stomach with Méanév kneeling beside him. Her mother and Zeyá had been friends since girlhood, and their children often played together. Méanév peered at Ésh's back now, and Náhgo realized it was bloody.

His grandson propped himself on his elbows. "*Námshim!* It is good you are here! You can help my wife care for my wounds."

Méanév smiled. "My silly husband was gored by a buffalo." With her lips, she pointed to the boys with the prickly pears.

Náhgo satisfied himself that the wounds were not serious. "The time for play is over, children." Even as he spoke, parents were coming to collect their sons and daughters.

Ésh frowned but stood.

"We need your medicine now, *nish*," Náhgo explained. "We are in danger. You must help me protect the People—your grandmother, most of all."

Náhgo had taught his grandson simple tasks before, like how to make offerings. But the boy always grew restless during these lessons; he wanted to play. Now, he looked at Náhgo's face and the faces of the other adults, and he seemed to understand. It was time to listen. It was time to act.

Their chief decided they should send out messengers to tell other bands about the *veho* sickness; but the rest of the village should remain here until they had prayed for guidance. Náhgo's apprentice and other men constructed the willow frame of the sweat lodge and gathered tanned buffalo hides to cover it. Ésh tended the fire that heated the stones they would need.

Instead of building a scaffold, Wotoná piled rocks on Hewovetas's body in hopes of trapping the evil spirit that had killed him.

Then she cleansed herself in the creek while Náhgo prayed that the young warrior would find the Hanging Road to the Land of the Departed.

When the sweat lodge was ready, Wotoná used antlers to carry the hot stones to the pit in its center. Then the chief, Náhgo, Wotoná, their apprentice, and Ésh shut themselves inside. Náhgo instructed his grandson to take sips from a little wooden bowl and then spit the water onto the stones till the lodge filled with steam.

Náhgo shook his buffalo-skin rattle and sang till sweat stood out on their skin. He asked the Sacred Powers for wisdom and the medicine to fight this sickness. Surely the Sacred Powers would not grant their People the buffalo they needed to survive and then force them to flee before the hides and meat were ready to travel. Surely the Sacred Powers would keep this evil spirit away.

The stones began to cool, so Náhgo's apprentice threw aside the buffalo robe door. He, the chief, and Ésh filed out to wash themselves in the creek. But when she tried to rise, Wotoná stumbled. Náhgo had to help her from the sweat lodge. In the sunlight, her face was tight with pain. At the sight, Náhgo's own heart began to race. Before they reached the creek, his wife fell to her knees and vomited.

A woman screamed. Náhgo glanced up only long enough to see that she had been watching the sweat lodge while she fleshed a hide. She dropped her scraper and ran for her tipi, crying: "It has found us!"

While the rest of the camp women panicked, Náhgo returned his attention to his wife. She refused to go back to their lodge. "It isn't safe," she argued. "I should remain here."

As the women collapsed their tipis, the chief muttered: "We cannot stop them now."

Náhgo's apprentice brought one of the hides from the sweat lodge so that Wotoná could lie down. Ésh stood nearby, still dripping with creek water, gaping at his grandmother.

"Fetch a hot coal and our medicine bundle," Náhgo told him.

The boy started and obeyed.

Wotoná moaned.

"Where does it hurt, *na-méo?*" Náhgo asked her.

"My stomach—my legs," she gasped.

Ésh returned. Náhgo showed him how to sprinkle bitterroot on the coal and pass his hands through the smoke. Then he directed the boy to place his palms on Wotoná's stomach and legs. He taught his grandson the healing song:

> "I know myself.
> I possess spiritual power."

Zeyá appeared. "Héshek is leaving!"

"She is thinking of her children," Náhgo reasoned.

"And our mother?" Zeyá touched her face. "I will not leave you, *náhko'e.*" Wotoná grasped her daughter's hand as Ésh worked to heal her.

Náhgo told his apprentice to go with the others. The women abandoned the racks of drying buffalo meat and the hides they'd stretched for scraping and tanning. They strapped their lodges and parfleches to pony drags and scattered with their children like a covey of quail fleeing from a coyote. The warriors trailed after them, powerless now: this was not an enemy they could see or fight.

Soon only Náhgo, Wotoná, Zeyá, and Ésh remained. Wotoná begged them to leave her, to save themselves, but they did not listen. "We do not know this is the same sickness, *na-méo,*" Náhgo said.

Soon he had to carry his wife to the creek, over and over, because her bowels could hold nothing. After the first few times, it was little more than dirty water, but it wouldn't stop. Terrible cramps seized her, and she was always thirsty.

Náhgo tried smoking his hands and Ésh's hands with sweet pine and dried mushroom instead of bitterroot. For more than thirty winters, Wotoná had helped Náhgo select and prepare medicines. When she could speak, he still asked her advice. They tried everything they knew, and Náhgo let Ésh administer it: cattail root, chickadee plant, yellow medicine.

They returned to the sweat lodge. They made offerings and pledges. Náhgo pleaded with the Sacred Powers to spare his wife, and Ésh shook his rattle to drive away the evil spirit. The boy repeated the healing song till his voice grew hoarse and weak:

"I know myself.
I possess spiritual power."

But Wotoná's lips turned blue, and her eyes appeared to sink into her head. Finally Náhgo could only cradle his wife's crumpled form in his arms. Beside them, tears streamed down Zeyá's cheeks. Ésh dropped the rattle and buried his face in his mother's dress.

Náhgo glared at his grandson. If Ésh had paid more attention, if he hadn't been so lazy, he would know how to use his medicine by now. He was a child of the New Life Lodge! Why was he withholding his power? Why wouldn't he act?

"She is your *grandmother!*" Náhgo yelled at the boy. "Why won't you help her? Why won't you do something?!"

The boy only hid his face and sobbed. Náhgo shouted and begged and wept till he looked back at Wotoná and realized she was already gone.

AMONG THE JUMBLED BELONGINGS her sister had left behind, Zeyá found their mother's best elkskin dress and her favorite shell earrings. She helped Náhgo wash Wotoná and clothe her for her journey. He laid his wife gently on a buffalo robe, painted her face, and braided her hair for the last time.

No—not the *last* time. This separation was only temporary, Náhgo reminded himself; he would see his wife again. He wondered how many winters he would spend alone before he could join her in the Land of the Departed.

Ésh sat and watched them prepare Wotoná's body with his knees drawn up to his chin and his eyes still leaking tears.

Zeyá asked: "Do you want to place anything with your grandmother?"

Her son hung his head. "I did not mean to kill her!"

Zeyá hurried to caress his pale yellow hair. "Of course not, *nae'ha*. We do not blame you."

The boy stared cautiously toward Náhgo. "But—"

"I should not have said those things to you, *nish*. This was not your fault. I was wrong about your medicine."

"Perhaps you used it all up when you returned to us," Zeyá suggested, trying to smile.

Or perhaps this was not the same child who had come to them in the New Life Lodge. But if Zeyá ever doubted that, Náhgo knew she loved Ésh anyway.

IN MANY VILLAGES, no one remained to care for the dead. As they rode to rejoin the rest of their family, Náhgo, Zeyá, and Ésh passed camps where vultures and coyotes feasted on human flesh. Abandoned lodges and funeral scaffolds littered the prairie that summer. Not only the Zizistas suffered; the terrible cramping sickness also struck down the Cloud People, the Inviters, the Greasy Wood People, the Rattlesnake People, and even their enemies the Wolf People.

The Zizistas had never been a large tribe. Now, more than half of their people were gone. Only a few thousand remained. Compared to what other families lost, the Sacred Powers did bless Náhgo: he lost only his wife and his elder brother.

Thousands of *veho* died as well; but the sickness did not stop them coming. No matter how many the cramps took, there were always, always more *veho*. On the far side of the mountains, one of them had found a yellow rock they all wanted.

Another kind of *veho* came too: soldiers who wore blue and did not simply pass through the lands of the People. These *veho* cut down pines from the foothills and used them to build square lodges near a bend of the Goose River. These *veho* stayed.

CHAPTER 30

To most Americans, the red man is, to this day, just what he was to the first settlers of this country—a being with soul enough to be blameable for doing wrong, but not enough to claim Christian brotherhood, or to make it *very* sinful to shoot him like a dog, upon the slightest provocation or alarm.

— Mrs. C. M. Kirkland, Preface to Mary Eastman's *Dahcotah* (1849)

É sh heard the barking first, quick like coyotes but deeper. Then he heard the shouts of men. His eyes widened. That was not Zizistas or any other language he knew. They must be *veho* words. He was not far from the bluecoats' village on the Goose River.

Quickly he finished his prayer to the rabbit, thanking it for its sacrifice. Then he slung his bow over his shoulder, lashed the rabbit's ears together with the tail of the squirrel he had shot, and ran as fast as he could away from the sounds.

He darted between pines and aspens and straight through bare autumn bushes, startling birds. They fluttered up and cried out in vengeance, alerting the *veho* and their dogs. The barking and the men's voices grew louder, pierced now by a horse's whinny. Ésh had heard that the *veho* used dogs to help them hunt, because they did not know how to call the animals to them.

What if they were not hunting animals? What if they were hunting *him*?

Ésh ran faster, certain the bluecoats were gaining on him, even when pain shot up his legs at the effort. The *veho* might eat him! They ate their own savior!

He leapt down into the deep bed of a stream strewn with yellow aspen leaves. The sand there caught his fall but slowed him: he slipped sideways and it slid inside his moccasins. He did not stop.

He could throw down the rabbit and squirrel to confuse the dogs; but they were too precious to him, and the dogs already had his scent. Ésh splashed up the stream that changed appearance with every bend and depth with every step. If only he could change into an eagle and fly away from the *veho*. He tried to stay to the shallows, since Winter Man had already chilled the water; but when Ésh crossed over the piles of small jagged rocks in his running, the sound seemed to announce him to the entire forest—surely the bluecoats would hear.

He could not outrun horses. He saw that a flood had washed deep into the banks of the stream, uprooting saplings and leaving the roots of larger trees dangling from the banks. Some of the spots were narrow, some quite—*there* was one large enough for him, shielded even more on one side by a fallen aspen.

He waded into the pool that guarded the new cave, grimacing and shivering as the cold crept up his buckskin leggings. When the water overtook the ends of his breechcloth and passed his knees, he held the rabbit and squirrel above his waist but glanced over his shoulder. The *veho* dogs were howling now. He dove forward, underneath the dangling roots—into something soft and wet and *warm*.

Ésh scrambled backwards in a crouch as the wolf's yip of surprise became a furious growl. But the yells of the *veho* and the barks of the dogs surrounded them; he could not escape the wolf without being captured. Ésh flattened himself against the stream bank, knocking off his quiver, the cool mud molding into his bare back. He dropped the squirrel and rabbit between his knees and tried frantically to draw his bow; but its top jammed up into the roots and its bottom stuck out into the stream. He yanked his knife from its sheath and met the moon-yellow eyes of the snarling black wolf as bravely as he could.

The animal bared its glistening white fangs in the shadows; but it did not lunge or snap. In fact, Ésh saw that the wolf could not open its mouth at all. Some sort of rope wound tightly around its muzzle. That was why the wolf was so angry. Its own sides heaved beneath its dripping black fur.

The sounds of the bluecoats and their dogs swarmed above and around them. Its fiery yellow eyes never left his, but the wolf turned back its ears now, ducked its head, and pawed desperately at the rope binding its jaws. Its face was already scratched and bleeding, and one of its front paws also bore teeth marks. Or perhaps they were the marks of the metal-jawed traps the *veho* used.

Still gripping his knife, Ésh dared to peer out through the shield of roots. Just across the stream sniffed the brown-and-white dogs with floppy ears and thin tails. The men wore hair even on their faces. This was the closest Ésh had ever been to a *veho*; he'd seen them only from a great distance before. They were very ugly.

He could not understand the *veho* words, and he could barely hear them above the dogs' barking and moaning. The bluecoats seemed to be yelling not only at the dogs but also at each other.

The wolf whimpered beside him, and Ésh begged the stream to rush faster, louder. He watched the morning sunlight reflect off the surface of the water, bounce up against the bank and the tree trunks, and dance there. *Blind them, Atovsz,* he prayed silently to the Sun.

Atovsz heard him: finally the dogs trailed farther down the stream, and the bluecoats followed. Ésh began to let out his breath; but when he glanced back at the black wolf, he realized it was creeping toward him, sniffing as fiercely as the floppy-eared dogs. He looked out toward the streambed—but the *veho* must still be nearby. He raised his knife as the wolf ventured closer, though it did not seem to understand. It ruffled the fur of his rabbit and squirrel with its breath.

The wolf was muzzled and defenseless; with a single slash to the throat, he could kill it easily. If he brought back a wolf skin before he reached even nine winters, he would be famous. How envious the other boys would be!

But what if he did not perform the proper ceremonies? What if he angered the wolf spirit? It might strike him lame, or take his own life in vengeance. What if he stayed in the Land of the Departed this time and couldn't return? Ésh didn't want to die before he'd found his medicine, before he'd done anything to make the story-tellers remember him. The risk was too great.

He watched the black wolf carefully: its ears flat, its body crouched and its tail tucked. Its wet coat showed just how skinny it was, and how small; it was only a young wolf, born that spring. He lowered his knife, since the animal could not use its teeth. He allowed it to approach and inspect him.

It inhaled his face, his unravelling braids, his chest, and the little deerskin medicine pouch tied around his neck. He wondered if the wolf smelled the camp dogs on him. He'd played with them after his morning bath, and they were mostly wolf. This animal sniffed his knife hand without interest, then concluded with his breechcloth. Its whiskers tickled his thigh, and Ésh sniggered.

The wolf backed away humbly and tilted its brows like a begging puppy. It hung its head, looped a large paw over its bound muzzle, and whimpered.

If he left the animal like this, it would starve to death, and that would certainly make it angry. If he wasn't going to kill the wolf, he should cut the rope.

It could open his throat. But as familiar as he was with the camp dogs, he knew the language of their bodies; he knew this wolf was submitting to his authority.

Still Ésh clasped his little medicine pouch. It contained the black-and-orange wings of a butterfly, so like the colors of this dark wolf with its fiery eyes. He recalled the prayer his big brother Háhkota sang in enemy territory. He whispered the words:

"Wolf I am.
In darkness
in light
wherever I search
wherever I run
wherever I stand
everything
will be good
because Maheo
protects us."

With the last breath, Ésh leaned forward, slid the blade of his knife alongside the wolf's jaw, and sliced off the rope. The animal pawed itself free of the tatters, licked its muzzle, and immediately lifted its head. Ésh retreated as far as he could into the mud bank, but the wolf's mouth kept coming.

In his panic, he dropped the knife. He could only squeeze his eyes shut and grip his medicine pouch. If this was what the Sacred Powers wanted, he would accept it.

He felt the animal's warm breath and bristly whiskers, heard the liquid sound of its jaws opening, and then felt the smooth wet press of its tongue against his chin, across his lips. He expected fangs to follow, but then the licking stopped.

He squinted his eyes open to see the wolf in its crouch, tongue still working but eyes fixed now on the squirrel and rabbit between his knees. It whined to complete its plea.

Fingers trembling a little, Ésh untied the cord linking the two animals, grasped the bushy tail of the squirrel, and tossed it to the wolf. It pounced and devoured the squirrel almost whole, tearing skin, crunching bones.

Before the wolf had even licked its snout clean, it began to stare longingly at the dead rabbit. Ésh scowled now. He would have nothing to show for his hunt! When he could have had the wolf's own skin!

But Grandfather had always taught him to share the best with others; the wolf was only reminding him. It would need strength to

run where the bluecoats could not find it. And the wolf did look pitiful, even hunched over what little remained of the squirrel with
blood smeared on its face like war paint.

So Ésh gave in. As the rabbit disappeared, he picked up a black
tuft of the wolf's shed fur and tucked it inside his medicine pouch.
He leaned under the roots to look up and down the stream for any
sign of danger. The sun's reflected pattern had faded. He heard only
the trickle of the water and a busy woodpecker somewhere nearby.

The wolf gave a sort of breathy *whuf*—softer than a bark—and
Ésh quickly returned his attention to it, worried that the animal
might expect him as the final part of its meal. But the wolf watched
him without demand. In the shadows, in the midst of that black fur,
its golden eyes seemed to glow like pools of flame. But fire could be
good as well as dangerous.

Still, Ésh decided he should escape before the wolf changed its
mind about eating him. He sheathed his knife, gathered his quiver
and bow, and ducked under the roots into the pool.

When he reached the other side of the stream, he looked back,
wondering if the black wolf might follow. Instead, it lay down inside
the little cave, crossed its bloodied paws, and rested its head there.
Perhaps the wolf was a spirit who would disappear back into the
Earth when he was gone. Ésh grinned and climbed the bank.

"WHERE HAVE YOU *BEEN?*"

Náhgo looked up from the hand drum he was lacing to see Zeyá
kneeling before Ésh. The boy always worried her—and Náhgo too
—when he disappeared like this.

"I was hunting," the boy answered breathlessly. He was smiling
as if he were proud of himself, though he'd brought back only mud.
He was covered in it.

"You went hunting by yourself?"

Ésh's smile faded, and he stared down at his filthy moccasins.
"Yes…" He knew he'd been disobedient.

"You know it isn't safe! Especially with the *veho* so close!" Zeyá grasped his shoulders, her face stricken with fear. "They would take you away with them! Is that what you want?"

"No!"

"Did—" Zeyá hesitated and dropped her hands. "Did you *want* to see them?"

"No! They are ugly!"

Zeyá sucked in a sharp breath. "You *did* see them!"

"It was an accident! And they did not see me!"

Zeyá held her son close for a moment and murmured her thanks to the Sacred Powers for bringing him back to her. Then she pulled away and clucked her tongue at the mud on him. But the corner of her lips turned up too. "Were you hunting prairie dogs *underground?*"

"No," the boy giggled.

"Go and wash yourself."

Ésh set his quiver, bow, knife, and medicine pouch beside Náhgo. He kicked off his moccasins, untied his leggings, pulled off his breechcloth, and ran to the river. Zeyá muttered her displeasure at his filthy clothing. She fetched fresh things from their lodge and took away the others to clean them.

Náhgo returned to his own task: wrapping more rawhide around the laces on the back of a drum. When he was finished, the hand-hold would take the shape of the morning star.

Ésh came back from the river still ringing out his hair. It had darkened since he was a baby: it was yellow in the sunlight and brown when it was wet. But his hair would never be black.

As the boy dried himself with the blanket Zeyá had left, Náhgo told his grandson: "Your mother is right, *nish*. It is dangerous for you to leave camp on your own."

Ésh pouted while he pulled the end of his breechcloth through the cord around his waist. "If the bluecoats caught me, I would escape."

"There is only one of you, *nish*—and there are many, many *veho*." Náhgo set down his drum. "Who would you call on to help you? You do not have your medicine animal yet."

Ésh plopped down beside him and grinned. "I think I do now."

He pulled a tuft of black fur from his medicine pouch, and he told Náhgo about the wolf.

As his grandson tucked the wolf fur back out of sight, Náhgo smiled too. "You did well, *nish*. The wolf will remember your kindness and your sacrifice."

The animal made sense for Ésh. Almost every day, Náhgo saw his grandson wrestling with the camp's wolf-dogs. The animals played rough; but almost as soon as he could walk, Ésh had matched their ferocity without fear—with laughter—baring his own little teeth in return. At first the dogs were wary, but soon they treated him like an honorary wolf-dog. His grandson did not try to scold or beat the animals into playing his way, nor did he retreat from their violence: he met them and matched them. Sometimes they let him win, because they respected him. Often Ésh bore their fang marks for days afterward; but he wore them proudly. He was nothing like the arrogant, cowardly *veho*.

Maybe his grandson's medicine was not as great as Náhgo had hoped; maybe Ésh would not be a savior like Sweet Medicine. But he could be Zizistas. That was enough.

PART VII
WOLF I AM

1851-1858

There must be in their social bond something singularly captivating, and far superior to anything to be boasted of among us; for thousands of Europeans are Indians, and we have no examples of even one of those Aborigines having from choice become Europeans!

—J. Hector St. John de Crèvecoeur,
"Distresses of a Frontier Man,"
Letters from an American Farmer (1782)

CHAPTER 31

It will be the commencement of a new era for the Indians—an era of peace. In future, peaceable citizens may cross the desert unmolested, and the Indian will have little to dread from the bad white man, for justice will be rendered to him.

— Father Pierre-Jean De Smet, on the Horse Creek Treaty (also called the Fort Laramie Treaty of 1851), *Western Missions and Missionaries: A Series of Letters* (1859)

There were two of them. They were watching everyone, but Ésh thought the bluecoats watched him most of all. That was why his arrows never quite landed where he'd aimed them.

The People, their allies the Cloud People and the Inviters, their enemies the Crow People and the Sósonée, and seven other nations —all of them had gathered on Horse Creek to have a council with the *veho*. For days and days, there had been feasting, parades, and dancing. That morning, men from each tribe had raced their horses.

Ésh and his horse were good enough to race, but some other boys his age had decided to test their skill with a bow instead. He had joined them, but even as he placed his arrows, he couldn't stop thinking about the two bluecoats who had come to watch the contest.

After an Inviter boy won, the two *veho* walked up to Ésh. He considered running, but he did not want to leave his arrows behind, and the bluecoats were surrounded by the People and their allies—surely they would not try to capture him here. The men's voices weren't angry; they only seemed to be asking him questions.

Ésh couldn't understand them, and he pretended not to hear. Then his mother was there, grasping his hand, tugging him away, fear behind her words.

"I haven't found my last arrow, *náhko'e!*" he tried to tell her, straining toward the next target. She kept pulling him after her, toward the camp of the Cloud People. It wasn't even the right way home. He tried to tell her this, but she hissed: "Do you want them to follow us?"

Ésh looked behind him. The bluecoats were still staring in his direction, but they weren't following.

His mother yanked him behind a Cloud lodge. "Didn't I tell you what happened when Chief Starving Bear only tried to *look* at the ring one of the bluecoats' wives was wearing?"

His mother had told him more than once. "Her husband attacked Starving Bear with a whip," Ésh muttered. "But didn't the *veho* call us here to make peace?"

"And the first thing they do is attack a chief! Your father is right: we cannot trust them. They also promised us food, while we are camped here and cannot hunt. But have they given us any food?"

The bluecoats claimed it was coming.

"Whenever you see a *veho*, whatever you are doing, you must run away, *nae'ha*—before they see this yellow hair."

The other boys would think Ésh was a coward! Before the contest, they had been talking about a Black Robe who had joined the *veho* camp. Ésh had heard of these holy men and their great medicine, how they wore dresses like women, but he'd never seen one, even from a distance. There must be a way he could join the other boys when they visited the Black Robe and proved they were not afraid of his powers.

"I will ask Háhkota if I can borrow his hat!" Ésh's brother had obtained it from a *veho* trader. He liked the way the hat shielded his eyes from the Sun. "I can hide my braids up inside it!"

"With such a hat, you would look more like a *veho*, not less."

"Then...I will wear a blanket pulled up over my head, like Grandmother used to do when she was cold!"

"When it is still warm? And even a blanket around your head would not hide *all* your hair." His mother touched a thumb to his yellow eyebrow. "What about these?"

"I will pluck them out like the men do!"

Her own eyebrows bunched up, her face pinched with pain. "And your beautiful green eyes?"

They *weren't* beautiful. Ésh hated them. He was tired of being special. He wanted to look like everyone else. "The *veho* won't see my eyes—I'll stay back! My skin isn't so different from yours!" He had the Sun to thank for that. "I'll rub bear grease and ashes in my hair to make it dark!"

While Ésh continued to protest, his mother led him back to the Zizistas camp.

"You said I was special, like Sweet Medicine! The Sacred Powers will protect me!"

Now his mother paused. Her gaze remained on the way ahead, but her voice grew quiet. "Someday, *nae'ha*, you *will* do great things. I am certain of it." Finally she glanced down at him, her eyes damp with tears. "But for now, you are my son—my only son—and I could not bear to lose you a second time." She started forward again, pulling him with her.

She stopped at a lodge he didn't recognize and scratched at the door-flap. A woman's voice invited them to enter, but Ésh's mother instructed him to wait outside for her. He crossed his arms over his chest and obeyed. He heard his mother talking to the owners of the lodge, a woman and a man, but he didn't listen. He peered in the direction of the contest. His arrow should still be there—he could run back, right now... Then his mother opened the door-flap and motioned for him to join her. Ésh sighed loudly and climbed inside.

His mother made introductions. She used his new formal name:

Mo'ohtáwo'neh, Black Wolf. But in private, she and the rest of his family continued to use his baby name, Ésh.

He knew the owner of the tipi the moment he saw her: White Cow Woman, the other member of the People who did not look like the People. Ésh had seen her at summer gatherings, but he'd never spoken with her. White Cow Woman had curly brown hair, blue eyes, and spots across her pale cheeks and nose. Her baby looked right, though, like her husband Raccoon. He sat beside her.

Ésh's mother distracted him from staring impolitely at White Cow Woman. "Until the council is over, I want you to stay somewhere safe. I know you will not want to remain with me all day long. So you can also come here." Ésh opened his mouth to argue, but his mother continued before he could speak: "Please, *nae'ha*—do not risk it."

Ésh narrowed his eyes. She was treating him like a baby. Even if he didn't have the protection of the Sacred Powers, he had two strong legs!

His mother sighed. "I must go help Héshek prepare our soup. Do you want to come back with me, or stay here?"

As an answer, Ésh dumped his quiver and bow on the buffalo robes, then flung himself against a willow backrest. His mother fretted over him for a few moments more but finally left the lodge.

While Raccoon stitched together a piece of folded buffalo hide —perhaps he was making a saddle—White Cow Woman gently rocked their sleeping child in her arms. She told Ésh in a whisper: "My husband will not let me go near the *veho* either." White Cow Woman looked happy about it; she was smiling as she glanced at Raccoon. "If they come looking for us, he will protect us."

"I am ten winters!" Ésh shouted back. "I can protect myself!"

He'd spoken too loudly: White Cow Woman's baby whined and shook his little fist. Both of his parents fussed over him, the brown head and the black one. Finally White Cow Woman offered the child her breast.

Ésh couldn't help staring at her. The skin of her chest was even paler than her face and hands. It was nearly white—so different from the red-brown skin of her baby.

Raccoon had risen to fetch a parfleche. After the man returned to his seat, Ésh asked him: "How did White Cow Woman come to live with us?"

Raccoon smiled with one side of his mouth, and he sounded like he was trying to hold in a chuckle. "It happened before *you* came to live with us." Raccoon opened the parfleche to reveal dried grass, which he began stuffing into his new saddle. "Eighteen winters ago, our warriors raided a camp of the Greasy Wood People." They lived to the south and east of the Zizistas, closer to the villages of the *veho*. "One of the women they captured was carrying a little girl on her back—a little girl with brown hair and blue eyes." Raccoon watched his wife and son, still smiling. "The Greasy Wood People had captured her from the *veho* only a little while before."

Ésh frowned. "But we made peace with the Greasy Wood People after that."

White Cow Woman spoke up: "I did not want to go back to them. And they did not ask for me. They knew I belonged here." She returned her husband's smile.

Ésh asked: "Do you remember being a *vehoá*?"

"No. Do you remember being a *veho*?"

"I was never a *veho*!" Ésh turned away from her.

In the morning, Ésh heard the giant *veho* gun booming like thunder, signalling that everyone should gather for the council. Everyone but Ésh. All day long, he had to stay within sight of his mother or White Cow Woman. Worst of all, the boys he'd thought were his friends did not come looking for him.

In the evening, Ésh's father, his grandfather, and the other men talked about the council. The bluecoats wanted one man to speak for each tribe, which made no sense to anyone but the *veho*. They wanted all the tribes to make peace with each other and to agree on the territories they claimed, which the *veho* promised never to invade. In exchange, the bluecoats promised each tribe gifts from their Great Father in the East. They would provide these gifts for fifty summers, as long as the *veho* wagons could travel to the West without trouble. Ésh's father argued that no amount of tobacco, coffee, or sugar would ever be enough payment for what the *veho* had already taken.

Before the cramping sickness, Ésh and his friends had ridden out and marvelled at the Great Medicine Trail. They'd delighted in the strange objects the *veho* left behind at each camping place, heavy things of wood and metal whose purpose they could only guess. Ésh found a cooking pot his mother was happy to have, and Méanév liked the bits of broken plate he brought her. The pieces were white painted with blue, and she fashioned them into earrings.

But the *veho* left behind other things too: the carcasses of buffalo and of their own animals who'd fallen down dead from exhaustion. On either side of the trail, the *veho* and their living animals took and took: they chopped down trees and devoured grass like swarms of locusts.

Earlier that summer, returning from a hunt, Ésh's father and his brother Háhkota had caught *veho* destroying two funeral scaffolds for firewood. They scared off the *veho* and laid the bodies to rest in a cave. Ésh had never seen his father and brother so angry.

Someone had named it the Great Medicine Trail as a dark joke, to acknowledge how the *veho* were changing the land. Once, there had been waving prairie grass along the Moon Shell River, grass that had fed countless animals who fed the People and their allies. Now, there was only a vast swath of bare earth along the river. Nothing would grow on this broad path because it had been trampled by so many feet and hoofs. At the slightest wind, a dust cloud would swirl up to sting your eyes and clog your throat and nostrils— a dust cloud made more of dried dung than of Earth.

The longer his father and the other men talked about the *veho*, the longer Ésh had to remain near his lodge like a captive, the more he stared at his yellow hair. His mother said he'd loved to watch himself in a mirror when he was little. Now, he could not bear the sight. Sometimes the other boys called him Toad Belly, because of his pale skin.

Ésh wished a rattlesnake had bitten this *veho* body and killed it on Painted Rock, so his soul could keep looking for a proper body.

He should find a rattlesnake tomorrow and ask it to bite him, so he could come back as a true Zizistas. He'd come back before. He could do it again.

But wouldn't he have to return as a baby, since all of the older Zizistas bodies already had souls? He didn't want to be a baby again. Instead of the same age, he'd be ten winters younger than Méanév, and then she'd never want to marry him.

As if she knew he was thinking about her, his friend sat down beside him, beneath the brush arbor his mother had made. Ésh smiled in surprise.

"We smoked the pipe with the Sósonée today!" Méanév told him. "Did you ever think it could happen? We adopted some of their children, and they adopted some of our children! I have a Sósonée brother now!"

"Did you see the Black Robe?"

"Up close! He is rather fat, but he is kind. He speaks a little Zizistas. He sprinkled water on me and my new brother."

"Water?" Ésh wondered. "Why?"

"It was some kind of blessing." Méanév shrugged. "Mother said it would be rude to refuse. Look what I got from a bluecoat!" She shook some sort of flat leaves from a little container, with shapes and people painted on both sides. "You play games and gamble with them. I can teach you."

Ésh decided that being a captive was not so bad when he had Méanév for company. She did not seem to mind that he looked like a *veho*.

CHAPTER 32

They had seen a few white men from time to time, and the encounter had impressed them with a strong desire to see no more… Their earnest wish was clearly to be left alone.

— George Gibbs, *Journal of the Expedition of Colonel Redick M'Kee, United States Indian Agent* (1851)

Carefully Ésh pressed the flat of his knife blade against the skin of his forearm and scraped the metal forward, dislodging the stinger with its little piece of attached honeybee flesh. Silly insects, didn't they understand that their sacrifice gained them nothing—he still robbed their hive—and cost them everything?

Grandfather probably had some herb or charm that would have protected him from the bees, but Ésh thought that would have been cowardly. Better that Méanév know how much pain he'd endured for her. Maybe he would ask Grandfather for something to cool the swellings later. Now, he did not want to miss Méanév.

He glanced up again, checking that the door-flap of the menstrual lodge remained closed and that no ants had found the honeycomb in its turtle shell bowl beside him. Then he returned to removing the stingers. He still remembered the morning four winters ago when Grandfather had explained to him about the women's use of that lodge. How ignorant he'd been then—what a child.

HE'D COME RUNNING BACK from racing buffalo rib sleds with the other boys, craving his mother's lily bulb porridge. He'd been frustrated when his grandfather stopped him from entering their family's tipi.

"If you are hungry, *nish*, I am sure Méanév's mother will have something for you. You must not go in now."

"Why not?" Ésh pouted. He needed fresh moccasins, too; his were soaked.

"I cannot enter either," Grandfather assured him. "You missed your father's announcement. He gave away a horse. While you were gone, Pákehe discovered she had become a woman. Your sister is inside now with your mothers, smoking herself with sage. Then she will go to the women's lodge for four days, just as your mothers do every moon."

"Why?"

"You know that men and women each have their own kind of medicine, Ésh. Usually this is good. But there are days during each moon when a woman's medicine is *too* strong. She must take herself away from men, or she may harm them."

For a moment Ésh hesitated, eyes widening. When he spoke, it was almost a whisper. "My sister is dangerous?"

Grandfather smiled. "Only for a few days each moon, and then only to men. If you wish to be a woman, go in." Ésh was not sure what his face looked like then, but it made Grandfather chuckle.

ÉSH STILL DIDN'T WANT TO BE A GIRL, but for them things were easy. All Pákehe and Méanév had to do to become women was to wait for something that happened naturally. He wouldn't be a man for many winters yet—and until then, he wouldn't be able to court Méanév without her mother running him off like a hissing goose.

He'd brought down a buffalo calf during the last hunt; that was a start. But he still had to prove himself in battle: he had to count coups and take a scalp. And if he really wanted the women to admire him, he had to dance in the New Life Lodge and offer his flesh to the Sacred Powers. It wasn't fair.

He hated the way the adults separated him and Méanév now. They had played together almost every day when they were children, even before they liked each other, since their mothers were friends. Now Méanév could keep company only with other girls, and Ésh had to limit his friends to other boys. Still, he hoped he'd be able to give her the honey without anyone objecting. He stayed back so that no one could tell he was watching the women's lodge, and in case any of their dangerous female medicine leaked out.

Finally someone pulled aside the door-flap of the tipi. The scents of sweet grass, juniper, and white sage drifted toward him, and Méanév emerged. She didn't look any different.

Ésh wasn't finished removing the bee stingers, but he grabbed the turtle shell bowl and stood anyway.

Méanév spotted him and smiled back. Arched upwards at the bottoms like crescent moons, her eyes seemed to smile too, the way they always did. Then she noticed all his welts, and her mouth dropped open.

Ésh inhaled proudly. "I did not flinch once." He held out the honeycomb.

"For me?" She touched her chest, just below the deer tail at her throat, just above where her breasts had begun to grow. That had started months ago. Her mother had added fringes to her dresses, but they did not hide the swells.

"For you." He knew how much Méanév loved the taste of honey, and how rarely she got it. He was so clever and thoughtful. He'd eaten only a *little* of the honey himself.

She accepted his gift, holding the turtle shell in one hand and brushing the fingertips of her other hand across his swollen shoulder, where the bees had gotten inside his shirt. "You must have been very brave."

"I was."

"So brave, we will have to give you a new name, I think."

That was only natural. He tried not to grin too broadly.

"What will it be?" Méanév mused.

Sáa-E'tóhtahe-he, Ésh thought. *He Is Not Afraid!*

"I have it!" Méanév declared. "'Many Stings!'" She laughed for only a moment before she took off running.

He scowled and chased after her. Several of the camp dogs barked in delight and joined their game; Ésh nearly knocked over a shield stand; and Méanév almost dropped the turtle shell. She ran laughing down the rows of corn by the river, which she had helped the other women plant that spring. Finally he backed her up against a cottonwood trunk.

She pretended to be very interested in the honey, though she couldn't stop giggling. If she was going to mock him, he would take it back! But as he stepped closer, Méanév dipped her fingers into the turtle shell and brought the honey to her lips. Ésh felt a new kind of itch—in his chest or his throat, he wasn't sure—and wondered what it would be like to kiss her.

Then her mother descended on him like a vulture. She swatted at him with her hide scraper, and he shielded his head as if the bees were still after him.

She dragged Méanév up the hill toward the camp, scolding, "Have you heard nothing I have told you these past four days?"

"It's Ésh, *náhko'e*," Méanév explained, following reluctantly, still giggling. She cradled the turtle shell under her arm, glanced over her shoulder at him, and pouted.

Her mother tugged harder. "You are no longer a child!"

NEITHER WAS HE, no matter what anyone else thought. Over his mother's objections, Ésh rode out to join the party of warriors gathering on the Flint Arrowpoint River. Two bands of Zizistas were camped with six other tribes, fourteen hundred lodges altogether. They had allied against two tribes from the East whom the *veho* had moved into their territory, in spite of the Horse Creek Treaty.

The warriors did not allow Ésh to actually fight. This was his time to learn, they said. What he learned was this: ten thousand arrows were like bee stings against one hundred guns. The Zizistas and their allies fled in retreat and decided not to attack the eastern tribes again. Ésh must wait for another chance to prove himself.

Then, *veho* passing in wagons abandoned an old, lame cow who could not even stand. An Inviter named High Forehead put the animal out of its misery, used its hide, and distributed its meat. Thirty bluecoats came with two enormous guns and demanded the "thief." The Inviters offered horses in exchange for the worthless cow, but the bluecoats refused. Their leader was an arrogant young man named Grattan who hated all Indians, and their interpreter was drunk. Soon the arguing became shooting. The bluecoats shot first, but the *veho* cared only about their own dead.

The next summer, six hundred soldiers attacked an encampment of Inviters and Zizistas on Blue Water Creek. The bluecoats massacred eighty-six people and captured seventy women and children. The *veho* burned all their homes and belongings; and when the bluecoats finally released the women, many of them wished they were dead.

Among the Inviters and the Zizistas, the young men wanted vengeance. But the chiefs and the old men like Ésh's grandfather argued to keep the Horse Creek Treaty that the bluecoats had already broken. Before the agreement was even a year old, before any of this fighting had begun, the *veho* had decided they would provide payment for only ten summers instead of the fifty summers they had promised. Each year, while the *veho* and their wagons and animals ravaged the land, the People and their allies would camp near the soldier fort called Laramie and wait and wait for the bluecoats to keep their promise. The Inviters who found the lame cow were waiting on this payment, and they were hungry; that was why High Forehead had killed the animal.

The Zizistas turned their anger toward the Wolf People, who were friendly towards the *veho*. (What gave them the right to call themselves Wolf People? That alone made Ésh want to attack them.) This time, the war leader let Ésh scout with his brother Háhkota. They had been practicing during the summer hunts, locating buffalo and antelope. Ésh's favorite part was returning to camp and howling to announce their success; scouts were called wolves. Now, he would finally be able to hunt an enemy, even if it wasn't the *veho*.

Ésh and Háhkota travelled in the valleys, climbing each rise carefully and watching for smoke or other signs. At last they spotted a coyote trotting along a ridge and glancing over its shoulder. When they crept up the hill, they saw their enemies' earth lodges in the distance, across the river. The Wolf People still lived as the Zizistas had in the days of Grandfather's grandfathers: their villages were permanent, and they were farmers more than hunters.

Between Ésh and the earth lodges grazed the village's herd of horses, who were guarded by a boy of perhaps fifteen winters. He slumped under the shade of a scrub oak grove, his chin to his chest in the afternoon heat. Most of his head was shaved; he wore only a strip of hair down the center. He was clearly one of the Wolf People.

Ésh could hardly contain his excitement. He pulled an arrow from his quiver. This would be so easy!

"What are you doing?" Háhkota challenged in a hushed voice, laying a hand over Ésh's.

Ésh frowned, lowering his bow.

"The angle is bad," his brother pointed out. "What if you only wound him? Or what if you do kill him—what will happen when the next boy comes to guard? He will find his friend dead and run to the village. He will warn them, and then the Wolf warriors will be ready for us. We will have ruined the raid for all the others. Our duty as scouts is only to find the enemy, not to seek glory for ourselves. You know this."

Yes, Háhkota had told him that, over and over. Ésh plunked the arrow back in his quiver and scowled.

"You are not even fourteen winters, Ésh. You have your whole life to be a warrior. I did not count my first coup until I was sixteen. Come."

Háhkota was simply afraid that his little brother might surpass him. Ésh trudged after him till they reached their horses. When

Háhkota crouched to unhobble his stallion, Ésh quickly doubled back and slipped over the hill.

He slunk into the scrub oak so that he could approach the guard from behind, treading carefully and without noise. When Ésh glanced up between the scraggly trunks, he saw Háhkota motioning frantically for Ésh to rejoin him on the other side of the rise. Ésh grinned and ignored him. The Wolf People's horses chewed grass and paid no attention to either of them.

Carefully Ésh crouched behind the enemy and extended his bow till the far end tapped the guard on the shoulder. The boy stirred but only slapped the place idly, as if he were brushing away an insect, then settled again.

Ésh had to bite his lip to keep himself from laughing in delight and pride. His first coup! And Háhkota had said he could not do it! Ésh backed away from the enemy, crept out of the oak grove, and scrambled up the ridge.

He was moving too quickly and not watching where he stepped. He must have kicked a small rock in climbing, which slid and knocked against other rocks. One of the Wolf People's horses stamped and whinnied in surprise, causing the others to panic. Ésh glanced back in horror to watch the guard start awake. The boy's eyes fixed on them almost at once.

Muttering under his breath, Háhkota pulled Ésh to safety before the Wolf boy could gather his bow. "I told you! I told you! Why did you not listen?" His brother dragged Ésh behind him, and together they rushed for their horses as the guard began yelling on the other side of the rise.

Shame filled his face with blood, and Ésh's throat and stomach tightened in fear. He and Háhkota might be killed—and for what? Ésh kept throwing glances over his shoulder. A gallop had never seemed so slow.

Finally they reached the camp of their war party. "The Wolf People know we are near!" Háhkota cried. "We must go back!"

The other men did not ask questions. They strapped their few belongings together, mounted, and fled.

That night in their new camp, while the others glared at Ésh, he demanded of Háhkota: "Why did you have to tell them? You could have said anything!"

His brother sighed. "In battle, our lives depend on each other, Ésh. If you are going to do only what is good for yourself, these men need to know."

They returned to their disappointed families: there would be no dancing tonight. Instead, the warriors planned when they would strike the Wolf People again—not too soon, or they would be expected. Ésh was not invited. No one seemed to care that he'd counted a coup. For a few days, even Méanév scurried away before their paths could cross.

Ésh was not the first scout to make such a mistake, Grandfather assured him. But this did not excuse Ésh's choice. "You remember that each of us has four spirits inside him, *nish?*" Grandfather chided. "You must learn not to listen to the Crazy Spirit or the Tantalizer. Listen to the Good Spirit and the Thoughtful Spirit. That is the way to become a man. That is the Zizistas way."

CHAPTER 33

I used to hate all white people, especially their soldiers. But my heart now has become changed to softer feelings. Some of the white people are good, maybe as good as Indians.

— Iron Teeth, a Northern Cheyenne woman, *Century Magazine* (1929)

É sh hardly noticed it till one of the other boys in the gambling circle pointed at him and laughed. "Look: Black Wolf is turning into a black wolf!"

He looked down to where his legs were crossed in front of him, and just as Mo'kesa had said, short thick hairs sprouted like grass from his shins, darker than the hair on his head.

The other boys sniggered too.

"The hair isn't *black*," Wóhkóóh argued. "It's brown—he's turning into a buffalo!"

Ésh left them with their bone dice, since he was losing anyway.

When he realized that similar hair was growing on his forearms, Ésh became worried. He had expected the hair in his armpits and around his *véto'ots* to change. But why was the rest of the hair on his body changing too?

What if he *was* turning into a buffalo? Their prophet Sweet Medicine had transformed himself into animals. But Ésh had no control over this. He didn't want to be a buffalo. Someone might chase him down and eat him by mistake.

Ésh tied leggings to the cord of his breechcloth and pulled on an antelope skin shirt. Háhkota was sitting in the shade of a pine tree near their lodge. He was making a bow using pieces of horn from a mountain sheep. The glue came from boiled rawhide clippings. His brother explained all this while Ésh pretended to watch him work.

The hair on Háhkota's arms and legs was so fine you could hardly see it. That was the way it was supposed to be. Maheo had given the Zizistas true hair on only their heads in order to distinguish them as human beings, as his People. Something was wrong with Ésh.

He searched their lodge and found the tweezers their father used to pluck out his eyebrows. But it would take days to remove each of his leg hairs that way. Finally Ésh settled on his mother's elk-horn scraper for tanning hides.

He took some of the peeled yucca root from the morning bathing place and carried it farther down the river where no one would look for him. He untied his leggings, rubbed the root fibers together for suds, and smeared them on his shins.

Scraping off the ugly hair proved difficult. He wasn't a buffalo hide. Not yet. He cut his skin, but he just gritted his teeth and kept trying.

Before he finished his left leg, a strange voice startled him, and an even stranger hand snatched away the elk-horn scraper. The man was a *veho*!

Ésh scrambled backward in fear, but he could go only so far without falling in the river. The *veho* did not raise the scraper like a club, and he did not seem to carry any other weapons. He must be a trader. So instead of trying to escape him, Ésh demanded: "Give it back!"

The man seemed to be speaking Zizistas; if Ésh concentrated, he could understand him, but the *veho*'s pronunciation was terrible. "Not until you tell me what you are doing."

Ésh had not been so close to a *veho* since the Horse Creek Treaty, and it was difficult to look at the man politely from the corner of his eyes. His skin was splotchy: pinkish across his cheeks and nose and pale elsewhere. A beard covered half his face, and his greasy brown hair reached only to his shoulders. He wore a red *veho* shirt and a breechcloth of black trade cloth with buckskin leggings and moccasins. He looked like he had seen about twenty-five winters, but with *veho* it was hard to tell.

"Answer me, Black Wolf." The man's tone was not angry, but Ésh scowled to hear his name coming from this stranger. "Yes, I know who you are," the *veho* continued. "I know your grandfather. My name is Robert Smith. The Zizistas call me Mé'hahts."

Ésh remembered now. Grandfather had been threatening to introduce him to this man for several moons. "You are the bluecoat."

The *veho* laughed. "Not anymore."

Ésh knew Mé'hahts had abandoned the bluecoat fort on the Goose River two summers ago, and that he lived with the People now. He had married a Zizistas woman. He wasn't a very good hunter, so Grandfather thought that if they traded him meat, Mé'hahts could teach them the *veho* language. The man could not betray Ésh to the bluecoats without betraying himself. The *veho* punished their soldiers who ran away.

Unlike Grandfather, Ésh had no interest in speaking the *veho* language. He didn't care what any of them had to say, least of all this bluecoat who thought he was a Zizistas now. He would never be Zizistas.

"Isn't this for scraping hides?" Mé'hahts peered at the elk-horn tool. "Why are you using it on your legs?"

"I am fixing them!"

"Fixing them?"

"They are hairy!" Ésh cried.

Mé'hahts laughed loudly. It was not good to hide all your feelings like the Sósonée, but this man had no manners. "They are supposed to get hairy! It means you are becoming a man!" Mé'hahts grasped one of his own leggings and tugged it up to his knee. "See?"

Ésh's mouth dropped open. The man's leg was as shaggy as a bear's. Generations and generations ago, the Zizistas had been bears; but they had become human long since. The *veho* were stuck somewhere in the middle. Ésh had heard they were hairy, but he had never imagined anything so hideous.

"You will get hair all over your body," Mé'hahts continued. "In winter, you will be glad to have a beard."

No, Ésh would not!

Next the man pulled open the neck of his shirt, exposing more hairs. "And on your chest."

Wide-eyed, Ésh stood. "I won't!" How could Mé'hahts's wife bear to touch him? He was disgusting! Ésh grabbed his leggings and fled back toward camp, not caring that the hairy man still had his mother's scraper.

"You cannot run away from it, Black Wolf! It is who you are!" Mé'hahts followed him like an insistent mosquito. "Where I come from, boys are *proud* when they start growing hair. You are lucky I am here to tell you these things, and to teach you English." He said the last word in his own language, and tripped over a cottonwood root.

"I do not want to learn your 'English'!" Ésh shouted back without turning, hurrying along the riverbank.

"How will you communicate when you leave?"

"I am not going anywhere!" Finally Ésh stopped, so that Mé'hahts could see he was serious.

"Right now, you do not have a choice, because you are a boy." The *veho* caught up to him, panting. "But soon you will be a man, and you can return to your people."

Ésh stared at him incredulously, then pointed his lips toward the lodges. "I am already with my people!"

"Look at yourself, Black Wolf." Mé'hahts seemed to be laughing at him again. "They should call you White Wolf! You are like me, not them. You are a cygnet, not an ugly duckling." Who said ducklings were ugly? "I do not know how you ended up in this nest, but you do not belong here."

Ésh glared up at the lying *veho*, who was hardly taller than himself, shorter than any grown Zizistas. In that way too, Maheo had set his People apart. "*You* are the one who does not belong!"

Mé'hahts looked away and sighed, a sound that still bordered on laughter. "I am here because I am lazy, I suppose. Here, work does not feel so much like work. Men's work, at least." He rubbed a squat thumb along the hide scraper he still held. "And if you fail, someone is always there to help you. I have never met such a generous people." Then his smile faded. "But this life cannot last, Black Wolf. Every year, there are fewer buffalo. Soon the Zizistas will not have enough to feed themselves. You must understand that."

The Sacred Powers would not abandon them. The buffalo would return. If his mother was right and he was special, Ésh might be able to help call them back. He opened his mouth to tell the stupid *veho* this, when he heard Grandfather's voice:

"There you are, *nish!* I am glad Mé'hahts found you." Grandfather paused, and Ésh glanced toward him, to see that Grandfather was staring at his soapy, bleeding shins in confusion. "What happened to your legs?"

ÉSH WAS FORCED TO LISTEN while Mé'hahts gave "English" lessons. Grandfather and Ésh's little brother Tahpeno also wanted to learn. Sometimes several children would come, and Tahpeno would puff up with pride like a prairie chicken as he translated all the ridiculous stories Mé'hahts told about how the *veho* lived and travelled. Ésh's aunt Héshek had given birth to Tahpeno the summer after the cramps; he wasn't even six winters yet, but he learned English even faster than their grandfather.

Mé'hahts made so many strange noises. Ésh and his grandfather practiced and practiced, and still their tongues struggled to form some of the sounds. Ésh hated the stupid, impossible language. It made no sense. The *veho* called themselves "white men," when they were closer to pink—and they called the Zizistas "red men," when they were closer to brown. The only English words Ésh needed to know were: "I am Cheyenne. Go away!"

He hated even being near Mé'hahts. After Ésh's scouting

disaster and his embarrassing new hair, he did not need this too. When Mo'kesa and his friends saw Ésh and Mé'hahts together, he mocked: "Toad Belly! You have finally found your real father!" And then they all laughed.

The other boys had long ago lost their fear of the power Ésh might have someday. He wished the wolf spirit would hurry up and show him why he'd returned in this body. He was tired of waiting for an answer, tired of the way people stared at him when another village camped beside his.

Háhkota was always kind to him; but like their father, Ésh's older brother was often away hunting or capturing horses. Their father never spoke up for Ésh, and his aunt Héshek was cruel to him in small ways she thought no one else would notice.

Mé'hahts did prove useful in one thing. As he had predicted, by the next season of New Leaves and Berries, the hair on Ésh's face grew more noticeable. So he accepted a "straight razor" and "strop" from the *veho*, who taught him how to use them. Ésh needed his own mirror now, to help him shave. To make it easier to prop the mirror where he wanted it, Ésh attached it to a thick piece of wood, with the bottom half carved into a handle. Mé'hahts said it looked like a "paddle." To Ésh's relief, the hair on his chest did not change very much. Only a patch at the center turned ugly, and that was simple to shave.

Mé'hahts kept pestering Ésh with questions about his "real" family. Mé'hahts always waited to talk about it till they were alone. He would speak in a low voice, as if he and Ésh were sharing a secret. "You cannot believe that nonsense about being born Cheyenne and dying and returning in another body," the *veho* insisted. "You cannot tell me you are not curious about where you *really* came from." Mé'hahts called the landmark where Ésh's mother had found him "Independence Rock" instead of Painted Rock.

When their village camped near the Rock again, Mé'hahts wanted to see the cave and the carvings that had been there the summer Ésh was born. Grandfather had shown him the cave when he was younger. Even then, the Rock had been covered in *veho* markings, so Mé'hahts would never find the right ones without help.

While Mé'hahts was whispering to him about this and Ésh was refusing to go with him, Grandfather walked up to them.

The *veho* looked guilty and tried to talk about something else.

But Grandfather had heard enough. He wanted to know what the markings in the cave said as much as Mé'hahts did. "Someday, this may be important, *nish*."

So Ésh came along; but he stayed at the base of Painted Rock. "To make sure no one steals our horses," he said. Ésh wandered till he found the pile of rocks that had been here since he was born, the rocks Grandfather had said must cover a body.

Not just *any* body: this grave probably held the *vehoá* who had borne the *veho* body Ésh now wore. It was so strange to think about. He'd never seen her face, but this *vehoá* had given him his yellow hair, his green eyes, and his pale, hairy skin. She had given him life just as surely as his real mother, and she had died doing it. When they were baby-sized, Ésh's hands, his feet, his head—*every* part of him had lived for nine moons inside this dead white woman who lay hardly a hand's breadth away.

Not even that far: peeking between the rocks on her grave, Ésh saw a bit of pale blue cloth. He knelt down. Could that be part of his mother's dress? What else did these rocks conceal? Might there still be enough flesh on her bones to see what she looked like? If nothing else, her hair would have survived. Would it be yellow like his? He reached toward the cloth. If he pulled...

He leapt to his feet instead. The *vehoá* in this grave was *not* his mother. His mother was Zizistas, just like him. Ésh found more rocks to pile on top of the *vehoá*, till he couldn't see the blue cloth any more.

When Grandfather and Mé'hahts came down from the cave, they wanted to tell Ésh what the markings said. Mé'hahts had copied them onto a rabbit hide.

"Some of it makes sense," he explained in a mixture of Zizistas and English. "There's a man's name and a woman's name: 'David

McAllister' and 'Sophie McAllister.' Those must be your parents. You're Scottish!"

Whatever *that* meant.

"What became of your father is a mystery, unless they were both buried together…" Mé'hahts continued, glancing over at the grave. "The date makes sense too: it says 'July 1841,' and you're fourteen years old. The strange part is this line." He pointed to it the way *veho* did, with his fingertip. "It says: 'Charleston, South Carolina.' That's a city—a very large village—all the way on the eastern ocean, on the far side of the *veho* lands. I thought everyone who travelled on the overland trail came from the nearer states like Illinois and Missouri. But it's clear as day. You're from South Carolina, son."

"I am *not* your son!" Ésh shouted, and ran to his horse.

CHAPTER 34

When white persons of either sex have been taken prisoners young
by the Indians, and lived a while among them, tho' ransomed by
their Friends, and treated with all imaginable tenderness to prevail
with them to stay among the English, yet in a Short time they
become disgusted with our manner of life…and take the first good
Opportunity of escaping again into the Woods, from whence there
is no reclaiming them.
— Benjamin Franklin, in a 1753 letter

Grandfather wanted Mé'hahts to teach them how to read the
veho markings themselves, but Mé'hahts's wife said they had
camped with Ésh's band long enough. She was expecting a child,
and she was eager to return to her own family.

Soon after Mé'hahts and his wife left, Tahpeno told Ésh that
Méanév wanted to learn more English. She'd come to a few of
Mé'hahts's lessons, but like the rest of the women, she was usually
busy. Méanév's father had been born among the Rattlesnake People.
He spoke not only their language and Zizistas but also some of the
language of the darker *veho* to the south. Her father had taught her

many of their words. Méanév liked all the different sounds, and she made them beautifully.

Tahpeno knew this because he was already teaching her bits of English. Ésh didn't care if his little brother was only six—Méanév was *his*! *He* would teach her English! One afternoon, as she came back from gathering plums, Ésh pulled her aside and whispered for her to meet him in his willow shelter that evening.

He had built his own little hut at the edge of camp, like his brother Háhkota and the other young men did, so they wouldn't be cramped in the same lodge with their families. When Méanév sat down with him, she left the door-flap open. They were only practicing their English, and laughing; but Ésh's face was very close to Méanév's so he could watch the position of her tongue against the roof of her mouth.

All of a sudden, Méanév's mother appeared. "You are not a loose Rattlesnake girl!" she yelled as she pulled her daughter out of the hut. "You are a Zizistas woman! Zizistas women are pure! Do you think you will attract a husband, behaving like this?"

"We only wanted to talk, *náhko'e*," Méanév protested.

"That is not all *he* wants!" Her mother pointed her lips at Ésh accusingly.

He said nothing because he had, in fact, been thinking of another thing their mouths might do besides forming strange words. But only thinking. Now, he knew he must speak. "She wanted my help learning English. But the truth is: Méanév was helping *me*; she's better with languages than I am. Your daughter is the smartest girl —woman—in camp."

"And what have you done to deserve her?" Méanév's mother demanded.

The question felt like a blow.

"Where are your scars from the New Life Lodge? Bring me a scalp. Recount your coups to me, and then you can court my Méanév. Until then, you are only a boy, and you have no right to be with her."

"Please, *náhko'e*…" Méanév kept her eyes lowered. "If he only sat beside our lodge in the evenings, and spoke to me through the wall, then I would not be in danger. You could watch over me."

Her mother squinted at Ésh in suspicion, but finally she sighed. "As long as he does not try to crawl *under* the wall." She pointed at Ésh again in warning. "Anything you stick under the wall, I will chop off! Do you hear me?"

When Ésh stopped sniggering—half in amusement, half in nervousness that Méanév's mother meant what she said—he agreed.

He loved the way Méanév could resolve arguments. She had been a peacemaker all her life. When the other children fought, she wasn't afraid to step between them. Everyone listened to her, no matter how angry they were, and she never became angry herself. More than once, she'd defended him when someone made fun of the way he was colored. Even under the weight of firewood on her back, in each lovely line of her face, with each graceful step she took, Méanév seemed to carry calm with her as effortlessly as the blue beads of her necklace. Blue for serenity.

Her name meant Summer, but Méanév did not remind Ésh of bustle or heat. She reminded him of still winter nights when the snow fell without sound and everything seemed to pause, even his own heartbeat. In those moments, he felt no fear, no pain. Only peace. Only anticipation.

THAT SUMMER, AN ARGUMENT BEGAN that Méanév could not resolve, because it involved the bluecoats. The *veho* complained that the People had stolen four of their horses, when the animals had been wandering the plains.

The People remembered how many had died because of the lame cow. For the sake of peace, the new owners of three of the horses returned them; but the fourth refused. The bluecoats seized this man, Two Tails, and two of his friends who were not to blame for anything but were simply Zizistas. When the warriors tried to escape, the *veho* recaptured Fire Wolf and shot Bull Shield through the head. Two Tails was only wounded. He reached his camp and brought the terrible news to the rest of the People.

The bluecoats took Fire Wolf to their fort on the Goose River. Mé'hahts had described this place to Ésh, including the terrible "guardhouse" where they kept their captives and even their own soldiers when they disobeyed or drank too much firewater: underground in "cells" so narrow you could hardly turn around, so shallow you couldn't lie flat, and so short you couldn't even stand up. "It's like being buried alive! And the *stench*!"

When Ésh closed his eyes at night, sometimes he would dream he lay bunched up in the cell next to Fire Wolf's, with walls tight around him—walls unlike any he had ever known—walls made of stone that no knife could cut. Ésh would start awake, and even his willow shelter would make him feel trapped. Then he would scramble out into the warm night, stare up at the great splash of stars overhead, and his heartbeats would slow again.

He was safe. He was free.

When Fire Wolf's family fled in fear, the bluecoats burned their lodges. And still they wanted more captives. Still the *veho* shot at the People because they were the People, killing War Shirt who had only ridden up to a "stagecoach" to ask for some tobacco, and then six more Zizistas who had thrown down their weapons.

The old men could no longer control the young men; in vengeance, they scalped a fur man and attacked a few groups of *veho* travelling west. (How Ésh wished he could have ridden with them! He was fifteen winters now—much wiser than he'd been at thirteen!) The warriors captured a *vehoá* and a pale little boy and brought them to Ésh's camp.

He knew he should stay away from them, because the warriors would return the captives as soon as the bluecoats returned Fire Wolf. If the woman saw Ésh with the People, she might tell the *veho*, and they might come for him. But Ésh had never seen a *vehoá* or a young *veho*. The Tantalizer proved impossible to resist. Ésh found himself creeping closer and closer to the lodge of Méanév's parents, where the *vehoá* and the little boy were staying, hoping to catch a glimpse of them.

Finally, the woman left the tipi, holding the little boy's hand in one of hers and wiping her eyes with a small white cloth. The boy looked about four years old. His hair was short and reddish, the color of a buffalo calf. The woman's hair was long and yellow, like Ésh's.

He had half expected her to wear a beard like *veho* men, but she did not. Ésh wondered if the woman's arms and legs were hairy too. Both were covered by her dress. She and the boy still wore their *veho* clothing, so simple and plain. It was stained with dried blood, but they did not appear to be injured.

Méanév's mother seemed to be pointing them toward the stream. Perhaps they would bathe and Ésh would be able to see more of the *vehoá*'s skin. He trailed them at a distance, careful not to let them see him.

The *vehoá* did kneel at the stream to wash the boy's face with her white cloth. Then she pushed up her sleeves. Ésh crouched nearby, trying to see her arms. But there was a willow blocking his view. Maybe if he…

The *veho* boy spotted him then. He gasped and came running. The *vehoá* followed at his heels, calling in her own language. She seemed to be addressing Ésh, not the boy.

Ésh closed his eyes, sighed, and stood. He tried to remember all the things Mé'hahts had taught him, but the woman's words flew at him like a swarm of bees. He recognized "help us"; mostly she was repeating variations of that.

The woman fell to her knees in front of Ésh, her yellow hair wild and loose around her tear-streaked face. She gripped the bottom of his shirt so hard he could feel the pull against his shoulders. He was wearing a *veho* shirt today, one his father had obtained from a trader. Ésh didn't like *veho* clothing very much, but his mother did, because it was easier to make and clean than animal skin. She also liked how the green shirt matched his eyes. So Ésh had decided to please her. Now, as the *vehoá* and the red-haired boy gaped up at him, Ésh regretted his choice.

The woman pleaded with him to "Take us back with you—help us get to the fort!"

The *vehoá* must think Ésh was a trader, or the son of a trader.

She must not understand that her stay with the People was temporary. "You will have what you want when my people have what we want," Ésh told her in English as best he could. "Until Fire Wolf is free, you must stay here."

Her blue eyes widened. She stared at Ésh's braids and his pierced ears as if she were noticing them for the first time. "What have they done to you?" Panic tightened her face, and the *vehoá* staggered to her feet. By now, many of the people in camp had stopped what they were doing to watch her. The woman snatched up the red-haired boy and clutched him to her chest as if she were protecting him from predators. "You will never make us like you!" she cried. "Never!"

Méanév stepped out of the crowd. Ésh knew his friend meant to help, so he motioned her toward them.

The woman's nostrils flared. She backed away from them and screamed: "I will *die* before I become a filthy savage!"

"No one will hurt you," Méanév assured the *vehoá* in English. Méanév tried to touch her arm, but the woman jerked away from her. Méanév's mother came to help her lead the captives back to their lodge.

The woman glared over her shoulder at Ésh, who had started to follow. He wanted to explain. "Traitor!" the *vehoá* hissed. She spat on the ground as if she were cursing his path. "Coward!"

Ésh thought he understood the first English word, that it was an insult. He certainly understood the second.

He shouldn't care what this crazy *vehoá* thought of him. She was his enemy.

Yet the sight of this woman with her yellow hair made Ésh wonder. Had his *vehoá* mother looked like her? And if she could see him now, would she hate him too?

THE BLUECOATS REFUSED to release Fire Wolf. The People treated their own captives kindly, not even guarding them, and the woman escaped with the little boy. But Fire Wolf remained a captive at the fort until he died that autumn. Whether he'd died because of the way the *veho* treated him or simply from grief, no one knew, because the bluecoats did not even have the decency to return his body. Fire Wolf, who had done nothing to them.

These were the people whose skin Ésh wore.

CHAPTER 35

The Cheyenne young women and young girls always wore the protective rope... All men, young and old, respect this rope, and anyone violating it would certainly be killed by the male relations of the girl.

— George Bird Grinnell, *The Cheyenne Indians* (1923)

A few nights after a messenger brought news of Fire Wolf's death, Ésh tossed first one way and then the next inside his willow shelter. He fought it as long as he could; but in the end, he could not deny the demands of his body: he would have to leave his comfortable bed, traipse out into the darkness, and relieve himself.

He threw aside the blanket door-flap and stumbled outside. He squinted and blinked in the light of the half-moon, wondering if he was dreaming. A man stood frozen in place, slightly crouched, holding the halter rope of Ésh's best buffalo horse. The man's hairstyle proved he was no Zizistas: cut short in front and teased with grease to stand on end, as if daring his enemies to scalp him. When the figure reached for its knife, Ésh knew it was no dream.

He dove at the man, wrestling him to the ground and straining for the weapon. "*Óoetaneo'o!*" Ésh shouted while he struggled.

"Crow!" Where there was one, there must be others; he must warn the rest of his village.

A great commotion sprang up around them as new voices echoed the shout. Ésh and his horse thief rolled back into his hut, collapsing it. Ésh was a good wrestler against boys his own age, but his enemy was full-grown. The Crow warrior was stronger. Ésh could not keep the knife from darting dangerously closer and closer to his flesh, till the blade sliced across his side. Ésh gritted his teeth at the pain.

His enemy tried to draw back and stab him again, but the knife slipped and dropped into the darkness. Both of them groped for it. Ésh felt only buffalo fur, the softness of his bedding. At last his fingers snagged on the base of his mirror on its thick stand—almost as good as a war-club. He grabbed the handle, turned his face away, and whacked the mirror against the head of the Crow warrior.

Ésh heard the glass shatter, and bits rained down on him. He scrambled out from beneath the moaning thief and crawled across the man's knife, still slick with his own blood. Ésh grasped its hilt with both hands and shoved the blade deep into his enemy's throat. He did not release the knife until the man stopped making choking noises and lay still.

The sounds of the fight were fading now; the other Crow had fled. Since the danger was past, Ésh finally had a chance to urinate. He kept his shirt pressed against the cut in his side, trying to slow the blood.

He let go only long enough to grip the Crow thief's spiky scalp lock and slice it from his head with an oval of skin. Then Ésh ran to join the others in the camp.

Asishk spotted him first. "Were you the one who called out the warning, Black Wolf?"

"I am the one," Ésh grinned. His smile faded as he looked toward the herd. "Did they take many of our horses?"

"Not so many as they would have, thanks to you!"

"You are hurt!" O'hek noticed.

"It is not serious," Ésh shrugged. "As for the Crow who tried to steal *my* horse…" Ésh held up the thief's bloody scalp by the greasy hair.

The others whooped in praise, their voices like sunlight in winter. As the news of his feat travelled, the ululations of women joined the men in a chorus. All for *him*.

"How did you know the Crow were attacking?" Asishk wanted to know.

"Did the black wolf return to you in a dream?" little Tahpeno suggested.

"Or was it a different spirit?" his brother's friend asked. The boys stared up at Ésh with a mixture of awe and fascination, as if he were the great Thunderbird.

"I had to urinate" did not sound very brave or remarkable. So Ésh acknowledged only: "A different spirit, yes."

"What did it look like?" Tahpeno begged.

"He cannot tell you a dream meant for him!" their brother Háhkota reminded Tahpeno.

Ésh's mother found him then and fussed over his wound. She sent Tahpeno to find Grandfather. Ésh pretended it didn't hurt; but in truth, he was grateful for the attention. He was feeling dizzy, and he had to sit down.

The others promised not to hold the scalp dance till he was well. Beaming with pride, Ésh's father stretched the Crow's scalp on a hoop for him so it would dry properly. Grandfather smiled too. "Two spirit helpers, and you are not yet sixteen winters! You may be a great medicine man after all!"

DESPITE THE MEDICINES of his mother and grandfather, a frightening heat sank its claws into Ésh's wound and climbed up his chest. This was worse than when a rattlesnake bit him as a child. In his misery, he wondered if the Sacred Powers were punishing him for lying about his discovery of the Crow warrior. But how could he tell the truth now?

In his misery, he pledged to sacrifice his flesh during the New Life Lodge. If only the spirits would allow him this secret, this victory, the other men would let him go to war with them again, and he could offer the Sacred Powers the scalps of many more enemies, including the *veho*. Even in his fever, Ésh prayed with his grandfather:

> "I do not claim to know anything.
> If I make a mistake, turn it into good."

The spirits heard and took pity. The heat left Ésh's body, and the wound in his side healed. It left a scar that was a great help when he told the story of his bravery at the scalp dance. And he had no trouble finding partners in the dances that followed, throughout that long winter.

The young women watched him with admiration now, giggling and fluttering away when he glanced toward them. Not only had he proven he was a warrior, many of the girls wanted to touch his yellow hair: the color of the Sun, the color of beauty and perfection.

He was careful to pluck and shave all the hair that grew in the wrong places. But Ésh knew he was not as tall as the other men. He also worried that he smelled wrong, especially in his armpits. No one else seemed to sweat so much. So he rubbed even more mint on himself than the other young men did. Each day, he chose his ear ornaments, arm bands, shirt, breechcloth, leggings, and moccasins with great care.

He grew bolder then and pursued his admirers, or waited where they gathered wood and water. He gave Méanév *most* of his attention; but he could not deny the other girls. He threw his blanket around them as the Inviters did in their courting. The girl would keep her eyes shyly on his braids, while his eyes caressed all of her, and he said things he forgot as soon as the words left his mouth.

His grandfather and parents grumbled at how courting had changed since the days when they were young. "When I courted your grandmother, I was too shy to even tug on her robe!" Grandfather admitted. "I was glad only to have her *look* at me!"

"I think it was the Big Cramps that changed things," Ésh's father said gravely. "These young men are afraid that if they do not please themselves now, they might never have the chance."

Ésh still found courtship more frustrating than pleasing. He could barely touch the women—certainly not the places he wanted to. They wore protective ropes wrapped around their waists and thighs to prevent it. Not only Méanév but all Zizistas women guarded their virginity like winter's last pemmican cake, and had mothers like mad dogs. Ésh couldn't afford any wives yet, so he had to be careful.

If only he were Rattlesnake! When they played camp as children, boys and girls also went into the bushes together and played freely with each other's bodies. If only he were Blackfeet! Their men could accost their women—even married ones—whenever they wished, and bragged about it.

Ésh knew that the self-control of the Zizistas was what set them apart from their enemies, and even their allies. Zizistas men respected their women. They did not waste their *exhastoz*. Even as husbands, they abstained often. This made the children they did create stronger. This gave the Zizistas greater medicine than any other tribe, especially in battle. This was why their enemies feared them.

But if he had been created during the New Life Lodge, out of Maheo's own *exhastoz*, then Ésh possessed more of that energy than anyone else. Surely he might waste a little of it.

He decided this when his band camped beside the Cloud People that spring. *Their* women were not afraid to be alone with a man. Cloud men actually encouraged their women to join with men from other tribes—even *veho* men—to take some of that foreign *exhastoz* into themselves, into their people. That was how the Cloud People increased their medicine.

Perhaps the Cloud women had learned how special Ésh was: many flirted with him. He chose a woman named Nataane, who was a few years older than himself, because everyone wanted her. She knew how beautiful she was, and she made him pursue her. Nataane understood some Zizistas, and Ésh spoke some of her language. Not that they needed many words.

When Nataane finally accepted his attentions, she taught him so much about kissing, she made all the work and waiting worthwhile. For the first time in his life, Ésh felt as if this *veho* skin truly belonged to him. Nataane made it tremble and swell with delight and anticipation.

Finally, she shoved him down among the chokecherry bushes and promised him *more* than kissing. But when she tugged aside his breechcloth, Nataane pouted. She seemed disappointed.

Ésh wanted to ask her what was wrong, but with Nataane on top of him, with her hands where they were, he couldn't remember a single word of any language. He could scarcely breathe.

"I thought your hair would be yellow here too," Nataane seemed to be saying, as she trailed her fingertips through his dark curls. "And you're not very large, are you?" She squeezed his *véto'ots*, which immediately sought to prove itself by growing larger. "Still…" She pulled her skirt above her lean thighs. She was *not* wearing a protective rope.

Ésh grasped her buttocks. He still couldn't breathe. This was it; this was *really* happening! To *him*! Nataane was rubbing herself over his *véto'ots*: he felt the strange wonderful—

No, no! Not yet! His *véto'ots* was still determined to prove itself: his *exhastoz* was already rushing into it. He wasn't even inside her yet! He had to make Nataane stop for a little while—he had to—

It was too late.

Nataane groaned—but not the way *he* was groaning—and pushed herself back to her feet. "I thought you were a *man*," she muttered. "You are nothing but a weak boy."

"Wait!" Ésh gasped. He knew from the times he'd played with himself (even though it was wasteful) that it wouldn't be long before he was ready again.

Nataane wasn't listening. She'd already disappeared.

He snapped fistfuls of leaves off the nearest chokecherry bush to clean himself up. But the leaves were small and thin, so it took him a few tries. Then he covered himself with his breechcloth again and ran after Nataane.

She was standing with two other Cloud women. When they saw

him, Nataane smirked and said something to her friends in their language that Ésh didn't catch. Whatever it was, they began laughing. He backed up a step. The women laughed even louder.

Ésh didn't have to understand the words to know they were laughing at *him*. He turned and fled back to his village.

Again and again, Ésh reminded himself that joining with a woman would only weaken him for hunting and fighting. He needed all his strength for both. The herds were becoming harder and harder to find, and the *veho* were clearly preparing for war: to the north and the south of the Zizistas villages, two great parties of bluecoats were travelling westward. The People would be ready for them.

When the warriors came to ask him, Ésh pretended to resist as a scout should. But as they dragged him away, he thought his heart might burst from happiness. He and Háhkota helped the other scouts watch the bluecoats' progress, laughing at how the *veho* went to war: with so many wagons and a whole herd of their wimpy buffalo trailing behind them, travelling along the ridges where anyone could see them. The soldiers could not even find their way without the help of the Wolf men.

The *veho* were still wandering westward when the longest days of summer approached. The New Life Lodge began, and with it Ésh's sacrifice, to thank the Sacred Powers for returning his life to him after the Crow warrior tried to take it. Grandfather prepared him, warning Ésh with a smile, "I am going to tickle you a little, now." Then he pinched up the flesh of Ésh's back and drove two skewers through it. Ésh clenched his fists and made himself joke: "That feels good!"

To each skewer, Grandfather tied the skulls of two buffalo bulls. Ésh had practiced this as a child, dragging pieces of wood around the camp instead. The skulls were heavier and the pain much greater now. Many times, he feared he could not take another step. But then he thought of Méanév and how ashamed he would be if he failed, how he dreaded facing her mother. At last the skulls' weight pulled the skewers free, and Ésh sank to his knees in exhaustion and relief. Grandfather helped him offer his torn-away flesh to the Sacred Powers and tended his wounds.

The pain did not bring him any visions. Ésh was disappointed. "Many men wait for years before a spirit comes to them," Grandfather reminded Ésh as he lay healing. "You have already seen two. You must be patient."

Grandfather did not understand. He did not know that no spirit had warned Ésh about the attacking Crow.

Soon Ésh was well enough to scout again. The two parties of bluecoats met near the mountains, and then together they turned east, toward the camps of the Zizistas. At last, the *veho* would pay for breaking the Horse Creek Treaty. At last, they would feel the Peoples' strength and leave their lands forever.

Two young medicine men, Ice and Dark, foretold a great victory. They led the warriors to a sacred lake, where everyone dipped his hands into the water. This medicine would make the *veho* bullets drop powerless to the ground when the People's warriors raised their hands, Ice and Dark promised.

The People had a few guns of their own—only a few: most traders refused to give them guns, no matter how many horses they offered. The guns they did get were very old and did not shoot straight or far. So Ice and Dark blessed their guns as well. Now they could not fail.

The war leaders chose the place where they would wait for the bluecoats: the wide valley of Turkey Creek, a safe distance from their villages. Old men like Ésh's grandfather fashioned arrows day and night.

Ésh and the other warriors selected their best horses and prepared them. They painted circles around their ponies' eyes to give them keen vision, hailstones on their rumps to make them fierce, and lightning on their necks to make them swift. The men sacrificed pieces of their own flesh to the Sacred Powers to ask for their blessings. The warriors did not touch their wives. Then they rode out to meet the *veho* horse soldiers, singing of the victory to come.

All morning they waited along the creek for the bluecoats who moved slower than turtles. The warriors rested and gambled for the shade of the cottonwoods and willows. Again and again, Ésh checked his bow and his arrows and the hoofs of his brown-and-white stallion. He must not let any bluecoats come close enough to see him and escape with their lives. He must show no fear. If Ésh proved himself, one of the warrior societies would finally invite him to join. There was nothing he wanted more.

Finally, scouts rode around the bluffs, turning their horses in circles to signal the enemy's approach. Ésh and the other men leapt onto their own horses and spread out across the valley, like a beaver's dam between the bluffs and the creek to stop the *veho*.

Just as the scouts had predicted, the bluecoats appeared at the end of the valley. Even though he was safe behind the leaders of all the warrior societies, Ésh's eyes widened as he watched the enemies' numbers grow. He had never seen so many *veho* together at once. They all looked the same, clothed in blue and glinting with metal.

The war leaders began to move forward slowly, confidently, raising their medicine lances, and Ésh and the others followed. He tried to count the bluecoats, although it was difficult from this distance. There seemed to be about three hundred of them. One for each of the People's warriors. Ésh wondered which *veho* he would kill. He wondered if the man's hair would be yellow like his.

The bluecoats' strange, insistent instruments sounded across the distance. Trailing great clouds of dust, the soldiers began trotting forward, their leader calling out things that the Zizistas warriors soon drowned with their own songs. Ésh made certain that his first arrow was positioned and pulled till his bowstring was almost taut. He reminded himself that he had no reason to be frightened: the People had the Sacred Powers with them, and the great medicine of Ice and Dark. He had only to raise his hand to stop the *veho* bullets from harming him.

Now the bluecoats' leader yelled something new, though they were still too far away to understand. Suddenly at the side of every *veho* flashed a reflection like the Sun. For a moment the light blinded Ésh, and then he saw three hundred long blades pointed at him, and the soldiers broke into a thunderous gallop. Were those *knives?* They were longer than any knife Ésh had ever seen. He glanced around at the other men, who had stopped singing and reined in their horses.

A Red Shield warrior gave voice to Ésh's confusion: "Why aren't they using their guns?"

A war leader with a long bonnet of eagle feathers kicked his horse to the front. He shook his lance and rode back and forth, while behind him the horrible blue flood bore down on them. "My brothers, we cannot turn back now!"

"We cannot stay!" someone else argued.

"This is the day we defeat the *veho!*" encouraged the war chief in the bonnet.

"Our medicine is against bullets! It will be useless against these long knives!"

"Then we will kill them before their long knives ever reach us!"

They all raised their bows or their guns and fired at the bluecoats. Many of the *veho* fell. But most of them kept coming, their long blades like the teeth of a great hungry monster.

The Zizistas warriors yelled only to their horses now, tugging on their reins to turn them. In relief, Ésh followed the other men. They were not fools. They must live to fight another day, when the signs were better.

The bluecoats chased them toward the shallow, sandy waters of Turkey Creek. Ésh and the other warriors spread out to make themselves harder to catch. As Ésh forded the creek with his paint, another horse whinnied in terror to their left. He looked over to see the animal floundering in quicksand, carrying a Kit Fox Soldier who struggled to stay on its back. The warrior reached toward him and called out.

Ésh glanced behind them, saw the bluecoats approaching, and did not stop. If he rode close enough to help the man, his own stallion would surely become stuck. Even if he did pull the Kit Fox Soldier up behind him, with two men weighing down his horse, they would not escape the enemy.

Ésh and his stallion galloped until they had lost the *veho* soldiers, until they returned to the villages. Others had reached them before

Ésh: he found the women packing as quickly as they could. As he searched for his family, he heard the other men urging their wives and mothers to take nothing: "The *veho* are coming! Which are more important, your lodges or your lives?"

Some risked staying till the sentries spotted the bluecoats. Many left everything behind but what they could carry. They fled both north and south, scattering as they did from sickness, so that the *veho* could not find them all. Instead of a great victory for the People, the bluecoats killed four warriors, wounded many more, and captured the son and nephew of a chief.

One of the slain warriors was He'heeno, the Kit Fox Soldier whose horse had been trapped in quicksand, the man Ésh might have saved. But no one mentioned Ésh's part in He'heeno's death; he did not think anyone else had witnessed the choice he'd made. At least the man had been only a son and a brother; he'd left no wives behind.

The next night, Ésh's mothers cried out and clutched one another, turning away from the southern horizon. Ésh looked up to see a red glow above the prairie. In the morning, great black plumes of smoke still scarred the sky.

Their family's lodge and the four hundred others abandoned in the flight from Turkey Creek were ashes now. Robes, blankets, and backrests—ashes. Parfleches full of clothing, tools, and medicines— ashes. Dried meat, berries, and roots the People had gathered throughout the summer—ashes, all because of the merciless *veho*. With so little food and so little to shelter them, how would they survive the coming winter?

CHAPTER 36

It was you who sent out the first soldier and we who sent out the second.
— Paruasemena (Chief Ten Bears) of the Yamparika Comanches, in a speech before the Treaty of Medicine Lodge Creek, October 1867

Whether they had taken refuge with the Inviters or the Cloud People, especially when they returned from a hunt without a single buffalo, long into the night the men discussed what had gone wrong in the battle. "Why did the medicine fail us?" the warriors whispered. "How did the bluecoats know to use their long knives instead of their guns?"

One night, Ésh was passing a crowded lodge—they were all crowded now—with the bottom folded up for the breezes. Someone inside promised the warriors answers. Curious, Ésh sat down outside to listen, seeing only the backs of the other men in the darkness. A few glanced toward him. Only one nodded in acknowledgment.

"Remember Alights on the Cloud?" the talker began.

Of course they remembered. Five summers before, he had been the People's greatest chief and warrior. He owned a hat, shirt, and leggings covered in metal like fish scales, which protected him through seven years of battles. The medicine of this iron shirt was so great, it seemed no one would ever kill Alights on the Cloud. Then the Wolf men shot him through the eye and tore off his iron shirt. They scalped him, opened his belly, and pulled out his entrails. They cut off his arms and legs and tossed them on the prairie for coyotes to eat.

"Why must you remind us?" one of the listeners asked.

"Because our grief then and our grief now come from the same source," explained the warrior at the center of the lodge. "That iron shirt came from the *veho* to the south. And when Alights on the Cloud died, wasn't White Cow Woman with the war party? Didn't she hold the reins of his horse as well as her husband's while they scouted?"

"What does that have to do with Turkey Creek?" another man asked.

"Someone warned the *veho* that their bullets would be useless!" the first man insisted. "It is the only explanation."

Murmurs bubbled up inside the lodge, voices without bodies in the shadows, growing united and angry.

Still someone doubted: "Who would have done such a terrible thing? Who *could* have done such a thing? No one speaks their language!"

"*Someone* does," declared the voice of the man at the center, as if he had been waiting for this question all along. "Someone who pretends to be one of us, though he is really a *veho*. All you have to do is look at him to see it."

The heads in front of Ésh turned, a few at first, then more, all of them scowling. He scowled back. They couldn't be talking about him.

The voices rippled inward now, away from Ésh. He could make out few words. He understood his name, however, and "He *does* speak their language!"

Ésh leapt to his feet in anger and disbelief. "I learned it only because my grandfather made me learn it! It tastes like dung in my mouth!"

He glanced around desperately for an ally, but no one defended him. How could these men believe he would ever betray them? The Zizistas were his people, not the *veho*!

This was worse than the boys who called him Toad Belly or the adults who stared at him in disappointment because he had no medicine. Those stares were like beestings, painful but quick to fade. These stares were like the bites of a hundred rattlesnakes all at once.

He fled into the night. He didn't know where he was going, but he refused to stay where no one wanted him. He left the last lodge behind, passed a sentry, and kept running. No one pursued him, but he could still feel the venom of their rejection gripping his heart.

The landscape became rocky, rock so pale it shone in the moonlight. Ésh veered and stumbled around the boulders, but he did not stop till the Earth dropped away in front of him. He barely caught himself, and the wind tried to push him over the edge. Below him, everything was darkness.

He staggered back a few steps and sank to his knees. The rocky ground tore into the bare flesh of his legs. If he threw himself from this cliff like a buffalo fleeing a hunter, would anyone care enough to retrieve his body?

Maybe someone *had* seen Ésh abandon He'heeno to the quicksand and the bluecoats. No true Zizistas would have acted so selfishly. The other men were right to doubt him.

None of the warrior societies would ever accept Ésh now—not the Elk Soldiers, not the Red Shields, not the Dog Soldiers, and certainly not the Kit Fox Men. And it was his own fault.

He yanked his medicine pouch from around his neck and threw it away from him, not caring where it landed. The black wolf he'd helped had been only a wolf—not a message. It had meant nothing.

His mother was wrong about him being the child who began during the New Life Lodge. She'd been wrong to take him in. He didn't belong with the People. He didn't belong anywhere.

Ésh plunged his hands into his horrible yellow hair and pulled as though he could tear it from his scalp. He slumped onto the unwelcoming ground and screamed. It was not a war cry.

. . .

HE MUST HAVE FALLEN ASLEEP among the rocks. When Grandfather found him the next morning, Ésh was curled on his side like a child. He had not dreamed. The Sacred Powers had nothing to say to him.

Ésh sat up stiffly. He could hardly bear to look at his grandfather. He wondered how long he'd been sitting on that rock. By the way the old man held himself and hesitated, Ésh knew he had heard the accusations. The news must have travelled through the camp: the People had lost the battle and their lodges had been burned because Ésh had betrayed them to the bluecoats.

"They are frustrated and hungry," Grandfather began. He did not move any nearer. "They have lost their homes. They need someone to blame."

Grandfather did not mention He'heeno. Surely he would have, if anyone knew that Ésh truly was to blame for his death.

"But this doubt will pass, *nish*."

"Don't call me that! Your grandson is dead! He died sixteen years ago!" Ésh pounded his fist against the boulder beside him. It hurt his hand. If he had medicine, he would have split it into pieces. "Haven't I proven how useless I am? I couldn't even heal my own grandmother!"

In response, the old man only grimaced.

Hot tears stung his eyes, so Ésh looked back toward the cliff, toward the landscape the Sun had illuminated below them: the wide course of the Moon Shell River and all the rocks bursting from the Earth. This should be a sacred place, these little mountains in the middle of the plains, where the World Below stretched toward the World Above. But he felt nothing.

Ésh thought of the little cave his mother had shown him so many summers ago, the place where his first body rested. That's what she had called it: his first body. But Ésh understood now. Those little bones had belonged to her true son. Ésh was only an impostor. *His* true mother lay at Painted Rock.

Or maybe the person under that pile of rocks had nothing to do with him. Maybe his true mother and father were alive and well. Maybe they'd abandoned him because they knew he was worthless.

The old man came to stand beside him. At the edge of his vision, Ésh saw him fingering his own abandoned medicine pouch. When the old man found words, they carried great sadness. "Maybe you are not the child Maheo gave us in the New Life Lodge. But you are still my grandson, Ésh. You are still Zizistas. You drew your first breath in our land. You grew up on my daughter's milk and the meat of buffalo. Your ears are pierced to mark you, and your body is scarred from your offerings. Only a few days ago, you rode out and risked your life for us."

Ésh closed his eyes. He knew he should tell Grandfather about He'heeno, but he could not bear the shame.

"Last summer, you killed one of our greatest enemies," Grandfather continued. "You have his scalp to prove it!"

"I *lied*!" Ésh stood quickly and wavered, so few steps from the edge of the cliff. He admitted: "Yes, I killed that Crow horse thief; but I did not have a dream warning me of his coming. It was an accident. I had to piss! *That* is why I went outside and saw him! You see the great medicine of your *veho* grandson!"

Ésh forced himself to glance at his grandfather. The old man's face looked stricken, as if painted with doubt and disappointment. When Ésh retreated to his willow shelter, Grandfather did not follow. But he kept Ésh's secret.

HIS MOTHER STILL DOTED ON HIM as if he were her true son. His big brother Háhkota was still kind to him. Their little brother Tahpeno still followed both of them around like a lost duckling, which did not bother Ésh as much as it had before. But outside of his family, the men eyed Ésh with suspicion now; and the same girls who had become giddy at his attentions fled without a word, as if he carried a sickness.

Ésh considered turning away from the Zizistas as they had turned away from him, living with another tribe. He could go to the Cloud People, and their women would make him forget. But if he ran, wouldn't the Zizistas think he was admitting his guilt? Exiled *murderers* took refuge with the Cloud People.

Méanév still smiled at him. He would stay for her.

Ésh began spending all day with his horses. They did not care if he looked like a *veho*. They welcomed him into their herd. Horses were also the best way to gain wealth, to prove to Méanév's brothers that he could support her. He would offer them so many horses, her family could not refuse him.

Even if he could not steal horses from the People's enemies with a war party, Ésh could capture the mustangs who roamed the plains and mountains. His first trip was unsuccessful. Then Ésh took back his medicine pouch from his grandfather and added a beaded horse charm from a man who had horse medicine.

Ésh had been riding horses on his own since he was four winters, and he'd been watching them all his life. But as he listened to the advice of the horse medicine man and his brother Háhkota, Ésh realized he still had things to learn. The horse medicine man taught Ésh how to help a mare whose foal was turned inside her, and his brother taught him how to accustom foals to human touch.

Háhkota said the best way to understand horses was to become one. So Ésh lifted their little brother Tahpeno onto his shoulders, and the boy became his rider. With the slightest changes in his balance, Tahpeno could direct Ésh to go forward, to stop, to turn left or right. This game taught them how horse and rider communicated without a sound, and it delighted them both.

Ésh grew better and better at taming wild horses. Watching their ears and their mouths, turning his body and breathing in the right way, he would convince the mustangs he meant them no harm. Not only did they accept him into their herd, they accepted him as their leader.

Some of the mustangs were more stubborn than others. Sometimes Ésh led them into a pond so that they couldn't buck when he climbed on their backs. Sometimes he tied a wild horse to a gentle mare: she kept the mustang from running off, and she showed him he could trust Ésh. If only the Zizistas would trust him like the horses did.

Ésh trained many of his horses as buffalo runners, to make the most of every herd the Sacred Powers gave their People. Hunters needed both hands to use their bows, and these horses understood just when to swerve close or pull away from their thundering prey. With the help of these horses, Ésh and the other hunters brought down buffalo after buffalo. Their flesh would feed the People, and their hides would make new lodges.

It was still a terrible winter.

IN THE SPRING, when his village camped near the Cloud People, Ésh decided not to pursue any of their women. He was afraid Nataane had told all of them about his weakness. He didn't want them to laugh at him again. He had also heard that the *veho* had made some of the Cloud women sick. This sickness would not kill you; but if you caught it, your *véto'ots* would drip green and feel like it was on fire every time you pissed.

Ésh must wait for Méanév. She'd learned about his previous visit to the Cloud women, and she hadn't been happy about it.

That summer, his seventeenth, Ésh danced during the New Life Lodge. Praying for a vision, he fasted four days and four nights. His grandfather pierced Ésh's chest with skewers and he leaned back until they tore free from his flesh.

When Ésh collapsed, there was only blackness. No spirits visited his dreams.

FINALLY THE WARRIORS SEEMED TO UNDERSTAND that even if Ésh was not one of them, he wished to be. Or perhaps the men would trust him as long as the enemy they faced was not the *veho*. He was certain now: no one knew he'd abandoned He'heeno. None of the warrior societies invited Ésh to join, but they let him accompany them on horse raids against other tribes.

When Tahpeno discovered they would attack as far as Sósonée territory, his brother begged: "Will you bring me back a spotted horse?"

Ésh promised he would.

But the mare he captured was far too fine an animal for

Tahpeno. As the raiding party returned, the camp girls came running to coo over the men's war prizes. Many lingered at Ésh's new mount. Black spots speckled her white coat from nose to rump.

Then Tahpeno's cry broke through the girls' chatter: "My spotted horse! My spotted horse!"

The black-and-white mare allowed Tahpeno to stroke her nose. Ésh held his tongue till the girls had hurried back to their lodges to don their best things for the victory dance. Then Ésh informed his little brother: "This horse is not for you, *ma'kos*. This is a horse for a man, not a boy."

For a moment, Tahpeno blinked up at him and waited, unsure, as if he expected Ésh to change his mind. When his voice came, it was weak. "Where is my horse?"

Ésh had been busy stealing this mare from the center of the Sósonée village, where only the best animals were kept. He'd had no time for any others. "There is not a horse for you, *ma'kos*."

Tahpeno's chin quivered.

Ésh sighed. "I will bring you a horse next time."

That night, a few of the girls let Ésh flirt with them again and agreed to be his partners in the dances.

The next morning, his grandfather, his father, his mothers, and Háhkota left no doubt how much his decision displeased them. They reminded Ésh of his promise to Tahpeno.

"I risked my life for that mare!" Ésh argued.

"A Zizistas man sees to the comfort and happiness of others first," Grandfather scowled at him. "Until you learn that, you will remain a boy."

"I *am* thinking of others! I will use that horse to capture more horses—to hunt the buffalo that feed this family!"

In truth, Ésh was thinking of the dancing the night before, and how much he wanted to do it again. With the spotted mare, he would fail neither in hunting nor in battle, and the camp girls would welcome his attentions.

. . .

Ésh did try to find another spotted horse for Tahpeno. But in the end, he had to settle for a paint, which his brother accepted without raising his eyes.

When Ésh returned from this raid, he found a strange man in his family's lodge, a man with a brown beard and ragged clothing, who stared wide-eyed into the fire as if he feared it might attack him. Ésh stood speechless just inside the door-flap. His grandfather and his mother stood as one to explain their guest.

"While you were gone, my sister and I found him wandering in the hills when we went to gather berries," his mother began. "He had no belongings. He was chasing grasshoppers and stuffing them in his mouth."

"He has a crazy spirit in him," continued Ésh's grandfather. "He keeps talking to himself about 'gold.'" The *veho* had recently found their chief metal on this side of the mountains, in the middle of the Zizistas and Cloud People's lands. Being *veho*, they asked no one before they swarmed toward the place and dug into the skin of Grandmother Earth.

"He would have died if we had left him," Ésh's mother concluded.

"And that would be good!" Ésh cried out in frustration. "He is a *veho*! He has no right to be here!" He threw aside the door-flap and swung himself back onto his spotted horse.

Grandfather followed him. "Ésh, wait." Grandfather grabbed the mare's reins.

Ésh clenched his teeth and did not look at him.

"While you were away, a messenger came as well. The council chiefs of the southern bands have asked for peace with the *veho*."

"Then they are cowards!"

"This was not an easy choice, *nish*. The chiefs do not want to give more lands to the *veho*, and they do not want to farm like women. But they have eyes, and they can see. The buffalo are disappearing. Soon we will need the gifts of the *veho* just to survive. It is useless to fight them. Their medicine is too strong."

Ésh yanked his reins from Grandfather's hands. "We have barely tried to fight! There will be another battle! And this time, we will win!" He dug his heels into his mare.

Ésh was glad for his hut, so he didn't have to sleep in the same lodge with the smelly *veho*. He considered sneaking back to his family's tipi in the middle of the night and scalping the man in his sleep. That would prove to everyone how Ésh felt about the *veho*.

But his mother and grandfather tended the man like a sick child till he was healthy, and then Háhkota returned him to one of the new *veho* villages on Cherry Creek. They were all fools to believe that looking after others applied to your enemy too.

In the next season of Animals Getting Fat, Ésh returned his latest tamed mustang to the horse herd and found the other young men scrambling onto the backs of the most pitiful nags (none of *his* animals). They were riding off gleefully to attack not the *veho* or the Wolf People but the camp women, who had been digging prairie turnips all day. This was one of Ésh's favorite games! The men could keep as many of the delicious roots as they could capture.

The women were prepared to meet them; they had taken shelter behind a rocky hill, laughing and tossing things at the men who tried to charge them. Just when Ésh spotted Méanév, someone bounced a piece of dried buffalo chip off his gelding's rump.

He cried out in mock despair at the wounding of his temporary horse, leaping to the ground and drawing the gelding after him with the bridle. "My poor Lightning!" he mourned, comforting the animal loudly as it stared at him in confusion. "How cruel these enemies are! There will never be another horse like you!" Ésh certainly hoped not; he was not sure if the gelding's sway back or potbelly was worse.

He used the horse as a shield to survey the terrain between himself and the women, Méanév in particular. While the other men rode back and forth on their sorry horses and taunted the women, Ésh began crawling toward his future wife.

Lightning brought himself back to life and trotted off in the direction of the horse herd. Ésh crept ever closer to the rocks protecting Méanév. She grinned at his approach, then lobbed a piece of dung at his head.

He clutched his wound as if there were blood gushing between his fingers, screaming and thrashing about. He looked up from time to time to see her giggling behind her hand. Finally, when his throat was hoarse, Ésh lay still with his face in the dirt, regaining his breath and chuckling to himself.

Still the battle raged. Ésh wished he'd lived longer. He decided that perhaps he was not quite dead. When Méanév was distracted, he dragged himself over the rocks and rolled next to her.

She narrowed her eyes at him, while the friend beside her kept giggling. "*You* are supposed to be dead."

He felt breathless again. How could her face be so familiar to him and yet more beautiful every time he looked at her? "I have a little life left in me," he managed to say, watching the smile flicker on her own lips.

"Should I scalp you?" Méanév gripped the top of his hair and thrust the edge of her root-digger against his forehead. "Would that convince you to stay dead?"

Ésh shook his head as much as he could in her grasp, excited and comforted all at once to be under her power. This was even better than having Nataane on top of him. It wouldn't be long now, before he had Méanév on top of him, and beneath him... Aloud, he said: "I have made a vow not to give up my spirit—until I do this." He leaned up so quickly she had no chance to dodge him and captured her mouth with his.

Méanév dropped her root-digger and gasped, which parted her lips. Ésh could not resist the opportunity to taste her with his tongue. Compared to the kisses he'd shared with Nataane, he showed immense restraint.

With effort, Ésh released Méanév and fell back against the ground. "I am content," he sighed, closing his eyes in surrender. "You can scalp me now." When Méanév didn't respond, he peeked with one eye.

He saw her friend staring at him as if he were a water monster. Méanév's gaze was fixed on the ground, her hand shielding her mouth. Ésh picked up her root-digger and offered it to her. Still Méanév did not look at him. For the first time he could remember, her eyes did not seem to be smiling. In the quiet, he realized the turnip battle had faded. He heard the sounds of the other men munching their plunder.

Méanév murmured to her friend, who took the root-digger from Ésh's hand. Without another word, they gathered their turnips and left him.

Ésh wondered if Méanév was still angry about Nataane. Should he tell her he'd *tried* for a coup but hit only air? That might be worse. Méanév might conclude that he was too weak to please her either. Maybe he was. How would he know, until he had the chance to prove himself?

Maybe Méanév was angry about Sheheso. He'd barely touched the girl's thigh! Sheheso should have known he was only having fun —and so should Méanév. She couldn't expect him to do *nothing* with the other girls while he waited moon after moon.

Or maybe Méanév simply thought he shouldn't kiss her where others might see. What did it matter, if she was going to marry him, and he knew she was chaste?

Perhaps Méanév wanted him to court her properly. So Ésh traded two of his best horses to a medicine man, who gave him a cedar flute that had never failed to charm. Ésh played it every night outside Méanév's tipi.

Except during the New Life Lodge, or when he was away from camp capturing horses. But he chanted her name in the wolf songs before his party rode out.

One evening during the Moon of Ice Forming, on their way to the enemy camp, his friend Hotohk dashed back from hobbling his horse to grab his blanket. When Hotohk returned, his blanket was wriggling and hissing—and stunk. From the musk, almost as strong as a skunk, Ésh knew that his friend had caught a badger.

Hotohk grinned at his hidden prize. "Now we can see our futures!" Because they were fierce hunters and made their homes in the Earth, badgers possessed powerful medicine.

Ésh hurried to prepare a bed of white sage while the other men wrestled with the badger inside the blanket. The animal snarled and squirmed, worked its head free, and flashed its fangs like a wolf's. It slashed its claws like a bear's straight through the blanket. Together, they held the badger down on its back on the bed of sage with its head toward the East and offered it a prayer. The animal stilled, blinking at them from its black-and-white face striped like war paint. The badger allowed them to kill it, surrendering its medicine.

Hotohk laid a hand on the badger's belly and thanked it. Then he sliced the animal open and cut out its organs, careful to let the blood pool inside its long, flat body. "There!" Hotohk declared when he had finished. "We will see how many of us are brave enough to return here in the morning."

They left the badger's body on the bed of white sage all night. Then any of them could go and look at his reflection in the blood. If he saw himself as an old man, he knew he would live a long life. But if he saw himself covered with sores, he knew a *veho* sickness would find him; and if he saw himself scalped, he knew he would die in battle.

Ésh lay awake most of the night wondering if he should look. Finally the Tantalizer won. As Ésh rose quietly in the dawn light, Hotohk smiled and encouraged him. Before he reached the badger, Ésh stripped off his shirt, leggings, moccasins, and breechcloth—he would see nothing unless he was naked. He undid his braids so his hair hung loose down his chest. Shivering, he approached the badger cautiously. He knelt at its tail, closed his eyes for a moment, and asked the badger to show him his fate. Then he opened his eyes and peered down into the blood-mirror.

Ésh scowled and leaned closer. At first, he thought the medicine wasn't working; he saw only himself as he was now. Then he realized that in the reflection, his hair was short. It barely reached his shoulders.

Dread seared through his chest. It *was* a vision. He wanted to run away, but that would not change the badger's truth. He would die as a young man, when his hair was cut.

Ésh staggered to his feet. His body had never felt so heavy, or so old. As he pulled on his clothing and returned to the place where the other warriors waited, he knew he could tell no one what he had seen. Still he longed to ask: *Are badgers ever wrong?*

PART VIII
RED INTO WHITE

1859

CHEYENNE NATION AND FORT LARAMIE

The usages of civilization were like the chains of slavery to him. To wear pants and jacket, to sleep upon a bed, and to eat bread, and salt meat cooked in an iron pan—all this was so strange—every thing so unnatural…

— George Peck,
Wyoming; Its History, Stirring Incidents, and Romantic Adventures (1858)

CHAPTER 37

We were like deer. They were like grizzly bears. We had a small country. Their country was large. We were contented to let things remain as the Great Spirit Chief made them. They were not; and would change the mountains and rivers if they did not suit them.

— Hin-mah-too-yah-lat-kekt (Chief Joseph of the Nez Percé), "An Indian's View of Indian Affairs" (1879)

Another winter or two, and Ésh would have enough horses to make Méanév his wife. Surely he could be her husband for a few years, before the badger's prophecy came true. He would give her a son, so she would always remember him. That was the only way anyone lived forever.

He was a coward to fear death. He should dread long life. As the Kit Fox Society sang:

> When a man gets old, his teeth are gone.
> I am afraid of that time.
> I wish to die before it comes.

If the southern chiefs were right, long life might mean something else, too. It might mean submission to the *veho*.

In his eighteenth autumn, Ésh and three other men rode out
from their village to capture mustangs. But no matter how many
tracks they followed, the wild horses eluded them day after day, till
the full moon became a sliver and grew fat again. Ésh and the other
men returned home with nothing.

Winter Man had arrived early this year. Ésh was glad for the
warmth of his family's tipi and of his mother's buffalo soup that
night. His brother Háhkota was absent; he must be hunting.

Usually when Ésh came back from tracking mustangs, everyone
wanted him to tell them in great detail what he had seen on his
journey. On this night, however, even Tahpeno was quiet. Was he
still upset about the spotted horse?

After Ésh set down his bowl, he dug through his belongings for
his courting flute. It was too late to coax Méanév outside, but
perhaps she would talk to him through the lodge wall as they had
when they were younger.

He pulled the flute from its case, and realized his mother was
watching him. When he glanced up, she looked worried. As they sat
bundled on their beds, the rest of his family kept their eyes lowered.
Grandfather poked idly at the fire.

"Is something wrong?" Ésh asked.

"You were gone almost a moon," his mother began, picking up
his bowl and playing with the horn spoon for a moment. Then she
laid her hand on his. "Méanév is married now, *na'eh*."

"*What?*"

"She became Háhkota's wife two days ago."

His own brother?

"I am sorry, Ésh."

How could she? How dare Háhkota steal her!

The rest of his family tucked themselves under their robes. But
of course Ésh could not sleep. He lay there thinking about Méanév
and his brother, alone in their tipi. Doing what Ésh had waited so
long to do. It made him sick. It made him furious.

Finally he pulled a buffalo robe around his shoulders and slipped out of the lodge into the bite of the autumn air. He heard movement behind him, and he turned to see his little brother. Ésh scowled. "Go back to sleep, Tahpeno."

The boy caught up to him. "Where are you going, *na'neh?*"

"Nowhere."

"Can I come with you?"

Ésh sighed a white cloud into the night air. If Tahpeno returned to their family's lodge, he might alert the others to Ésh's absence. Besides, he might know which tipi was Méanév's. "Do you *promise* to be quiet?"

The boy nodded eagerly. He walked with Ésh till they found Méanév's new tipi. Above the lining, the tanned hides stretched around the poles seemed to glow. The fire inside cast indistinct, tantalizing shadows.

Fortunately, the stump of an old pine stood nearby, providing the perfect place to hide and watch the door. Ésh crouched behind the trunk, motioning for Tahpeno to do the same, and pulled the buffalo robe tight around himself.

"What are we doing, *na'neh?*" his little brother asked too loudly; Ésh was trying to listen for any noises inside the tipi.

"We are going to play a game, *ma'kos,*" Ésh whispered. "We will pretend we are ghosts."

Even in the moonlight, Tahpeno's eyes looked very wide. "Won't we make the real ghosts angry?"

"If we do," Ésh smiled, "do you remember how to scare them away?"

"But what if I *can't* fart?"

Ésh chuckled at the worry in the boy's voice. "Then I will be here to protect you. Now be quiet." Ésh found a pebble and threw it hard at the side of Méanév's new lodge. When Tahpeno started to speak, Ésh had to shush him again. He kept his eyes on the tipi.

Háhkota pushed aside the buffalo robe door-flap to see what had made the noise. He looked fully clothed. Ésh was both relieved and a little disappointed that he had not interrupted anything.

What did Méanév see in Háhkota to like? He was a decent scout and horse trainer, but he'd taken only two scalps. He was annoyingly humble, and so shy around women, he would probably let Méanév wear her protective rope for a full moon without a single complaint. He had probably been *talking* to her all night. Ésh tried not to snigger.

Háhkota leaned out of the lodge and peered to one side, then the other. "Is someone there?" he asked. Ésh heard Méanév's voice inside the lodge, but he couldn't understand her words. Háhkota gave up and closed the door-flap.

Tahpeno stared up at Ésh expectantly, teeth chattering since he had not brought a robe. "Should we whistle like ghosts too?"

"No. Be quiet." Méanév could not find out *who* was disturbing her—what would she think of him? Ésh picked up another pebble and tossed it at the lodge.

The flap opened again, more slowly this time. Méanév stood in the doorway, only a silhouette against the light of the fire inside. An impossibly lovely silhouette. She did not look for very long before she closed the flap and disappeared inside.

Ésh threw a third pebble, but now no one appeared. He frowned, waited, tried again. Still Méanév and Háhkota ignored him. Ésh glared at the lodge till he had an idea. He turned to his brother. "*Ma'kos*, if you do what I tell you, I will let you ride my spotted horse."

"Really?" Tahpeno grinned.

"Only if you do what I tell you."

"Do I get to be the ghost now?"

Ésh nodded. "I want you to run to the lodge and scratch, then run back to me."

His little brother hurried over to the tipi, then stood for a moment, glancing back over his shoulder and shivering. When Ésh nodded, Tahpeno reached out a hand and scratched the doorway beside the buffalo robe.

The door opened quickly, so quickly that Háhkota grabbed their little brother before he could escape. Ésh clenched his teeth and crouched lower to the ground, barely peering around the stump. The boy should have scratched at the side away from the door!

"Tahpeno?" their big brother asked, as Méanév climbed out of the tipi behind him. "What are you doing?"

"I am sorry!" The boy squirmed, and then started bawling like someone much younger than nine winters. "I didn't mean to scare you! Don't let the ghosts take me! Our brother said I could ride his spotted horse!"

Ésh groaned quietly into his hands. After such a betrayal, he would never let Tahpeno touch his mare again.

"Ésh told you to do this?" he heard Háhkota ask. Ésh looked up to see their little brother nodding. "Where is he?"

Tahpeno looked right at Ésh.

He thought about fleeing. Then Méanév laid a hand on Háhkota's arm. The intimacy of the gesture infuriated Ésh but transfixed him too. She said quietly: "Let me talk to him, *na-eham*." Husband.

On the other side of the stump, Ésh stood and turned his back to the lodge. He adjusted his buffalo robe and crossed his arms as if he were simply gazing at the moon. But while Méanév's footsteps approached him, a hundred exclamations and demands roared through his head:

I have twice as many horses as Háhkota did when he was eighteen!

You could not wait for me? I waited for you!

You married while I was away because you were ashamed! You betrayed me!

If you realize your mistake and divorce him, I won't take you back!

How long have you loved him?

Do you love him?

Did you ever love me?

When Méanév stood next to him, what came out of Ésh's mouth was: "Is it because I look like a *veho*?"

"No, Ésh, no..." Then she lowered her eyes, as if ashamed of her lie.

He let himself look at her. The pale moonlight concealed her true beauty; but it offered him enough to choke his throat.

"I do not know," she admitted in a murmur. "Maybe the skin you wear does explain why you..." Méanév hesitated.

"Why I what?"

"Why you interrupt!" There was no shyness in her now. "Why

you use a little brother who adores you as a plaything for your own amusement! Why you are envious instead of happy for your older brother and your friend!" She sighed, and her voice quieted again— quiet, but emphatic. "In courtship, in war, so often you think only of yourself, Ésh."

He opened his mouth to defend himself, but she did not let him. Who was being selfish now?

"I watch you with your horses, and I see that you can be patient. I see that you can be kind. But you must learn to be that way with people."

And this was how she would teach him, by denying him what he wanted most, the only thing he had ever wanted? He had only a few years left on Earth—how would he ever find another woman like Méanév?

"I think your mother is right, Ésh: I think you can be a great man, a man we will all remember. But not like this. When you can give what you have without expecting anything in return, *then* you will truly be Zizistas."

None of that mattered now!

Ésh could not listen to any more. He did not wait for his traitorous little brother. He stalked back to his lodge and threw aside the door-flap, not caring how much cold air he let in. One of his mothers whimpered.

As Ésh dug his belongings out from underneath his backrest, Grandfather sat up and rubbed his eyes. "Ésh?"

He did not answer.

"What are you looking for?"

"I am going to fast until the Sacred Powers show themselves to me."

"Let me help you. Wait until—"

"I have waited long enough!" Ésh grabbed his knife.

"This is not the way to approach them, *nish,*" Grandfather insisted. "You must ask humbly. And you must prepare yourself properly. You cannot do it alone."

"I do not want a spirit who comes when *you* ask! I want a spirit who comes when *I* ask!"

"*Nish...*" When Ésh didn't listen, Grandfather stood and reached toward him.

Ésh yanked himself away. "Let me go!" When Grandfather went silent, Ésh looked back at him, to see his whole family sitting up now, watching him in the firelight. Ésh said nothing, but threw his quiver over his shoulder and wedged his way through the door. He dropped the parfleche he'd been carrying.

Tahpeno was standing outside and picked it up, his eyes lowered. His face was wet with tears. "I am sorry, *na'neh*," he mumbled. "I did not mean to—"

Ésh took the parfleche and did not wait for him to finish.

CHAPTER 38

That night, while I slept, I dreamed that a wolf came to me, and spoke, saying: "My son, the spirits to whom you have cried all day long have heard your prayers, and have sent me to tell you that your cryings have not been in vain."
— George Bird Grinnell, *When Buffalo Ran* (1920)

É sh left his spotted mare and his other horses in the herd. Guided only by moonlight and memory, he walked away from camp, putting the glow of the tipis far behind him.

At dawn, he stopped to cut enough white sage to fill his parfleche. He kept walking till he found a high hill on the south side of a river. He drank long and deep of the water. At the top of the hill, he deposited his buffalo robe and weapons, then prepared a bed of the white sage. All day long, Ésh sat on the sage, turning only to follow the Sun. For the next four days, he would allow himself neither food nor water.

"Why haven't you come back to me?" he demanded of the black wolf he had seen all those years ago and the spirit who had sent it. "I trusted you! I freed you and gave you my hunting. Then your People accuse me of betraying them, and you do not reappear. You do not defend me. The woman I loved marries my own brother, and you do nothing!"

Amongst the grasses, the sagebrush, and the pines far in the distance, nothing stirred in answer, not even the wind.

"I accept the fate I saw in the badger's blood," he told the Sacred Powers. His voice was not as steady as he would have liked. "I know I must die young. But you cannot expect me to die a virgin! Is this because I play with myself? Is that why you are punishing me, because I have wasted the precious *exhastoz* you gave me? What am I supposed to do with it? What good has it ever done anyone?"

Grandfather had taught him to pray:

"I know myself.
I possess spiritual power."

But those words were a lie. Ésh was no savior. He was no one. He was nothing.

"I refuse to die as I am now: unknown and distrusted!" Ésh shouted to the spirits. "Show me my medicine! Give me a purpose!"

The Sun hid himself behind a great cloud.

Ésh could become a suicide warrior: he could ride out without weapons and give his life to strike fear into the hearts of the enemy. Then his name would always be remembered. The People would sing songs about his bravery, and they would be sorry they had ever doubted him.

Night fell. Ésh rested on his stomach atop the bed of sage with his head toward the East, laid out like the badger flipped over. He shivered in the cold, and he did not dream.

The second day, it rained—little spears that felt like ice. His clothing went from wet to stiff as it dried. No matter the weather, his hunger, or his thirst, he could not move from the white sage—not if he wanted a vision.

The Sun set, and Ésh lay face-down for the second night. Again no spirit came to instruct him. The next morning, instead of staring at the Sun, he kept glancing down toward the river, longing to drink. His throat felt dry as bark. His lips were cracked and sore.

Méanév claimed the color of his skin had had nothing to do with her decision not to marry him, but Ésh did not believe her. Nor could he blame her. Who would choose anyone who looked the way he did? Flirting was one thing—he was a curiosity; but in the end, he'd disappointed even Nataane. He was too short, too hairy, too pale.

Why had the Sacred Powers cursed him with the body of a *veho?* He stared down at the ends of his ugly yellow braids, at his ugly hairy legs. His throat tightened with more than thirst.

The Sacred Powers had nothing to do with this—nothing to do with him. He was not the child of the New Life Lodge. *This* was the only body he had ever inhabited. The wolf he had seen as a boy was no message—only a hungry, frightened animal. The Sacred Powers spoke only to Zizistas. Only to Maheo's chosen, beloved People.

Who could love a *veho?* Sometimes they were clever, but they were not wise. Children laughed at stories of *veho*'s foolishness. The *veho* killed even each other without thought, so they were cursed with hairy faces.

Like his own face, which sprouted with stubbly hair even now. He had not brought his razor with him.

In spite of their ugliness and ineptness, the *veho* were braggarts. They thought they had a right to any woman they wanted. They could not control their desires. They had no patience. They were loud. They said what they thought without considering anyone else's feelings. If they were kind, they were only pretending because they wanted something. They were liars. They cared only about themselves and possessing things. They were selfish.

He was all those things; he had done all those things. Méanév had only told him the truth. Grandfather knew it too.

The fourth day dawned, and still no spirit had come to him. "What do you want from me?" he begged the Sacred Powers in a hoarse voice. "What do I have to do to become Zizistas?"

When he received no answer, Ésh ripped off his shirt and snatched up his knife. He pinched up the skin on one shoulder as hard as he could, dragging it away from the muscle beneath. He gritted his teeth and used his knife to slice off the pinched skin. He held up the bloody piece to the Sun and the rest of the Sacred Powers. "Is *this* what you want?" he cried. He pinched up the flesh on the other shoulder and sacrificed it too. "Or is the skin of a *veho* not acceptable to you? It is all that I have! It is all that I have to give you!"

There was not one darting rabbit or soaring hawk Ésh might have taken for a sign. Angrily, he dug a hole with his knife at the eastern end of the sage bed. He dropped the pieces of his flesh into the Earth and shoved the soil back over them. Then he lay down on his stomach again and hid his face—less in humility and more because he was dizzy from the effort and pain.

He was also afraid the Sacred Powers might see his tears, but none came. He'd drunk nothing but a little rain for four days, and now he couldn't even cry, no matter how much his eyes ached.

He shuddered from more than the cold. His hand clawed out and found the edge of his buffalo robe. He dragged it over him, grimacing at how the motions pulled on his fresh wounds. His useless sacrifice.

Tomorrow, he must return to camp—a failure. Unwanted by his *veho* family. Unwanted by the Zizistas. Unwanted by the Sacred Powers. He might as well cut off his hair and let himself die of thirst right here. No one would miss him. But he was too weak to rise and find his knife. He only lay there shivering between the sage and the buffalo robe till he slid into sleep.

At last, he dreamed.

First, he caught a scent that reminded him of the little pink flowers that grew on thorny bushes, though this scent was stronger. Then, he heard the beautiful voice of a young woman singing. He did not understand the language, yet each note glided over him like honey soothing his wounds. The girl sounded so near, as if she were kneeling where he had buried the pieces of his skin. Finally, she spoke words he did understand—in English: "Your flesh is more than acceptable. But I prefer it *on* your body."

The intimate way the girl whispered sent a shiver of pleasure through his skin. He opened his eyes to dawn light, but it illuminated only white sage and his own folded arms. He tensed to raise his head, but delicate fingers seemed to sink into his hair, caressing him but also holding him in place. "Not yet, my love—but soon."

He hesitated, desperate to see her but afraid she would withdraw her touch.

"The wolf will show you the way," the girl promised as she stroked the back of his neck, light as butterfly wings.

Ésh could bear it no longer. He must know what she looked like. He raised his head—and the girl darted away. He saw only her back as she vanished into the morning mist: a flash of green skirt and hair that nearly brushed the ground. Hair like a waterfall of honey, like the colors of Sun and Earth together.

Ignoring the dull pain of his wounds, Ésh pushed himself to his feet. The buffalo robe dropped from his body, exposing his chest and arms to the morning cold. Dizzy from his fast, he staggered and nearly fell again. The fog was thick around him—how would he follow the girl? He looked down to where she'd been kneeling. The earth was undisturbed; she hadn't left a single footprint.

Of course not; she was a spirit. But not a Zizistas spirit—with hair that color, speaking English, she was the spirit of some *vehoá*. Ésh frowned. What were the Sacred Powers trying to tell him, sending him such a vision? Were they saying he did not deserve a Zizistas woman, only a white girl? What good was a wife who could not tan a hide or build a tipi?

Yet how he longed to see the girl's face, to feel her fingers on his skin again, to sink his own fingers into that hair like honey…

Ésh stepped from the bed of sage, longing to follow her but not knowing how. Then, ahead in the fog, a dark shape took form: a black wolf padding toward him, head low, yellow eyes cautious. *"The wolf will show you the way,"* the girl had said!

Ésh did not wait. He did not snatch up his shirt or any weapons. He was running even before the wolf turned and fled. At first, Ésh saw the bushy black tail ahead of him. Then even that disappeared into the fog.

Desperately Ésh turned his eyes to the ground, trying to pick out the wolf's tracks. But if it was a spirit like the girl… Ésh glanced ahead again. In the distance, pines rose above the fog. Perhaps the wolf had been racing *there*?

Then, in the depths of the fog, a man's voice called out in English, followed by a horse's whinny. Ésh's breath caught in his throat. Ahead in the fog, a line of shadows marched. *Bluecoats.*

The girl and the wolf had tricked him! They wanted the *veho* to capture him!

Ésh scrambled behind a nearby outcropping of rocks. The bluecoats did not follow. They were moving away; they hadn't seen him. Grateful for the cover of the boulders, he watched the soldiers pass as the fog began to lift. Three men rode horses; a few drove wagons; most walked.

They reached the edge of the pine grove, and one of the riders shouted for them to stop. He seemed to be their leader. He dismounted his fine black horse—as black as the wolf that had led Ésh here. As its owner tied it to a tree, Ésh peered at the animal across the distance. Was this a sign—a gift—a challenge? He'd never captured a horse from a *veho* before.

Ésh looked back in the direction he had come. He had arrows and a knife by the bed of sage. He decided not to go back for them. How much braver to face the bluecoats just as he was: unarmed, without even a shield. That would impress the Sacred Powers, and all the girls he would tell this story to.

Even if the young woman with the voice and hair like honey *was* his fate, that did not mean he couldn't amuse himself with other girls until she appeared—or that he couldn't take other wives.

The bluecoats began to take axes to the smaller pines. For the larger trunks, they used long toothed strips of metal. Ésh made sure none of the men were looking toward him, then darted from the rock outcropping to the grove. A bend of the river ran alongside it, and he allowed himself to stop and drink. He was still weak from hunger, but that would make his feat all the more impressive.

Ésh approached the *veho* silently, careful of each step, using the pines to hide himself. He paid special attention to the bluecoat who'd been riding the black horse. The man had strode away from his animal and lit a cigar. None of the other *veho* stood close to the black horse; they were too busy attacking the trees. This would be easy.

Finally Ésh reached the pine where the black horse was tethered. Ésh let the gelding sniff his hand. The animal's dark eyes showed no fear, only interest. Ésh slipped the horse's rope free of the branch and urged him to walk forward. The gelding obeyed. Ésh glanced toward the bluecoats and smiled. None of them had seen him.

He wanted to take off the horse's *veho* saddle, which was bulky like the saddle of a child. But he must be careful not to attract the soldiers' attention. He led the black gelding a little deeper into the trees and reached for the girth. Then he started at the sound of shouting. Removing the saddle would have to wait. Ésh swung himself onto the gelding's back and squeezed his sides.

A gun fired behind them, but the bullet missed its mark. Ésh and the black horse tore through the grove and emerged into the open grass. He must retrieve his weapons. He glanced back to confirm that the bluecoats were not yet free of the trees. Then he turned the black gelding around the side of the hill where he'd fasted the past four days. He dismounted, tied the horse to a large sagebrush, and crept up the hill. He kept close to the ground so the bluecoats would be less likely to notice him.

But as soon as he'd reclaimed his knife, he saw two soldiers on horseback coming straight for him. He'd have to leave his shirt. He snatched up his quiver and bow and raced back toward the black gelding. The men pointed their guns and shouted at him in English. Ésh did not pay much attention; he could guess what they were yelling without stopping to translate, and it was nothing he needed to hear.

He positioned an arrow and let it fly, but he was trying to shoot at a moving target while escaping downhill over rough ground. Instead of lodging in his enemy's gut, the arrow pierced the man's arm. Still he howled.

The other one sounded angrier now. Before Ésh could reach his horse, pain seared across the back of his hand. The bullet only grazed him, but it made him drop his second arrow.

Ésh grabbed a third one; but the men were upon him now, pouncing from their saddles. The *veho* who'd shot Ésh landed on top of him, knocking them both to the ground. Ésh groped to unsheath his knife—to no avail; the bluecoat with the arrow in his arm kicked the blade out of Ésh's hand. The other one struggled to pin Ésh's limbs as if he were a hide to be tanned. The man's thumbs dug into the fresh wounds where Ésh had cut away his skin, igniting a double blaze of pain.

This wasn't fair! Any other day, Ésh could take two *veho* easily; but he was weak and stiff from four days of fasting. His muscles refused to obey him; they only shrieked and shuddered in protest. Lacking any other defense, Ésh turned his head and sank his teeth into the bluecoat's hand.

The man yowled, but Ésh did not have very long to enjoy the sound. The other soldier swung the butt of his gun at Ésh's head like a club, and the world went black.

CHAPTER 39

You might as well expect all rivers to run backward as that any man who was born a free man should be contented penned up and denied liberty…

— Hin-mah-too-yah-lat-kekt (Chief Joseph of the Nez Percé), "An Indian's View of Indian Affairs" (1879)

Somewhere too close, laughter exploded from the silence, jarring Ésh awake. Every part of his body began to ache at once. Even his groan was weak. His legs bent, he lay on his back somewhere flat, hard, and intensely cold. When he opened his eyes, false shapes swam above him in the darkness.

His nose awoke as well, and immediately he wished it had not. He gagged on the reek of urine and vomit, but there was nothing in his own stomach to cough up. He'd gone without food and water so long, he doubted he was responsible for either stench, but the fact was no comfort. He tried to breathe through his mouth, but he could taste the foul air.

Most of the pain collected on the side of his head where the bluecoat had struck him. Ésh tried to lift his right hand from his chest, but he dragged his left with it: something hard and cold

bound his wrists together. His skin was stiff from the graze wound
and hampered by a cloth binding, but he maneuvered shivering
fingers above his left ear. Instead of his hair, they touched another
cloth. He palmed his way along the cloth to find that it went in a
band all the way around his head.

With effort, he lifted his neck to pull off the wrapping—and
knew immediately that something more than the blow was wrong
with his head. He tried to ignore the throbbing above his ear and
decide what else was different. His head felt *lighter*. He plunged his
fingers into his hair to discover that most of it was gone.

Panic closed his throat. The badger's prophecy was coming true.
He must escape *now*. He sat up, too quickly. His feet kicked into
something; the wounds on his shoulders flared like flames; and a
nauseating and deafening ringing attacked his ears, as if thousands
of tiny pebbles were hurtling through a rock crevasse inside his
head.

He collapsed back where he had been, one of his elbows striking
a hard surface beside him and his head banging into another behind
him. He gasped the putrid air in and out till the dizziness subsided.

His whole body felt strange: heavy and contained. His slightest
movements were restricted in unfamiliar and disconcerting ways.
When he'd tried to sit up, he'd been pinched and squashed.

Dread shivered through him like the cold. He touched his
shoulder where his bound hands had landed and felt trade cloth
instead of animal skin. Awkwardly he slid his fingers across his
chest. No medicine pouch met them, only two straps leading from
his shoulders to his waist and an outer layer of trade cloth. The
metal loops bit into his wrists as he twisted his hands desperately to
feel his trapped hips, *véto'ots*, and thighs.

He, a Zizistas warrior, was wearing a pair of the *veho*'s enclosed-
rump-things! His hair and his medicine pouch were not enough—
they had taken his breechcloth! Inside these rough cloths of theirs,
he was naked and defenseless.

He wrestled with the coat they'd put on him. It was hard to do
anything with his wrists attached by loops of metal, and he realized
that even if he succeeded in yanking the coat and shirt mostly off,

he wouldn't be able to pull them beyond the metal loops. He also kept banging his elbows against hard places on either side of him that must be walls. He groaned in frustration and sat up again. This space was as narrow as a man and not even long enough for him to lie flat in.

His feet weighted uncomfortably with *veho* shoes, he worked himself into a crouch on what felt like a packed dirt floor. He rose uneasily—and before he straightened out his legs, his head smacked into some surface above him.

In a daze, he staggered forwards. Fortunately he thrust out his bound hands; almost immediately he crashed into the wall that had been at his feet, a wooden one that gave very slightly. At the impact, the ringing inside his head doubled.

When the sound became a soft but still aggravating trill, his nose sensed new air. He lifted his face till he found an opening in the wall and caught a scent from outside. Wood smoke, along with a trickle of warmth and a faint dance of light. Yet he heard none of the familiar night sounds. Nor was there any kind of breeze. Beyond this wall must be another.

As he pressed his face into the small hole, trying to see the fire, his nose smashed against something blocking it. He dragged his hands up to discover that there were three upright sticks made of metal attached to the outside of the opening. Through them, Ésh gulped in the warmer air as if it were tea. His mouth and throat felt as dry as rawhide. At the thought of nourishment, crippling stabs writhed in his stomach.

The slow currents of new air began to clear his head. He could hear the noises that had woken him more clearly now. They originated overhead: muffled voices and another burst of laughter. He wondered if the bluecoats were laughing at him, at his failure as a warrior.

He would show them. He would escape. Within their metal loops, he turned his wrists and flattened his palms against the wooden wall. Slowly he pushed his hands across its surface, spreading out his shuddering fingers to search every part of it in the darkness.

High or low, middle or edges, he found nothing except the small, divided opening. He kept groping along the three other walls, which were made of stone. The surface above him felt like wood and was just as featureless as the walls. He did not believe his fingers; he kept searching, no matter how the metal loops chafed at his wrists and limited his movements. What good was a lodge without a door? There had been a way in; there must be a way out…

Ésh returned to the wall with the opening and wrapped his fingers around the strange metal sticks. He gripped them and yanked forward and backward. At least this wall responded a little to his efforts; but if it was a door, how did it open? His greatest force barely made the wall-door jiggle; and with this new, violent motion, the ringing inside his head came roaring back.

Desperately he squeezed the metal, as if his hatred could melt it. Then, with a sound that began as a growl and ended as a roar, Ésh turned to hurl himself backwards. Almost immediately, his shoulder slammed into the opposite wall and his bones jarred violently inside him. The defeat infuriated and exasperated him even more. He began to pummel his entire body against the sides of the space, screaming as though his voice could shatter wood and stone.

With each impact, his whole frame convulsed and recoiled until his legs refused to assist him. His knees collapsed without warning, and Ésh slumped against one of the stone walls. For a moment he half-stood, half-crouched there, desperate to continue the battle he knew he would lose.

He was completely trapped—inside these walls, and inside these clothes. His skin and his insides were crawling with that smothering, terrifying closeness. But even as he pleaded for it, strength drained from him, and he was powerless to do anything but choke back sobs.

Maybe he had gone crazy and could no longer tell what was up or down or hot or cold or in or out. Maybe he was already dead; and this was where dead *veho* went. Mé'hahts had told him once about a place called Hell…

Ésh's shivering body slid down the rough, frigid wall onto the flat, frigid floor. The space was so narrow, the toes of his shoes bent against the opposite wall, and his knees were shoved back against his chest. So narrow he could hardly turn around; so shallow he couldn't lie flat; and so short he couldn't even stand up.

The truth sank into him like icy claws. He realized where he must be. The bluecoats must have brought him back to their fort on the Goose River. They must have shut him inside one of the underground cells Mé'hahts had described.

This was where Fire Wolf had died. Fire Wolf, who might be buried in this floor, whose soul was trapped here for all eternity because the *veho* had not buried him properly. The bluecoats would keep Ésh in this cell till he died too, till his soul was trapped too—if he even had a soul...

But *veho* did not have souls.

Was that what the vision of the honey-haired girl had meant? The Sacred Powers were saying he belonged with the soulless *veho*? When the black wolf led him to the bluecoats, was he supposed to kill them, to prove he was Zizistas? He had tried!

None of this is real, Ésh told himself. *This is all still a vision in order to teach me a lesson. I have learned it, Maheo!*

What have you learned? a voice in his head seemed to reply. The voice was both his and not his. It must be the Thoughtful Spirit Grandfather had told him about.

Ésh held his breath to listen, and now the voice of the girl in his vision echoed back to him. Maybe she was his Good Spirit. She repeated: *"The wolf will show you the way."*

At first, Ésh was angry. *I DID follow the wolf! That's why I'm here!* What else could the girl have meant, but to follow the wolf?

What did the wolf show you ten winters ago?

Ten winters ago? When he'd been a boy and he'd given the black wolf his hunting? When he'd freed the wolf, even knowing it might kill him?

The wolf had shown him how to be a Zizistas, how to be kind instead of selfish—how to think about the comfort and happiness of others first, as Grandfather had said. But again and again these past ten winters, Ésh had thought only of himself. He'd counted coup on the young Wolf guard and ruined the raid. He'd abandoned

He'heeno to the quicksand and the bluecoats. He'd kept the horse he'd promised to his little brother.

Ésh could not go back and choose to be a better scout the day of the raid. He could not go back and save He'heeno either. But he could try to make things right. Though the Kit Fox Soldier had not been a husband, his mothers and sisters had depended on him for meat and for hides. Ésh could tell He'heeno's family the truth. He could offer them everything he had.

Except for his spotted mare. Ésh would give her to Tahpeno. If he ever escaped from these *veho*.

Ésh struggled to remember the way Grandfather had taught him to pray. *Have pity on me and pardon my mistakes,* he begged the Sacred Powers. *I am only a child. I need your guidance. I need your strength.*

I know I have been selfish—that I have not acted like one of your People. But I will change. I will follow your way. Let me show you that I can be kind— that I can choose the happiness of others. Don't let me die like this. Don't leave me in this place.

Beneath his closed lids, his aching eyes were as dry as his throat. No tears rose. But with a trembling voice, Ésh sang the prayer he had chanted in enemy land so many times before—the prayer of a good scout:

"Wolf I am.
In darkness
in light
wherever I search
wherever I run
wherever I stand
everything
will be good
because Maheo
protects us."

I beg of you, do not forget me... Give me another chance to be Zizistas...

CHAPTER 40

The mountain men of this country do not have scurvy, because they are not crowded, have plenty of fresh air, are subjected to no continued labor or exposure, being strongly inclined to lead a lazy Indian life…
— Assistant Surgeon E. W. Johns, "Sanitary Report, Fort Laramie" (1858)

A creaking noise assaulted Ésh's ears, and he cracked open one eyelid. He saw a faint light, but nothing like the Sun. A man held the light above his head. The man was a bluecoat.

Ésh closed his eyes again, sighed as if he were releasing his soul, and sank further into the ground. It had not been a vision. He remained a captive of the *veho*. Before he could prove himself to Grandfather, to Méanév, or to the Sacred Powers, he would have to escape.

The bluecoat was talking to him. The meaning of the English words sank in slowly. Many of them Ésh did not understand, but he could pull together the general intention. "Do you know where you are? This is the guardhouse at Fort Laramie. I am Dr. Johns, the post surgeon. I've brought you a pot of beef tea."

Ésh squinted up at the man. He passed his light to a younger bluecoat who stood behind him, calling the other man "Private." This second *veho* watched Ésh warily, one hand ready on a pistol. Private seemed afraid of Ésh, but the first man wasn't. Doctor, he'd called himself. Ésh remembered that was something like a medicine man. The doctor wore brown hair on his upper lip. He unfolded a little seat and settled himself where the wooden wall with the opening had been. That wall now gaped wide, but beyond it stood another wall.

The doctor reached outside of Ésh's vision and produced a cup of steaming liquid. The meaty smell of it made Ésh's dry throat contract with longing. With an effort that made his muscles scream and his head throb, he used the walls of the narrow cell to push himself into a sitting position. The doctor tried to help him, but Ésh shrugged away from his touch. He did accept the cup and gulp its contents. The doctor filled it again from a pot and spoke while Ésh drank the second cup.

"I have been trying to convince Major Day that you do not belong down here with the drunkards, that this cell is injurious to your already fragile health. He is understandably reluctant to trust you. You stole a captain's horse, impaled a sergeant, and *bit* a corporal. But allowances must be made. I can only imagine the hellish existence you've led—tortured and starved. No wonder your mind is addled and you cannot distinguish friend from foe. How long did the savages hold you captive?" When Ésh didn't answer, only drained the last of the tea, the doctor continued: "It must have been *years*, judging by the length of your hair."

Ésh shoved the cup at him. "I want it back," he croaked in English.

"You *do* remember how to speak," the doctor smiled. He filled the cup a third time and returned it to Ésh.

"I want it back!" Ésh repeated.

The doctor frowned at the cup in Ésh's hands. "I did give it back."

"Not this—my hair!" One of these *veho* could use it to put a curse on him. Maybe they already had. He'd never felt so weak in his life. "Where is it?"

The doctor glanced behind him at Private. Both men looked confused. "I imagine your hair is floating down the Laramie with the rest of the refuse."

"And my clothes?"

The doctor hesitated. Again he looked to the other bluecoat.

The weakness of his body irritated Ésh more with every passing moment. He wanted to strangle these bluecoats. All he had to fling at them was his voice. "You will return my things!"

"Young man, did you understand *nothing* I just said? If you wish to leave this cell, you must cease this belligerence."

Since Ésh had no idea what that meant, he returned to the tea that tasted like meat. It was finally starting to ease the ache in his stomach and settle the buzz in his head. Without drawing their attention, he glanced behind the two bluecoats. All he could see were more walls. Somewhere there must be a door that led outside. But the men were blocking his escape, and Ésh doubted his ability to stand, let alone fight.

The doctor kept talking. "Sergeant Steine or Corporal Beatty might still succumb to the wounds you inflicted. It will be weeks before their recovery is certain. In the meantime, you would do well to show some contrition. We are *trying* to help you, but we need you to be more cooperative. Shall we begin with your name?"

"Black Wolf." He pushed his cup back at the doctor. "I am Cheyenne."

"Not your Indian name—your *real* name."

"*Black Wolf*," Ésh said louder and more slowly.

The doctor stared at him. "Have you been a captive so long you've forgotten your real name?"

Ésh held up his wrists, still trapped in the metal loops. "*This* is the first time I am a captive!"

The doctor frowned. Even his mustache seemed to droop. "But you look as if you haven't eaten in days, and your body is covered in deliberate scars."

"I starved myself! I cut myself, or I asked others to cut me! I am not like you white cowards—I am not afraid of pain!"

The bluecoats' eyes looked as wide as buffalo chips. The doctor sat back in his seat. The other man had drawn his pistol and pointed it at Ésh. He shook his head. "You said it yourself, Doc—he's mad. He belongs in an asylum."

"I said no such thing." The doctor reached out of Ésh's vision again and came back with a blanket. "He belongs in my hospital."

"He ain't safe."

"That is for Major Day to decide." The doctor laid the blanket next to Ésh, then produced an empty white pot. "This is for—well, it's so you can keep this cell cleaner than the drunkards do." He set the pot on the blanket and held up another object. "There is water in this canteen."

Ésh took it at once, pulled the plug, and drank greedily.

Next, the doctor handed him a plate of green leaves. "Watercress to start. Eat *slowly*, or you're liable to make yourself sick."

As if Ésh had never broken a fast before.

The doctor held up a metal tool, one Mé'hahts had been fond of. "Can I trust you not to stab anyone with this fork? Including yourself?"

Ésh didn't answer, only snatched it out of his hand. He did not use the fork as a weapon—not yet. If he was to regain his strength and escape these *veho*, he had no choice but to attack the watercress first.

"Once you've eaten, I'll need to examine your wounds again and change your dressings."

Ésh glared at the doctor and turned the points of the fork in his direction.

The man narrowed his eyes. "If you do not cooperate, I *will* chloroform you, young man." He promised to return later. He shut the door and left Ésh alone.

∽

THE MORNING AFTER HIS GRANDSON left their village, Náhgo had ridden out and located him on the hill where he was making his sacrifice. Ésh hadn't been difficult to find; he'd been shouting at the Sacred Powers. Náhgo had sighed but returned to camp. Perhaps a spirit would take pity on his grandson. Or perhaps Ésh would starve himself for four days and receive no visits at all—but perhaps that was exactly what he needed to learn humility.

On the fifth morning, Náhgo rode out again with a spare horse to retrieve his grandson. He knew Ésh would be weak after his fast. But before Náhgo reached the hill of his grandson's sacrifice, he saw a party of bluecoats approaching. Náhgo hid the horses and himself and watched the soldiers pass. When he saw the body of his grandson on one of their wagons, his heart nearly stopped beating.

At first, Náhgo thought Ésh must be dead. Blood stained his yellow hair, and he lay motionless on the pile of wood. But one of the mounted bluecoats kept watching Ésh as if he might spring up at any moment. The man had his bloody arm in a sling. That made Náhgo smile, because he suspected his grandson was responsible.

Náhgo followed the bluecoats at a distance till he was certain they were returning to their camp on the Goose River—Fort Laramie, Mé'hahts had called it. Náhgo hurried back to the village to tell the others what he had seen. Zeyá collapsed to her knees and began wailing, certain she had lost her son. Tahpeno sobbed too. No matter how poorly Ésh treated him, the boy still loved his brother.

The news of Ésh's capture also distressed Háhkota and Méanév. Náhgo decided to go to the fort and plead for Ésh's release. He and Háhkota selected five fine horses to offer in payment. They knew the chances were slim that the bluecoats would let him go, but they had to try. Zeyá insisted on coming with them.

Náhgo knew the soldiers would ask how Ésh had become Zizistas. Náhgo found the rabbit skin on which Mé'hahts had recorded the words from the cave on Painted Rock, and he tucked it in an elk hide pouch to bring with him.

That night, Náhgo, Zeyá, and Háhkota slept in the sad village outside the fort. The people in these tipis—Inviters and a few Zizistas—did not follow the buffalo. They were the wives and children of the fort's scouts and interpreters. They were warriors whom firewater had made crazy, who were no good for anything but begging now. Some of the women who no longer had men to care for them sold themselves to the soldiers. Náhgo feared that if the *veho* won control of this land, all of the People would become like this.

Háhkota and Zeyá waited in the village with the horses. Náhgo would go first to ask about Ésh. The bluecoats should not view an old man as a threat. He carried no weapons. But as Náhgo approached, a soldier who had been pacing stopped to ask his business at the fort. Náhgo said he wished to visit the trader, which was not a lie. Seeing he carried no hides, the sentry narrowed his eyes in suspicion, but he allowed Náhgo to pass.

He had not seen this fort since before Ésh's birth. There had been no bluecoats here then, only fur men. The old fort had been small and enclosed by wooden walls, with high places to look out for threats. But these soldiers feared nothing. Their fort had no wall, no way to protect themselves but their own numbers.

The soldiers' wooden lodges surrounded a field of mud and dead grass. Here, a group of bluecoats practiced how to walk and hold their guns, with one man on a horse shouting what to do next. As Náhgo watched the soldiers aiming their weapons across the Goose River, he wondered which of them had aimed those guns at Bull Shield and War Shirt. He wondered how soon they would be aiming at the People again.

He continued on. A dog ran over to bark at him, as if it were another sentry. Náhgo ignored it. A young *veho* boy stopped to gape and was startled when Náhgo said in English: "Good morning. I look for the trader. Do you know his lodge?"

The boy pointed to a structure of stone and earth not far ahead. He would have followed Náhgo, but a *vehoá* hurried out of another lodge and called him inside.

In front of the trader's lodge, two *veho* wearing buckskins and smoking pipes sat and chatted. Beside them, a woman stitched together a moccasin. She looked like she might be Zizistas, but she wore a dress made of *veho* cloth. They barely glanced at Náhgo as he stepped up into the trader's lodge.

The inside smelled of tobacco, fish, and other strong things Náhgo couldn't name. Trade goods seemed to climb up the walls: blankets, shawls, shoes, gloves, saddles, guns, knives, pots, sack after sack of food. There were three *veho*. One inspected the skins an Inviter offered, and another made marks in a book.

Náhgo approached the third man, who was stacking small metal containers. Náhgo cleared his throat and began: "Pardon me."

The man turned. He didn't look much older than Ésh, but the lower half of his face was covered with hair. "Yes? What do you need?" He glanced toward Náhgo's hands and seemed confused that they were empty, that he'd brought nothing to trade.

"I am Náhgo of the Cheyenne. I look for my grandson. His name is Black Wolf. He is eighteen years old." Náhgo hesitated. He knew this would make no sense to these *veho*. "His hair is yellow like your hair, but it is long, and his eyes are green."

As Náhgo had expected, the man frowned.

"Soldiers who cut wood, they carried my grandson to this fort yesterday."

The *veho*'s eyes went wide. "Stay there." He scurried over to one of the older men, whose beard was starting to turn grey. "Mr. Ward, sir! This Cheyenne says he knows the new prisoner! The one who bit Corporal Beatty!"

Ésh had done *what*?

"He says the prisoner is his *grandson*!"

The older man, Ward, had Náhgo repeat himself in Zizistas. Ward spoke it about as well as Náhgo spoke English, but he still wasn't satisfied. "You mean he was your *adopted* grandson—your captive?"

Náhgo shook his head. "My daughter and I found Black Wolf when he was a baby, at the place you call Independence Rock."

"You *stole* a baby?" gaped the younger man.

"He was alone. His first family, they left him behind. Black Wolf has been Cheyenne all his life." Náhgo studied the trader's face. He did not look unkind. "What will you do with him?"

"That is not my decision to make. But I will speak to Major Day on your behalf. He is the post commander—the chief of this fort."

Ward led Náhgo to the fort's largest lodge, made of wood painted white. He asked him to wait just below the place that was both inside and outside. The space reminded Náhgo of the arbors his daughters would build in summer. When Ward reappeared, he brought a thin bluecoat with him who had seen perhaps sixty winters. Ward introduced the man as "Major Hannibal Day."

At the sight of this chief bluecoat, Náhgo's breath caught. The man looked like a ghost, like a spirit who had refused to remain in the Land of the Departed and returned to his body instead. His eyes startled Náhgo most—pale as ice and set deep in their sockets. But the man's strangeness did not end there. His thinning hair, his thick mustache, and a beard he wore underneath his jaw like a noose were shocks of white against his leathery skin and the dark blue of his coat. He stood as straight as the trunk of a dead pine, his chin tilted up and one thin eyebrow raised just enough to express his displeasure.

This was the man who held Ésh's fate in his hands? Even his name declared it: Day, the trader had called him. Zeyá had suggested the name Ésh for her son because it meant Sky, but it also meant Day. If the boy remained with these *veho*, would he resemble this walking ghost in forty winters?

The cold eyes fixed on Náhgo, and the tight mouth opened to speak: "Mr. Ward has told me of your *relationship* to our prisoner."

Other bluecoats, a handful of pale children, and even *vehoá* were beginning to gather around them to watch and listen. Náhgo hated to beg, especially with such an audience, but he loved his grandson more. "Please: my grandson is only a foolish boy. Foolish boys do not think before they act. If he harmed one of your warriors—"

"He harmed *two* of my warriors and attempted to steal valuable government property," interrupted the chief bluecoat.

Náhgo swallowed. "What is your punishment for this?"

The chief bluecoat did not answer; he continued as if Náhgo had not spoken. "He also refuses to give us any other name but Black Wolf. What is his real name?"

Ésh was not a name to share with enemies, and Náhgo knew it was not what the man wanted. "His real name is Black Wolf."

The chief bluecoat sighed and turned his frightening eyes away, but only for a moment. "What is his *white* name?"

Náhgo thought of the rabbit skin hidden in the pouch at his waist, the skin that bore the names from the cave. But if these bluecoats knew Ésh's *veho* name, it would only give them another reason to keep him. "My grandson has no white name. He has never been white."

A grey-haired *vehoá* had come from inside the lodge to stand behind the chief bluecoat. She did not look cruel.

"Please—his mother cries for him."

At Náhgo's words, the face of this *vehoá* pinched with sadness. From the crowd, he heard both murmurs of sympathy and chuckles of mockery.

The chief bluecoat answered: "Your squaw is not that boy's mother. He belongs with his own kind. He is no longer your concern." The man turned as if their conversation was over.

Náhgo called after him: "I have brought five good horses to give you, if you will let my grandson go!"

The people in the crowd went quiet, as if they were holding their breaths.

"Only a savage would offer horses in exchange for a child," the chief bluecoat muttered as if to himself. He stepped toward the inside of his lodge.

"Our best horse, if you will let his mother say good-bye!"

Somewhere in the crowd, a *vehoá* whimpered as though she had lost her own child. A male voice murmured something like: "That sounds fair to me."

The chief bluecoat stopped and glared at the soldiers as if he were trying to locate the source of the male voice. The grey-haired *vehoá* laid a cautious hand on his arm. "Hannibal, surely we might…"

The chief bluecoat cast another dark look into the crowd, then turned his head to the trader. "Mr. Ward!"

"Yes, Major?"

"Tell the Indian and his squaw to return tomorrow. Promise him nothing."

CHAPTER 41

Crazy Horse said, "I am no white man! They are the only people that make rules for other people."
— Interview with He Dog, *Oglala Sources on the Life of Crazy Horse* (1930)

The doctor returned as he'd promised. He held up his light and peered through the little opening into Ésh's cell. "Did the beef tea and watercress agree with you?"

Ésh pulled the blanket tighter around himself and did not answer.

"I'm going to open the door, but first I'll need you to return the fork."

Ésh gritted his teeth and gripped the little weapon tighter underneath the blanket. He'd been hoping the man had forgotten about it. Instead, the doctor passed his hand between the metal sticks in expectation.

Ésh knew jabbing the man would accomplish nothing; his hands were still linked together, and he was still too weak for a fight. Ésh pushed aside the blanket and clamped the fork between his teeth. He used the walls of the cell to maneuver himself to his feet, which was difficult when one of his hands always had to follow the other. Finally, he slapped the fork into the doctor's palm.

"He could still hit us over the head with his chamber pot, Doc," worried Private from outside the cell. "He could still bite us!"

"That is why I have retained your services, Private." As he opened the door, the doctor informed Ésh: "An old Indian came to the sutler's asking about you. Said he was your grandfather."

Ésh held his breath. Grandfather had found him. He'd cared enough to look. But he must be ashamed that Ésh had allowed himself to be caught. *Ésh* was ashamed. He was a pitiful excuse for a warrior.

The doctor blocked his path, examining Ésh with his light. "Major Day—he's our chief, if you will—has decided you may leave this cell and even speak to your 'grandfather' tomorrow. There are conditions, however. You will obey my commands and any others put to you. Do you understand?"

Ésh curled his hands into fists. His arms were stiff from the way the metal loops restricted their movements. "I understand I am your captive."

"I hope, in time, you will consider yourself our guest. But if you attack me or Private Shea or anyone else, you will be returned to this cell forthwith. Lastly, to preclude escape, you will wear a ball and chain. The Major was adamant on that last point, even after I explained that you are barely ambulatory. Do you think you can manage a flight of stairs?"

Ésh squinted at the doctor. How was he supposed to answer when the man used so many words that meant nothing to him?

"They're the only way to the surface."

Ésh would manage this "flight" if it killed him. Better to die in the sunlight than in this unnatural cave.

The doctor walked ahead of him through a door into another space, glancing back frequently to check Ésh's progress. Muscles aching, each step heavy and halting, he shuffled and staggered in his *veho* shoes. In a corner, a man was snoring loudly, curled up in a blanket on the floor. The doctor continued past him to a wooden structure that climbed into the ceiling above them. Faint light drifted down. The doctor stepped onto the steep wooden path. With Private close behind him, Ésh followed, panting at the effort of the climb.

They emerged into an upper space where a fire in the center wall gave out heat and light. Two more bluecoats stood waiting for them. Reluctantly, one held out a small metal tool. "You sure you want to do this, Doctor?"

"I'm sure, Sergeant." The doctor took the tool and inserted it below one of the metal loops trapping Ésh's hands. With a pop, his arms were suddenly free. Ésh flexed his wrists gratefully. Private gripped his pistol more tightly.

The doctor took up a cloth sack that had been hanging on the wall. The bluecoats were watching Ésh warily, but the doctor commanded one of them to open the door, and he obeyed. Private urged Ésh outside.

Ésh did not need the prompting. He wobbled like a newborn foal down a short wooden path and nearly toppled into the mud. Then he stopped and found his balance. He turned his face to the Sun, closed his eyes, and breathed deep of the cool air.

"Come around the back, please." The doctor led him down a slope, closer to the Goose River. "I need to see how your wounds are healing."

Ésh sighed loudly but allowed the doctor to examine the injury on his head and the graze on his hand. He did not exactly trust this *veho* medicine man, but he'd brought Ésh food and freed him from that cell. Why would the man have done those things if he meant to harm Ésh?

"Now the wounds on your arms."

Ésh shrugged off his coat and wrestled with the straps looped over his shoulders, refusing the doctor's help. Then he pulled the two shirts over his head. He felt not only the caress of the autumn air against his bare skin but also what was missing: the weight and brush of his braids. He might hate its color, but the length and style of his hair had marked him as Zizistas for more than eighteen years. These *veho* had taken that away from him. He could not reclaim his braids as he might a stolen horse. How much longer did he have before the rest of the badger's prophecy came true? Months? Days?

"Your grandfather said you are eighteen years old," the doctor commented. "Is that correct, to your knowledge?"

Ésh nodded. He guessed the man's own age to be something over thirty.

"Your parents must have been with the very first wagon train." The doctor stared at the six piercings in each of Ésh's ears. No *veho* could take those away from him. "You're an interesting study on how a European body can be molded by primitive practices and diet. Apart from your scars and your recent starvation, you seem to be healthy." The man smirked. "Your reticence makes your intelligence a bit more difficult to assess."

Ésh kept glancing surreptitiously at Private. Every time he looked, the view was the same: the man's gun remained pointed at him.

The doctor examined the cuts Ésh had made on his shoulders and seemed satisfied with their current appearance. Then he asked Ésh if his head still ached and if there was anything wrong with his vision. The doctor never seemed to run out of questions. "If you've lived with the Cheyenne all your life, how did you learn English?"

"A soldier who escaped this place."

The doctor frowned, then raised his eyebrows. "A deserter. I'm glad *one* of them made good use of his freedom." He looked toward the Goose River. "Before we attach your leg irons, I thought you might like to bathe. We could heat up some water for you, but our interpreter tells me Cheyennes bathe every morning no matter the weather, so perhaps you would prefer..."

Instead of answering with words, Ésh managed to kick off the awkward shoes they'd put on him and proceeded down the river-bank in his socks.

"I *was* going to suggest our usual bathing place, a bit farther up the..." The doctor trailed off when he realized Ésh was already wresting open his trouser buttons. "Oh, very well."

Fortunately, Ésh had been able to examine one of these enclosed-rump-things before, so he knew how they fastened. At the end of the Horse Creek Treaty, several chiefs had received coats and trousers. Many had adapted the coats into their attire. No one liked the trousers.

"Don't you try and swim away!" Private called, still following. "I'll shoot! I will!"

Ésh ignored him. He dropped the trousers and stepped out of them.

From the direction of the fort, on the rise, a woman's voice squealed in alarm. Ésh glanced back to see a *vehoá* and her daughter scurrying out of sight. Did *vehoá* never see their men naked? He wasn't even naked yet; the bluecoats had given him some kind of white under-trousers that reached nearly to his ankles and covered a great deal more of him than his breechcloth would have.

Before Ésh could start on these buttons, the doctor retrieved a white block from his sack. "Do you know what this is?"

Soap, Ésh remembered—his mother had obtained some from traders. He peeled off the under-trousers and his socks, then accepted the soap. At last, Ésh waded into the river up to his knees. The water was almost painfully cold, but he welcomed the bite—the chance to cleanse himself of the itch and smell of the *veho* clothes. He only wished he had a razor to scrape off his new beard.

The doctor fell silent. Private kept threatening to shoot Ésh if he took another step forward. Ésh amused himself by advancing, causing the young soldier to panic, then backing up obediently, and repeating the process. He stopped not because the doctor cleared his throat in reprimand but because the little game exhausted his sore muscles.

When Ésh leaned over to dampen the soap, he heard a feminine whistle behind him, followed by: "Will ye look at that arse, Maureen?"

Ésh gazed over his shoulder to see two *vehoá* descending the riverbank, carrying great piles of clothing with them.

"Don't mind if I do, Rosanna," the second woman chuckled. "Wouldn't mind a view of t'other side of him, neither."

"Mrs. Lenox, Mrs. Heagan," the doctor greeted them. He did

not sound very welcoming. He stood with his arms crossed and his back to Ésh. "Perhaps you could take your washing a little—"

The women did not retreat. Nor did they stop grinning. They set down their burdens on the riverbank only a few paces from Ésh. "But this is our spot, Dr. Johns!"

"And it has such a *breathtaking* view!" When she said this, the second *vehoá* was staring directly at Ésh.

He frowned. The cadence of their words was unfamiliar, but the women's faces seemed to express delighted admiration. Apparently these *vehoá* found him attractive. He contemplated turning around for them. Then he remembered Nataane's scorn for the unimpressive size of his *véto'ots*, which had shrunk further in the cold. Better to let the women admire his backside and imagine.

He didn't find *them* attractive, but neither were they repulsive. Before his vision of the girl with the voice and hair like honey, he'd never even considered coupling with a *vehoá*. The possibility intrigued him now and inspired a tingle of excitement. But such exploration would have to wait.

While he washed—and pretended to wash—Ésh glanced from horizon to horizon. He knew Grandfather was somewhere nearby, but where? He saw only bare ugly earth, the ugly lodges of the bluecoats, and the pristine mountains in the distance, already white with snow.

Ésh stared longingly into the meandering current of the Goose River. In an instant, he could dart forward and dive into the water. He might or might not take a bullet from Private. Of one thing, there was no doubt: he was surrounded by dozens of other bluecoats eager to recapture him.

Even if he managed to elude the soldiers, where would he go then? He knew there was a village of Inviters near the fort, but they would likely betray him to the bluecoats for a few gulps of firewater. He had little chance of surviving very long on his own, weak as he was, naked and weaponless. After the Sun disappeared and true cold set in, if he was unable to start a fire, he might well die before morning.

He *would* escape. But he must wait for the best opportunity, till

he had a greater chance of success—once his strength had returned
and he'd stolen a knife at least. If these bluecoats had intended to
kill him, they would have done it already. Perhaps they wanted him
to lead them to the winter camps of the Zizistas. He would trick
them in the end. He would show them *he* was the better warrior.

So Ésh rinsed the soap from his body and hair and mounted the
bank again, careful to keep his backside to the still-giggling women.
He accepted a cloth from the doctor so he could dry himself. The
man pulled new *veho* clothes from his sack. "Where are *my* clothes?"
Ésh demanded.

"I believe Corporal Beatty, Sergeant Steine, and Captain Smith
cast lots for them—trophies, if you will."

"My medicine pouch? My knife, arrows, and bow?"

"The same, I'm afraid."

Ésh glared back, understanding one thing: these bluecoats were
thieves.

"I know you are accustomed to buckskins and breechcloths, but
you won't need them any longer, son. You must adapt yourself to
our customs—to the customs that should have been yours these past
eighteen years." The doctor glanced disapprovingly at one of the
vehoá, who was creeping closer to gather up the clothing Ésh had
discarded earlier. "Foremost amongst those customs is: cover yourself in the presence of females." The doctor pushed a new pair of
under-trousers at Ésh.

Since even *veho* clothes were preferable to shivering, Ésh pulled
them on.

"We shall also have to find a new name for you; we cannot keep
calling you 'Black Wolf.'"

One of the *vehoá* called with a snigger: "How about 'Adonis'?"

"Thank you, Mrs. Lenox," the doctor replied loudly, though he
did not sound grateful at all.

He insisted on wrapping cloths around Ésh's wounds again.
When Ésh was dressed in fresh clothing and the old uncomfortable
shoes, the doctor led him back up the bank to the fort. There, near
the entrance of the lodge where they'd held him captive underground, stood a frightening bluecoat. He seemed more ghost than

man, with pale eerie eyes and startling white hair. Private snapped his hand to his forehead and addressed this bluecoat as "Major."

Major took an instant dislike to Ésh as well. "So this is the boy who thinks he is an Indian."

"Yes, sir," answered the doctor.

"Why is he outside the guardhouse and not yet in leg irons?"

"They make changes of clothes a bit difficult, sir."

"Did it not occur to you that he might have escaped during your little outing? Did it not occur to you that, having lived as a savage, he is accustomed to being filthy?"

The doctor opened his mouth to reply, then shut it again.

"From this moment forward, you and Father Vaux will see that he wears his irons *at all times.*"

"Yes, sir."

Slowly, Ésh realized what they meant by "irons." Major stood next to a large metal ball and a jumble of metal loops. The man fixed his eerie eyes on Ésh and pointed at the irons. "Come here, boy."

Ésh didn't move. His heart seemed to plummet into his stomach. Behind Major, he saw something he'd not noticed when he first emerged from the Earth. A bluecoat sat perched on a wooden frame like he was riding a horse. But the man's arms were bound behind him in metal loops. His feet were crossed beneath him and trapped by more metal loops. He was gagged, and one of his eyes was red and swollen.

If the *veho* did such things to their own men, what torture did this Major have planned for Ésh? He should have seized his chance to escape, no matter how unlikely his success.

"I thought you said he understood English, Doctor."

"He does, sir." The doctor urged Ésh forward, and Private poked him in the back with his pistol till Ésh was standing next to the irons.

He could hardly breathe now. He'd endured pain before, but he'd always known what was coming, and the pain always had a purpose. He tried to flee, but the doctor reached out to grip his shoulders from behind. Another bluecoat crouched down and

snapped shut the largest metal loops around Ésh's ankles. The man
tugged, then stood up again.

In confusion, Ésh glanced to the doctor and Major. Was that it?

"You'll have to learn how to walk in them, how to keep your
balance," the doctor told him. "Rather than drag the ball behind
them, some men prefer to carry it." He nodded toward the round
metal object. "But be mindful you don't reopen your wounds."

Major was still staring at Ésh with his arms crossed over his blue
coat. "I was a captive of the red devils myself once, in the 1812 war.
I've fought against the Sauks and the Seminoles too. I can understand how that life of wildness might appeal to a boy. But now, you
must put away childish things and cast off your savage habits. It is
time to accept your destiny and become a man. A white man. Such
a man cannot call himself 'Black Wolf.'"

"I agree, Major," interjected the doctor. "I thought perhaps
Father Vaux might suggest—"

Major did not wait for him to finish. "From this point forward,
your name shall be 'John White.'"

When Ésh only frowned at him, Major thrust gloved fingers
beneath his chin. Instinctively, Ésh jerked backward, but his feet
tangled in the metal loops, and he fell hard on his buttocks.

"Repeat it!" Major commanded. "'John White'!"

Ésh grimaced and muttered: "John White."

"Remember it." With that, Major left them.

The doctor knelt next to Ésh. "Are you all right?"

His backside was screaming, but Ésh said: "Yes."

"Let me help you up."

This time, Ésh accepted his aid. As soon as he'd achieved his
feet, a yellow-haired *veho* boy about Tahpeno's age came running
across the field to them.

"Did Major Day and Black Wolf have a fight?" the boy cried.
"Did I miss it?"

"You missed nothing, E. P.," the doctor assured him. "And we
aren't to call him Black Wolf any longer. His name is John White
now."

The boy pouted. "I like Black Wolf better."

"That is neither here nor there."

The boy bent quickly at the waist, then straightened and held out his hand to Ésh. "I am pleased to make your acquaintance, Mr. White. My name is Exeter Pusey Vaux. But I don't like it much either, so people just call me E. P. You're going to come live with me!"

The doctor explained: "You are to dine and take lessons with our post chaplain, Reverend Vaux, E. P.'s father. However, you will sleep at the hospital."

"Is this *really* heavy?" the boy asked, tugging on the metal loops that linked the iron ball to Ésh's ankles.

Ésh bent to test it, then shrugged. "It is as heavy as the skull of a buffalo bull."

The boy squinted at him. "As the *what?*"

"I think he said: 'the skull of a buffalo bull,'" offered the doctor.

"Your l's sound funny!" the boy informed Ésh.

Ésh scowled. This boy had no right to insult him—when he himself pronounced words differently than the doctor, who pronounced words differently than Major, who pronounced words differently than the *vehoá* at the riverbank! Just let any of them try to speak Zizistas!

"I think Mr. White is doing remarkably well," the doctor said. "How would you like it if suddenly everyone around you were speaking Greek?"

CHAPTER 42

BALL AND CHAIN. This punishment, still recognized as legal by the Army Regulations, has been adjudged in sentences from an early period, generally in cases of soldiers convicted of desertion, or of aggravated offenses characterized by violence, and in connection with the punishment of imprisonment. In some cases it has been imposed continuously for long periods... The court has generally fixed the weight of the ball at from six to forty, (most frequently perhaps twenty-four,) pounds, and the length of the chain at from three to six feet...
— Lieutenant Colonel William Winthrop, *Military Law* (1886)

É sh learned to take short steps so he wouldn't trip on the metal loops binding his feet together. The doctor called them "shackles" and the metal loops attaching Ésh to the heavy ball a "chain." This was long enough that Ésh could carry the ball over one shoulder. First he knelt, and then E. P. helped him lift it. Ésh held onto the chain with both hands to take some of the weight off his shoulder.

Finally Ésh began to move forward, across the field toward the chaplain's lodge. As he passed, the bluecoat shackled to the wooden horse watched him enviously with his one good eye. Private still considered Ésh a threat; he followed and did not put away his gun. The doctor accompanied him too, grimacing sympathetically.

E. P. gazed up at him in wonder. "I bet even Hercules wasn't as strong as you!"

Ésh didn't recognize the name, but he understood. "This is nothing," he panted. "This is only *one* buffalo skull. When I was fifteen summers, my grandfather pierced my back and I dragged *four* buffalo skulls behind me till my skin tore."

The boy gaped at him. "Your *grandfather* tortured you?"

"It was not torture. I asked him to do it. It was a vow I made."

E. P. looked to the doctor for confirmation, and the man nodded. "Mr. White has the scars to prove it. I've seen them."

"May *I* see them?"

Before Ésh could answer, the doctor chuckled. "Later, perhaps."

The boy frowned, then asked: "Did your grandfather pierce your ears, too?"

"No."

"Why don't you have long hair like the Indians who come to the sutler's store?"

Ésh almost stumbled. He cast a dark look at the doctor. "Ask *him.*"

"I needed to treat your head wound, and... I didn't think twice about it." The doctor hesitated, and his voice became quieter. "Your hair was important to you, wasn't it?"

Ésh did not think he needed to answer.

In another part of the field, a bluecoat made the clear, insistent sounds Ésh had heard before, only they sounded a bit different each time. Now, he could see the sounds came from a gold instrument played with the mouth. "Mess call!" E. P. informed him.

They reached the lodge where the boy lived with his father the chaplain. *Veho* dwellings looked nothing like the homes of the Zizis-tas. For one thing, their shapes were wrong. Some were made of wood, a few of stone, but most were fashioned out of mud. "Adobe," E. P. called it, when he saw Ésh eyeing the material.

It reminded Ésh of the Wolf People's earth lodges, only uglier and more likely to collapse. Ésh decided to set down his iron ball so it wouldn't slide off his back and through a wall by accident. If a tipi fell on you, you could survive; but Ésh did not want to be smothered by one of these mud houses. That was no death for a warrior.

Inside, they heard voices arguing: the frightened and pleading voices of women and the steady—but equally unhappy—voice of a man. The doctor waited for a lull, then called: "Father Vaux? It's Dr. Johns and the—uh, your new pupil."

The voices ceased. The wooden door of the lodge opened, and a stern man of about fifty winters emerged. He stared Ésh up and down and did not seem to like what he saw.

A *vehoá* whose hair was turning grey hovered in the doorway behind him. She was both looking and not looking at Ésh. "Will you dine with us, Dr. Johns?"

"Thank you, Mrs. Vaux, but I really must return to my hospital."

Trepidation pinching up her face, the woman asked Ésh's guard: "Private Shea?"

"Yes, ma'am. Thank you, ma'am. Major Day told me I weren't to leave Mr. White's side."

Mrs. Vaux let out her breath, then disappeared inside.

"Major Day christened our guest 'John White,'" the doctor explained to Vaux. "Or rather, he wishes *you* to christen him John White."

Ésh watched the doctor stride away, feeling more uneasy than ever.

"Were you baptized during your time with the savages, Mr. White?"

Ésh had planned to look at Vaux, in case something in his posture or expression gave Ésh an idea what he was asking. Instead, his gaze stopped at the new occupant of the doorway: a yellow-haired girl of about fifteen winters who stood staring at him with her mouth open.

"Has a white man poured the waters of eternal life over you?" Vaux persisted. "Perhaps it was a Papist, wearing a black robe?"

"No."

"Then we shall have to select a sponsor for you."

The girl in the doorway stepped forward at once. "May I do it, Father?"

"No, Sylvia, you may not!"

The girl shrank back.

"Come inside now, Mr. White," Vaux commanded. "Mind our doorways and our furniture with that ball of yours."

Ésh maneuvered it inside and sat down at their "table," Private following at his heels. Vaux introduced his wife and his children. E. P. was the only boy, but there were five girls. The youngest were Virginia, Laramie, and Omega, who was hardly more than a baby.

The eldest girl, Victoria, was a few years older than Ésh. She didn't touch her food. Her jaw clenched, she watched him as if someone had asked her to dine with a rattlesnake. Even across the table, he could see her nostrils flaring with each furious breath; and he knew such open hostility must mask a deeper fear. In spite of the bland "bread" and stringy "beef" they were making him eat, Ésh couldn't help smiling. Mrs. Vaux might be afraid of him too, but she'd chosen to treat him like a child. Victoria understood that even shackled and guarded, a Zizistas warrior was a Zizistas warrior.

Sylvia, the girl from the doorway, did not take her eyes from Ésh either. The longer Ésh's attention remained on her sister, the more she tried to attract it. Finally Sylvia leaned behind E. P. and told Ésh in a loud whisper: "Victoria *hates* Indians, because Lieutenant Grattan was going to marry her."

"Twenty-four arrows weren't enough for you," Victoria muttered. "You *mutilated* him. We had to identify him by his *watch*."

Over his mother's objections that such talk was "not fit for the dinner table," E. P. pointed out: "It wasn't Cheyennes who killed Lieutenant Grattan. It was Sioux. They're different." Ésh was impressed that the boy realized this.

"They are all *savages*," Victoria hissed.

"Mr. White isn't a *real* savage," E. P. argued. "He's like Romulus and Remus, only he isn't a twin." He frowned and turned to Ésh. "Are you a twin?"

"What is 'a twin'?"

"Two brothers who are the same age."

"I am not a twin. But I have a brother the same age as *you*."

E. P.'s eyes went as wide as the cup he was holding. "Really? What's his name?"

"Tahpeno."

"And he's a real Indian?"

Ésh did not appreciate the implication that he himself was not a real Indian, yet he found the boy strangely endearing. Unlike most *veho*, E. P. was eager to learn. *He* was not Ésh's enemy—at least not yet. "Tahpeno is a Cheyenne, yes."

"Can he come visit?"

"That is out of the question, Exeter!" his father declared. "It is our duty to civilize Mr. White. He must be reborn and forget everything that has come before. *We* are his only family now."

These people would *never* be his family.

After everyone else left the table, Vaux told Ésh about his gods, who were a father and a son. Fortunately, he did most of the talking and didn't expect Ésh to say much. Inside his trouser pocket, Ésh caressed the handle of the knife he'd stolen when no one was watching.

Then Mrs. Vaux returned, glaring at him, one hand on her hip, and held out the other hand. Ésh tried to pretend he didn't know what she wanted, but finally he had to surrender the knife.

Vaux stopped talking about his gods and started in with things like: "We take you into our home, and *this* is how you repay us?"

Ésh had never asked them to take him in—*he* wanted to put this place far behind him and never think about these people again.

Except maybe E. P. While his father raged, the boy stood watching Ésh with his chin trembling. When his father paused to take a breath, E. P. begged: "Please don't send him away, Father! He didn't hurt anybody!"

Vaux banished Ésh anyway. He told him to spend the evening "contemplating his sins." In the morning, if Ésh was "contrite," Vaux would permit him to enter his home again. E. P. ran off with tears in his eyes.

Private took Ésh and his ball to the hospital, which was made half of adobe and half of wood. Instead of the doctor (who was out), his wife greeted them. She showed Ésh to a space she called a ward. "We'll see what tomorrow morning's sick call brings; but for now, we have all our patients in the other ward, so you can have this room to yourself, Mr. White."

The ward contained four objects resembling beds. They did not touch the Earth and were covered by itchy *veho* blankets. At least the space was warmed by a fire; and there were openings in the walls showing the outside, so in spite of his shackles and ball, he did not feel so trapped. Private remained with him, and Ésh heard voices in other parts of the lodge, but mostly the doctor's wife left him alone.

Ésh lay down to rest and plan his escape. He also scratched at his beard. He'd never let the hair grow so long before. He did not like it at all.

Another bluecoat came to replace Private. The second guard was also called Private.

The doctor returned. He sat down on the bed across from Ésh and sighed. "I heard what happened at the chaplain's house."

Ésh did not take his eyes from the ceiling. "Do you mean when his daughter said that I killed—"

"I mean: You stole a knife."

Ésh shrugged. "I need to shave."

"I do not think you appreciate the precariousness of your position, Mr. White."

Ésh glared at him. "That is *not* my name!"

"I know you are unhappy here. I know you must be overwhelmed by all these new words and objects and faces. But you must restrain your savage impulses. Do not strike out, and do not attempt escape. You will not succeed. You will only make Major Day reconsider his decision. This fort and this treatment"—he glanced down at Ésh's shackles and ball—"is a paradise compared to the alternative."

Ésh narrowed his eyes. "What is this 'alternative'?"

"It's called an asylum. I know that word doesn't mean anything to you. I hope it never does. The one Major Day suggested—the one directed by a West Point classmate of his—it's no place for madmen, let alone sane ones."

Ésh sat up. "This fort and this 'asylum' are not the only choices. Why do you not let me go?"

"You may *think* that is what you want, Mr. White, but returning to the Cheyenne is not a solution. You would have a few more years with them—that is all. The Indians' time is ending. A few painted warriors on horseback will not stop the advance of civilization. You are young. Before you are old, white men will cover this continent. Sooner or later, you must learn to live with us. Give us a chance, Mr. White. See this as an opportunity to experience everything you've been missing these past eighteen years—all the comforts and wonders civilization has to offer."

Ésh stared pointedly at the ugly wall made of dirt beside them.

"I have heard many Indians die of hunger and cold during winter."

Only because the *veho* were killing so much game and chopping down all the trees.

"Give us till the spring, then. Keep your head down and obey every command to the letter till Major Day orders these irons removed. If you still wish to leave, I will help you."

"Why?"

"Oh, I expect something in return. Your knowledge of a vanishing way of life is absolutely unique. I want to take down what you know, write a monograph." The doctor pulled something out of his coat pocket. "For instance, the circular design on this 'medicine pouch' of yours…"

Ésh snatched the little deerskin bag away from him. "You are all angry when *I* take what does not belong to me, but *you*—"

"I didn't take it; I got it back. And it wasn't easy!" He watched Ésh loop the medicine pouch's cord around his neck. "That design, it's made from flattened and dyed porcupine quills?"

Ésh tucked it beneath his shirts. "Yes."

"What does it *mean*?"

"You are ready for your first lesson about the Cheyenne?"

The doctor stood. "Just let me fetch a pencil and a notebook."

Ésh did not wait. "The first thing I will tell you is this: a man's medicine is for him. No one else."

The doctor stopped in the doorway. He opened his mouth to protest but wisely shut it again. He sighed. "Do you truly wish to shave?"

"Yes."

"Then I will *lend* you a razor—I will remain in the room while you use it and take it back when you are finished."

"Fine."

The doctor returned with a little mirror, a cup, a brush, a razor, and soap. He remained as he'd said while Ésh cleaned up his face and throat. When he was finished, Ésh stared down at the razor and wondered if trying to steal the knife had been such a good idea after all. "Will I still see my grandfather tomorrow?"

"I prevailed upon Father Vaux's Christian forbearance and persuaded him not to tell Major Day of your theft."

"I understand only half of the words you say."

The doctor chuckled. "Yes, you will still see your grandfather tomorrow. But do not put anything else in your pockets. Understand?"

Ésh nodded. He closed the razor and handed it back to the doctor. At "supper," he eyed the knives but did not take one. These *veho* ate not when they were hungry but at certain periods of the day when their instrument called them together.

To Ésh's amusement, two bluecoats he recognized sat at the other end of his table during the evening meal. As soon as they recognized him, the men looked like they wanted to leave again. The hand of one was wrapped in a white cloth and the other's arm was in a sling, because of the wounds from Ésh's teeth and arrow.

That night, he checked his medicine pouch to ensure that nothing was missing. His beaded horse charm seemed undisturbed. Only fragments of the black-and-orange butterfly remained, but his mother had given him those wings when he was a baby, and they'd always been as fragile as they were beautiful. Staring at the tuft of its fur, he wondered again why the black wolf had led him to the *veho*.

It was hard to rest on this strange bed in this strange place with his feet shackled. He never stopped planning how to escape, even though there were Privates guarding him all night.

He thought about what he would say to Grandfather. *It is my fault I am here with this iron ball on my legs. If I had listened to you—if I had approached the spirits properly—the veho would not have captured me. Maybe I do belong here with them. It is like in the children's stories: the stupid, selfish veho does not listen, so he suffers.*

There were some advantages to remaining here. He did not have to face Méanév and Háhkota yet. He did not have to tell He'heeno's family how he'd abandoned their son and brother. While he remained among his enemies, Ésh did not have to be kind or think of others' happiness.

The *vehoá* with the voice and hair like honey visited him again that night. The moment his nose caught the scent of roses, he tried to open his eyes. He saw only a glimpse of her beautiful hair before she leaned close to kiss one of his eyelids and brush the other with her thumb. Blindly he reached out to touch her. The girl teased her fingers over his hand and whispered: "This is how you'll know you've found us."

"'Us'?" Ésh asked.

The girl vanished before answering his question, but she left him a gift: a black-and-orange butterfly like the one in his medicine pouch. This creature was whole and strong, opening and closing its wings. The butterfly remained perched on his hand, caressing the same skin the girl had touched, till sleep closed his eyes.

CHAPTER 43

I was born upon the prairie, where the wind blew free and there
was nothing to break the light of the sun. I was born where there
were no enclosures and where everything drew a free breath. I
want to die there and not within walls.

— Paruasemena (Chief Ten Bears) of the Yamparika
Comanches, in a speech before the Treaty of Medicine Lodge
Creek, October 1867

When the call of the bluecoats' gold instrument awoke Ésh,
the butterfly was gone. Dawn light showed through the
openings to the outside, but no one came to fetch him. He decided
to turn over and continue resting. Escape would be useless till he
was strong enough to survive, till he'd found a way out of these
shackles.

When a second call awoke him, Ésh opened his eyes to find E. P.
standing over his bed.

The boy chewed his lip. "You weren't going to scalp me, were
you? With the knife?"

This veho is not your enemy, Ésh reminded himself. *He is simply a boy.
You can make him happy so easily. He is good practice for Tahpeno.* Ésh sat up

and tugged at the yellow hair on the top of E. P.'s head. "Your hair is so short, it would not be worth taking. But your sister, *she* has good hair for scalping."

The boy gaped for a moment, till he saw from Ésh's grin that it was a joke. Then E. P. smiled too. "Which one of my sisters?"

"The one I saw first yesterday."

"Sylvia?"

"Sylvia."

The boy sniggered. "I think she fancies you."

"This 'fancies,' it is a good thing?"

"Not if you want to scalp her! She might let you!"

"I was not going to scalp anyone," Ésh assured him. He kicked at the iron ball still chained to his ankles. "I wanted to free myself from this thing."

E. P. frowned. "You need the key."

Ésh realized Private was gone. He peered at the boy. "Do you know where the key is?"

"In the guardhouse."

"Can you bring it here?"

The boy shook his head. "They won't let me in the guardhouse."

"They let you in here."

"Dr. Johns said it was O.K. But he's not in charge of the guard-house. I tried to see you, when I first heard you were there, but they wouldn't let me enter." He chewed his lower lip again. "Can I still see your scars?"

"Yes." Ésh pulled off his two shirts and told how he had earned the scars on his arms, his chest, his back, and his side. E. P. especially liked the story about the Crow who had tried to steal Ésh's horse.

Then the boy pointed to the little pouch around his neck. "What's that?"

"It is my medicine pouch," Ésh answered, although the doctor was leaning against the doorframe behind the boy now. "There are important things inside, like the hair of a black wolf and the wings of an orange butterfly. The things make me strong and quick."

E. P. reached out to the pouch. "May I—"

Ésh closed his hand around it. "Each man has his own medicine. This is mine."

The boy pouted for only a moment before the doctor spoke: "Your grandfather is outside, Mr. White."

E. P. wanted to come along, but the doctor told him to remain inside. Ésh pulled his shirts and his coat back on, then dragged his iron ball outside. There stood not only his grandfather but also his mother.

"*Náhko'e!*" Ésh gasped, hobbling toward them. "*Námshim!*"

His mother ran to him and tightened her arms around him as she hadn't done since he was a child. "What have they done to you, *nae'ha?*"

"I am all right, *náhko'e.*"

"But your hair—and what is this thing?" She pulled away to stare down worriedly at the iron ball.

"It is so I do not escape. It is nothing."

"What do they plan for you?" asked Grandfather.

"They want to keep me here until I learn to be like them. If I disobey them, they will send me to a place that is even worse."

His mother sniffled.

Grandfather looked behind Ésh, who followed his eyes to see that the doctor was standing at a distance, watching them. "What if the bluecoats knew your *veho* name? Would they send you to your *veho* family, do you think?"

Ésh scowled. "I have only one family."

His words made his mother smile, but Grandfather said: "You know that is not true, *nish*. You have wondered why you do not look like us since you were a boy. I know you have. This is your chance to find the people who brought you here."

"But they are dead!"

"Maybe your *veho* mother and father are gone, but you must have a *veho* grandfather, an aunt—maybe even a brother."

"We don't know where they are!" Ésh pointed out. "We don't even know their names."

"Do you remember the marks inside the cave on Painted Rock?

How Mé'hahts copied them onto a rabbit skin? I kept it for you." Grandfather pulled it from an elk hide bag at his waist. "These words could lead you to your other family."

Ésh only stared at the rabbit skin. His mother was weeping now.

"I am *not* saying: 'You do not belong to us' or 'We do not want you,'" Grandfather explained. "I am saying: 'I think you must do this.' I am saying: 'When your journey is finished, I hope you will return to us.'"

"Please come back, *nae'ha*," his mother sobbed.

"Of course I will come back! I do not want to go!" But Ésh did not want to remain at this fort either, with Vaux scowling at him and Major yelling "John White" at him and this ball he must always drag behind him.

"If you go among the *veho* to learn about your first family, you will learn many other things too," Grandfather reasoned. "You will learn how the *veho* live in their own lands. You will see if there is any good in it. You will learn how they think. You can bring this knowledge back to our People. You will be able to tell us stories for many winters to come. Maybe your stories will help us win when we must fight them. Or maybe your stories will convince us that it is time to stop fighting. You will be the greatest scout our People have ever known—one who has travelled deeper into *veho* territory than a scout who looks Zizistas ever could."

Grandfather was right. Grandfather was always right. The first part of the badger's prophecy had come true: Ésh's hair had been taken from him. He would not live to see it grow long again. Before death found him, he must do one great deed. Something that would help his People in a way only he could. What greater deed could there be than to slip into enemy territory, learn their secrets, and return to his People with that knowledge? If he did this, they would never forget him, and he would live forever.

Ésh accepted the rabbit skin from his grandfather.

His mother embraced him again. Then she retrieved a large parfleche she'd packed. Inside were jerky and pemmican, two animal skin shirts, two breechcloths, two pairs of leggings, and three pairs of moccasins. She'd also brought him a buffalo coat. Ésh smiled, thanked her, and touched her scarred, tear-wet face. "*You* will always be my true mother."

This set her to weeping even harder.

"Even if you decide to stay with your *veho* family," Grandfather said, "you will always be my grandson."

"I *will* return to you," Ésh promised. His grandfather began to lead his mother away before Ésh remembered. "*Námshim!*"

He turned. "Yes?"

"Please give my spotted horse to Tahpeno. Not to look after until I return—to keep."

Grandfather smiled. "I will tell him."

Ésh must still make amends to He'heeno's family, but that he must do in person. That would have to wait.

The doctor came to inspect the contents of the parfleche. He pretended to admire the fine beadwork and quillwork of Ésh's mother and the pattern she'd painted on the rawhide case. But the doctor was probably making sure Ésh's family hadn't given him any weapons. The doctor saw the rabbit skin in Ésh's hand. "What's that?"

"Do you know how to read?"

"Of course."

"The person who left me in the cave on Independence Rock, he also left these words." Ésh handed the doctor the rabbit skin. "I think they are the names of my white mother and father."

For several moments, the doctor only stared at the words, mouth agape. "So much for my monograph." He looked up. "We have to get you to Charleston."

MAJOR WAS ANGRY to learn about the rabbit skin. He accused Ésh and his grandfather of lying—they'd known Ésh's "real name" all along. But in the end, he agreed that Ésh must go to Charleston. Whoever had left him at Independence Rock might be dead, or they might be in Oregon, or they might be in California. These places were too large to search. But when *veho* followed the Great Medicine Trail, they usually left family behind in the East, or at least neigh-

bors who could answer Ésh's questions. In Charleston, he might find
nothing, but he might find everything.

The doctor was something of a captive himself; he had to
remain at the fort, so he could not accompany Ésh to Charleston.
But in a few more days, another bluecoat would be going on "leave"
to a village called Savannah, which was near Ésh's destination of
Charleston.

This bluecoat was called Lieutenant Gates, and he let Ésh know
exactly how he felt about this duty: "You may look white on the
outside, but I know what you really are. You give me any trouble
whatsoever, I won't hesitate to shoot you."

While Ésh waited to leave, he had to sit every day and hear
more about the *veho* gods from Vaux. He attended "Sunday service,"
where everyone sang and Vaux made a speech about how to behave.
At least the bluecoats and their women called Ésh "Mr. McAllister"
now, because that was the name from the cave on Independence
Rock. He liked it better than Mr. White.

Ésh enjoyed the long glances of many of the "laundresses" and
young Sylvia. He returned them. But when Vaux realized what was
happening, he thundered: "No white man looks at a white woman
that way unless he intends to marry her! And I will become a Papist
before I allow *my* daughter to marry the likes of you!"

Apart from this bit of advice, Ésh didn't know the rules about
vehoá. He certainly couldn't risk having to marry one. Looks would
have to satisfy him for now. Besides, it was hard to chase after
anyone while dragging an iron ball. And the Sacred Powers had
shown him the young *vehoá* with the voice and hair like honey for a
reason. Maybe she awaited him in this Charleston.

E. P. didn't want him to go, so Ésh spent as much time as he
could with the boy, answering his questions and telling him stories.
He also listened to the boy talk about himself. Ésh realized there
were no other boys E. P.'s age at the fort, only young soldiers; and
his father was so busy "preaching and teaching" that he seemed to
forget about E. P.

Ésh was surprised to learn that the boy (and all his younger
sisters) had been born at the fort. Their parents had been born in a

place called England, which lay on an island far across the eastern sea. The name McAllister meant that Ésh's white father, or at least one of his ancestors, belonged to a people called the Scots who lived on the same island, but farther north.

Ésh was only beginning to understand how many lands the *veho* occupied. Like the tribes of the plains and the mountains, some of the *veho* were allies, and some made war on each other. But until a few generations before, none of them had been born in *this* land; they had brought the battles here on themselves.

E. P. taught Ésh many new words and helped him with his pronunciation. Ésh helped the boy make his own medicine pouch. Nothing in the bag was blessed by a medicine man, of course, and E. P. would have to hide it from his father: "He'd call it 'pagan idolatry.'" But the fact that his medicine pouch was a secret seemed to please the boy all the more. He begged Ésh for a bit of his hair to put inside. Ésh was flattered, and he decided this would be all right because E. P. did not know the curses to say over hair.

Still he warned the boy: "This has great power. You must keep it safe."

E. P. nodded solemnly.

As this yellow-haired boy followed him about and stared up at him with such admiration, Ésh wondered if he would live long enough to tell his own son stories like the ones he was telling E. P. But if the badger's prophecy was true, Ésh would be fortunate to have a son at all.

The second time the doctor allowed Ésh to use a razor, he thought about shaving his head. Then he would have to live long enough for the hair to grow back—in the badger's blood, his hair had been short, but he had not been bald. Yet Ésh knew it would be cowardly to do such a thing, just as it would be cowardly to escape and return to the Zizistas before he'd accomplished his scouting mission. He must do what no other member of the People could do. He would live as long as the Sacred Powers wished him to live and no longer.

At last the bluecoats freed him from the iron ball. Ésh collected his parfleche, which the doctor and his wife had kept for him. He was especially grateful for the buffalo coat; a sprinkling of snow had fallen the night before. Ésh promised to send a letter to let the doctor know he'd found his white family. Ésh couldn't write or read yet, but he hoped this was something he could learn during his time among the *veho*.

Ésh embraced the weeping E. P., then climbed onto the "mail wagon" beside Lieutenant Gates. The mules pulled away from the fort and carried them eastward, toward Charleston. Toward Ésh's *veho* family. And maybe toward the girl with the voice and hair like honey, too.

THE END of *Lost Saints*.
But The Lazare Family Saga continues…

Have you guessed that "the girl with the voice and hair like honey" is Tessa's daughter Clare? She was eight years old when we left her in 1851; but by the time Ésh meets Clare in 1860, she'll be seventeen. If you want to know what happens next, *Native Stranger*, Book Three of the Lazare Family Saga, is available for Kindle, in paperback, in hardcover, and as an audiobook performed by the incomparable Dallin Bradford.

I spent three decades researching, writing, revising, and publishing this series. If you're glad I did, please take three minutes to help other readers discover my books. You can do that by leaving a review of *Lost Saints* on Amazon, Goodreads, or BookBub or by recommending The Lazare Family Saga on social media. This makes an enormous difference to an indie author like me. Thank you!

If you'd like to chat about my series, email me at elizabeth@ elizabethbellauthor.com.

AUTHOR'S NOTE

This novel would be considerably weaker if not for the honesty of the priests and priests' lovers who shared their stories in my sources. Especially heartwarming, heartbreaking, and helpful in my understanding of Joseph and Tessa were two collections of interviews: Clare Jenkins's *A Passion for Priests: Women Talk of Their Love for Roman Catholic Priests* (1995) and Jane Anderson's *Priests in Love: Roman Catholic Clergy and Their Intimate Friendships* (2005). One particular account has haunted and guided me:

> We'd spend some of the night together in the same bed, but we never, ever had intercourse. He was afraid of sex. If he thought he was getting too excited, he would get really upset. I've never seen anybody so brainwashed. ... He was absolutely petrified of having an orgasm. I mean, that would have been the end of the world for him. And to my knowledge, he never did. (Jenkins, p. 83)

While selfish hedonism is equally destructive, I wanted to explore what happens to our psyches and the people we love when we're taught to fear happiness and hate our own humanity. I've had readers call Joseph cowardly, even cruel. To me, he is a tragic figure, the victim of centuries-old belief systems determined to destroy his personhood. All his life, the merciless voices of dogma and racism have whispered inside his head: "You are worthless. You are power-less. You exist only to serve God and your betters." Loving an equal has no place in this hierarchy. Technically, Joseph is a "tragic mulat-to," although Catholic guilt ultimately proves stronger than racial self-consciousness. Joseph's journey isn't finished, however; he will reappear in the last two books of The Lazare Family Saga, *Native Stranger* and *Sweet Medicine*.

Bishop Ignatius Aloysius Reynolds and **Thornton** are taken from life. Bishop Reynolds really did try to claim **Father James Wallace**'s three sons as Church property. **Andrew**, **George**, and **James Wallace** really did obtain passes to play at a ball in order to aid their escape to Canada, along with Andrew's fiancée.

All the people who accompany David's family westward are also historical, including the members of the Jesuit missionary party and their guide, mountain man **Thomas Fitzpatrick**, whom the Indians called "Broken Hand." The emigrants of the 1841 Bidwell-Bartleson party were the first to travel overland to California. After they split with the Jesuits, they had neither a guide nor an accurate map. Amazingly, **George Shotwell** was the party's only casualty. In actuality, only a mule drowned during the North Platte crossing. However, in subsequent years, river crossings would claim hundreds of emigrant lives, and hundreds of women would die of childbirth complications on the trail.

In his journal, **John Bidwell** lists the members of the emigrant and Jesuit parties as well as the mountain men who accompanied them part of the way before striking out on their own. He mentions that "The trappers for the mountains are the following—Jas. Baker, Piga (a Frenchman), and Wm. Mast." Nothing else is known about Piga; but that is not a French name. Bidwell was probably guessing at the spelling. I altered it and invented the man's fate. I am indebted to Doyce B. Nunis, Jr. for *The Bidwell-Bartleson Party: 1841 California Emigrant Adventure: The Documents and Memoirs of the Overland Pioneers* (1992), an outstanding collection of primary sources, including drawings Father Point made on the trail.

A note on genetics: If a White person has a child with a partner whose ancestry is partly White and partly Black, the child will always inherit less melanin than and thus be lighter-skinned than the mixed parent. This is because darker skin tone is dominant; it does not "hide" or skip generations, and the White parent's genes can only dilute the mixed parent's contribution. However, before genetics were understood in the 20th century, the idea of a "throwback child" who resembled a dark-skinned ancestor was a powerful fear for mixed-race people passing as White. Even men of science thought it possible. Parents who are both mixed race Black and White can have a child who inherits their "lightest" genes and appears more White than either of them. Or their child can inherit his parents' "darkest" genes and appear more Black than either parent—but only if both parents are mixed.

The Cheyenne words I use in the text are taken from dictionaries of the language, although I have often chosen simplified spellings for ease of pronunciation. I wanted to give a flavor of the language without tripping up the reader. For example, in the modern Cheyenne alphabet, the Cheyennes' name for themselves should technically be spelled "Tsétsêhéstâhese"; but when said aloud, this sounds like "Zi-zis-tas."

I followed a similar principle with personal names: they are a sort of shorthand. In the end, simplicity outweighed strict authenticity. Most Cheyenne given names are inherited, thus invoking the medicine of the individual's ancestor. But Cheyennes also have more personalized nicknames.

With the exception of my own Black Wolf, any Cheyenne character whose name is given in English was a real person, and their actions are based on recorded events. These include **Starving Bear, White Cow Woman** (also called Kiowa Woman)**, Raccoon, Fire Wolf**, **Ice**, **Dark**, and **Alights on the Cloud** (also translated as Touching Cloud). **Two Tails** would become the famous Chief Little Wolf. **High Forehead** was a real person, but the other Lakota characters are fictional.

Inspired by Blackfeet author James Welch's marvelous novel *Fools Crow* (1986), I often retain Cheyenne terminology. The *veho* are of course white men. The Zizistas or "the People" are the Cheyenne themselves. The Inviters are Sioux, specifically Lakota; the Cloud People, Arapaho; the Wolf People, Pawnee; the Greasy Wood People, Kiowa; the Rattlesnake People, Comanche; and the Occupied Camp People, Apache. The Crow and Blackfeet are the same, and the Shoshoni are a cognate.

The Moon Shell River is the North Platte; Goose River, the Laramie; Flint Arrowpoint River, the Arkansas; and Turkey Creek is Solomon's Fork of the Republican River. To this day, no one knows why Colonel Edwin V. Sumner ordered a saber charge at the Battle of Solomon's Fork. The white scabs sickness is smallpox, and the "Big Cramps" in 1849 is cholera.

The healing song "I know myself..." and the Kit Fox Society song are from George Bird Grinnell's "Notes on Some Cheyenne Songs," which appeared in *American Anthropologist* 5.2 (1903): 312-322. The "Wolf I Am" prayer is from Karl Schlesier's *Wolves of Heaven: Cheyenne Shamanism, Ceremonies, and Prehistoric Origins* (1987). The "turn it into good" prayer is from Edward S. Curtis's *The North American Indian*, Volume 6 (1911).

Badger blood divination was practiced by many Plains tribes. I discovered it in Grinnell's *The Cheyenne Indians: Their History and Ways of Life*, Volume 2 (1923). The practice is also mentioned in Rodolphe Petter's *English-Cheyenne Dictionary* (1915) under "augur." The most complete Cheyenne dictionary was compiled at Chief Dull Knife College and can be found online at http://www.cdkc.edu/cheyennedictionary/index.html

I use several Cheyenne kinship vocatives, that is, terms of address for family members: *nae'ha* (son), *náhko'e* (mother), *nish* (grandchild), *námshim* (grandfather), *na'neha* (older brother), *ma'kos* (younger brother), *na-eham* (husband), and *na-méo* (my love).

Major Hannibal Day, born in Vermont in 1804, was the post commander at Fort Laramie from September 1859 to May 1860. As a Brevet Brigadier-General, he would have a horse shot out from under him at the Battle of Gettysburg. He would retire the following month after forty years of service. Day's history with Indians is noted in Major William S. Powell's *Officers of the Army and Navy Who Served in the Civil War* (1892). I have described Day's other-worldly appearance based on photographs taken by Mathew Brady's studio during the Civil War and now held by the National Archives. You can see them here: https://catalog.archives.gov/id/529029

Assistant Surgeon **Edward W. Johns**, born in Maryland in 1827, was first stationed at Fort Laramie in April 1858. In April 1861, he would resign in order to join the Confederate States Army. He would serve as the Medical Purveyor in Richmond, Virginia. Page 19 of the July 1860 Federal Census for the "Fort Laramie Reservation in the Territory of Nebraska" (now in the state of Wyoming) lists Dr. Johns (age 33) and his wife "S. A.," as well as S. (**Seth**) **E. Ward**, the post sutler, who had been trading in the vicinity of Fort Laramie since 1851.

The same census page lists **William Vaux**, the fifty-three-year-old Episcopal post chaplain, who was English by birth. His wife is listed only by her age (43) and the initial W. Their children are **Victoria** (21); **Sylvia** (15); **Virginia** (11); **E. P.** (10); **Laramie** (5); and **Omega** (3).

Vaux left two contradictory accounts of the death of **Lieutenant John Grattan** and his twenty-nine men in a confrontation with a village of Brulé Sioux over an emigrant's cow (August 19, 1854). In October 1854, Vaux reported to Bishop Jackson Kemper on

> the most unprecedented massacre... Upwards of 1,500 warriors rushed upon them, and in the most brutal manner assassinated the whole command, mutilating their bodies in the most savage and barbarous way...and further designed to attack and burn the fort, putting to death every white person, and actually marched on this fiendish mission... The shocking spectacle of the mangled and gory bodies lying over the place of slaughter was exposed for two days... ("Fort Laramie," *The Spirit of Missions* 20, 1855, p. 40-41)

Yet in October 1855, during the official investigation, Vaux wrote to Major (Brevet Lieutenant Colonel) William Hoffman:

> In reply to your inquiry as to my knowledge of the character, &c., of the late Lieutenant Grattan... Mr. Grattan, I know, had an unwarrantable contempt of Indian character... Often...have I reproved him for acts which I conceived highly improper, such as thrusting his clenched fist in their faces, and threatening terrible things if ever duty or opportunity threw such a chance in his way.

Vaux calls Grattan "one who has so sadly fallen a victim to his temerity...an undue reliance on his own powers," and probable intoxication.

While I have pulled other names and ranks from the 1860 Fort Laramie census, I have invented any details. For a more extensive bibliography and for a glossary, please visit my website: https:// elizabethbellauthor.com/

ACKNOWLEDGMENTS

I am deeply grateful to my critique partners and beta readers: Maron Anrow, Ida Bostian, Christina Campbell, Anna Ferrell, Elizabeth Huhn, Mary Overton, and Lillian Rouly. To Courtney Brkic, Stephen Goodwin, and Mary Kay Zuravleff for their feedback when the Cheyenne chapters were my thesis for the Masters of Creative Writing degree at George Mason University. And to my multitalented editor, Jessica Cale. Any remaining errors and questionable choices are *mea culpa*.

Publishing independently can be a lonely, terrifying, and humiliating endeavor. Everyone who supported *Necessary Sins* made me feel like a real author at last. A thousand thank yous to Danielle Apple, Piepie Baltz, Sharon Brewer, Amy Bruno, Ruth Hull Chatlien, Camille Di Maio, Stephanie Dray, Allyson Ellis, Nicole Evelina, Kathleen Grissom, Susan Gromis, Tinney Sue Heath, Beth Honea, Sarah Johnson, Daniella Levy, Nalana Lillie, Amy Mannette, Diane Moyle, Susie Murphy, Marina J. Neary, Susan Peterson, Kate Quinn, Hannah Ross, Deborah Lea Serrano, Laura Somers, Carla Suto, M. K. Tod, Tammy Underhill, Dana Wright, and Grace Wynter.

David Fitz-Gerald delighted me by sleuthing out E. P.'s full name (either Exeter Pusey or Exeter Purdy) and by uncovering more details about the Vaux family. Thank you to Sharlene Martin Moore for lending me her design expertise. To Erin Davies for letting me reveal the cover of *Lost Saints* on her Historical Fiction Reader Facebook page.

Thank you to Eliza Knight, whose online workshop "S.E.X.:

Writing the S.ensual E.vocative X.perience" gave me the confidence to write the love scenes Joseph allowed me.

I am grateful to Don Rawitsch, Bill Heinemann, and Paul Dillenberger, who created the Oregon Trail computer game that occupied me for many happy hours as a child and who are therefore responsible for many of the Lazare-McAllister family's woes.

To the historical interpreters at Colonial Williamsburg, especially Hope Smith. To librarian Sandra Lowry at Fort Laramie National Historic Site. To my parents, John and Lynne Becker, for coordinating their vacations with my settings.

To the Cheyenne people, who have survived epidemics, wars, and genocide yet maintain their unique, vibrant identity. To all the Native individuals who have shared their nations' histories and ways of life with outsiders. The work of Lakota author Joseph M. Marshall III greatly informed my understanding of Plains tribes, especially *The Lakota Way* (2002) and *The Day the World Ended at Little Bighorn* (2007). Living historian Michael Bad Hand allowed me to step inside an authentically furnished tipi at Fort Laramie. His books *Daily Life in a Plains Indian Village, 1868* (1999) and *Plains Indians Regalia & Customs* (2010) are invaluable, and his posts let me time travel even through Facebook. I am also thankful that I live near the Smithsonian Institution's National Museum of the American Indian. Not only their fantastic exhibits but also their special events, including plays and musical performances, have allowed Native art, thought, and values to enrich my life year after year as I wrote and revised this novel.

ABOUT THE AUTHOR

Elizabeth Bell has been writing stories since the second grade. At the age of fourteen, she chose a pen name and vowed to become a published author.

That same year, Elizabeth began The Lazare Family Saga. New generations and forgotten corners of history kept demanding attention, and the saga became four epic novels. After three decades of research and revision, Elizabeth decided she'd done them justice.

The first book of The Lazare Family Saga, *Necessary Sins*, was a Finalist in the Foreword Indies Book of the Year Awards. The second and third books, *Lost Saints* and *Native Stranger*, were Editors' Choices in the *Historical Novels Review*.

Upon earning her MFA in Creative Writing at George Mason University, Elizabeth realized she would have to return her two hundred library books. Instead, she cleverly found a job in the university library, where she works to this day.

Elizabeth loves hearing from readers and chatting about writing and history. Visit her on social media or her website:

https://elizabethbellauthor.com/

Made in the USA
Monee, IL
02 December 2023

47710937R00236